DECEPTION ISLAND

R.S. Burnett grew up in the Falkland Islands and began his writing career with the Islands' weekly newspaper, *Penguin News*. After moving to London and spending over a decade working for the *Daily Mirror* and in Formula 1, Burnett is now a freelance journalist and lives once again in the Falklands.

𝕏 @RobBurnett
⊙ Rob.Burnett

R.S. Burnett

DECEPTION ISLAND

HarperCollins*Publishers*

HarperCollins*Publishers* Ltd
1 London Bridge Street
London SE1 9GF

www.harpercollins.co.uk

HarperCollins*Publishers*
Macken House, 39/40 Mayor Street Upper
Dublin 1, D01 C9W8, Ireland

First published by HarperCollins*Publishers* Ltd 2026

1

A catalogue record for this book is available from the British Library.

ISBN: 978-0-00-869647-4 (PB)

This novel is entirely a work of fiction. The names, characters and incidents
portrayed in it are the work of the author's imagination. Any resemblance to
actual persons, living or dead, events or localities is entirely coincidental.

Set in Minion Pro by HarperCollins*Publishers* India

Printed and bound in the UK using 100% Renewable
Electricity at CPI Group (UK) Ltd

Deception Island is located in the Drake Passage, sixty-five nautical miles north of the Antarctic Peninsula. The first documented sighting was by British sealers William Smith and Edward Bransfield aboard the vessel *Williams* in January 1820.

It earned its name thanks to its misleading appearance, as the outer coastline hides a large natural harbour within, which is in fact a flooded volcano caldera.

The island served as a sealing and whaling station until 1931, and thereafter as a research base. In 1967 the volcano erupted, followed by a second eruption two years later which wiped out the scientific stations.

It could erupt again at any moment.

Prologue

Four years ago

Fitz sucked in a long, deep breath and ran over the details of the operation again in his mind. His eyes were locked on the horizon, his ears filled with the buzz of the diesel engine that was powering his Offshore Raiding Craft motorboat through the choppy black waters of the Arabian Sea.

Despite the hour and the darkness, the wind on his face was warm. For a moment he flashed back to his honeymoon, just eight months ago, when he and Abbie had hopped around the Greek islands for a fortnight. As a boy who'd grown up in a one-street village on the Black Isle in the north of Scotland, warm wind was something he'd never quite got used to. It just didn't seem natural.

He held his KS-1 assault rifle across his chest, knowing its chamber could soon be glowing red hot. He felt fear, anxiety and excitement all at once as the moment neared. If the intel was correct, soon he would see their objective rising up over the horizon, its lights twinkling in the darkness.

Intelligence reported there were between eight and twelve on board, including the target. Fitz had prepared his men to face at least twenty. The enemy would have plenty of weapons, but they were unlikely to be expecting a raid. Not out here on the high seas in the middle of nowhere. Not after all this time. He hoped their long run of evading capture had made them – *him* – complacent. Nevertheless, he expected it to be what the Fleet Contingency Troop of J Company – the Royal Navy's board and search specialists for counter-piracy and counter-narcotics operations – classed as a 'Level Three' boarding. The most difficult of the three categories, it meant facing an openly hostile crew that would violently attempt to repel any boarding party. In fact, he expected the resistance to begin before they even got close to the ship, followed by close-quarters fighting once they managed to get aboard. It was the very task the Royal Marines Commandos had been created for.

He looked at his watch, its face glowing green in the darkness. The vessel should be in sight soon. He flipped down the night-vision binoculars fixed to his helmet, then glanced to his left and then his right. The two accompanying boats were still with them, each carrying eight Marines, with seven more on his own craft. He wondered if it was possible they could get through this without losing a single one of them. He pushed the thought out of his mind. This was no time for emotion or hesitancy. He must do what needed to be done. There would inevitably be fall-out – unless by some miracle they could somehow pull this off without firing a shot. Perhaps the threat of force would be enough? But even as the thought flashed through his mind, he knew it was a forlorn hope. These fanatics wouldn't go down without a fight. Not now. Not after everything they'd done in the name of their 'Holy War'. Innocent men, women, and even children. They wouldn't hesitate to fire on a unit of heavily armed Marines – they'd probably relish it. Especially if their lives or escape depended on it.

The craft motored on. Fitz had no qualms about sending his men into danger, because he'd be right there with them. They were armed, they were equipped, and they were trained. This is what they did. They weren't looking to hurt anybody, but there would be no hesitation in using force if the situation called for it. Not for a second.

For two months now, his team – a detachment from Four-Two Commando – had been out here conducting drug raids. Just last week, Fitz and his unit had tracked a dhow in a six-hour operation, which culminated in his men seizing the vessel at gunpoint. After a search, they found a hidden compartment behind a false bulkhead. The 800 kilograms of crystal methamphetamine stowed away out of sight was estimated to be worth more than £15 million. That had been their fifth raid of the summer. Most of the crew back aboard HMS *Montrose* were under the impression tonight's op was another drugs raid. They were wrong.

Then he saw it. A light. Then it was gone again, hidden behind the wave they were about to crest. The boat rolled up as it powered through the water and he saw it again. The craft crashed down on the other side of the wave and the spray rained down on him. He didn't flinch as he kept his eye on the light. *This was the moment.*

As they got closer, more and more of the vessel came into view. It was a small cargo ship just over 100 feet long, with a dark green hull and a white bridge rising up at the stern. An array of aerials and dishes crowded the roof over the bridge. The deck seemed to be largely empty, save for what looked like four or five large packing crates, lashed down. The first task was to confirm they had the right target. Fitz strained his eyes as he looked through the binoculars until he was satisfied. There, painted in white lettering against the dark green of the hull were the words 'ST GEORGE, PORTSMOUTH'.

He tightened his grip on his rifle and spoke into his radio.

'Target confirmed. Mission is go. Mission is go.' His voice was measured, calm and clear. He and his men were on their own now. The buck stopped with him, but he had no doubts about his team's ability to deal with the threats they were about to face.

It was time for the next part of the op. He made a call over the radio, and within a minute he could hear the faint hum of the Wildcat helicopter as it approached. If the ship's crew hadn't heard it yet, they would in the next thirty seconds.

They must have been within 200 metres of the vessel now, and still he could see no activity onboard. The little ship seemed to be at peace, anchored and sleeping as it bobbed gently in the swell. He narrowed his eyes. It seemed *too* quiet. He hoped they were all asleep below decks, and that his men would be able to board and have them all at gunpoint before they woke. He tightened his jaw. *It wasn't going to be that easy.*

The black of the night was pierced by the tracking lights of the Wildcat and the thwock thwock thwock of the rotor blades slicing through the still, heavy air. Fitz felt the downwash from the aircraft as it buzzed overhead towards the target.

He glanced back at the vessel and saw activity. Movement. They'd been rumbled. He felt his heart rate go up, and the familiar metallic taste in his mouth as his adrenalin began to surge. There was no turning back now.

Then he heard another noise. The diesel engine on the ship spluttered and grunted into life. Apparently they were going to try to make a run for it. It didn't matter. His men knew what to do. He looked up and saw the Wildcat move into position, its powerful searchlight beaming down onto the vessel, which was now a blur of motion, men running around on deck – one dumping something over the side – as it slowly began to move in the water.

The gunner aboard the Wildcat fired two rounds of warning

shots ahead of the boat. The message was clear, but the *St George* didn't stop.

Another blast of warning fire.

Still the vessel continued to motor.

Fitz knew what would happen next. The sniper on the Wildcat now adjusted his aim as the helicopter swung around. He began firing at the rear. After three heavy barrages of gunfire, the diesel engine was silenced.

Then the gunner stopped firing. The message came over the radio, 'All yours, Zero.'

'Copy that,' he replied as he flipped up his binoculars. Then, 'Two Zero Bravo, deploy. Three Zero Bravo, deploy, deploy, deploy.' Again his voice was calm, in control. In response the starboard-side Offshore Raiding Craft peeled out of formation and began a wide arc away from the ship. The port-side ORC mirrored the movement in the opposite direction. Fitz's boat headed straight for the ship as the helicopter hovered overhead, illuminating the scene.

Then he heard gunfire. *Crack, crack, crack.* The first bursts sliced through the night like a whip. Someone had spotted the boat circling in on the vessel's starboard side. The Marines began returning fire, as did the gunner aboard the Wildcat.

Fitz hoped the gunfire would continue to be confined to one side of the vessel. If it stayed that way, it might allow his boat to approach – and perhaps even board – before they were discovered. He reached down for his radio. 'Two Zero, get around to the bow and cover Three Zero. Now.'

'Yes, sir,' came the response.

He watched the ORC off to port pick up speed as it circled around the ship. Still the gunfire was confined to the starboard side. If he could keep the crew occupied long enough, the port-side company might still be able to get aboard undetected; the gunfire might actually help them by masking the sound of their engine.

Fitz was within seventy-five metres of the ship now, and he could see more and more detail. The peeling paint. The small crane on the main deck, forward of the bridge. The radio aerials and LEO receiver dishes for their internet connection. The lights were on in the bridge now and figures were moving around hurriedly, though he couldn't identify any of them. 'Where are you, you bastard?' he muttered under his breath.

'Ladder team, make ready,' he shouted over his shoulder.

As the other two boats got closer, he knew the chances of one of his men being hit became ever greater. There was another burst of machine-gun fire from the ship, followed by the sharp *crack, crack, crack* of his men responding with their assault rifles.

Just fifty metres now.

If they could slip aboard, they could disable the crew before anyone got hit.

Forty metres.

Another burst of gunfire. He heard the cry as one of the bullets found its target. The radio message confirmed it. 'I'm hit!' He couldn't tell who it was. In almost every way, it didn't really matter. Not right now.

Thirty metres.

More gunfire, two short bursts from the automatic weapons the crew were using. Two more anguished cries sliced through the darkness. He clenched his teeth and clung onto his rifle.

Twenty.

We're going to make it, he thought as they got closer and closer. His mind switched into the next stage: get the ladder connected, climb aboard, get six of his men with him. Fan out either side to form a pincer movement on the crew shooting at the boats, order them to stop firing, and take them down if they refused. Then go cabin to cabin on the vessel in search of their real quarry. He highly doubted their target would be out on the deck with his crew. No – hiding down below or taking shelter somewhere in the cargo hold was more his style.

Ten metres.

'We're taking heavy fire here. Three men down, three men down,' came the call on the radio. It was in vain though – Fitz couldn't divert now. It was too late for that. They were all in. *Come on*, he silently pleaded as his craft approached the floating enemy fortress ahead.

Behind him, Lieutenant Broomfield was manoeuvring the ORC right up against the hull of the *St George*. As soon as they were close enough, Marines Kilner and Gould pivoted the ladder up towards the top of the hull. It was just about to catch when the heavy swell seemed to pull the earth away beneath them and the ladder clattered against the metal of the hull and bounced off it.

'I'm hit! I'm hit!' Fitz heard over the radio following another round of fire from the crew.

He winced as the two Marines steadied the ladder and, this time, anticipating the movement of the boat on the rising wave, lifted it and hooked it over the side of the ship. *Contact*.

'*Go!*' Fitz hissed as two of his men began to scramble up the ladder. They'd made it without a shot being fired on their side of the vessel. The diversion of the two other boats and the helicopter had worked. It was a minor miracle, he thought – but that was the exact moment their luck ran out.

Maybe it was the sound of the ladder clattering against the hull in a lull in the gunfire a few moments earlier. Maybe one of the crew was smart enough to assume there might be a second front to this battle. Maybe it was simply chance. But as Kilner was just six feet from the top of the ladder, a figure appeared over the side, towards the bow of the vessel. By the time Fitz saw him, it was too late. The figure had leaned over, raised his gun and fired. Two short bursts. Fitz heard the cry and then watched in horror as the momentum of the bullets ripped Kilner from the ladder. Even before he landed with a splash in the cold, black water just yards from the boat, Fitz had taken aim, and with two quick shots had taken down the shooter.

But where there was one, there were bound to be more. 'Go! Go! Go!' he shouted again to his men as they began scrambling up the ladder. In just a few seconds, Gould was at the top, ready to defend the next man to come up. They had a bridgehead.

Kilner, somehow still conscious, was thrashing his way towards the boat. Fitz hoped his body armour had done its job. Two men leaned over the side ready to haul in their injured colleague. Once he knew Kilner was being dealt with, Fitz turned away, his mind already on the next phase of the op.

He pulled himself up the ladder, climbed over the railing and jumped down onto the main deck. His men were already closing in on the ship's crew from either side. Fitz counted seven men. Two returned fire and were instantly downed. At that point, sur-rounded and realizing the situation was hopeless, the other five surrendered.

Fitz assessed the crew, each of them now on their knees in a line on the deck, hands behind their backs and secured with cable ties. Two of them were shaven-headed, the other three with close-cut, military-style haircuts. All five were wearing jeans and trainers, underneath army surplus camouflage jackets.

He wasn't here. *Hiding below, just as I thought.* He looked down at the five faces, then closed right up to the one who looked the most scared. 'How many men on board, and where is your boss?' he asked.

The man refused to meet his gaze and said nothing. Fitz didn't waste his breath trying again.

'Two Zero Bravo, with me,' he said. 'One and three, you know what to do.'

He was desperate to get his injured men proper medical attention back at the support ship, but he knew he couldn't do that until the enemy vessel was secured, and every single one of its crew members located and subdued. Especially their leader.

At his command, the Marines not tasked with first aid or guarding the prisoners fanned out around the ship and began going room-to-room, the way they had a thousand times before. This was bread and butter to them. Usually it was hidden stashes of drugs they were searching for. Not today.

Fitz remained up on deck supervising. One by one, each part of the ship was declared clear over the radio. Two more prisoners were taken without resistance – it seemed the fanatical devotion to their leader displayed by several of the men on deck earlier did not extend to every member of the crew, especially when confronted with a unit of Marines whose rifles were still glowing red hot.

But as each room was cleared, Fitz began to worry that their real target had evaded them yet again. It wouldn't be the first time the most wanted man in the world had slipped through the fingers of the British government.

But then Fitz's radio crackled again. 'Sir, we've got him.' He recognized Gould's voice, and felt a mixture of relief and excitement reverberate through his body. *We've got him.*

*

Fitz made his way below deck, following Gould's directions, until he arrived at an outer cabin deep in the belly of the vessel, with seven other Marines waiting outside.

The man they were hunting lay within.

The architect of a violent arson and bombing campaign against Muslims living in Western Europe and the United States, Julian Lindfield – better known to all by his adopted public profile of Father Richard 'the Lionheart' Milton – had been on the run for almost six years, all the while continuing to terrorize, murder, and spread his message of hate and fear throughout the world. Time and again he had avoided arrest in missions like this, somehow escaping just before his would-be captors arrived. He had been caught once, seven years previously, while hiding out in a flat in Manchester. That was two years after his first large-scale operation, when he bombed six mosques in London simultaneously, with a death toll in the dozens. 'Leave or you will burn' had become his macabre catchphrase, and the message directed at every Muslim – and every non-white citizen – in the West, which he posted after each attack on the only online platforms that hadn't yet banned him.

He'd been caught, tried, convicted and imprisoned. But he had escaped from Belmarsh Prison after just ten months of a life sentence. After that he'd slipped away, aided, it was thought, by his supporters and troublingly numerous and wealthy financial backers. After that, word was he never again set foot in any nation state, basing himself permanently onboard his ship. It was rumoured he never left it, and the ship never entered port or left international waters, or ever stayed in one place for more than one night. Fuel, food, and supplies were all ferried out to it from support vessels arranged by his allies, and he directed all his violent operations from his office on board. Permanently on the run, he brought terror to the world and taunted his would-be captors.

Fitz knew of two previous Four-Two Commando operations that had failed to apprehend him. On both occasions the *St George* was nowhere to be found when the Marines arrived. Did he have a mole inside the Intelligence services? Perhaps. Fitz had been worried that someone had once again tipped him off that he was in danger tonight, and that maybe he'd left the ship for the first time in years. Or that he'd left weeks, months, or even years ago, the ship now simply a decoy.

'He's in there, sir.' Gould nodded to a metal door with a porthole in the top half. Fitz steadied himself for his first glimpse of the monster. He looked inside and could see Milton sitting on the bed. He was alone. He was more overweight than he looked in his online videos, Fitz thought, but was wearing one of his signature T-shirts: black with white gothic lettering that read: MUSLIMS – LEAVE OR YOU WILL BURN. His shaved head and black beard – going grey at the chin – further confirmed this was the man the world had been hunting for the last six years. He had a disconnected look in his bright blue eyes, as if he couldn't really bring himself to believe that this was happening. Perhaps he'd thought himself untouchable, his years of evading capture having emboldened him. His rigorous precautions should probably have protected him for even longer. But there he was, surrounded, alone and helpless. A rat in a trap.

'We haven't been in yet, sir, as per your orders.'

Fitz nodded and, keeping his eyes and rifle trained on Milton, had one of his men crank open the door. He stepped inside and surveyed the room: the crumpled bed sheets, the desk littered with mobile phones and two laptop computers, and the enormous flag of St George hanging up in front of the video camera Milton used to make his online videos, spreading his message of hate, and taunting the world's security services after each deadly attack carried out in his name.

'Julian Lindfield. You are under arrest,' Fitz said calmly.

The prisoner broke into a smile and began to laugh. 'You know, that is the stupidest thing I have ever heard.'

'Get on your knees,' Fitz instructed. His voice steady, assured.

'I will not surrender to you like some common criminal. If you want me, you come and get me.'

'Don't make this any more difficult than it has to be. There's half a dozen Marines outside that door, your men are all out of the picture and you're surrounded. Now put your hands behind your head. Slowly.'

'Do you know your Bible, my son?'

Fitz knew this was all part of Milton's schtick. He styled himself as a man of God, even attaching the 'Father' prefix to his name, though he'd never actually been ordained by any church.

'I said, hands on your head.'

'If you did, you'd know the book of Isaiah – chapter thirteen, verse fifteen: "All who are captured will fall by the sword."'

Too late Fitz saw the flash of black in Milton's hand as he pulled the gun from under the bed sheets and squeezed the trigger.

Before any of the men outside the room could react, they heard first one shot, followed by another just a split second later.

*

BBC News report, the following morning:

The Ministry of Defence announced this morning that Richard Milton, the terrorist who was responsible for a string of deadly attacks on Muslim targets in Europe and the United States, has died, after committing suicide during a raid by British Special Forces sent to capture him on his ship, the *St George*.

An MoD spokesman said intelligence reports had located the vessel off the Gulf of Aden in the Arabian Sea, and a team of elite Royal Marine Commandos had been dispatched to arrest Milton, whose real name was Julian Lindfield, and who has been the subject of the largest and longest-running manhunt since the operation mounted against Osama Bin Laden.

During the raid, Mr Milton shot and killed one of the boarding party, before turning the gun on himself. The MoD says his body was buried at sea. Photographs and video clips, purportedly of Mr Milton's body, have already begun circulating online.

The body of the Royal Marines officer he shot is being repatriated this morning. He cannot be publicly identified until next of kin have been informed.

Four other Marines were also shot in the raid, but are recovering at a British military facility in Oman. Their injuries are not thought to be life-threatening.

Milton is estimated to be responsible for the deaths of more than 2,000 people, beginning with a coordinated attack on six London mosques nine years ago. In a video statement released online shortly afterwards, he said it was simply the first of many more attacks his group planned to carry out, unless what he called his 'manifesto' was adopted by the British government, and those of other Western European nations, as well as the United States. His demands included the deportation of anyone practising the Muslim faith, and the closure of all mosques and Islamic religious centres. 'Muslims – leave or you will burn,' he said, the words that became his sign-off for each one of his video statements.

The British government had been under heavy pressure from the international community to locate and arrest Milton, after he escaped from the maximum security Belmarsh Prison six years ago and continued to carry out attacks while on the run. The United States have been particularly forceful since Milton's group carried out an attack in Madrid eighteen months ago that killed the US Ambassador to Spain, David Marston, and his nine-year-old daughter.

Intelligence sources told the BBC the so called 'Cross of St George' terror group, which was headed up by Milton, will have been severely weakened by the death of its leader and the capture of seven of his top lieutenants in the raid.

Chapter 1

Leading Hand Abbie Błaszczykowski-Fitzroy crossed her legs and tried to avoid the gaze of the chaplain, which wasn't easy given he was barely two feet away from her. The two of them were crammed into his tiny cabin aboard the Royal Navy Type 23 frigate HMS *Northumberland* as the ship cut its way through the grey seas of the South Atlantic en route to a joint military exercise with the Chilean Navy.

Why had she even agreed to this? She wasn't religious – despite her mum's best efforts – and the last thing she wanted to do was talk about Drew. He was gone. It hurt like hell, even four years later, and no amount of chats over tea and biscuits with the chaplain would change that. But she'd promised Brewster she would try. As the chief boatswain's mate, or 'the buffer', as he was known on board, Brewster was her immediate boss, and pretty much the only person who could convince her to do anything at all now Drew was gone.

'So how have you been feeling this week?' the chaplain asked in a gentle voice.

She looked down at the blue carpet, faded and fraying at its edges. She wondered, for the first time, whether it was officially navy blue. 'Same as last week, Bish,' she said quietly, feeling the warmth from the mug of tea in her right hand.

He wasn't actually a bishop of course, but in the Navy everyone was known by a shorthand version of their job. No matter the ship or the individual concerned, the chaplain was always called 'Bish', and Abbie – as a seaman specialist, or 'sea spec', in the Warfare branch – was known as a 'dabber'.

He nodded slowly and stirred his tea. 'You know it's going to take time.'

'It's been four years,' she said plaintively.

She closed her eyes and fell back in time to the day that had changed her life, just six months after she'd first joined the ship. She'd woken up and checked her phone, hoping for a message from Drew. There was nothing. Instead she had begun scrolling through Facebook and had soon come across the news story. The terrorist Richard Milton had been killed in a raid by British Special Forces. She read on and froze when she reached a key part of the story. 'During the raid, Mr Milton shot and killed one of the boarding party . . .' Her heart had sunk through her feet. Somehow, she'd known. It was Drew. She was certain of it. Horribly, sickeningly, dreadfully certain.

Still, she'd silently prayed her intuition was wrong, but within the hour she'd had the most awful news she could imagine confirmed when the captain had called her into his office and relayed the news in a haltingly awkward manner. She was a widow. A widow at twenty-five years old. Widows were supposed to be old ladies. Not sailors in their mid-twenties.

They'd tried to prevent it, but pictures had leaked on the internet within hours: gruesome images of Milton's horribly mangled face – what was left of it. Abbie had told herself she wouldn't look, but of course she did. She hadn't known what she would feel, but if she was hoping to find some level of consolation – or even some sick pleasure – in seeing him dead, she was mistaken. She felt nothing but revulsion, both at the grisly photographic evidence and all that it – all that Milton – stood for. Everything he'd done, everyone he had killed. But Drew above all. He'd robbed her of her partner, her lover, her best friend – her life.

'At least he died doing something so noble,' someone had offered, as if that was supposed to be some kind of consolation. He was *gone*. Ultimately it didn't matter whether he had been killed bringing the world's most wanted man to justice, or been hit by a bus while out buying a pint of milk. In the end the result was the same. The pain was just as brutal.

'There's no time limit on grief,' the bish offered, in his gentle voice.

She blinked and looked up at him, back in the present. She noticed for the first time that he was somehow ageless. His face was smooth, devoid of the creases, lines and wrinkles that came with age, and yet he was completely bald. He wore a set of thin spectacles with gold rims which were currently perched on his hairless head. He could have been anything between twenty-five and forty-five.

'I know. I just thought by now it might be getting a *little* bit easier,' she said.

'But you don't think it is?'

'No,' she said. 'And I know I'm running out of time.'

He cocked his hairless head to the side. 'What do you mean?'

'People are fed up of me moping around,' she replied. 'Even my family. I know what they say about me. "It's been so long. Why can't she just get over it? Move on?" And that pisses me off. I can't just *get over it*. I wish people would stop saying that. My husband is *dead*. Gone. And everywhere I look I see happy couples, and I *hate* them.' She balled her left hand into a fist. 'I hate them because they're so lucky and they don't even know it. They take it for granted. And I'm left with no one.' She looked back down at the carpet as she felt a wave of grief roll back over her. '*Get over it,*' she said again. 'Would you just get over having your heart ripped right out of your chest? Having your life destroyed like that?'

The bish said nothing.

'But people don't want to hear that. They think you'll get over it a little bit more every day until the pain's all gone. Like it's a bruise that will just fade away to nothing. They want you to be over it – not just for you, but for themselves, because people don't like having to deal with other people's emotions. It makes them uncomfortable.'

She looked up at him again. 'Have you ever noticed how people apologize if they start crying? "I'm sorry, I'm getting emotional," they say. Why do they have to be sorry for that?' She didn't wait for an answer. 'It's because it makes *other people* uncomfortable. We're all such people-pleasers.' She shook her head again. 'But after four years, I'm just . . . exhausted. I'm exhausted of having to carry this all by myself. Of trying to *move on,* for everyone else's benefit.'

The bish nodded gently but didn't interrupt her flow.

'But I can't "move on". I can't "let go" or "get over it", or any of the other bullshit things people have spouted at me over the last four years. I can't do that because in a weird way it keeps him alive. Getting over it, letting go, moving on – doing that would mean he'd be slipping away from me. I can't let go. I can't move on. I don't want to. I don't want to let go of him.'

There was silence again in the little room. She was suddenly aware she was breathing hard, her jaw tight, her left hand still balled into a fist. She tried to release some of the tension and sipped her tea. 'Have you ever lost anyone? Anyone close to you?'

'My mother,' he said. 'Two years ago. A stroke.'

'Right, so then you *know* – you know how hard it is. If someone you love dies, they don't just die once. They die again and again, every single day. Every time you wake up and start to come to, there's that blissful moment – just a fraction of a second – when you don't remember. Then it hits you all over again: he's *gone*. And the pain of it all comes flooding back and you just want to shut your eyes and shut it all out again. But you can't.'

She wiped a tear from her eye.

'And you know the other thing? It's not just the hurt, the pain, the grief. It's the anger. I'm so *fucking angry*, Bish.' It briefly occurred to her that she probably wasn't supposed to use such language with a man of the cloth, but she didn't care. 'And I know it's not the Christian way, I know you're supposed to turn the other cheek and all that – but I will never, ever forgive that bastard Milton for what he did. And if he was here right now, I'd go up to the arms store, get a rifle, and shoot him dead.'

She looked up at the chaplain, meeting his gaze again.

'I'd make sure he knew who I was and what he'd done to me, and then I'd kill him. I don't care if I went to prison for the rest of my life. I'd do it for Drew.'

'And you think that's what Drew would want? Vengeance?'

She let out a deep sigh. 'I don't know.' But that was a lie. She did know. She knew he'd want nothing of the sort, but that didn't stop *her* feeling the way she did.

'What about going to Hell?'

'It's easier to scare someone with tales of Hell if they actually believe in it.'

The bish smiled. 'Okay, forget Hell, forget God and forget the Bible. How about some Eastern wisdom. Do you know what Confucius said about revenge?'

She shook her head.

'"Before you embark on a journey of revenge, dig two graves."'

'Meaning what?'

'Meaning revenge won't give you what you want. In the end, you'd only be hurting yourself.'

'I dunno, Bish. Right now, I think it would feel pretty fucking good. When I close my eyes I can see him in my mind's eye.' She let her eyelids drop. 'Cowering. Afraid. Made to feel what every one of his victims felt in their final moments. Maybe then I'd get some closure.' She sank back in her chair and tipped her head back, looking up at the ceiling. 'Maybe then I'd be able to *move on.*'

'Look,' the bish said, 'I know it hurts. I know it hurts like hell. But I've been around a little longer than you' – yes, but how *much* longer? – 'and there's something the self-help book pedlars don't want you to know.'

She tilted her head back down.

'I'm sorry to tell you this, but for most people, there *is* no such thing as closure. You just have to keep going and, little by little, day by day, eventually you *will* grow around it and chip away at the pain.' He held out his hands in front of him. 'And that's all there is to it. It's hard and it sucks and it won't be a linear process – you'll have good days and bad – but that's the truth.'

'But that's just it, Bish,' she replied, looking him in the eye again, tears forming in hers. 'It feels like all I ever have are the bad days.'

Chapter 2

Hugo Ridley flicked a stray piece of lint from his waistcoat and plucked an apple from the fruit bowl on the sideboard in his glass-walled office. He took a bite of the succulent fruit and savoured the taste for a moment before sliding behind his desk and sinking back into his ergonomic chair. He opened the secure email portal on his laptop and was confronted with a dozen fresh intelligence reports which had piled up over the weekend – a weekend he'd spent on a very agreeable shoot up in Scotland at the estate of an old family friend.

He sighed. So much admin. A part of him missed the old days, when he'd had far less power but a lot more excitement. It was the circle he could never square: he preferred being out in the field to being chained to a desk, but what he craved above all was power, advancement. And he knew that meant being here. Pulling the strings rather than dancing to someone else's tune.

One of the reports was marked 'DECEPTION ISLAND'. The time stamp told him it had come in early Sunday morning. He was irritated that he was only reading it now – he would have to remind the duty staffers that he was always to be alerted to any intel regarding that installation, no matter how trivial, no matter the time of day or night.

With a click of the trackpad, he opened it and began to scan the text, his mind filtering out the superfluous words so he only took in what was necessary.

'Distress call . . . Deception Island . . . 0200 hours . . . alert state RED . . . Major explosive eruption expected within twenty-four hours . . . request full evac . . . HMS *Protector* dispatched in response . . .'

Hmmm, he thought as he took another bite out of his apple and processed the information. He would need to get in touch with the base commander – and then brief the captain of *Protector*. This was a mildly vexing development, if not entirely unexpected. He had planned for it, after all. There was a procedure in place. A protocol. He'd designed it himself. And he knew Major Turner, the base commander, would already be putting it into action. Nevertheless, it would be prudent to check in with him. Ridley was careful like that. In his job, it was a necessity.

He scanned the rest of the contents of his inbox for anything else urgent while he crunched on his apple, but a buzz from his pocket interrupted him. His service phone. Well, one of them, anyway. The vibrations of this one did at least indicate something potentially more interesting than another routine intelligence report. It was a device he only used for a limited number of select contacts.

Still, he thought ruefully as he reached inside his jacket pocket, there was no *ceremony* to anything anymore. He was too young to have actually experienced it, but he longed for the golden age of espionage. A time when he would have received information from the field in the form of a coded message hidden in a dead drop, or via a monotone voice reading out numbers on a static-filled radio frequency as he sat in an attic room with an earpiece in, his pencil and codebook at the ready, deciphering the information as he went, with just a bottle of Scotch to keep him warm. He'd even settle for a teleprinter machine clattering into life in a secret and secure radio room, its clandestine message then conveyed to him by a pale young secretary who would be going to great lengths to hide her crush on him.

The *tradecraft*, the sense you were conducting business in a way no one else could, the romance of it all – he'd arrived in the job far too late for any of that. Now it was all so mundane. A message on a mobile phone. Just like any Herbert out there on the street. End-to-end encrypted message services were so secure these days, there simply wasn't the need anymore for their own network of secret satellites or radio transmitters or teleprinters in secure rooms. More's the pity, he thought as he pulled out the phone from his pocket and tapped in the code to open it.

He stopped chewing.

The delivery method of the message may have been mundane, but its contents were not. He stared at the single word that had popped up on his screen, wishing it would somehow morph into something else or disappear entirely.

It was a wish made in vain.

He glanced around his office. Despite his nostalgia for the lost age of his profession, and his yearning for the excitement of his youth, he was proud of how far he had come. He'd moved up the ranks with speed, managing to sidestep the usual perils that stymied careers like his. He'd even been called a 'high flier' by senior management in one of his most recent performance reviews. But he knew the moment he saw the message he'd have to go and see *her*. She would not take it well. He also knew that, if handled poorly, the code word staring back at him from his phone could represent the end of his career. The pitfall that finally arrested his rise.

But then, he knew he wouldn't handle it poorly. A lesser man might have been worried. But not him. This wasn't disaster. This was a blip. He'd wanted more excitement, hadn't he? And he was about to get it. He remembered the warning his housemaster Mr Garrett used to dole out: 'Be careful what you wish for, boy.'

He picked up the landline phone on his desk and dialled the number. A pause as it rang and was then answered. 'I need to see her. Is she free?'

Five minutes later, he was at an innocuous-looking outer office. A beige sofa on one side, a desk with a secretary on the other. He coveted it all. The status, the power, the trappings. The secretary.

'You can go in,' she said in a quiet, velvety voice.

He nodded as he approached the heavy oak door, knocked and then walked straight in.

The woman on the other side of it ignored him, continuing to read whatever was on her computer screen.

He surveyed her and her office. In contrast to the anteroom – all sleek furniture and not a stray speck of dust to be found – her office was a mess, a series of dumping grounds for piles of folders and papers, books and boxes. Her desk was the same – her laptop was perched on a stack of manilla files, and she'd carved out a space directly in front of her where her A4 notepad rested. With a surreptitious flick of his eyes, he tried to pick out some key words on the pages – old habits die hard – but her scribbles were indecipherable, her handwriting as messy as she was.

Next to the notebook was a brown McDonald's takeaway bag, also resting on a stack of papers. He could see the dark patch of a grease stain creeping up from the bottom. It disgusted him.

Still she hadn't looked up from her screen. He noticed she was wearing two pairs of glasses – one with pink frames perched on her nose as she read, and another turquoise pair lodged in place in her thick grey hair. He wondered if she knew the second pair

24

was there. He could imagine her hurriedly turning over papers and rummaging through her bag or desk drawers looking for them.

He was irritated at the thought. He'd long ago reached the irrational point that inevitably comes when you work for a boss you don't respect, when he found almost every aspect of her being annoyed him. The way she addressed him, the idioms she used, her colourful jumpers – it was as if she was deliberately trying to be conspicuous. Even her gait triggered irritation in him now.

He waited as patiently as he could. She was perhaps the only person in the world who could make him anything approaching nervous. Despite the fact he had little respect for her professionally, and even less liking for her personally, she was still his boss. She still had power over his advancement – or otherwise.

Eventually she flicked her eyes from her screen to him. The only signal she would give that it was time for him to start speaking.

'Something's just come in. It's Deception Island.'

'Oh, the eruption? Yes, rather unfortunate, but you have a procedure for this, I take it?'

So she already knew that part, he thought, once again irritated that he was only finding out now.

'No ma'am,' he tried to hide the involuntary wince that followed whenever he used a term that acknowledged her superior rank. 'There's something else.'

'Go on.'

'It's . . .'

'Come on, come on, spit it out.'

'I've just received a coded message.' He swiped open his phone and held it up for her to see.

She pulled the set of spectacles she was wearing up off her nose and added them to the pair wedged into her hair.

The message read: 'ELBA'.

Her face hardened, her eyes narrowed. 'When did you receive that?'

'In the last fifteen minutes.'

'And since then?'

He shook his head. 'Nothing. They've gone dark.'

'I was under the impression this situation was under control,' she said coldly. 'You assured me, in fact.'

He shifted uncomfortably on his feet.

'Need I remind you how embarrassing this would be if—'

'You need not.' He coughed. 'Ma'am.'

'We're talking about British sovereign territory here.'

'I know that.'

'If this isn't handled—'

'It will be,' he interrupted.

She resumed her sentence, her tone harder. 'If this isn't handled, it won't just be you and me on the chopping block. There will be enquiries, hearings, resignations. Could bring the whole bloody thing crashing down.'

'I'm aware of that.'

'There's a patrol ship en route already, I gather?'

He nodded. '*Protector*.'

She slid her glasses back down onto her nose. 'Then I suggest you find a way to get onboard that ship before it arrives.'

'Yes ma'am.'

'And I don't want to see you again in this office until this is dealt with,' she paused, 'one way or another. Do I make myself clear?'

'Perfectly.'

'Good.'

'There's a transport flight leaving Brize Norton in,' he checked his watch, 'just over two hours. That will get me most of the way.'

'I'm sure you'll figure out the rest. A *high flier* like you,' she said icily.

'Yes ma'am.'

'Good.' She returned to her computer screen. The meeting was over.

Ridley retraced his steps, past the secretary, down the hallway and two flights of stairs and then back to his perfectly ordered office, a plan already forming in his mind as he went.

There were a number of ways he could resolve this, but there was one that appealed to him immediately. This was a very specific situation, and he knew it would require a very specific solution. He needed to check the whereabouts of one of his assets. He remembered seeing something about a training exercise. *That could be it.* He returned to his desk and with a few clicks of his mouse he began pulling up the details. He was searching for one name. When he found it, he allowed a thin smile to creep across his face.

He began putting it together in his mind. *Yes, it could be done.* Christ, it was going to cost a fortune, but it could be done. It would have to be. There was no alternative now. The bill would be in the hundreds of thousands. There would be hell to pay for that. But *she* would back him up. She had to. Assuming he could resolve it, of course. If he didn't, he knew she'd cut him loose in a heartbeat. Throw him to the wolves to save her own skin. If he couldn't sort this out, they would need someone to pin it on. That would be him. He couldn't let that happen. He wouldn't.

He needed to make some calls. Fast. First he needed to call *Protector* off. That would involve pulling some major strings at Northwood – they wouldn't like that one bit, especially as the ship would be well over halfway there by now, and his asset was more than six hundred miles away. It wasn't perfect, but he would make it work. Once those wheels were in motion, he'd have to get himself on that flight south leaving in just a few hours.

He picked up his landline and began to dial. He glanced back at the reports piling up on his screen. They would have to wait. Excitement was back on the agenda for now. He saw Housemaster Garrett again, wagging his finger. 'Be careful what you wish for, boy.'

Chapter 3

Abbie stood out in the rain, leaning against a railing as she watched the Royal Marines Commandos training on the helicopter deck at the stern of the ship. They were hitching a ride on *Northumberland* as part of the joint exercise, and would soon be deployed to conduct mock raids on the other vessels, by boat and helicopter.

She watched as they continued their drills. As far as Abbie was concerned, they were the finest fighting force in the British military. Drew had been one of their number, and she'd been so proud of him.

'Have you sent your application letter yet?'

She turned to see Petty Officer Paul Brewster watching her as she in turn watched the Marines. He was the only person other than Drew to whom she'd confessed her ambition of one day joining the men she was now so closely observing.

Brewster had assumed the impetus came from Drew, but in fact, it had been Abbie's dream long before she ever met her husband. Her father had served in the Royal Air Force, as his father had before him. Abbie always knew she wanted to follow her dad into the military – but the Air Force wasn't for her. She wanted to join the elite. The absolute best of the best: the Royal Marines

Commandos. As a girl she'd read every book she could get her hands on, every biography from retired Marines, every volume charting their daring exploits in battle.

She'd been dismayed to learn that women weren't allowed to join – but when this ban was lifted, she resolved that one day she would apply to the training programme. It was a daunting prospect – she knew that the training was tougher than for any other branch of the military. She also knew that each year more than twenty-five thousand men applied to join the Royal Marines. Only four hundred made it. So far, not a single woman had been successful. Abbie harboured secret hopes of being the first, and yet something held her back from applying. Was it fear of failure? Fear of the gruelling training programme that broke 98 per cent of the men who attempted it?

Probably a bit of both. But that wasn't all. After Drew died, she'd lost focus. Focus and confidence. With him gone, everything seemed a bit pointless. He'd been so encouraging. It had taken her a long time to even tell him about her dream. She worried he'd try to warn her off or, worse still, mock the very idea.

But he'd done neither. In fact he'd become her cheerleader-in-chief. And, at his urging, she was readying herself to take the leap and apply. And then he'd died.

For the first few months she was too grief-stricken to do anything other than keep herself alive. That was how it had felt. Any further ambitions seemed ludicrously unachievable. As the months went by, she began to function a little better, but with each passing month and year, her dream seemed to get a little further away. It never died, it just got smaller and smaller in her rear-view mirror.

The presence of the Marines detachment on board ship had brought it back into sharp focus. And after one pint too many, when they'd been ashore in Cape Town on their way south, she'd confessed all to Brewster. Just like Drew, he'd encouraged her to dream again and apply for the training. She'd even filled out the application form but couldn't quite bring herself to send it, despite Brewster's urgings.

'Do you know how many people apply? The odds are terrible. *And* I'm a woman,' she said, as the Marines continued their drills on the flight deck.

'Someone's got to be first,' he said. 'Why not you?'

'Can we not get into this, please? I've just had an hour with the bish talking my ear off.'

'It's good for you,' he replied. 'I know you – if left to your own devices, all you'd do is lie in your bunk scrolling through pictures of Drew on your phone. You need to—'

'Do *not* say I need to "move on",' Abbie warned.

Brewster held his hands up. 'I wasn't going to say that. I know better. Anyway, look lively – new captain wants to see us in his cabin.'

Captain Harris had joined the ship just three weeks earlier. Abbie had yet to meet him, other than a few times they'd passed in the passageways of the ship, and he'd offered a quick 'hello'.

'Both of us? What about?'

'You'll find out when we get there.'

'You mean you don't know,' she replied with a smile.

'Don't make me court-martial you for insubordination, Blaz,' he said, rolling his eyes.

They made their way back inside the ship to the captain's cabin. Brewster knocked sharply on the door.

'Come in!' came the enthusiastic reply.

Abbie followed Brewster inside. The room was lined with pine panelling and the same blue carpet as the bish's little office. There was one small porthole above a built-in sofa which had a coffee table in front of it with two small armchairs either side.

31

A conference table with six chairs was off to the right, with the captain's desk in the corner. She noted there were three brightly coloured finger paintings pinned up above his work space. A young father away from home.

He rose from his desk and motioned towards the sofa and chairs. 'Thanks for coming. Please, have a seat,' he said.

He held out a hand towards Abbie. 'I'm sorry we've not had a chance to properly meet yet, but you know how it is. New vessel, trying to get around to everyone takes time.'

'Of course, sir,' she said as she shook his hand. He was a trim man, she guessed late thirties or very early forties, with light brown hair that would have been curly if he allowed it to grow any longer, and a big square face that reminded her of a Disney prince.

She saw him glance at the name tag on her chest, a cotton rectangle Velcroed to the left-hand side of her dark blue uniform.

'That's quite a name you've got there. How do you pronounce that?'

'Blaz-sy-kov-ski, sir. My great-grandfather was Polish,' she said, reciting a well-practised explanation. 'Came over in the war. A pilot. Flew with the RAF.'

'Jolly good.' He paused. 'And the "Fitzroy" bit?'

'My husband's name. Added it on when I got married.'

'Ah yes.' He shifted in his seat and averted his eyes. 'Terrible business, all that.'

'Yes, sir,' was all she could think to say.

'And you never thought of just taking his name entirely? For the sake of convenience, if nothing else.'

She could tell it was an awkward attempt at a light-hearted comment, but she couldn't help but bristle.

'Are you married, sir?'

'I am.'

'And when you got married, would you have taken your wife's name and changed your own – for the sake of convenience?'

Brewster shot her a glance that she knew meant she had over-stepped the line when speaking to a senior officer, but Harris nodded uncomfortably and said, 'No, no. Quite right. See your point.'

There was an awkward moment of silence, which Harris broke with a clap of his hands. 'Anyway,' he said, 'new orders. Forget the training exercise. Cancelled. For us at least. We're heading south.'

'Oh?' said Brewster.

'Yes. Antarctica. Deception Island, to be precise. I believe you know it?' he said, looking at Brewster.

The buffer nodded. 'Spent about two weeks there, must be, oooh, six years ago. Was on *Clyde* at the time. Stopped off there to help carry out some maintenance work on the station. Used to be a cold weather training facility, until they closed it down. Bit of a spooky place. Why are we going there?'

'Evac job.'

'Evac? I thought the place was deserted?'

The captain shook his head. 'Evidently not. There are ten researchers there. And they need pulling out. Fast.'

'Why the hurry?' asked Abbie.

'Deception Island isn't really an island,' the captain said. 'It's a sunken volcano and, according to the seismic data, it's about to blow.'

He stood and retrieved a print-out from his desk and began to read. 'Alert state: RED. Major explosive eruption is expected within twenty-four hours. Large ash plumes expected to exceed ten thousand metres above sea level.'

'Volcano? In Antarctica?' Abbie said.

Brewster nodded. 'Yeah. It blew in the Sixties as well. Caused an avalanche which cut right through some of the old buildings down on the shoreline. Then the lava came after that. You can still see where it went straight through the middle of the main hut like a hot knife through butter. They had to evac then. Only just got them off in time. The blast totally buried the Chilean base in ash and rock – they say the best wine cellar in Antarctica is buried down there.'

'So who's there now?' Abbie asked.

'Just those ten researchers, monitoring volcanic activity, and undertaking some kind of wildlife study,' said Harris, returning to his seat. 'Chinstrap penguins, or something.' He turned to Brewster, 'Not much else down there, I gather?'

'Not much,' he replied. 'They closed the training centre about five years ago, I think. Years back, the place was a whaling station, so there's still plenty of junk from that around – the old huts, the digester tanks, boilers, separators, harpoons, stuff like that – but that's about it. There was a wreck of one of the whaling boats grounded on the beach. There's still an old church from those days, too. And a graveyard,' he added.

'What's the access like?' Harris asked.

'There's a big natural harbour, which is really the flooded crater of the volcano. It's pretty cool, actually.'

Harris nodded.

'So why us?' Brewster asked. 'There must be someone else closer? A fishing boat? Research vessel? Something?'

'That there may be, but we've been told to go, and go, therefore, we shall,' the captain said. 'We're getting underway now, and should be there in about,' he checked his watch, 'twenty-four hours. And when we get there, I want you two to lead the shore party.'

Brewster nodded. 'Of course, sir.'

'Good. There's one more thing – you'll have a little company. There's a visitor on his way down who'll be coming with you.'

'Oh?'

'Some chap from Whitehall. The Foreign Office, I think; the message was a little vague. He's insistent we don't go ashore without him for some reason yet to be communicated to me – I suspect it's something to do with the territorial situation. The island is claimed as sovereign territory not only by His Majesty's Government, but also by Chile and Argentina. There's probably some arcane statute of international law we have to comply with to avoid giving an inch in terms of the British claim. We might need to leave some formal notice in writing. Make sure the flag's still flying. Let everyone know we'll be back once the trouble has passed. Leave the key under the doormat, so to speak.'

'When's the volcano supposed to blow?' Abbie asked.

'They can't say for sure, but we're in radio contact with the base and their best guess is some time in the next thirty-six hours. Could be sooner, could be later, but the base commander has reported it's started "venting", which is apparently a bad sign.'

A knock at the door halted the conversation.

'Sorry to interrupt, Captain,' the officer said, craning his head around the door. 'But you're needed on the bridge.'

'What is it?' Harris asked.

'It's Deception Island, sir – we've lost radio contact with the base.'

Chapter 4

'When did we last hear from them, Walker?' Captain Harris asked as he entered the bridge, closely followed by Abbie and Brewster.

'Two hours ago, sir,' the officer of the watch replied. 'Routine check-in. Green here,' he said, nodding at the comms officer, 'spoke to a Lance Corporal Robertson.'

'He reported venting continuing,' Green said. 'And they've started having tremors. I told him we'd be there in twenty-four hours.'

'When was next check-in due?'

'Oh-seven-hundred.'

The captain glanced at the clock. Almost an hour ago. 'And?'

'Nothing but static, sir. We're still trying, but we've got nothing.'

'Do we think it's already blown?'

'We don't think so. There's a seismic monitoring station on James Ross Island and they say they've not picked up anything significant yet.'

'And they'd know?'

'So they tell me, sir.'

Harris nodded and turned back to Walker. 'How far out from Deception are we right now?'

'About thirty hours.' The officer beckoned the captain over to his navigation terminal. 'We're having to go around a nasty-looking storm here,' he said, pointing to a spot on the screen directly between the ship and the island. 'It means at least an extra six hours sailing to skirt round the edge of it.'

'How bad's the storm?'

'Sea state eight. Fifty-knot winds, forty-foot seas. Very rough.'

Abbie watched the captain purse his lips as he thought through his options. A few moments later he began issuing orders. 'Walker, course change, please. Get us on the most direct route to the island. Storm or no storm.'

'Yes, sir.'

'Green – get on to Northwood. Tell them we've lost contact with Deception and are heading there at full speed. Find out if they've got any other way to contact the base – sat phone, anything – and keep trying them on the radio. Clear?'

'Yes, sir.'

Harris turned to Abbie and Brewster. 'It's going to be a bumpy ride. Send out the word – get everything lashed down and secure.'

Brewster nodded.

Abbie followed him out of the room as the captain picked up the mic and addressed the ship through the tannoy system.

'Good morning, *Northumberland*. Commanding officer speaking. I just wanted to take a couple of minutes to tell you what we'll be doing next. Our tasking is to the far south. It will be cold. It will likely be rough for a sustained period. We can expect ten-metre seas. We need to make sure we're on our A-game. So you need to be prepared and ready.'

Abbie made her way back down to the deck below behind Brewster, who began shouting out orders to his charges to make the ship ready for what lay ahead as he went room to room.

'We're expecting some fruity seas . . . It's gonna get

rough – really rough . . . If it moves, tie it down . . . Look at the state of this place. It's shit! Get those pictures down off the wall . . . Are you secure for sea state eight? Come on team, you can be *so* much better than this . . . Go and secure the mess for sea. You joined the Navy to *do* stuff, so get fucking moving . . . All it takes is one big wave . . .'

Abbie busied herself tying things down, stowing away anything that moved. She knew Brewster was a stickler and was determined to not give him any reason to find fault with her work. Once she was finally satisfied, she had time to return to her bunk – known as her 'rack' on board ship. She pulled out her smartphone and connected to the ship's Wi-Fi, which was provided by a low earth orbit satellite system that gave them access wherever they were in the world. She searched for 'Deception Island' and began reading through the entries.

The island was notable for its unique geography: the flooded volcano caldera in the centre that formed the harbour was surrounded by a ring of rock, with cliffs lining most of the outer coast. There was just one break in the rock: a narrow entrance called Neptune's Bellows which led into Port Foster.

The large natural harbour made it an ideal base for sealers, who hunted the fur seal population almost to extinction in just five years in the 1820s. The whalers came later, hunting and slaughtering the animals ashore for some twenty-five years until that industry collapsed too in the 1930s.

Abbie was surprised to learn the island had also seen some minor military action. The 'Deception Island incident' was a territorial skirmish in 1953 when, in response to Argentine attempts to build a naval base on Whalers Bay, Royal Marines had been dispatched to the scene to reassert British sovereignty. They captured two Argentine prisoners, seized their flag and equipment, and burnt down the Argentine and Chilean bases before leaving.

The first volcanic activity was witnessed in the 1840s when an American sealer reported the southern shore was 'in flames'. And in the 1960s two big eruptions destroyed the scientific stations that had been established after the Second World War, leaving the whole island abandoned for almost thirty years.

An abandoned Antarctic whaling station prone to major volcanic eruptions? It seemed an odd place for nations to be fighting over, Abbie thought.

She wondered about the researchers trapped on the island now, waiting for rescue or the volcano to blow, whichever came first. Were they hunkering down in their base, nervously watching for signs of the eruption? Were they even still alive? She hoped they could reach them in time.

She looked up from her phone when the ship seemed to surge up into the sky and then drop away beneath her, her stomach lurching up as it did so. She heard a crash from the next cabin – clearly someone had failed to follow Brewster's instructions and get everything squared away. He wouldn't be happy about that.

Then the ship rolled up and back down again as her stomach did more somersaults. They'd hit the storm.

Chapter 5

The big ship reared up over another towering wave and crashed down on the other side, the hull creaking and groaning with the strain as Abbie held on and prayed it would be over soon.

For hour after hour the dull grey vessel had doggedly forced its way through the storm. Abbie had never experienced seas like it. She had thought Brewster was being over-zealous with his barked orders to stow away anything that moved, but she now knew he'd been right. The fact that a structure as massive as a Royal Navy warship could be tossed about so effortlessly was a brutal reminder of the power of the ocean. The vessel creaked and cracked and clattered and crashed its way through the onslaught, being lashed by ferocious winds and driving rain as it remorselessly drove on into the violence.

For some reason, Abbie felt compelled to go out on deck, to fully experience the power of the storm swirling around her. She pushed open a hatch and stood out there alone, holding on tightly to a guardrail as the water – a mixture of rain and sea-water – came for her again and again as the ship rolled and pitched. The noise was overwhelming. Elemental. The wind howled, the waves crashed, the ship groaned. She stood her ground, getting wetter and wetter as she and the ship fought through the storm together. She relished the battle. The wind roared at her, so she roared back, summoning her grief and her anger, to rage at the elements. For once, she allowed herself to get completely lost in the emotions. With no one else daring to brave the conditions out on deck she dropped the facade she carefully maintained and gave in to it all. She bellowed back at the wind and the rain and the waves and thought them powerless over her despite all their might. She'd been going through a storm far worse than this for years now. A little rain couldn't hurt her now. Nothing could hurt her like that again.

She closed her eyes as the water lashed over her, Drew's face in her mind's eye. She'd been waiting all her life to meet him. Looking back, she felt like she'd simply been marking time through her childhood, her teen years and her early days of adulthood, until Drew came along. A young life spent existing, rather than living. She'd been a lonely child – despite being one of three sisters, she never felt the connection her older siblings seemed to share. She *was* close to her father, but less to her mother, who followed her dad around the world to his overseas postings and spent her days bitching about the other wives, attending church, and secretly drinking gin. Abbie had to follow too, of course. A year in Cyprus, two in Germany, then Belize, then back to Germany. People said military kids were good at making friends because they moved and changed schools so often. And Abbie's two sisters, Lauren and Beth, were. But somehow she'd never quite picked up the art herself. Sure, she had friends, but never what she would have called a *best* friend, someone to tell her deepest secrets to. She didn't find that connection until many years later when she met Drew. Only then did she finally have someone who was just hers. And she was his. They were a little team together against the world. It had taken her more than twenty years, but at last she'd found him.

And then Richard fucking Milton had taken him away.

And as that thought hit her once again like the eighty-foot waves crashing against the hull of the ship, she felt again the urge she'd confessed to the bish. She could feel her rifle in her hands, see his disgusting face through her sights as she aimed her gun, her finger closing on the trigger . . .

Another wave hit, the ship smashed against it, and for a moment her hand slipped on the rail. She flashed open her eyes. Drew was gone. Milton was gone. The gun was gone. The storm was getting worse. It was time to go back inside.

But before she could take a step towards the hatch, another wave slammed against the bow of the ship with even more violence. And as the big vessel rolled down the other side of it, she heard a crash from the helicopter hangar at the stern, followed by the painful screech of metal on metal. Half a beat later, the hatch nearest her was flung open and half a dozen flight engineers burst out onto the deck.

She held the hatch for them as they raced for the hangar. Normally she'd throw a disparaging comment their way about their general level of incompetence – which they'd return with interest – but the looks on their faces told her now was not the time.

Instead she stepped inside and pulled the hatch shut behind her, dulling the noise of the wind and the rain and the waves. Suddenly a high-pitched alarm sounded, followed by a warning over the tannoy system: 'Flood alarm. Flood alarm. Flood alarm.'

Abbie rolled her eyes and shivered at the prospect. *Northumberland* was an old ship. Leaky. She wasn't worried by the flood alarm – she'd heard it before aboard this vessel – but she knew it meant bailing out by hand. And that meant standing in freezing cold seawater for God knows how long. It seemed incredible that on a multimillion-pound warship, bailing out water by the bucket was still the most effective way to prevent a flood, and yet it was true. At least aboard this old ship.

She double checked the hatch was shut tight then made her way down into the ship where she knew she'd be needed to help out. She found Brewster directing operations, summoning buckets and brooms and ordering sailors to form a human chain to start bailing out the excess water. Abbie was set to join the chain when Brewster caught sight of her. 'Blaz. We're taking on water in the portside chain locker. Need you down there and bailing out on the double.'

Abbie froze. The chain lockers were, as far as Abbie was concerned, the most hateful places on the entire ship. Right down at the bottom of the hull, they housed the two huge anchor chains. There were two, one on either side of the ship, and they were both dark, tight and cramped. She could already feel the panic rising within her, her heartbeat getting faster, her mouth drying. Tight spaces. She hated them.

'Come on, look lively!' Brewster shouted at her as the buckets of water were passed up the human chain.

'The chain locker? Really?' she asked, hoping she could somehow get Brewster to deploy her elsewhere.

'Did I mumble?' he replied. 'Yes, the chain locker. Can't have that filling up with water. And they need someone small to get down to the bottom. That means you.'

Abbie paused for a moment.

'Look, I know it's a shit job, but this isn't up for discussion, Blaz. It's a JFDI request.'

'A what?'

'Just fucking do it. Now get a move on!'

She took a deep breath and climbed down the nearest ladder to the deck below, the panic rising in her with each step she took to get lower down in the ship.

As she made her way down, the tannoy system blared into life again. 'Can I remind you that the whole of the upper deck remains out of bounds,' the tinny voice said.

From further down the passageway, she heard someone reply, 'Cheers, dickhead! As if we didn't know!'

She arrived in the anchor windlass room – the space that housed the capstans and winches that raised the anchor. Three of the crew were scooping up water with buckets while a fourth – his name was Piper – waved Abbie over to a hatch in the floor.

'We've got water in the chain locker,' he told her. 'None of us can get down far enough – we can't fit past the chain, but you should be able to squeeze through.'

Abbie glanced down into the hatch. It seemed to spiral down forever, like a tunnel to the centre of the earth. She felt like it was getting narrower and tighter before her eyes, closing up into a point. She fought the urge to rear backwards away from it. *No*, she told herself, *you must*.

Piper handed her a head torch on a strap, which she slipped over her forehead.

'We'll lower these down to you,' he said, pointing to a couple of buckets on ropes.

Abbie nodded. She couldn't speak; all her concentration was focused on forcing herself down the tiny hole in front of her.

She took a deep breath and slid into the hatch, finding her feet on the ladder, then dropping down, rung by agonizing rung. Several decks down, she reached the chain locker itself. Without allowing herself to stop and think about it for even a second, she continued her descent down the ladder holds. She looked down and could see the water sloshing around at the bottom. She was almost at the very bottom of the entire ship, but the hardest part was yet to come. The heavy link chain was resting, coiled on top of itself in loops. But at the point just below her it had settled in an odd position, jutting out towards the wall. There was just enough of a gap between the chain and the ladder for a small person to slip past, before the gap opened up again below the pinch point.

Abbie tried to fight the terror rising up inside her. She could feel her heart beating inside her chest, like a V10 engine at full tilt. She was almost hyperventilating. She had to get a grip. She closed her eyes, but all that did was transport her back to that day on the beach.

It was bad enough navigating the warren-like passageways of the ship – and the tight-fitting bunk she squeezed herself into every night. But her desire to succeed in the Navy – and her childhood dream of joining the Marines – forced her to fight through her claustrophobia. She couldn't give them any excuse to pass her over. One long-standing requirement was that no Royal Marine could suffer from sea- or air-sickness. She didn't think a crippling fear of confined spaces would have helped her chances.

So she had never told a soul. She buried her fear as deep within herself as she could. She developed a coping mechanism that helped her battle through it every time it threatened to over-whelm her. She took her military training and used it in her own personal fight with her phobia. As she breathed in and forced herself down past the chain, she could feel the wall pressing on her chest and the chain at her back as the space closed in around her. She was thousands of miles from that bloody beach, yet she could still taste the sand in her mouth.

It took tremendous concentration, but she was determined not to give in to the panic. '*Per mare, per terram*,' she said under her breath. '*Per mare, per terram. Per mare, per terram.*' She whispered it to herself over and over like an incantation as she fought through the panic and pushed past the chain and down to the bottom. The first bucket was lowered down behind her, and she set to work filling it with the ice-cold water before yelling back to Piper to haul it up. Christ the water was *freezing*.

She repeated her mantra to herself silently whenever she felt she was about to lose control of her fear. '*Per mare, per terram.*' *By sea, by land.* The Royal Marines' motto. It kept her focused on her lifelong ambition. Something to think about rather than the tiny space she was squeezed into at the bottom of the ship. '*Per mare, per terram,*' she mouthed again silently as she hauled out another bucket of seawater and fought the overwhelming urge to pull herself up and out of this hateful place as fast as she could.

Chapter 6

Once the ship had been made safe and the captain had reduced their speed through the storm, there was time for dinner in the mess and then bed. Abbie had strapped herself into her rack, pulled out her phone and scrolled through the photo album marked 'Drew'. She'd flipped through her collection of photographs of him for the thousandth time, until she felt herself slipping out of consciousness as the ship rolled its way through the ocean. She let sleep take her, Drew holding her hand and hugging her tightly to keep her safe as she dreamt.

The next thing she heard was Brewster's voice.

'Blaz! Wakey-wakey. Captain wants us on the bridge.'

Abbie resisted, trying not to wake completely. She just wanted to hold onto Drew for a moment longer.

Brewster banged on the door. 'Chop-chop!'

Reluctantly, she blinked open her eyes. The ship seemed calmer than before. It was still rolling and pitching in the swell, but not with the ferocity of the night before. She glanced at her watch. She'd slept right through the night.

She hauled herself out of her rack, threw on some clothes, pulled her hair back and knotted the elastic band she used as a tie around the back. She opened the door to find Brewster on the other side.

'Come on, quick as you like,' he said.

They made their way to the bridge where they found Captain Harris, a pair of binoculars in hand, scanning the horizon.

'Sir,' Brewster said to announce their arrival.

The captain handed the binoculars to Brewster and pointed out the forward window. After a few moments, Brewster handed them on to Abbie. She put them to her eyes and tried to focus. She scanned the horizon until she spotted it: peeking through the mist and the rain was a snow-topped ridge.

'Mount Pond,' said Brewster. 'The highest point on Deception Island. We're here.'

Harris nodded.

'So why have we stopped?' Brewster asked.

'Three reasons. First, the very fact that it could blow any minute means I can't put the ship in that danger. If the volcano blows while we're in the harbour, we'd be a sitting duck. We will be keeping *Northumberland* a safe distance away at all times. Second, with the seas this rough, I wouldn't risk sailing through the harbour entrance anyway.'

'But the entrance to the harbour is half a K wide, isn't it?' said Abbie, remembering her internet research from the night before.

'Yes,' said Brewster, 'but there's a rock, two and a half metres below the surface, right in the middle of the channel. This island is full of hidden surprises.'

Harris nodded. 'It would tear the bottom off the bloody hull. So we'd have to avoid that, which puts us far too close to the rocks either side. At least in this weather.'

'Why do we need to go into the harbour? Can't we come alongside somewhere else?' Abbie said.

Brewster shook his head. 'No. Almost the whole outer coast is cliffs, either rock or ice. There are a couple of breaks in the rock, but the swells out here make landing a boat impossible. The only place you can get ashore is in through the harbour.'

'And thirdly,' Harris continued, 'we're still waiting for our friend from the Foreign Office.'

'Do we know when he's arriving?' Abbie asked.

The captain glanced at the clock on the wall. 'He should already have landed at Mount Pleasant. From there he's doing a chopper relay with *Lancaster*, then *Protector*, then to us.'

'Seems like a lot of fuss for an evac job,' said Brewster.

'The Royal Navy likes fuss, Brewster. I thought you'd have realized that by now.'

'So we wait?'

The captain nodded. 'We wait. In the meantime, please get yourselves and the RIB prepared so you'll be ready to go as soon as he's arrived.'

Abbie nodded and turned to leave, but didn't make it more than a few steps before they all heard it. It sounded like a bomb going off and seemed to reverberate through the hull of the ship itself like a wave in the steel.

Captain Harris raised the binoculars to his eyes. 'Smoke.'

'Looks like we're out of time,' Brewster said.

Abbie watched the captain clench his jaw as he thought through his options.

'Green,' he barked to the comms officer. 'Get on to North-wood. Tell them what we've seen and find out where the hell our visitor is. Now!'

'Yes, sir.'

'Could we send the helicopter in?' Abbie asked.

Harris shook his head. 'Damaged in the storm. Out of action for the moment.'

Abbie remembered the crash and screech of metal she'd heard

coming from the hangar the night before, and the look of panic on the faces of the flight engineers.

Harris turned to face her and Brewster. 'I don't like putting my ship or my ship's company in danger, but there are people in trouble down there. We have a duty to help if we can.'

'Yes, sir,' Brewster said.

'Sod the Foreign Office. I want you two on that RIB now. Get over there, grab them and get back to ship ASAP. Understood?'

'Yes, sir,' Abbie and Brewster said in unison.

Chapter 7

Abbie and Brewster motored away from *Northumberland* and towards the island on a Pacific 24 Mark 4 rigid inflatable boat, Abbie's hands on the wheel, Brewster standing to her left. The boats had room for two crew and six passengers – assuming all six were carrying weapons and full kit. Abbie and Brewster had neither – just Gore-Tex foul-weather jackets on over their uniforms – and so they should be able to squeeze all ten scientists on board at a pinch.

Abbie followed the wisps of smoke still rising from the top of Mount Pond. She hoped they could be in and out before the volcano stirred again. The danger was very real, but also kind of exciting. She wondered why the captain had specifically asked for her for this job. Usually he would have left it up to Brewster to pick a 'volunteer'.

The choppy seas forced her to moderate her speed, but even doing just fifteen knots they were soon in the shadow of the island, its cliffs rearing out of the black sea like the impenetrable stone walls of a medieval fort. It was an imposing sight – intimidating, even, as if it had been purposefully designed to cower anyone who dared approach.

'Why do you think the captain asked for me on this?' Abbie

asked. 'I mean you – it makes sense. You've been here before. But me?'

'You're one of our best sea specs, Blaz, and probably the best boat handler on board. Those facts may or may not have been noted to superiors in reports from your boss.'

She aimed an appreciative smile at Brewster.

He shrugged his shoulders in return. 'I'm just sayin'.'

'And calling me into his office like that? I think that's only the second time I've ever been in there. A lowly dabber like me, why not just pass on the orders through you?'

'You know this new breed of officer,' Brewster replied. 'All cuddly and friendly. All about the personal touch these days. They want to know everyone on board. Names and faces. It's his first command,' he added. 'They're always super keen when they first get their own ship.'

'I guess so.'

'And perhaps he knows that you're meant for bigger things,' he added. 'Maybe he just wanted to size you up.'

Abbie thought about it. In truth, she should be moving on by now. Moving up. She thought back to the Marines training on the heli-deck. Was her grief really holding her back? Or was it just an excuse? Was she just scared?

'I can't get promoted,' she replied. 'The captain would have to learn how to say my name first.'

Brewster stifled a grin. 'Give 'im a break. I've known you for years and I still can't get it right.'

'It's easy,' she said. 'Just ignore some of the consonants. Here – say it back with me: Blaz-sy-kov-ski. And don't forget the Fitzroy.'

Brewster shook his head. 'Don't suppose they get your coffee mixed up with anyone else's at Starbucks. Not with a name like that.'

She laughed. 'I tend to just go with "Abbie",' she said. 'They can usually manage that.'

Brewster closed his eyes tightly, as if summoning all his concentration. 'Diniyar Bilyaletdinov,' he said slowly and deliberately. 'I can say that one,' he added proudly.

'Who the hell is that?'

'He used to play for Everton,' he replied.

She shot him a look. 'Oh, so *that* you can pronounce?'

He grinned back at her.

'I looked it up, you know, after I got married. There's an app – you can see how many people in the country share your name. Apparently I'm the only one.'

'*Shocking*,' Brewster replied sarcastically. 'I'm *shocked*.'

She shook her head and rolled her eyes at him.

'Listen, Blaz,' he said, his tone suddenly more serious. 'When we get back, I want you to send that application in.'

'Yeah, yeah, I will,' she waved a hand at him dismissively.

'Don't fob me off like that,' he said. 'I mean it. Look, you're the best dabber I've got, and it would be so easy for me to keep you. But you've done your time. You're ready. And I don't want to be sitting over a beer in another Cape Town bar in ten years' time, listening to you whine to me about how you never went for it.'

She sighed. 'I just don't know. No woman has *ever* passed that training programme. Ever.'

'So what?'

'What if I can't do it?' Her mind flashed back to a Royal Marines Commando recruitment advert she'd seen a thousand times on TV when she was younger, and played a thousand more on YouTube. It showed a young hopeful taking on an assault course. There was one particular moment that haunted her. The kid – and he seemed to get younger every time she watched it – splashes his way through a muddy trench, his face already a picture of anguish, until he reaches an instructor who yells at him, ordering him down on his knees before shoving the poor lad under the surface and into a sort of underwater tunnel. The film stops in freeze-frame and a caption asks if *that* is the viewer's limit of endurance.

The film plays on, the trainee flailing in the water and then hauling himself through the tiny, claustrophobic tunnel. The angle changes to show him shimmying through from the rear, his shoulders scraping the sides, his knees hitting the rocks on the bottom, his head millimetres from the top. Was that *her* limit?

To compound the terror, a split second later the film shows his trouser leg getting caught on something – a sharp rock or a metal rod (she could never quite tell what it was, despite her repeated viewings). He yanks and yanks but it won't come free. He's starting to panic, his eyes ablaze with fear, bubbles filling the screen as he lets out muffled cries under the water.

It was unbearable for Abbie. She backed herself to be every bit as strong in body and mind and every bit as determined and resourceful as anyone else applying to that programme – but that image always stayed with her. And she knew it wasn't just an advert. She'd discovered it had been filmed at the Lympstone Commando Training Centre in Devon, and the underwater tunnel was an all-too-real part of the course. If she was even lucky enough to be selected for training, she would have to take it on – and beat it.

It seemed such a silly thing to be holding her back, but that didn't make the prospect any less terrifying for her.

Eventually the poor lad manages to free his trouser leg and pulls his way through the rest of the tunnel before he's yanked out of the water by an instructor and sucks in a desperate breath of air.

Another caption asks if *that* is the viewer's limit.

The recruit shakes his head, trying to reorient himself as an instructor yells at him to compose himself.

Another freeze frame, another caption, this time telling the viewer not to even bother filling in the application form if this is beyond what they could endure.

And it wasn't just her chronic claustrophobia holding her back. She'd lost so much drive, so much of herself, when Drew had died.

'So what if you can't do it?'

Brewster's comment snapped her back into the present.

'Ninety-eight per cent of the men who apply can't do it. There's no shame in not making it through the toughest military recruitment process in the world. I couldn't give a toss if you don't pass. The shame is in not even applying,' he said.

She nodded slowly. 'I know, I know.'

'I mean it, Abbie.'

She noted the use of her first name. He saved that for when he really wanted to make a point.

'Promise me you'll send the form in. Or I'll do it for you – or at least I would if I could work out how to spell your bloody name.'

She shot him a look.

'I can never remember, is it just one "t" in Fitzroy, or two?'

She laughed. 'Okay!' she said. 'Okay. I promise I'll send it in as soon as we get back. Happy now?'

'I'll be happy when we get this lot off the island and get back onboard ship.'

They motored on towards their destination, the cliff faces getting bigger, *Northumberland* getting smaller behind them.

'See that old lighthouse on the point there?' he said gesturing to a red and white structure that towered up out of the black rock. 'Head for that.'

She nodded. 'Does it still work?'

'Don't think so.'

As they got closer to the lighthouse, she could see the gap in the cliffs begin to reveal itself, like a mouth slowly opening. Just five hundred metres wide, it was the only break in the ring of otherwise impenetrable rock that made up the island. The only way in or out of the harbour that lay within. But still they couldn't see inside, the mist hung like a curtain over the entrance to the harbour, as if the island was hiding its secrets within.

'Neptune's Bellows,' Brewster shouted, nodding at the gap. 'That's what they call it. Raven's Rock is right in the middle, just two metres below the surface.'

Abbie remembered the captain's warning: *It would tear the bottom off the bloody hull.*

'Caught out plenty of ships coming through here before it was mapped,' Brewster added.

'This place is straight out of an Indiana Jones movie.'

'You feeling penitent?' he smiled.

They reached the narrows, passed the lighthouse off to their right and motored through the fog. The interior of the island began to emerge as they came out the other side of the mist curtain, the two great slabs of rock dwarfing them on either side. It felt almost magical, like they were entering a forbidden kingdom through a giant gateway.

The mist seemed to lift as they made their way through the Bellows, and the howl of the wind fell away as they became shielded by the mountains that ringed the island. Very suddenly, the waters were calm. Steam swept across the surface and wafted ashore, lending the whole scene an eerie, ghostly feel.

'That's the steam from the magma just under the surface heating the seawater,' Brewster offered. 'It was like that when I was here last time, only not so noticeable. I guess it's heating up with the volcano about to blow.'

'Spooky,' Abbie replied. 'Feels like we're heading into an

episode of *Scooby-Doo*.' She was trying to sound casual but there was something unnerving about this place. She felt a creeping sense of unease building with every moment as they were swallowed up by the island.

Now shielded from the worst of the ferocious southern winds by the ring of rock surrounding them, they could suddenly hear a new noise. An altogether more worrying one echoing off the cliffs. An alarm.

Abbie glanced at Brewster.

He raised his eyebrows to confirm he'd heard it too. 'Eruption warning?'

'Must be.'

They motored on.

Abbie knew from her internet research that the harbour was around five miles long and almost as wide, encircled by the rock of the island itself. It was almost like a lagoon, with the narrow channel they'd entered through the only way in or out.

'We're now in Port Foster, the crater of the volcano that forms the natural harbour. That's Penfold Point ahead of us,' Brewster said, pointing to a craggy rock face that jutted up out of the water, high and lifeless. 'And to the right is Whalers Bay, where the first sealers set up camp in the 1820s. It's the same spot where later they hauled up the whales and slaughtered them. And that,' he added, nodding to the mountain peak that towered over the scene, threatening and austere with its snowy top and black slopes, 'is Mount Pond.'

Abbie nodded and took in her first view of the interior of the island. It seemed like somehow colour hadn't made it this far south: the only two hues she could see were the black of the volcanic rock and ash that now encircled them, and the white of the snow and ice that covered the mountain tops and, in some cases, stretched right down to the shore. The whole scene was in monochrome, as if God had run out of paint as he neared the ends of the earth.

Her first view of Whalers Bay only compounded the feeling that she was looking through some kind of ghostly portal directly into the past. The black sand beach was littered with ageing wooden huts and discarded pieces of rusting debris: pipes, oil tanks, anchors and harpoons, which were slowly being eaten away by the wind and the cold and the salty sea air. The wreck of a small wooden ship was rotting away on the shoreline.

Further inland there was a church spire and, just visible through the rising mist, a small collection of perhaps three dozen weather-beaten crosses erected in a tidy group. The island's graveyard. The huge sun-bleached whale bones scattered along the beach only served to add to the macabre scene. Ash, bones, killing apparatus and destruction: the whole island was imbued with a feeling of decay and death.

'See that big hut that's collapsed right down the middle?' Brewster said.

She nodded.

'That's Biscoe Hut. British Antarctic Survey. That big hole is from the last eruption. First an avalanche was triggered when the lava melted the ice up the mountain, then the lava flow itself arrived.'

The hut had simply been torn in two, the remnants of a tin roof sagging down either side of the gap the lava had cut. It looked like it was about to collapse entirely at any moment.

To the southeast of the beach there was a concrete slip that extended all the way down below the waterline at one end, next to a dilapidated warehouse.

'That was the slipway for the whale carcasses,' Brewster explained. 'They'd harpoon them out on the open ocean, tow them in here to the harbour. Then they'd winch them up the slipway and use these massive knives and hooks to strip off the blubber, and then finally remove the meat and the bones. It's called flensing.'

It all sounded so barbaric. She tried to picture the scene, imagining those hardened whalers slicing and hacking away at the mighty creatures on this very shoreline. She felt suddenly repulsed by this deathly little island, which appeared to her to be little more than a butcher's yard on a grand scale.

'You can see the big winch in the middle there,' he said pointing to a rusted-up series of cogs at the top of the slipway. 'They had smaller hooks on chains either side to hold it steady while they worked. Then they'd take the blubber and boil it up in those massive tanks you can see there. That's how they got the oil.'

The hulking tanks sat, bloated and squat on the black beach. Once full to the brim with the bloody spoils of the whalers' war against their prey, they now hunkered down beneath the watchful gaze of the surrounding peaks, slowly rusting away. One was tilted at an angle, its collapse already in progress.

'How do you know so much about all this?' she asked, slightly surprised at his detailed knowledge of all the grisly details.

'I was here for two weeks. No internet, no TV. But they had books. I can read, you know,' he said sarcastically before rolling his eyes at her.

She smiled.

Round to the northwest was the only modern structure within view: a single-storey building, about the size of a large bungalow, clad in dull green corrugated iron and topped with a green tin roof. It sat next to a wooden pier that ran out into the harbour. It seemed oddly out of place among the rusting detritus of previous centuries, like a new car parked in a scrapyard.

'Head for the jetty,' Brewster said, raising his voice over the sound of the alarm which was getting louder as they got nearer to shore. 'That's what they call the beach house – used to be one of the training centre buildings. It's where we stayed. I presume they still use it. There's a second building further up the side of Mount Pond.'

'Looks like it's undamaged,' she said.

'I guess that bang we heard from the ship was just the opening act,' Brewster replied. 'The old girl just clearing her throat.'

Abbie turned the wheel and cut the power to the engine as they neared the jetty. As the RIB silently glided up to it, Brewster stepped off the boat and tied up, with Abbie following as they began walking towards the hut.

With the engine silenced, the only sound now was the deafening alarm. It was echoing off the rock walls that surrounded the harbour, which amplified and multiplied it. Abbie winced at the urgent, invasive, aggressive noise. Now they were inside the confines of the harbour, the wind was much quieter than when they were out on open water. The island seemed protective and claustrophobic all at once. A welcome port in a storm, but not one you'd wish to shelter in for a moment longer than was necessary.

Despite the inescapable and pulsing alarm assaulting their senses, somehow it was too quiet. 'Hey Buffer,' Abbie shouted as she scanned the scene. 'Where is everyone?'

Chapter 8

Abbie and Brewster stood on the wooden jetty, the alarm slicing through the crisp sea air around them. There wasn't a soul in sight.

'You'd think someone might have come out to meet us,' Abbie said.

'Hello?' Brewster called out as they trip-trapped down the wooden dock towards the black beach. '*Hello?*'

As they got closer to the dull green building, they could see one of the external doors flapping back and forth in the wind. Brewster turned to Abbie and raised an eyebrow. Above the door was an orange warning light flashing on and off in time with the pulsing of the alarm. They continued up to the building and stepped inside, finding themselves in a large boot room. Abbie pulled the door shut behind them to stop the flapping. The alarm seemed even louder inside the hut. There were thick red jackets on hooks, and pairs of trainers scattered on the floor. Someone had been here, and recently.

'Weird,' said Brewster quietly. 'Hello?' he called. 'Anybody home?'

There was no response other than the piercingly loud alarm. It was like some sort of bug, burrowing through their ears and directly into their brains. BwaaaaaaaaAAAAAAAAHHHHHHH. BwaaaaaaaaAAAAAAAAHHHHHHH.BwaaaaaaaaAAAAAAAA HHHHHHH.

'We need to get that thing shut off,' Abbie called to Brewster. He nodded in full agreement.

They walked through the boot room into what was clearly a mess hall.

'Hello?' Brewster shouted again.

Abbie surveyed the scene. There were two half-eaten meals on the table – it looked like a full English breakfast had been interrupted – cutlery dropped next to the plates, and two half-drunk cups of coffee. She put her hand against one of the cups. 'Cold,' she said.

'Looks like they left in a hurry,' Brewster replied.

'What?' Abbie said; the alarm was so loud that she couldn't hear him.

'*THEY LEFT IN A HURRY,*' he repeated, shouting over the alarm.

'I guess you don't hang about if you know the volcano's about to blow,' she shouted in reply.

Brewster nodded.

They walked through the room into a corridor that led into the rest of the building, which they soon discovered included a shower room with four stalls, two single bedrooms and four twin rooms. There were personal items in all: clothes, stereos, iPads, and pictures of family members pinned up on the walls. One room had a topless calendar. Both beds in two of the twin rooms were made, as was the one in the larger of the two single rooms. The beds in all the others looked like they'd been left in a hurry: the sheets, duvets and pillows left haphazardly strewn on the mattresses.

Further on there was some kind of laboratory with a desktop

computer on a bench and two units that looked a little like printers. Each housed in one half of a suitcase, the machines consisted of a big roll of paper on a reel with an arm over the top, and a box with buttons, dials and switches to the right.

'For the seismic activity?' Rachael said.

Brewster nodded. 'Guess so.'

Next to the lab was what looked like a comms room. They both clocked the radio base unit humming at the end of a wooden bench, its dial glowing yellow. Abbie looked around the room for some control that might silence the alarm but, seeing nothing she walked across to the bench and checked the frequency, then picked up the mic. 'Testing, testing,' she said, a sound echoed in real time through her and Brewster's handheld units.

'The radio works,' she said. 'So why did they go dark on us?'

Brewster shook his head.

There was a white box, about the size of a carton of cigarettes resting on the bench next to the radio unit. Abbie followed the cable coming out the back of it as it went up and then through the wall. She looked through the little window and followed the cable to a white slab of plastic perched on a shipping pallet, angled up towards the sky. She recognized it as a Low Earth Orbit internet system, similar to that used onboard the ship.

'And looks like they have internet,' she said.

He nodded. 'So where is everybody?'

They stood looking at each other.

'The open door, half-eaten meals, porch a mess, radio perfectly operational, and no sign of anyone,' Abbie said. 'What the hell's going on here?'

'They must have gone up to the other building,' Brewster offered.

'Yes, but why in such a hurry?'

'Maybe they thought this building wasn't safe? With the volcano and all?'

'But surely they wouldn't want to be going *up* the mountain and closer to the eruption? Being down here on the shore makes more sense.'

Brewster shrugged.

'And they must have a radio up there too, so why haven't they called us on that in the last twenty-four hours?'

'Maybe it's broken?' he said. 'Or the eruption cut the signal somehow?'

'Perhaps, but the one here works fine – surely they could have taken it with them? Or come back to send us a message once the initial danger had passed?'

Brewster had no answer to that.

'Is there anywhere else they could have gone?'

'There are a couple of old huts dotted around the island,' Brewster said. 'Most of them derelict for decades – all the old whaling ones, anyway. Some of the old research huts might be in better nick – the ones not buried under ten tons of ash – but they haven't been used since the Sixties, so probably not much better.'

'So they must be in the other building, right?'

He nodded.

'Then I guess we'd better get up there and see if there's anyone home.'

'This fucking alarm is doing my head in,' Brewster shouted as they headed back the way they came.

It was only when they walked back through into the boot room that Abbie noticed another door leading off it that they hadn't spotted on their way in. She pushed it open with some difficulty, and found what she thought at first to be a second radio room, but quickly had to reappraise her take. The room was windowless, the door thick and heavy. She felt for a switch on the wall inside the door and flicked it on. Two fluorescent strip lights blinked into life. Across the length of the far wall was a long wooden bench with one office-style chair facing it and a second knocked onto its back. On top of the bench sat another radio and an array of small boxy monitors, like CCTV units, stacked double height. There were eight screens in all. She looked behind her, then back at the screens. One of them was showing the outside of this very room. The one underneath it had a view of the jetty where their boat was tied up. All six others were showing nothing but static, as if the cameras that fed them had been knocked out or disabled.

'You remember this?' Abbie shouted.

Brewster shook his head.

On the desk she found a dark blue hardback notepad, flipped it open and began scanning the entries.

'Some kind of logbook,' she said. 'Looks like a record of shift times. People clocking on and off.' She frowned as she read on, then flipped back through the pages to the front of the book. Each day was the same, going back months. 'Why would you need twenty-four-hour shifts?'

'For monitoring the volcano?' Brewster suggested as he pulled open cupboards and drawers.

'I guess so. But what about these other screens? What do you think they were showing?'

Brewster shook his head.

Abbie closed the book. 'Come on then—'

'Jesus!' Brewster exclaimed, cutting her off.

She turned to her right, where he was standing next to a six-foot-high metal cabinet. He was holding one of the doors open and peering inside.

'What is it?' she asked.

'Gun cabinet,' he said. 'And, by the look of it, it held some serious shit.'

'Held?'

He nodded as he turned to face her, pulling the other door open for her to see inside. 'Whatever was in here, it's all gone.'

She scanned the cabinet, row after row of empty gun racks.

'I thought this was a volcanic research facility,' she said quietly.

Brewster shook his head and pointed to his ear. He hadn't heard her over the noise of the alarm.

'Why they hell would they need all that for a research facility?' she said, louder.

'I told you there was something off about this place,' Brewster said, shutting the doors.

'Yes but what? What the hell's going on here? And why would you need a room like this?'

'I don't know,' Brewster said, shaking his head, 'but somewhere on this island there are a shit-load of guns – and we don't have any of them.'

They stood for a few moments as they thought through the implications, the pulsing of the alarm the only sound audible. With every note it sounded, it seemed to be getting louder, reverberating through their skulls, slowing their brains, ramping up their anxiety.

Abbie looked back at the screens and something caught her eye. At first she wasn't sure what it was, but something was different. Something was off. But what was it? It was as if her subconscious had picked up on something awry but was refusing to share it with her conscious brain. She looked at each screen in turn. The six showing static were just as they had been before: nothing but an electronic snowstorm. She looked at the one showing the outside of the room they were standing in. Again, it looked the same as it had before. Then she shifted her focus to the last one, the camera showing the jetty. *That was it.*

'Come on,' Brewster shouted. 'We're getting out of here. We'll head back to the ship, update the captain and decide what to do from there. We can't stay here unarmed if there's people with weapons out there. Let's go,' he said, turning towards the door. 'Now.'

Abbie shook her head. 'That might not be possible,' she said as she pointed at the screen. Brewster turned to look. The tiny black-and-white screen was showing its view of the jetty. Their boat was gone.

Chapter 9

They ran out of the room, through the porch and out of the building and thudded down the jetty. But even before they reached the end, they could see there was no sign of the boat.

'What the hell?' Brewster said.

'You sure you tied it up?' Abbie asked.

'Of course I did! You saw me do it.'

'Then where the hell is it?'

It had been less than fifteen minutes since they'd landed. But now, as they stood on the end of the dock casting around the expanse of the harbour, there was simply no sign of their boat. How could it have simply disappeared? Even if Brewster somehow hadn't tied it up, it couldn't have drifted far.

'Unless . . .' she was thinking fast. 'Unless the researchers saw the boat and just took it to get the hell out of here?'

'But without us? Why would they do that?'

Abbie raised her eyebrows and shook her head. 'I don't know. Maybe they panicked?'

'Get on the radio to the ship,' Brewster said.

Abbie pulled her radio from its clip on her belt and held it up to her mouth. '*Northumberland*, this is Błaszczykowski-Fitzroy. Błaszczykowski-Fitzroy to *Northumberland*, do you read?'

She held the radio close as she listened out, but got nothing but static and empty airwaves in response. She shot a worried look at Brewster before she tried the radio again. '*Northumberland*, this is Błaszczykowski-Fitzroy. Błaszczykowski-Fitzroy to *Northumberland*, do you read?'

Nothing.

'These bloody things are shite,' Brewster said, before trying his own radio with the same result. He gestured at the mountains surrounding them. 'We'll never get a signal down here.' The geography of the island meant that they were at the bottom of a huge natural bowl made of solid rock. 'We'll have to get to higher ground.'

Abbie shook her head and began walking back down the jetty. 'Or we could just use the radio in the hut,' she said.

'Smartarse,' Brewster replied as he turned to follow her.

She marched back inside the building as the alarm continued to blare, and straight to the radio room. She picked up the mic and repeated her message. '*Northumberland*, this is Błaszczykowski-Fitzroy. Come in, *Northumberland*.' Again there was silence. She tried again. '*Northumberland*, do you read? Come in, *Northumberland*.' She shot Brewster a worried look. 'It doesn't make sense – this radio must have got signal, otherwise why was it here?'

He nodded at the radio base unit. 'Doesn't matter if there's a signal if the radio isn't working,' he shouted back over the noise of the alarm.

She looked at the small grey box. It was lifeless, its dial no longer glowing yellow. She hit the on/off toggle three times, but to no effect, before tracing the power cord back to the wall. She unplugged it and tried a different socket, but nothing would bring it to life. 'It was working *literally* five minutes ago,' she said, with no real expectation of an explanation from Brewster. 'Wasn't it? I'm sure the dial was on? Or did I imagine it?'

He shrugged, but she was already pushing past him, heading for the mysterious CCTV room they'd found. There was another radio in there. She pushed the heavy door open and flicked the light switch, but the room stayed pitch black. She flicked it back and forth, but there was nothing but darkness.

She was trying to think straight, work it all through logically, but the incessant and unbearable noise of the alarm was like a spike pushing into her brain.

Each blast started low before building, building, building in volume and pitch, until it reached its crescendo: the point of maximum noise and the most hateful note of the cycle, where it held for a fraction of a second – though it felt like longer and longer with each repetition – before it ceased, then began the sequence again.

BwaaaaaaaaAAAAAAAAHHHHHHHH. BwaaaaaaaaAAAAA AAAHHHHHHHH. BwaaaaaaaaAAAAAAAAHHHHHHHH.

Abbie felt like each stabbing note was cutting off the synapses in her brain, stopping her train of thought in its tracks. She tried to block it out, tried to focus – *what had happened to their boat? And why had the power gone off?* – but the alarm wouldn't let her.

BwaaaaaaaaAAAAAAAAHHHHHHHH. BwaaaaaaaaAAAA AAAAHHHHHHHH. BwaaaaaaaaAAAAAAAAHHHHHHHH.

It was like trying to think while someone was slapping you repeatedly in the face.

BwaaaaaaaaAAAAAAAAHHHHHHHH. BwaaaaaaaaAAAAA AAAHHHHHHHH. BwaaaaaaaaAAAAAAAAHHHHHHHH.

She closed her eyes as if that would help dull the sound.

If only the fucking thing would stop just for a moment.

Abbie shouted, 'WHAT THE HELL—' but suddenly the noise she was trying to overcome ceased. The alarm stopped.

There was silence.

Chapter 10

'The power's been cut,' Brewster said, somewhat redundantly as they stood in the doorway.

'Maybe their generator was damaged in the eruption?' Abbie offered.

'Or maybe,' Brewster said more quietly, 'someone has knocked it out deliberately.'

'Why would anyone do that?'

He shook his head. 'I don't know, but there's something very weird about this place.'

'It's not a bloody haunted house,' Abbie said. She was trying to stay calm and rational – that was imperative – but he was right: there *was* something very weird about this island. First the whole *Mary Celeste* vibe of the deserted mess hall with the half-eaten meals and no one anywhere to be seen; then their boat going missing, and now the power cut. Clearly someone was messing with them, but who? And why? The truth was it didn't matter; the only thing they could do was get a radio signal. There would be a rational explanation for everything else. There had to be. 'Come on, let's go,' she said firmly. 'We need to get to higher ground, get somewhere our radios will work. Or find another base unit.'

Brewster furrowed his brow. 'There's another radio room up

at the second building up the hill. At least there was. And anyway, the path up there is the only way to higher ground. The cliffs are too steep down the rest of the beach.'

'Right then,' she said, trying to sound anything other than freaked out.

'Hang on,' Brewster said. 'Let's try the generator first. Maybe it's just tripped out.'

She nodded. 'Good idea.'

He led her along the beach, the peak of Mount Pond towering over them ahead, the huge oil tanks rusting away to their right. Abbie's eyes were scanning the bay and the beach, looking for any signs of life. In amongst all the old derelict buildings, and the rotting and ghoulish remains of the whaling station, there were a hundred places someone could be hiding, watching them.

Someone had taken their boat – it was the only explanation. What she could not explain was why someone would want to do that.

She was all too keenly aware of their exposed situation: they were alone, unarmed, and cut off from back-up. They'd found some kind of surveillance room that once also held a substantial cache of weapons – weapons that were now missing. That was clearly an active, working room. A room set up for watching *something* – something possibly highly dangerous, judging by the armoury they'd found.

'You said this used to be a training base, right?' Abbie said, trying to take the sting out of the situation by talking it through.

'Right.'

'So maybe there are no guns. Maybe they just never took away the cabinet when they closed the base?'

'Possibly. But what was that room about with all the CCTV screens?'

'For watching the volcano?'

'Maybe,' said Brewster sceptically.

They made their way from the beach house, past a maze of ancient pipework and whale oil apparatus and then past the old British Antarctic Survey hut which, close up, Abbie could see was on the verge of collapsing: its timbers rotting away, the glass in the windows on the east side having long since fallen out and smashed, the rusty tin roof well past saving.

At the west end of the bay, set onto a concrete pad just in front of the sheer rock face that lined the beach, was a small tin shed, some four metres by three.

'Generator,' said Brewster. 'Runs on diesel.'

He cranked open the metal door and peered inside. 'Dead.'

'Well, let's get it going again.'

Between them they located the fuel valve and the choke handle, but the starter switch elicited no response. After three attempts, Abbie began investigating, and soon found the cause of the problem.

'Brewster,' she said quietly, 'the fuel line's been cut.'

He came and crouched down next to her, and she pointed to the break. This was no fraying over time, or corrosion from weather – or anything natural or accidental. This was a clean and deliberate slice through the line.

They looked at each other, once again at a loss. Neither one of them felt the need to vocalize the fact that apparently someone was sabotaging them at every turn. Someone, it seemed clear, who was intent on not letting them leave this island.

'I guess we're going up the hill,' Abbie finally said. It was their only rational course of action. She tried not to think about the fact that might be exactly what someone wanted.

Brewster nodded.

They pushed on along the beach. Abbie flicked her eyes left and right. Was someone watching them right now? Was there someone crouching behind one of the old buildings or rusty tanks, watching and waiting for . . . for what? The more she thought about it, the more she became convinced they'd got themselves caught up in something much bigger than a simple rescue mission.

What of the mysterious Foreign Office guy? Was the captain right – had they wandered into the middle of a territorial dispute? Harris had said Chile and Argentina both claimed the island, along with the UK. Had one of them *invaded*? Had the British known it might be coming and had a detachment of Marines at the ready to repel it? That might explain the armoury and the surveillance equipment, at least. Perhaps the Marines had seen the invading forces and leapt into action, leaving their meals half eaten. But would the MoD really go to such lengths to protect this weird hunk of volcanic rock in the middle of nowhere? It just seemed fanciful. Mind you, hadn't the whole Falklands War kicked off with the occupation of a whaling station at South Georgia? Perhaps it was all a prelude to something bigger.

Maybe it was all about something as mundane as oil. Most wars seemed to be, these days. Abbie had heard stories that the US was already sniffing around and trying to drill for oil in the Antarctic. Maybe there was oceans of it underneath all this volcanic ash as well.

But if she and Brewster had found themselves in the middle of some kind of conflict, where was everyone? Why wasn't the Chilean or Argentine flag flying over the little settlement on the beach? Why hadn't they been greeted at the jetty by some officious major spouting anti-British rhetoric at them in halting English? And what of their boat disappearing? And the power cut? None of it made any sense.

They approached the half-derelict remains of what had once been the island's church. It had greying timber cladding, a tin roof the same colour as the ash beach that surrounded it, and a spire reaching up into the heavens at one end. There was a little porch on the southeast side underneath the spire, and a lean-to jutting out from the west end at the back. Clearly it too had been left to rot, and half the roof had already collapsed, while several more sheets of tin were flapping in the wind, ready to be ripped off in the next gale. The cross that had once sat proudly atop the spire was now hanging upside down and lopsidedly against the tin.

Even God had abandoned this island now.

On the shoreside of the building were a couple of dozen headstones and crosses set into the ground in three rows – the graveyard Abbie had spied from the boat. It was close enough to the harbour for the steam to roll over the graves, as if the spirits of the dead were being lifted from their final resting places.

'This is the spookiest shit I've ever seen,' Abbie said.

'Biggest cemetery in Antarctica, apparently,' Brewster replied.

Abbie looked down the rows. There was one obelisk-like stone monument in the middle, bigger than all the others at almost six feet tall. It was surrounded by several other smaller ones, as well as some flat headstones. The majority, though, were simple wooden crosses. It seemed oddly fitting that the only people Abbie and Brewster had encountered on this forgotten and decaying island were long dead and buried.

'Who were they?'

'Whalers, mostly.' Brewster pointed to the large stone obelisk. 'That's a memorial to ten men lost at sea. Norwegians, I think.'

He walked on down the line as Abbie stopped to read the details on the stone. She crouched down and squinted, but time and the harsh climate had made reading the names inscribed all but impossible.

'What the fuck?' Brewster muttered.

Abbie looked up to her left where he stood, now at the end of the row of graves.

'What the *fuck?*' he repeated, his brow creased in confusion.

'What is it?'

'Jesus, Abbie, you need to see this.'

'What?' She crunched her way towards him, being careful not to step on any of the graves as she went. 'What is it?'

He didn't even look at her, he just nodded his head to where he was staring.

At the end of the line there were three freshly dug graves. One was already filled. Next to that were two identical shallow trenches cut into the ash surface of the beach, two mounds of earth next to them as they awaited their intended occupants.

At the head of the first – the one that had already been filled – there was a cross made from what looked like two bits of driftwood.

She leaned in and read the writing that had been painted onto the cross.

K. Turner – 1/9/2026

'Today's date,' Abbie whispered.

The open grave next to it had a similar cross planted at its head. This time with the inscription *H. Ridley – 1/9/2026.*

She finally looked at the third. Also still open, also with a simple wooden cross marking it. She narrowed her eyes to read the words painted on the wood.

Again, it had today's date. But above that – no, it couldn't be, it *can't* be. But somehow it was. Somehow, above the date on a wooden cross marking this freshly dug grave, was the inscription: *A. Błaszczykowski-Fitzroy.*

She reared back as if it was a wild animal about to strike at her.

'*What the fuck?*'

Chapter 11

Four years earlier

For the second time in two months, Abbie stood at the graveside of a man she loved.

First her father had gone, and now Drew. It just wasn't fucking *fair*.

Drew's had a been a sudden, unexpected and brutally quick death. A single devastating thrust of a knife deep into her heart. Her father, meanwhile, had taken months to die. A dripping tap of pain and sadness that was too awful to bear, yet which she simultaneously prayed wouldn't stop. She, her mother and her two sisters had been forced to watch as he got weaker by the day, the pancreatic cancer eating away at him, stealing him from them – from her – little by little. Every day another little piece of him gone.

He'd been feeling overly tired for some time but had, typically, not mentioned it. Eventually her mum noticed something wasn't right and persuaded him to go and see the doctor. Some troubling blood-test results triggered a biopsy. And then the worst news was delivered by her mum in a tearful phone call. Pancreatic cancer. Stage four. That meant it had already spread to other parts of his body. There was nothing they could do. And that was the trouble with that particular cancer – it killed 95

77

per cent of the people who got it, because it was almost un-detectable in the early stages when it would be treatable. In many cases, by the time it was discovered, it was too late.

He was given only weeks to live.

Abbie was given compassionate leave from the ship and moved back into her childhood bedroom to help her mother care for him, with her sisters coming up on rotation, fitting it in around their own jobs, husbands and children.

'I knew you'd come,' her mum had said. 'You always were your father's shadow.'

Together they looked after him round the clock. No longer able to make it upstairs, the dining room became his 'ward', a proper hospital bed taking the place of the table, which was moved to the garage.

Eventually even that arrangement wasn't sufficient to cope with his needs as his body shut down, bit by bit. They'd found a hospice that looked a little shabby but was staffed with excellent nurses and carers. And so that was where he ended his days. Where Abbie watched him drain away before her very eyes, until she got a phone call in the middle of the night from the duty nurse. 'You might want to come in . . .'

She and her mum made the journey in record time and sat with him through the darkness. Before the sun was up, he was dead. He was only fifty-nine.

She didn't know how she would have coped without Drew to comfort her through her grief. He sat up with her when she couldn't sleep, hugged her when the pain was pulling her down, and wiped away her tears.

He'd been there, steadfastly by her side at the funeral, and had held her hand tightly through a hundred conversations at the wake she'd much rather not have had.

He'd been her rock.

And now, as she stood at Drew's graveside, she had no one. He'd been there to carry her through her father's death, but now there was no one to help her through his. Despite the presence of her mum and her two sisters, she felt utterly alone. Normally she would have sought comfort from her dad. She'd always run to him, ever since she was a little girl. *Your father's shadow.* But he was gone too.

And as the little urn containing Drew's ashes was lowered into the hole, she felt a new wave of loneliness wash over her. She'd always been something of a solitary person through her childhood and young adulthood. Drew had finally changed all that, but now she'd lost him too and the sense of abandonment was overwhelming. She never imagined she'd find someone like him, and to have him ripped away hurt far more than any loneliness she'd felt before they'd met. She felt the breath being forced from her lungs as the dirt was sprinkled on the urn and the minister said a short prayer. That bit had been her mum's idea and Abbie had been too numb to object. Drew had already lost his parents and had no siblings. A lone cousin was the only member of his family who came. She felt like every little clump of damp soil was pinning him down, suffocating him. She felt it too, that unmistakable and terrifying feeling of being trapped. Buried.

She wanted to get down on her knees and scoop him out, brush off the dirt and hold him close. It just wasn't fair. None of it was fair.

Chapter 12

Abbie blinked and looked back at the grave in front of her, as if doing so might somehow clear or reset what she was seeing. Because what she was seeing just couldn't be possible. She was standing on one of the most remote islands in the world – an island that barely thirty-six hours earlier she'd never even *heard of* – looking at a freshly dug grave with today's date and her own name carved into the cross marking it.

It couldn't be coincidence. True, they didn't have a manifest of the researchers based on the island, but the odds on there being one with her *exact* double-barrelled name – not to mention the same initial – seemed long in the extreme.

The discovery threw up a welter of questions, chief among them: how would someone have known she was coming to this island, when just hours earlier she hadn't even known herself? Indeed, *no one* had known she would be coming here. And even if someone had known, why on earth would someone dig a grave for her?

Abbie felt a chill run down her spine and reached out to Brewster.

'I don't get it,' he said. 'You have any relatives it could be?'

She shook her head. 'None. We combined our names when we got married. My relatives are all plain old Błaszczykowskis.'

'And look at the date!' he said, pointing to it and frowning up at Abbie in confusion. 'That's today.'

She nodded. 'I know.'

'What the fuck does it mean?'

She shook her head slowly. 'I haven't got a clue.'

'You think someone knew you were coming?'

'I guess so. But how? *We* didn't even know we'd be coming until last night. The captain didn't even know.'

Abbie felt as though she'd slipped into some weird parallel dimension – as if the passage through Neptune's Bellows was a misty portal to another world, another time, or both. A world in which she was already dead and about to be buried.

'And who the hell are "H. Ridley" and "K. Turner"?'

Abbie could do nothing but shake her head. 'I don't know.' She looked around them. 'Seems they weren't expecting you, though. And you're the one who's been here before.'

He nodded but said nothing for a moment. Then, 'So what do you want to do?'

She took in a deep breath. 'I want to get off this fucking island.'

Chapter 13

The bizarre and macabre discovery of the freshly dug graves didn't alter their immediate plan. They still had no choice but to go up to the second building to see if the radio was working there. If not, they had to go further up the mountain anyway and find somewhere their handheld units would work.

But before they moved, Abbie unzipped her dark blue Gore-Tex coat, reached inside to her shirt and ripped off the Velcro name tag fixed to her chest. She knelt down, scooped aside a few handfuls of dirt next to the grave, placed the tag in the hole and then buried it.

'What are you doing?' Brewster asked.

'If someone here is about to try to kill me, I don't want to make it too easy for them,' she said.

He didn't object.

She stood, brushed off her hands, zipped up her coat and they began to walk.

Abbie was trying to keep calm – she knew there simply *must* be a rational explanation for what they'd found down by the church, but for the life of her she couldn't work out what it was. And it was hard not to be freaked out – after all, how often do you come across your own grave, open and waiting for you?

They crested a rise in the ash track, which widened out and led to a sort of plateau on the mountainside on which the second building was positioned. It was clad in green tin, just like the beach house down by the jetty, only this one was a little smaller. The track continued around to one side of the hut and then further on up the slope. She couldn't see the back of the building, but it appeared to be set into the rock of the mountainside itself at the rear.

As they crunched their way cautiously along the ash path, there was still no sign of anyone to greet them, friend or foe. And unlike at the beach house, there was no door flapping in the cold wind, no flashing light at the entrance, no deafening alarm. It was quiet. Dead quiet.

Brewster led them around to the main entrance and then paused, unsure what to do next.

Abbie made the decision for him. She pulled down the handle on the metal door and pulled. It was so heavy she found she really had to put her back into it to move it. Like the one leading to the surveillance room down at the beach house, it was clearly reinforced.

If this was some kind of trap then she knew she was about to walk right into it – and she'd feel pretty bloody stupid if so – but she also knew that if anyone was waiting for them, they would have seen them approaching from the beach anyway, so there was little point in trying to hide their arrival.

'Hello?' she called. 'Is anyone home?'

She was greeted only with silence.

They were standing in a large entrance hall. Just as at the beach house, there were boots and trainers lying haphazardly on the floor, some heavy-duty red polar jackets hung on hooks, and not much else. Abbie pushed open the other door which led into the rest of the building, and they found themselves in a central corridor, with two skylights set into the roof, letting in the sun. Abbie tried the light switch but, just as at the beach house, there was no power.

Brewster stayed to investigate the boot room further as Abbie tried the first door on her left and found herself in a canteen/mess room. It was smaller than its equivalent down at the beach house and, unlike that one, there were no abandoned plates of food or half-drunk cups of coffee. The plastic chairs were tucked neatly under the tables. There was a flat-screen TV mounted on one wall opposite another two doors.

Through one, Abbie found another lab, and through the other, an industrial kitchen, which contained two long steel benches on wheels, side by side and about six feet apart. One had a collection of what she first assumed were cooking utensils, until she got closer, when she saw they were in fact work tools. A wood saw. Screwdrivers of different sizes. Several pairs of pliers and two claw hammers. They were sitting on the surface next to a box which, upon closer inspection, contained other DIY aids: rope, plastic cable ties, gaffer tape, a box of nails, a reel of twine, some electrical fuses and a tape measure.

Had someone been doing repairs in the kitchen?

She saw something had been spilt on the vinyl floor. Something that had once been liquid but was drying fast in a wide arc around the two steel benches.

The colour. The texture. There was only one thing it could be.

'Is that . . . blood?' Brewster asked. He was standing in the doorway behind her, staring down at the floor.

Abbie stepped back away from the stain. 'I-I think so.'

She glanced at the steel bench closest to her and saw more red stains on its surface, along with dents in one end. On the floor next to it were four lengths of rope, each with knots in them and two frayed edges at either end.

'What the hell?' Brewster began picking up the tools on the other bench one by one and examining them. 'Looks like a DIY dentist's surgery,' he said, holding a pair of pliers up to the window to see it better in the sunlight.

'Your dentist always strap you down to a bench, does he?' Abbie said, nodding at the ropes on the floor.

'Some kind of field hospital?' Brewster offered.

'You think they were trying to save someone?'

'Maybe.'

Brewster picked up a saw. It too was covered in dried blood. 'An emergency amputation?'

'Could be.' Abbie went to inspect the ropes. 'But why tie them down?' she said, picking one up and running it through her hand.

Brewster turned his head this way and that. 'No sign of any anaesthetic. Maybe they had to.'

There was something else on the floor by the ropes. Abbie looked closer. It looked like someone had spilled, what, coffee beans, perhaps? No, they were too big to be coffee beans. She dropped the rope, bent down and picked one up, and turned it over between her thumb and forefinger. It took her a moment to realize what it was, but when she did, she dropped it in disgust.

'What is it?' Brewster asked.

Abbie frowned in confusion and horror. 'Fingernail,' she said quietly. 'They're fingernails. Covered in blood.'

'What?' Brewster put down the saw and walked around the bench to join her.

Abbie nodded at the scene before them. Then something else caught her eye in the shadow underneath the bench. She frowned. 'What is *that*?'

She pushed the bench back a couple of inches. And there it was. Lying there on the blood-soaked floor was a human finger.

'This isn't a field hospital,' she said, looking slowly from the bloody digit to the fingernails, to the rope, the tools and the bench, and finally back at Brewster. 'This is a torture chamber.'

Chapter 14

Ridley watched the snow-capped ring of Deception Island appear over the horizon as the helicopter chomp-chomp-chomped its way over grey seas towards the naval vessel anchored some five miles off the coast.

He had hoped never to set foot on this blasted island ever again, yet here he was, back at the bottom of the world.

As the helicopter set down at the stern of the ship, Ridley waited for a crewman to slide open the door, then he unclipped his safety belt and stepped out onto the deck. One of the ground crew directed him back to a safe distance, and then the engine note of the aircraft increased again and the pilot immediately lifted it back up into the sky, swung it around through 180 degrees and powered away.

'Welcome to HMS *Northumberland*, sir,' the man shouted over the roar of the departing helicopter.

Ridley nodded. 'I need to connect to your Wi-Fi and I need to see the captain.'

'He's waiting for you in his cabin. Follow me.'

A few moments later, Ridley stepped inside the room and held his hand out.

'Captain Harris?' he said.

Harris nodded as he stood and shook hands. 'And you are?'

'Ridley.' He didn't volunteer whether this was his first or his last name. 'I believe you're expecting me.'

Harris nodded again. 'Please, have a seat. Cup of tea? We could have someone from the mess get you a sandwich or something? When did you last eat?'

Ridley shook his head. 'I need to check in with the office and then I need to get over to the island ASAP.'

Harris pointed to a sheet of A4 paper pinned to the board above his desk. 'Wi-Fi login,' he said.

Ridley pulled out his phone and entered the details. 'Do you have your helicopter ready?'

Harris shook his head. 'Was damaged in the storm last night. Still being repaired. Couple of hours away from being airworthy, I'm afraid.'

'That's too long. A boat then? I need to get over there toot sweet.' His phone was connected and began to buzz repeatedly as his messages came flooding through.

Harris cleared his throat. 'I've already sent a boat team across.'

Ridley jerked his head up from his phone. 'You *what?* Did you not have orders to wait until I arrived?'

Harris nodded. 'I did.'

'And yet you disobeyed a direct order and sent a boat anyway?'

'That's correct. We heard an explosion – an eruption. There was smoke, and we'd lost radio contact with the base. We couldn't stand by and wait. By the time you arrived, it may well have been too late. I wasn't willing to risk the loss of life. I presumed your coming here was administrative, anyway, something to do with the territorial claim?'

'You presumed wrong,' Ridley snarled. 'Who did you send?'

'Our CBM. Petty Officer Brewster. And one of the sea specs.'

'Which one?'

'The one you asked for.'

Ridley paused for half a beat. 'Well, that's something. When did they leave?'

'About an hour ago. I ordered them to get ashore and evac the base as quickly as possible.'

'And?'

'They aren't back yet.'

'Any radio contact?'

'Not yet.'

Ridley shook his head in frustration. Yet again he had to deal with others' incompetence and their inability to follow simple fucking instructions.

He pursed his lips and stared at Harris. 'You've made a grave error here, Captain. I just hope I'm not too late – for your sake.'

'What do you mean?'

Ridley shook his head again. 'You should have followed your orders,' he said, without elaborating any further. 'I need a number of things from you, and I need them quickly,' he continued. 'You have another RIB, I take it?'

'We have one more, yes, but—'

'Have your team prepare it for me. You've got ten minutes.'

'Now hold on a moment. What exactly is going on here?'

'I will also need a weapon.'

Harris frowned. 'What for? This is a civilian rescue, is it not?'

Ridley sighed in frustration. 'We're wasting time,' he said.

Harris stood his ground. 'I'm sorry, but I'm the captain of this ship. You come aboard demanding boats and weapons, and you haven't even told me what's really going on.'

Ridley rolled his eyes impatiently. 'What's going on here, Captain, is that you disobeyed a direct order. And now I will need to clean up a mess you've only made worse.'

'What mess? What is all this about?'

'I'm not authorized to give you that information,' Ridley said, his tone cold and unwavering. He paused for a moment and looked first at the captain and then around the room. Harris was young to have his own ship – and he'd only had it for three weeks. As wet as they come. Ridley noted the finger paintings above his desk. Clearly he had young children too. Lots to lose. 'This is your first command, is it not?' he asked.

Harris nodded. 'It is.'

'Would you like it to be your last?' He let the words hang as he stared, unblinking, at Harris. 'And they gave you this old thing? Hardly the pride of the Royal Navy, is it?' he said, the look on his face a mixture of pity and faux sympathy.

'She has her unique challenges,' Harris replied. 'But we make do.'

Ridley looked sceptical. 'I heard this old thing is leakier than the Cabinet Office. Next stop the scrapyard.' He paused. 'Let's hope the same isn't true for her CO.' Another pause. 'Now, I need a boat and I need a weapon,' he said in a low, slow voice. 'Or do I need to get on the phone to London and speak to Northwood? Or should we bypass that and go straight to the minister?' Ridley enjoyed flexing his bureaucratic muscles. He could have made any number of calls to a higher authority to get Harris into line, but he found it all the more pleasing to achieve the same result simply with the threat. Ridley calculated it wouldn't take much to get his way.

There was a momentary silence. Then Harris looked away. 'I'll have a crew ready for you in fifteen minutes,' he said.

Ridley shook his head. 'No crew. I'll take it myself. Alone.'

'You know how to handle—'

Ridley held his hand up to stop the captain. 'I do.'

Chastened, Harris went to leave the room.

'Oh and Captain,' Ridley called after him. 'No one is to follow me to the island after I leave. You will wait here at anchor until I return. Is that clear?'

Harris nodded and stepped out of the office, closing the door behind him.

Ridley felt a buzz from his pocket and pulled out his phone. His face hardened as he read the message, forwarded on to him from the office. An intercept – no, several. 'URGENT . . . possible imminent attack . . . Project Reichstag . . . a lot of chatter in the last 48 hours . . .' *Project Reichstag? What was that?* He took a breath. This whole thing was getting worse by the hour. He needed to get ashore. Fast.

Chapter 15

'We need to get out of here,' Abbie said.

She looked at Brewster who stared back at her. She saw fear in his eyes, and felt it rising up inside her, too. She knew Brewster wasn't a coward – far from it – but now he and Abbie were facing the unknown and the unexplainable.

The alarm, the secure room with the CCTV screens, their boat disappearing, the power going off, the graves – and now this: human fingernails, a severed finger. Blood. There was surely no other conclusion to be drawn: someone had been tortured in this room.

Had one of the researchers simply snapped? Been driven insane by the isolation of being trapped out here on this sunken volcano in the middle of nowhere? Perhaps they'd cracked and embarked on some horrific violent rampage. Maybe that explained why there was no one to greet them at the jetty – perhaps the rest of the scientists were hiding. Or dead.

'Let's split up and try and find that radio,' Brewster said.

Abbie nodded. She walked back into the central corridor that led through the building like a spine, and headed for one of the two doors they hadn't yet tried, while Brewster went for the other.

Abbie's door was right at the far end and had a small porthole window in the top half. It was gunmetal grey, and clearly made of very thick steel. She peered through the window, but could see only another door – it looked identical to this one – about six feet away. The rest of the room looked like it was nothing but bare painted concrete from floor to ceiling.

She pulled the heavy door open and stepped inside. The room was small. Too small. She felt the familiar panic as her claustrophobia began to take hold. Within seconds she could taste the sand in her mouth. She tried to fight it, tried to hold it off and ground herself in the present, but it was no good. She was losing the battle. She could feel it pressing down on her limbs, suffocating her, gripping her tightly.

She was nine years old again, and back on that awful beach. They were on holiday back in England to visit family. Abbie's father had been based in Cyprus at the time, and they'd come back to the UK for a two-week break in the late summer.

They'd been staying with her Uncle Keith and Auntie Carol in Newquay. Abbie had hated it. Her older sisters Lauren and Beth were about the same age as her cousins Ellie and Stevie – and the four of them had quickly formed a gang. Little Abbie was most definitely not a part of it. As usual, she was left out – and no amount of cajoling from her parents to include her had any effect.

Three or four days into the holiday, they'd gone on a day trip. Two cars, buckets and spades, a cooler box full of sandwiches. She still remembered the name of the place. *Fistral Beach.* She shuddered at the memory.

Her sisters and cousins were busy building their sandcastle. An extensive job all directed by her bossy eldest cousin Ellie, who was barking out orders to the other three. It was all turrets and channels and walls and moats.

The adults had erected a plethora of windbreakers and beach chairs nearby. Plastic cups and bottles were produced.

Abbie didn't even try to join in with the castle building. She couldn't be bothered with the drama that would inevitably ensue. Her cousins and sisters being mean to her, followed by the shouting of parents.

Instead she went down to the water looking for crabs. She wandered along the shoreline, spade in hand, until she'd found one. She watched it scuttle up the beach. 'Hello, Mr Crab. How are you today? Where are you off to in such a hurry? Are you late for lunch with Mrs Crab?'

She followed it as it made its way along the beach. Soon she couldn't even see her sisters and cousins. She was glad to be on her own as she watched the crab go about its crabby business, until she found herself between the sea and a row of sand dunes. She dropped to her knees, took her spade and began to dig. She would dig all the way down to Australia, she decided, as the crab crawled off down the beach. Away from Lauren, away from Beth and Ellie and Stevie and Auntie Carol and Uncle Keith. Away to somewhere where *she* was the one with friends. The one in the gang. She dug and dug and dug, down and down and down, her hole swallowing her up as she went. She had no idea how long she'd been digging for – she didn't care. She was happy to be occupied. And she still had a long way to go before she reached Australia.

She turned and took another spadeful from the shoreside of her hole, and that was when the sand dune above her suddenly collapsed, the sand pouring in on top of her like liquid cement. Before she even had time to realize what was happening, she was trapped. Stuck fast. And soon the sand was everywhere, in her mouth, her nose, her eyes, her ears. She'd been buried alive and she couldn't even scream. She couldn't move and she was choking, her mouth full and dry.

Up until that point she'd made her way through life with the parental safety net there at all times to protect her. Whatever bad thing happened, Mum and Dad would always be there to make it better. That was the one certainty you had as a child. But as she lay trapped and fighting for breath, she suddenly realized no one even knew where she was. Not her cousins, not her sisters, not her parents. No one. Her safety net was gone.

The horror gripped her, primal and terrible.

She cried and cried, her tears soaking into the sand as she lay trapped and terrified in the darkness, pinned down under the great weight of the load above her.

She stopped after a while, her limbs lifeless and her tears spent.

And amid the terror, the panic and the horrifying certainty that she was utterly alone, one odd thought kept coming back to her: *I'm going to be in so much trouble.*

Two things saved her life: one, a passing dog-walker had seen her playing just moments before the sand dune collapsed, and two, an RNLI patrol unit was stationed just 200 metres up the beach. The dog-walker had raised the alarm and she was dug out in minutes – though it felt to her as though she'd been trapped for hours as she lay crushed by the enormous weight in the dark, panic surging through her tiny veins.

As she was pulled out and fell sobbing into the arms of one of the lifeguards, they asked where her parents were. She was still choking on the sand in her mouth and couldn't yet speak – but it didn't matter. Before she could answer, she saw her mum and dad running down the beach towards her.

Her mum was in near hysterics and was crying just as hard as Abbie was. The lifeguard handed her over to her mum, who clutched her tight. They cried together, her dad wrapping them both up in a hug and stroking her hair, gently telling her everything was okay now.

The lifeguards and the dog-walker were thanked profusely, and her dad carried her back to the makeshift camp of chairs and windbreaks, where Uncle Keith and Auntie Carol were already starting to pack things up.

'You mustn't go wandering off like that,' Keith had said sternly.

'All right, Keith, she knows that,' her dad had said as he hugged her a little tighter.

'But *why* do we have to go?' Lauren had asked in a whiny voice.

'Because your sister has had a terrible fright and we need to get her cleaned up,' her mum had said as bottles were returned to cooler bags and camping chairs folded up.

Abbie could tell her sisters were pouting, not only put out that their day at the seaside had been curtailed, but also because – for once – Abbie was the centre of attention with both parents. Her mum couldn't stop fussing over her. Abbie later realized that was, in part at least, a way of assuaging the guilt she'd felt at her child having come perilously close to suffocating under a ton of sand while she sipped gin in a deckchair.

They drove back to the house and Abbie was put in the bath, where her mother washed sand out of every conceivable hiding place on her body. Once cleaned up, Abbie stuck like glue to her father's side. If he went to the kitchen, she followed. If he went back to the living room to read his paper, she was at his feet. As an adult, Abbie realized this must have been a little hurtful to her mother, but she always gravitated to her dad when she was upset. She had always felt closer to him. *Your father's shadow*. It was entirely accurate after that day in Newquay.

She'd been incredibly lucky – but from that moment on, small spaces of any kind triggered abject terror in her.

She had to get out of this tiny room, on this miserable little island at the bottom of the world. She had to get out now. *No.* She had to fight the fear. She needed to look for the radio.

She opened her eyes, grabbed hold of the door handle to steady herself and took a deep breath. '*Per mare, per terram,*' she whispered to herself as she tried to control her breathing. Control the panic. '*Per mare, per terram. Per mare, per terram.*'

Another deep breath.

She darted her eyes this way and that, trying to scope the room as quickly as possible so she could get out.

There was a sturdy wooden table with one wooden chair tucked neatly underneath it on the left-hand side of the room, next to a window with frosted glass. On the other side was a metal bunk with a thin mattress and an even thinner blanket on top. *Another dorm room?*

She walked between the bed and the table to the door at the other end. She pulled it open and found herself facing two more doors. One led into a tiny wet room that she couldn't even bring herself to walk into – it was just far too small – and the other opened onto a small outside yard.

There was no sign of a radio or anything else useful.

'Nothing here,' she called out. 'You found anything?'

She listened out for a reply but none came. 'Brewster?' she said a little louder, then held her head still to listen for a response. Still nothing. *Where was he?*

She turned, glad of a reason to leave this tiny, claustrophobic room, and went in search of her boss.

She made her way back down the corridor to the room she'd seen him enter. The door was heavy. She pushed it open and found herself in another control room – a larger version of the one they'd found down at the boathouse: a long bench with banks of square TV monitors stacked two high – all of them now black and dead – with three office chairs, one of which was on its side. On one wall was a large map of the island – Abbie estimated it must have been six foot by six – with the land mass marked out into different sectors. Next to that was another large gun cabinet. Empty.

Brewster was standing at the far end of the room to the right of the wall-mounted map, where the dull grey breeze-block wall bent round a ninety-degree corner. He was stock still, and staring intently. 'Didn't you hear me calling?' she asked.

He didn't reply. As Abbie got nearer, she could see why.

This corner of the room housed the radio base unit, which was mounted on a small steel bench.

And slumped on the floor, directly in front of it, was a dead body.

Chapter 16

The man lying before them was wearing Royal Marines fatigues. He was on his back in a pool of blood, his left arm folded awkwardly behind him, his head propped up against the wall, his lifeless brown eyes staring up at them. He was young, early twenties, Abbie guessed, with a small nose and a doughy face. The patch on his fatigues revealed his name: Berkeley.

She could clearly see two bullet holes in his chest and another in his thigh; the blood that had soaked through his uniform was already drying around the wounds.

'Jesus Christ,' Abbie breathed. 'Pulse?' she asked, almost as a reflex – it was clear just by looking that the man was long dead.

Brewster shook his head. 'Nothing. He's cold.'

He stepped back and nodded at the radio set. 'Must have been trying to call for help when they got him.'

'Whoever "they" are,' Abbie replied. She stood stock still as she took in the sight before her. She realized it was only the second time she'd ever actually seen a dead body in the flesh. The first had been her father, but that was very different. Maybe her years of grief, of trying to shut herself down from too much emotion – highs or lows – just to get through the day had dulled her senses, inured her to the violence, but she was surprised she didn't find it more shocking.

'Wait,' she said, a thought suddenly occurring to her. 'Check his hands.'

Brewster nodded. He knew what she was getting at. He reached down for the left hand. It was cold, but intact. The right was the same. 'No digits missing,' he said.

'So whoever that finger belonged to is still out there somewhere.'

'Along with whoever removed it.'

'Unless that was him,' Abbie said, nodding at Berkeley.

'Either way, we need to get out of here, pronto,' Brewster said. 'Whatever the fuck this is, we now *know* there's someone loose with a gun out here. And we don't know who or why or what. Let's get back to the beach now and find a way off this place before he gets us too.'

Abbie shook her head. 'We can't. The boat's gone, remember?'

'Okay, so what do you suggest?'

'I don't know.'

'Come on, Blaz. Improvise, adapt, overcome. Think like a Marine!'

Abbie took a breath. *What would Drew do?* she thought. She could picture his 'thinking' face: his brow slightly creased, his eyes narrowed. She found herself mimicking it as she tried to work through their options.

'The way I see it, we have two choices,' she said. 'We can head further up the mountain and try to get radio signal, or we can go back down to the beach and try to find our boat. I say we go up. Get on the radio, establish a line back to ship. Tell them what we've found.'

Brewster shook his head. 'Negative. We go back down to the shore. If we can't find our boat, there must be another one down there.'

'And what if there isn't? Then we'll have to come all the way back up here to get radio signal. Going back to the beach is just a waste of time.' Abbie could feel the edge of frustration in her own voice.

He held up his hands. 'I'm just trying to get us off this island as quickly as possible.'

'So am I!' she shot back, fighting to control her temper.

'You want to wander around on the trail? Anyone could be out there! Whoever got that poor bastard could be right around the next corner waiting for us.' He shook his head. 'I told you: let's go back down to the shore and look for the boat.'

'But whoever got this guy' – she jerked her head at the dead body – 'could just as easily be down *there* waiting for us.'

'You're right,' Brewster conceded. 'But who knows how far up the mountain we'd have to get for a radio signal. I'm in charge here and I'm telling you: we're going back to the beach. Now.'

'I'm afraid I'm going to have to insist you stay for the time being.'

Abbie and Brewster spun round in unison to face the owner of the voice: a tall, lean man wearing black combat trousers and black boots, with a rifle slung across his chest, his finger on the trigger. He was standing in the doorway with his feet planted firmly, blocking the only way in or out of the room.

Chapter 17

'You must be Błaszczykowski-Fitzroy,' he said, pronouncing Abbie's name flawlessly. He didn't move from his spot blocking their exit.

He knows my name, she thought with a chill as she remembered the open grave.

'Which makes you Brewster.'

He was handsome, in a smug sort of way, Abbie thought, with a strong jawline, short black hair that fell lightly across his forehead, above green eyes and a mouth that was even now in a half-smile. Abbie guessed he must be mid-forties, but he looked as if he kept himself very fit.

'Who the hell are you?' Brewster asked, his body stiffening up with wariness and fear.

Abbie eyed the stranger's gun with envy. *Why hadn't she and Brewster come armed?* Because they were supposed to be rescuing some researchers, not fighting a war, that's why.

'I'm the chap who's going to get you out of this alive,' he said, his half-smile threatening to go all the way. His accent was southern, posh. Officer class. Abbie guessed public school before Aldershot or Oxbridge. 'I'm the chap who you should have waited for before coming ashore here.'

'You're the one who works for the Foreign Office?' Abbie asked.

'Something like that.' The smug smile again.

'All you FCO guys carry KS-1 assault weapons, do you?' she said.

'Only those of us who need to,' he replied. 'And it's the FCDO now, my dear.'

My dear. Abbie winced inwardly at his choice of words, but said nothing.

'How did you get here?' Brewster asked.

'On a RIB, same as you. Only you seem to have been a little careless with yours. Where is it?'

Brewster looked away. 'We're uh . . . we're not sure. We tied it up, then ten minutes later it was gone.'

The stranger pursed his lips. 'Hmmm. This might be worse than I thought. Why haven't you radioed back to the ship?'

'The power's off, and our handhelds won't work. We need to get to higher ground,' Brewster replied.

'What's your name?' Abbie asked. 'Since you already know ours.'

'Ridley.'

Abbie's mind flashed back to the other empty grave they'd found down at the cemetery. The name etched into the bone cross. 'RIDLEY'. This was getting weirder by the minute.

'Now, what have you found? Time is critical here.' He still hadn't moved from his position in the doorway, and his hand still gripped his gun.

'You're a spook?' Brewster asked.

'Tell me what you've found,' the stranger repeated, ignoring his question – which, Abbie thought, rather answered it anyway.

'Hold on,' she said. 'We want some answers first. If you are who you say you are, show us some ID.'

"Fraid I left my wallet back onboard ship. Didn't think I'd be needing much cash out here,' he said glibly.

Abbie's face remained impassive. 'Where have you come from?'

'London,' he sighed. 'I flew down from Brize Norton overnight to Mount Pleasant, then hopped from there to the *Lancaster*, to *Protector*, and then to *Northumberland* by helicopter today. When I arrived, I discovered you two had disobeyed a direct order and come ashore. I asked the captain very nicely to lend me another RIB. And here I am.'

'What's the captain's name?' Abbie asked accusingly. It wasn't much of a test – the names of Royal Navy captains weren't a secret, but she was running out of ideas.

'Captain Harris. Captain Timothy Phillip Harris. Now of HMS *Northumberland*, as of three weeks ago.' He tilted his head to one side. 'Satisfied? Can we get on with it now?'

'Not yet. We want answers first,' she said. 'What's going on here? Have we walked into some kind of territorial dispute?'

He shook his head. 'No, no.'

'Then what the hell is this place? A frozen volcano with sur-veillance rooms, gun cabinets, armoured doors, and now this,' she gestured towards the body at their feet. 'This place is no vol-canic research base, so what the hell is it?'

'It's a prison,' he said simply.

Abbie remembered the claustrophobically tiny room she'd found just before Brewster called her in to see the body of the mur-dered Marine. The thick steel door with all the locks, the frosted glass, the spartan furniture. It wasn't a bunk room – it was a cell.

'What the hell kind of prison is all the way out here?'

Ridley was getting visibly irritated. He was clearly used to people obeying orders without him having to ask twice, but Abbie stood firm.

'A special prison,' he said. 'A prison for just one inmate.'

'Who?'

'You don't need to know. Yet. Now, I need you to tell me very quickly where you've been since you arrived, and what you've found.'

'Hang on. A prison for one inmate – how do we know *you're* not the inmate?' Abbie asked.

Ridley sighed irritably, as if the very idea was beneath contempt. 'Because I could have shot you the moment I walked in here,' he said, raising his rifle an inch to emphasize his point. 'How would I have known you weren't supposed to land on the island without me? And how would I know your names?'

She considered his answer. Someone on this creepy island definitely *did* know her name. The grave marking proved that. And they knew Ridley's too. Unless he was lying, and was just calling himself that because he knew they'd seen the graves . . . ?

'Come on, tell me what you've found,' he repeated.

Abbie still wasn't ready to cooperate yet, and was irritated when Brewster began to answer.

'We landed at the jetty and searched the beach house. Whoever had been having breakfast there got spooked by something or someone – it was empty when we arrived. Then the power went off. That was just after we saw our RIB had disappeared. We couldn't get a radio signal, so we came up here to see if this one was working . . .' He paused and looked at the body next to the radio unit. 'That's when we found him.'

'Go on.'

'We also found an empty munitions store down at the beach house, and there's another one here,' he said, nodding at the cabinet on the far wall. 'No weapons in either.'

'Mmm-hmm.'

'There's something else,' Abbie said. 'Did you come past the church on your way up here?'

'Yes. Why?'

'Did you happen to stop for a look at the cemetery?'

He shook his head.

'There's a grave down there,' she paused and took a breath, 'with your name on it.'

Ridley shrugged. 'It's not an uncommon name.'

'No, no. You don't understand.' She took a step forward. 'Not an old grave. A *new* one. As in, freshly dug. Open. With a cross with your name on it – and today's date.'

Abbie watched him closely as he considered this information, the half-smile returning to his face. Bizarrely, he seemed to find the revelation amusing.

'Not only that,' Abbie went on, 'there's one next to it with *my* name on a cross. Also dated today. So, if you have any idea as to what the hell is happening and why someone has dug a grave for me, then I'd appreciate it if you'd clue us in on the whole story. Now.'

'Wait, say that again.' Ridley frowned. 'There's a grave with *your* name on it?'

Abbie nodded. 'Yes. Apparently someone knew we were coming.'

She watched him taking this on board and assessing her. His eyes narrowed and his jaw tightened as he thought it over. Up to now, he'd been in total control, but she could tell this was something he clearly hadn't anticipated. She saw a tiny crack in his confident facade for the first time. Perhaps that was why he finally volunteered some more information.

'The situation is this,' he began. 'The prisoner being held here has escaped. I received a coded message to that effect just over twenty-four hours ago. That's why you were supposed to wait for me before coming ashore.'

'So if it's a prison, where are all the guards? I'm guessing he was one?' Brewster said, glancing again at Berkeley.

'They were all Marines.'

'How many were there?'

'Eight. The message I received from the base commander informed me the prisoner had escaped, and that he and his men were going to bring him back.'

'But what if he was already off the island by the time they knew he'd escaped?'

'Impossible. There is no way off this island, other than by boat through the harbour entrance you came in through. And no boats were kept here. Basic security measure. The only access was from outside.'

'He could have taken ours,' Brewster offered.

'That was my first thought, too – but where would he go with that? There's a bloody great warship just outside the narrows – they would have seen any boats, and they haven't. Plus, there are no other vessels in the area, and he's hardly going to get a thousand miles to Argentina in a RIB, is he?'

'So what happened to our boat?' Abbie asked.

Ridley sucked his teeth. 'I'm not sure. But it doesn't really matter now. What matters is getting the prisoner back under lock and key.'

'And what about the graves?' she asked. 'Yours and mine?'

Ridley pursed his lips. 'It's possible he knew I'd be making an appearance. Pulled that stunt to frighten me, perhaps. He'd have enjoyed that – we go way back.'

'And mine? How could he possibly have known I'd be coming? And why would he want to kill me?'

'That,' Ridley conceded, 'I can't yet answer. But it doesn't change anything. We have an escaped prisoner. We must get him back under lock and key.'

'He must be down on the beach,' Brewster said. 'It must have been him who nicked our boat, then took out the power.'

'But if he's down there, where are the Marines?' Abbie asked.

'I don't know. But our first job is to find them,' Ridley said.

'No,' Brewster shook his head again. 'Now we know there's an escaped prisoner running around with at least one weapon, we need to get back to the ship on the double. Let's take your RIB, brief the captain, and then decide what our next move is. We can send the Marines ashore to handle the prisoner.'

'No,' Ridley said simply with a quiet but unshakeable authority. 'No, that's not what we're going to do. We're going to stay here and help out the CO, and get this all sorted out and squared away. *Then* we'll go back to the ship. Need I remind you we're under a certain amount of time pressure here – imminent volcanic eruption and all that – so we need to get to it, PDQ,' he added casually.

'But we've got a full detachment of Marines on the ship. Why can't we send them in to sort this out?' Brewster asked. 'I don't understand.'

None of this seemed right to Abbie. The explanation about the prison made sense – but only served to throw up even more questions. 'Who was being held here?' she asked quietly. 'And why did you have them hidden all the way down here?'

Ridley clenched his jaw tightly. 'All right,' he said curtly, apparently aware he had to give them a little more at this point to get things moving. 'Before we go any further, I must remind you that you are both subject to the Official Secrets Act of 1989, and that breaching the terms of it will ensure you are dishonourably discharged, could see you imprisoned for up to two years and fined an amount that could bankrupt you and your family for generations. This island, its facilities and activities all fall under the Act. You will never speak publicly or privately about what you have seen and will see here. Ever. Is that clear?'

They stood in silence.

'Is that clear?' he repeated.

'For Christ's sake, yes!' Brewster replied.

'As I told you, this place is a prison. A special prison. A prison for just one inmate.' Ridley took one hand from his gun, yanked open a Velcro opening, reached inside his jacket and pulled out a smartphone. 'A prison he could never escape from,' he continued, 'and where no one would ever find him.'

'Find him?' Abbie said.

Ridley unlocked his phone and began tapping at the screen. 'This facility is a prison built to hold one man, and one man only.'

'Yes but *who?*' Brewster asked. 'And why? Why go to all this bother? Why not stick him in a normal prison?'

'Because we're not talking about a normal prisoner,' he said. 'The only inmate of HMP Deception Island is a man named Julian Lindfield.'

Abbie knew the name instantly, but it didn't make any sense. It just wasn't *possible*. The disbelief and confusion fought with the feelings of rage and hate surging through her veins as she tried to take in what Ridley was saying.

Brewster shook his head, unable to place the name.

Ridley held his phone screen up for them to see. A man with a shaved head and a greying beard looked back at them. A face Abbie saw every single night when she closed her eyes.

'But you may know him better by the name Richard Milton.'

Chapter 18

Ridley had returned his phone to his pocket, but Abbie could still see the face – it was seared into her brain like a screen burn and she saw it every day of her life; every morning when she woke up, and every night when she lay in bed trying to sleep. She saw it every time she thought of Drew. In her head their faces were now almost as intertwined as their fate – or what she had *thought* was their fate.

Every single day, she'd cursed every god she didn't believe in that Milton had taken the coward's way out and killed himself. He had robbed her twice. Firstly by taking away her beloved Drew, and then by committing suicide and taking away her chance to stick a knife in him and *twist*.

And now to learn that that evil, calculating, cowardly monster was still *alive?*

'But . . . he's . . .' She was unable to finish the sentence.

'Dead? Yes, that's what you were supposed to think,' Ridley said flatly. 'And in most ways, he is. Dead to the world, dead to everyone. And we must keep it that way.'

'They said he killed himself. That night, when . . .' Drew flashed across her mind's eye. The image she had of him in his final moments on that ship. She tried to banish it again. '. . . when they caught him.'

'Yes, that is what was said. That is not what happened. He was taken into custody. And then he was brought here. Eventually.'

'They said they'd tested the DNA. There were those leaked pictures. I saw them!'

'And what did you actually see?'

'I saw the pictures, I saw his body – his face.' She shuddered as she remembered the brutality of it.

He nodded. 'As you were meant to. As everyone was meant to.'

'You mean . . .'

'Yep. Faked,' he said casually. 'Faked, then "leaked".' He even raised his hands and waggled his fingers to indicate the inverted commas around his last word.

'And his DNA? They said the Americans were demanding it? Proof, I mean?'

'You don't need to be dead for someone to take your DNA,' he shrugged.

Abbie reeled. Four years of rage and grief were bubbling up inside her and had nowhere to go. She curled her fingers tightly, clenching her fists. Her nails dug into her palms and her knuckles went white, the skin straining over her bones as her hands trembled.

And then a sliver of hope hit her. When Drew's body had been sent home, that coffin in the back of an RAF transport plane, she'd gone to Brize Norton to meet it. It had been a beautiful day: blue skies, a gentle breeze. It hadn't fitted the image she'd had in her head of dark clouds and rain lashing down as she greeted the aircraft on the tarmac. But they hadn't wanted her to see him. They said it would be too upsetting – the gunshot wounds. She'd agreed. She just hadn't been able to bring herself to do it. She didn't want to remember him like that.

And as she stood there in the control room of this prison built to hold that monster Richard Milton – a man she'd thought had been killed on that same dreadful night four years ago but who she now discovered was in fact alive – the realization hit her: *she'd never seen her husband's body.*

She took a step forward. 'Since you know who I am, I am going to assume you know why I'm asking you this, but I need you to tell me now *exactly* what happened that night.' Her expression was determined, her jaw set. She knew he must be aware of her connection to all this. 'I want to know everything. Most of all, if Milton is alive, then is . . .' she could barely get the words out, '. . . is my husband still alive too?'

Chapter 19

Six years earlier

It wasn't Abbie's scene at all, but somehow she'd been persuaded to go on a speed-dating night in Plymouth with some of the other sea spec ratings from the HMS Raleigh training unit at Torpoint in Cornwall.

She'd agreed mainly because she thought it would be funny to watch her two mates, Charlie Middleton and Rico Warren, get shot down by a succession of women. That, and they'd promised her there would be beer. She was still hesitant, but Charlie had appealed to her better nature.

'Look,' he'd said. 'If me and Rico go by ourselves, we're just another couple of wankers. But if we come in the place with you, all the other women there will think we must be all right if another woman's hanging round with us.'

'You think?'

He nodded. 'Psychology, innit? If you're with us, it's like we're "pre-approved" by womankind. You'll be our wing-woman. It can't fail!' He flashed her a grin.

She was still sceptical, but she had nothing else on that evening, and Rico clinched it when he offered to pay for her drinks.

'And think about this,' he'd added. 'You'll clean up!'

'How do you work that out?'

Rico smirked. 'Just tell them all you're a seaman specialist and they'll be queuing up.'

Abbie rolled her eyes. 'If I had a quid for every time I've heard that one.'

And so they arrived at the pub and followed the signs downstairs to what, on Friday and Saturday nights, was the 'club room'. It was all black walls and ceilings, and there was a DJ booth in one corner, disco lights and smoke machine at rest.

A series of tables had been lined up down the middle, a chair on either side. It looked like the scene of a summit between two warring nations, Abbie thought. *The battle lines had been drawn.*

Rico went to fetch the first round, while Abbie and Charlie assessed the room. It was crackling with nervous energy, little clusters of friends huddling together, the lads trying to look cool, the girls for the most part ignoring them. It reminded Abbie of a school disco. She'd always hated those. There were a couple of guys standing alone at the bar, closely nursing their pints and scrolling through their phones in a desperate bid not to look too alone and awkward.

Then she spotted him. He looked just as nervous as she felt, standing uncomfortably with a bottled beer while the three mates he was with cast furtive glances at the women entering the bar.

He was handsome. Short and stocky. But his nervousness was what really caught her eye. He looked like a kindred spirit.

They were one round deep when a short blonde woman wearing leopard print trousers called for quiet and explained how it was going to work. The women would sit and the men would then change seats every four minutes. Leopard Print Lady had a timer on her phone and would announce when it was time to move.

Charlie bought them another round and Abbie took her place on the battlefield. The first two guys – a software developer named Colin and a very tall man named Richard who worked in 'ad sales' – were pleasant enough. But she wasn't sad when the buzzer went off.

And then Drew sat down and Abbie felt her heart rate tick up a notch.

'Sorry about this,' he said, as if his very presence was an imposition.

She laughed – why had she laughed? – never mind. *Just say something!* 'Your mates drag you along to this, too?' she asked.

He nodded, and nervously took a sip of his beer. 'I'm Drew.' He had just a hint of a light Scottish accent.

'Abbie,' she replied.

'So what do you do?'

'I'm in the Navy. Just about to finish my training. You?'

'Oh, what branch?' he asked. 'I'm in the Marines.'

Abbie felt herself almost swooning at that. And then they were off: she had a hundred questions for him and he started to open up. The awkwardness, the nerves, evaporated.

And then, all too soon, Leopard Print Lady's phone was buzzing. Time up.

Abbie never took her eyes off him as he rose apologetically and moved to the next table.

She felt a little sorry for the other guys she chatted to after that. She was at best only half listening to them and couldn't help but glance over at Drew every few seconds, already feeling a pang of jealousy when any woman opposite him smiled or laughed – or, worse still, when he laughed back.

After the official game of musical chairs was over, he didn't even wait for Leopard Print to distribute the little envelopes with the results in (they usually used a smartphone app but the signal wasn't strong enough in the basement room, she explained). Instead, he walked straight up to Abbie and – even though she

115

could tell he was once again dying with nerves – asked if she fancied grabbing a drink somewhere else. She couldn't get her coat on quickly enough. As they left the bar, she could feel the eyes of a dozen jealous women on them. It was the first time she'd ever felt like that. He'd already made her feel more special than every guy she'd ever met combined.

She winked at Rico and Charlie as she went. 'Good luck, boys,' she said.

'But you're supposed to be our wing-woman!' Charlie called after her.

She and Drew found another pub round the corner, took a table in the back, and sat drinking pints of cheap lager together and talking. Somehow, they were soon holding hands. And that was that.

There had been the physical attraction, of course – and that had been unlike anything she'd ever experienced before. The strength of her need to be with him, physically, had shocked her. She hadn't known she was capable of that depth of feeling. Luckily, his need for her was just as strong. But as wonderful, as fulfilling, as exciting and blissful as the sex was, she was even more overjoyed about their compatibility on a mental and emotional level. Something that, looking back, was there from almost the moment they met, and only grew as they spent more and more time together. She'd finally found her best friend. For the first time in her life, she felt at peace when she was with him. She felt like she never had to explain herself, never had to try to be something or someone she wasn't. It was just so easy. So right.

She never told anyone that, though, because she hated being the cliché. 'Looking for my best friend who I fancy the pants off,' as a million dating app profiles read. But it was true. Him and her against the world. They didn't need anyone else. It was strange, but she couldn't even really remember him proposing – probably because it barely needed talking about. He didn't really have to ask – she felt they both knew it was inevitable. The only questions were when and where. And she barely cared about either, as long as she got to have him forever.

She hadn't enjoyed much of the performative side of the wedding, but at the end of the day, when they'd hugged everyone there was to hug, danced awkwardly in front of their family and friends, cut the cake, and Drew's best man had come perilously close to upsetting her grandparents with his speech, they had retreated to the bridal suite at the hotel, and closed the door. She'd always felt that very moment was when their marriage had really begun. The door to the outside world shut. Just the two of them. Just the way they liked it. He'd turned to face her, a sparkle in his eye. They were both grinning.

She couldn't believe her luck to have found him – and to have their whole lives ahead of them.

Chapter 20

Ridley narrowed his eyes.

Abbie watched him closely, looking for any sign of a reaction to her question. She wasn't at all sure this guy would tell her the truth, but she would sure as hell be watching every flicker of his eyes, every twitch of his mouth, every tiny movement of his face that could give away a lie.

'All right,' he said. 'I'll tell you exactly what happened.'

She folded her arms across her chest as she listened.

'That week we'd got some new intel on the whereabouts of Milton's ship. It seemed to check out. The prime minister authorized a kill or capture order, and the Commandos were sent in.'

'And then?'

'Four Two Commando stormed the boat, then Major – your husband, confronted Milton. Before he could detain him, Milton shot him. Twice. Then the other Marines rushed Milton, took him down and then did what they could for your husband. Unfortunately, it was too late. I'm sorry, but yes, he is dead.'

Abbie was crushed. Just for a split second, she had allowed herself to dream he might still be out there somewhere – perhaps even here on this island – and that she might see his smile again, feel his touch, have the last four years of pain and hurt and anger melt away in his arms.

But now it felt as though she'd lost him all over again. She felt weak. Unsteady.

'So why the lies?' She was breathing fast, asking questions to try to deflect some of the pain. 'Why were we told Milton had killed himself?'

'We weren't left with much choice on that.'

'No choice? Why not? You'd caught him,' she paused. '*Drew* had caught him.'

'And then what were we supposed to do with him?'

'Put him on trial.'

Ridley shook his head. 'You're talking about the most dangerous man in the world. His trial would have become a circus – a stage on which he would grandstand, pontificate, quote scripture, attack the state, refute the legitimacy of the court, whip up his pathetic band of supporters with his hate-filled bile. Just imagine it: wall-to-wall coverage of his dangerous nonsense in the papers and every night on the TV for weeks, months. His fans picketing the court, misspelt placards and poorly thought-out chants led by skinheads with tannoys. It would have been his best publicity in years, and all paid for by the state. Don't forget, we knew what he would do – we had his playbook from his first trial. Only this one would have been turbo-charged. He had nothing to lose.'

'But people are repulsed by him, by what he's done,' Abbie said. 'People *hate* him.'

'*Most* people. The overwhelming majority of people, even. But some agree with every word he's ever said, every action he's taken. Look at his band of sycophants and followers. Look at his sources of finance. You can't pull off the atrocities he did without a lot of money. He had backers. Very wealthy backers. Some of whom are way beyond our jurisdiction. It's a dangerous time. Recessions, inflation, poverty, cost of living through the roof, people struggling to make ends meet. Strikes everywhere you look. People always lash out when that happens – they gravitate to radical thinking. *If the old ways have got us here, why not try something else?* Look back in history and you'll see it every time there's an economic slump – support for the far right and the far left goes up. His trial would just have added fuel to that fire. We couldn't let it happen.'

'So you locked him up with no trial and threw away the key?'

'We had no choice.'

'You did. You made the choice.'

'The Americans were livid after he killed their ambassador in Spain. They roared through Whitehall demanding vengeance, justice, and Milton's arse on a silver platter. Of course, at that point we didn't have him. They were screaming bloody murder – and gave us a month to find him or they would do it for us.'

'So why not let them?'

'What? And let the *Americans*' – he almost spat out the word – 'clean up our own mess?' He shook his head. 'No, no. This fellow was one of ours. Up to us to sort it out. Not the done thing to let the Yanks do it. Whitehall wouldn't have worn it. We still have our pride, you know.'

'But still – building a prison for him? On this island? In the middle of nowhere? I mean, this is just . . . unbelievable.'

'It was only meant to be temporary,' Ridley said. 'Problem is, it would have been far more . . .' he paused while searching for the right word, '. . . convenient, shall we say, if he'd died while resisting arrest – even if he didn't resist, if you catch my drift. It was a kill or capture order, with the emphasis very much on the former. Seems the Marines we sent to do the job didn't fully understand that.'

Now she felt a flash of anger at Ridley. He'd just insulted her husband. 'Or perhaps they understood exactly and simply didn't want to be a part of it,' she said coldly.

'Either way, when they took him alive, we were stuck with a problem.'

She shrugged. 'If you wanted him dead, why not just kill him after he was caught?'

'My dear girl,' she winced at his patronizing choice of words, straight from the Eton school yards, 'whatever you may think of your government, *that* would have been going too far.'

She shook her head in disbelief. 'What's the difference?'

'It's a matter of etiquette.'

'It's a matter of balls, you mean,' she said. It was astonishing the moral acrobatics this man was performing to justify his actions. 'You should have called me. I'd have fucking done it for you,' she added.

Ridley smiled. 'Dying in the crossfire of an operation to capture him is easily explained, and easily believed. Whereas arranging for him to accidentally slip off the back of an aircraft carrier in the Indian Ocean is somewhat less so. Besides, everything was already in place: the stories – and the pictures – prepped. In light of all that, it was decided to proceed with the original plan. And that just left the issue of what to do with the chap himself.'

'And *this*' – she gestured around them – 'was the answer?'

'Yes,' he said firmly. 'The briefing operation about his demise had already begun. Someone was a little over-eager to get it out there. We would've looked like fools to have backtracked on that, and with the world watching. So we decided to stick him here while we worked out what to do with him. It was only ever meant to be a temporary solution. But then it seemed to be working so well.'

'But why not just lock him up back home somewhere?'

Ridley scoffed. 'It would have got out. *He* might have got out. He'd done it before, after all.' He shook his head. 'No, no. Not an option.'

'So instead you pack him off to a tiny island miles away from anywhere and leave him here?'

'We did it with Napoleon. It worked then.'

'That was two hundred years ago!'

'Yes, one of the Foreign Office's newer ideas,' Ridley said drily. He smiled, clearly pleased with his wit. 'And the French themselves were terribly keen on this sort of thing. Dreyfus and all that. Devil's Island. They did it for years.'

'But why here?'

'We took him to Diego Garcia at first, but then that became a bit of a hot potato – politically speaking – so we had to find somewhere else. This place was perfect for a number of reasons: it's miles away from anywhere, it's not on the way to or from anywhere significant, and since the whaling industry stopped, it's not used for anything. And look at it.' He gestured to the giant map on the wall. 'It's a natural fortress. Only one way in or out, and the rest of it defended like a castle.'

'But what about the volcano? You must have known that might be a problem.'

'That's the best bit!' Ridley exclaimed. 'Ever since those two eruptions in the Sixties that caught those researchers out and destroyed the huts on the beach down there – and buried the Chilean base entirely – no government or scientific organization was willing to risk sending anyone here. And it gave us an excuse to ban cruise ships from visiting. That meant we had it all to ourselves.' He smiled that smug smile again. 'His Majesty's Government still controls a handful of tiny islands all over the world – the last relics of the empire.' He looked wistful, nostalgic.

'This one turned out to be perfect for our needs. And we already had the training facility here. Bit of tweaking – put in the containment cell, surveillance and all that, and voilà: our very own, one-man Guantanamo Bay. Or Wormwood Scrubs-on-Sea, as the chaps in the office call it. It was perfect.'

Ridley was interrupted as an unmistakable sound sliced through the air outside.

Gunfire.

Chapter 21

The three of them stood stock still, ears pricked up like meerkats. There it was again – the CRACK CRACK CRACK of rifle fire. There was a reply half a beat later, then another burst in response. This wasn't Marines popping off warning shots to force the prisoner to surrender – this was a firefight.

'Sounds like they found him,' Brewster said.

'Discussion over,' Ridley added, looking directly at Abbie. 'You two are trained in small arms, correct?'

They both nodded.

'Those are Royal Marines out there taking fire. Are you going to just leave them to it, or are you going to help your naval colleagues?'

Abbie knew he was manipulating them. He couldn't have known about her Commando ambitions, but he would know the sense of duty she and Brewster felt deeply as sailors in the Royal Navy. The bond with their fellow service personnel. He would know there was simply no way they'd leave them if they could help. Abbie looked at Brewster. He caught her eye and slowly nodded his head. She did likewise. It was decided.

'But we're not armed,' she said. It was less an argument against helping, and more simply a lament.

Ridley unzipped the front of his jacket and produced a Glock pistol – standard issue for Marines. He handed it to Brewster.

Milton's face flashed across Abbie's mind. The thought occurred to her that if she had a gun, she could even be the one to fire the fatal shot – if it came to it. She felt a surge of adrenalin at the prospect.

'What about me?' she asked.

'Just stay with me,' Ridley replied. 'Don't worry, we'll get you a gun.'

With that he turned and made for the exit. Brewster and Abbie followed.

Ridley pulled open the main door slowly and peered outside. The cold air rushed into the porch and Abbie shivered as she felt it wash over her.

There was another burst of gunfire, and another reply.

'It's not coming from the beach,' Ridley said. 'Sounds like it's up the mountain.'

'That makes sense,' Brewster replied. 'Other than by boat from the beach, there's only one way out of Whalers Bay – Hektor Pass. A narrow path that leads up to the north of the island. It snakes up Mount Pond.'

'They must have him pinned down somewhere,' Ridley added. 'Let's go. Sooner we get him back, the sooner we can get off this bloody island. Brewster, Captain Harris tells me you know this place. I suggest you take the lead.'

Brewster nodded and led the way as they began walking up the mountain on the gravelly ash and rock pathway that a previous eruption had left, the lava having cut through the rock on either side as if it was made of paper.

The gunfire stopped. Abbie thought that was a good sign: it likely meant they'd managed to recapture him. But she also knew better than to assume anything – particularly when it came to

Richard Milton. A man who, twenty minutes ago, had been dead and buried.

She still couldn't quite believe it was all true.

'How come it's never got out?' she asked as they made their way up the trail. 'A secret like this? I mean, it's incredible! And people talk.'

'Maybe they do, maybe there are rumours,' Ridley replied. 'But would you believe it if you weren't here to see it? The internet's full of rumours, conspiracy theories – oddballs convinced the government is tracking them through their phones or conducting secret mind-control experiments on the general population. All that rubbish is superb cover. Helps us enormously in all sorts of ways.'

That smile again. She didn't return it.

'And even if anyone did want to talk, they couldn't. Official Secrets Act. Their military career would be over, and a criminal conviction would follow. A prison sentence would be a surety. Would you risk it? Give up everything just to blow the whistle on the fact we're holding a mass-murderer here?'

He had a point.

'As I said, it was the perfect solution.'

'Until now.'

'What?'

'Until now – until the volcano woke up.'

'Something of a curve ball,' he conceded as they crunched along the ash path, 'but we'll handle it.'

'Wait, wait, wait,' Abbie said, shaking her head as a new thought occurred. 'Our orders were to come and evac everyone. We were told we were rescuing civilian researchers, not a detachment of Marines and a terrorist who's supposed to have been dead for four years. Don't you think we would have noticed when we turned up?'

'That is precisely why you were supposed to obey orders and wait for me.'

'But how was that going to work? The handcuffs on Milton might have been a bit of a giveaway.'

'We'd have used the old Mossad/Eichmann routine.'

'The what?'

'Milton would have been drugged – knocked out and taken aboard ship as a casualty. Then we would have kept him isolated. The rest of the Marines would have worn civilian clothing, and told to have minimal contact with the crew on board. The captain would have been informed. For everyone else, it would have been "need to know".'

'And you'd have taken him where?'

'As I said, that is need to know. And you don't.'

'I guess that poor Marine back at the radio didn't need to know either?' Abbie said.

'Yes, that is unfortunate,' Ridley conceded.

'Tell him what else we found,' Brewster said over his shoulder as they continued up the mountainside.

Abbie nodded and explained what they'd seen in the kitchen. The blood, the tools. The human finger.

She saw Ridley take it all in and try and make sense of it.

'He always was a sadistic bastard,' he said.

'He's a monster,' Abbie spat. It was an impulse. She hadn't consciously realized what she was saying until the words were already coming out of her mouth.

She saw Ridley stifle another smile. *Why was he smiling at her?*

'So what do you think happened?' Brewster asked.

'The guards operated on eight-hour shifts, two on shift at any one time. I presume Milton somehow escaped, killed the poor fellow by the radio, and then tortured the other one to extract information. Presumably about how to get off the island.'

127

'And then what?'

'Maybe he didn't hear what he wanted to? Probably took off up the mountain when he heard Major Turner leading reinforcements up the hill from the beach house; the rest of the Marines bunked down there when they weren't on duty.'

Abbie stopped. 'Major *who?*'

'Turner, the base commander.'

The third grave. The one already occupied.

'I'm sorry . . .' she began.

Brewster stopped too and looked back uneasily.

Abbie continued: 'But I think Turner is dead.' Again she watched Ridley's reaction. Again she could see he was trying not to show one.

'And why do you think that?'

'Those open graves with our names on them? There was a third. It was already filled. Turner.' She didn't have to spell it out any more clearly.

Abbie was still freaked out by the discovery they'd made in the graveyard. When she had seen the three freshly dug holes, she hadn't known who Turner and Ridley were. Now those mysteries were solved – but that still didn't explain the one with her name on it.

Ridley looked up the mountain as his jaw stiffened. 'Well, Turner may be gone, but his men are clearly still in the fight, so we must go and help them.'

They pressed on, but cautiously. Abbie estimated they had only been climbing for fifteen minutes when Brewster stopped and held his left hand up. The three of them froze and stood in absolute silence as Brewster assessed what he saw ahead.

From Abbie's vantage point at the rear of the trio, she couldn't see anything at all, save for the black rock which lined the path and which narrowed even further up ahead of them. She peered around Ridley and Brewster, and caught a flash of camouflage green.

That was when Brewster slowly turned around. The colour had drained from his face. He said nothing, but nodded his head up the hill to indicate they should see for themselves.

First Ridley and then Abbie craned their necks around the kink in the rock. She instantly understood Brewster's reaction and pulled a hand up to her mouth as she took in the bloody and shocking scene in front of them. A pile of Royal Marines lay awkwardly on the ash, their blood-stained uniforms already hardening in the icy cold.

They were dead. They were all dead.

Chapter 22

Dead and cold and left in a pile. From their wounds, it seemed obvious to Abbie that they'd simply been picked off as they came round the corner of the path. Shot down before they realized what was happening.

The three of them scrambled back down the path to the safety of a rocky outcrop that gave them cover. Abbie saw fear again in Brewster's eyes, but something closer to irritation in Ridley's. She sensed it was more about a tactical setback for him, rather than the people behind the bodies. They were numbers on a spreadsheet, little figures to be pushed around his field map back at his office in Whitehall or wherever he really worked. If he was mourning anything, it was the loss of some highly trained 'assets' – as he would no doubt call them – and the time he would now lose to resolve the situation.

'He must have got ahead of them up the mountain, then just mowed them down when they followed,' said Brewster breathlessly. 'But why would they all walk straight into a trap like that? If they knew to follow him up the mountain pass, they must have known they'd be vulnerable. The whole path is like a tunnel, and he already had the high ground. It doesn't make sense.'

'Did you notice they'd all been stripped of their weapons,' said Abbie.

'Jesus,' said Brewster, his face still ashen.

'He must be armed to the teeth.'

'Time for us to get out of here on the double,' Brewster said. 'Keep as close to the rock as you can – we have to assume he's watching the path. Maybe the fact we're leaving will mean he'll leave us alone, but we can't take that chance – he could still try to pick us off.'

Abbie nodded.

'Leaving?' Ridley said, his tone firm. Commanding. 'Who said we're leaving?'

Brewster looked at him incredulously. 'We have to! Me and Blaz would have been out of here the moment we found the armoury if we'd had a boat. Now we have one, and we *know* there's a lunatic on the loose on this island carrying more guns than a Texan on the fourth of July, and who's already murdered a whole unit of Marines. We've got to get out of here. Now.'

Ridley shook his head and pulled an apple from inside his combat jacket. ''Fraid not, old chap,' he said, before casually taking a large bite. 'My orders are to get Milton back under control. We don't leave until we have him locked up again and snug as a bug in a rug.'

'Are you *mad?*' Brewster hissed. 'He's probably sitting up there right now, his eye at the sight, his finger on the trigger, just waiting for us to bimble round the corner so he can add us to the pile of bodies up there.'

'I have no intention of getting shot today, Petty Officer Brewster. But we will stay here and deal with this fellow right here and now. And you will both stay too. That is, if you at all value your careers and your livelihoods. Believe me, one word in the right ear and I could have you court-martialled and dishonourably

131

discharged before your feet touch the ground. Out on your ear. Do not pass go, do not collect two hundred pounds.'

Abbie watched Ridley as he munched on his apple. He seemed so calm. Relaxed. It was unnerving.

Brewster changed tack. 'Let's get some back-up over from the ship, quick sharp then,' he said evenly.

Ridley shook his head again as he took another bite of fruit. 'Negative. We'll do this alone.'

This was too much for Brewster. 'What? *Why?* The captain can have a dozen Marines choppered in here in fifteen minutes. Then we just surround him and force him to surrender. Easy. Why not?'

'Two reasons. One: containment. This fellow is not supposed to exist. This *prison* is not supposed to exist. For four years, knowledge of it has been tightly controlled. I've issued strict orders to the captain that no one else is to come ashore. He is to sit at anchor until we return to the ship. And Captain Harris is a man who understands the importance of following orders.' He paused for a moment. 'At least now he does.'

'But why can't we call up for some help? You said no one could talk, even if they wanted to!'

'First rule of keeping a secret: only divulge it to someone if you absolutely have to. Keep the circle as small as you can.' He took another bite of his apple. 'Secondly – and perhaps more pertinently – we've got no radio signal. Even if I wanted to call for back-up, there's no way of doing it until we're on higher ground.' He threw his apple core over his shoulder. 'Besides, there's three of us and only one of him. Those are pretty good odds to me. I hardly think we need all the king's horses and all the king's men to detain one chap.'

'That's probably what that poor lot thought,' Brewster protested. 'And we only have two guns!'

'Details, my dear boy, details,' Ridley said dismissively. 'Come on, let's go and get him. It's not like we're facing an army, is it? It's only one fellow, and we're British for God's sake.

'This is absolute madness,' Brewster protested. 'Absolute fucking madness.'

Abbie watched the exchange between the two like it was a tennis match. But Brewster was right, this *was* madness.

'Do you have a problem with authority, Petty Officer?' Ridley asked.

'Only when the authority in question is being completely fucking idiotic,' Brewster replied.

Abbie tensed up.

'You will do as you're ordered,' Ridley said, his demeanour hardening. 'Or there will be consequences.'

Abbie watched Brewster closely. She could tell he wasn't ready to back down.

'Why do we even need to recapture him?' he said evenly. 'There's no way off the island and the volcano's gonna blow at any minute. Why not leave him to his fate?'

Ridley shook his head. 'We can't take that chance,' he said. 'What if another vessel comes past? What if he gets a flare off? Gets picked up? No. We stay and we deal with him. I'm not setting foot off this island until he's back under lock and key.' He looked Brewster straight in the eye. 'And neither are you.'

Brewster stared right back.

Abbie was almost holding her breath.

'Come on, Blaz,' he said finally. 'We're getting out of here.'

Abbie thought of Drew. She thought of Milton, that monster, running around out there. Escaped. Free.

She didn't move. She took a deep breath. 'No,' she said simply.

Brewster stopped and turned towards her. 'What?'

Abbie shook her head. 'No.'

Brewster stepped in close to her, ignoring Ridley and speaking only to her. 'Blaz, this is absolute madness. We're not prepared or equipped for this, and we don't know what the hell we'd be facing.'

'I do,' she said. 'I know exactly what we're facing.'

Brewster's face softened.

He was one of the few people Abbie had confided in about the whole sorry business. She'd told him plenty about how hard it had been – how hard it continued to be for her.

'Look,' he said quietly, 'I know this is personal for you – as personal as it gets – but this is crazy.'

'I know,' she replied. 'I know it's mad, and if you order me not to comply with this guy,' she nodded at Ridley, 'then you know I'll follow that order.' She paused and took another deep breath. 'But I'm asking you – I'm asking you as a friend not to do that. You know what that bastard did to me, and God knows how many others. This is my one chance to look that monster in the eye – to get him locked up again. I can't be *this* close and just walk away. I can't risk him getting free and doing to someone else what he's done to me. I just *can't*. Maybe this could get me the closure I need. Seeing him behind bars again – maybe that's what I've needed all this time. To see him beaten.'

Brewster began to shake his head.

'Please,' Abbie said, 'I need this.' She looked up at Brewster, her eyes wide as she waited for his answer.

He sighed heavily and looked from Abbie to Ridley and then back to Abbie. 'The *second* this looks like going south, we're out of here. No arguments. Understood?'

Abbie nodded. 'Thank you,' she mouthed quietly.

He nodded back.

'Jolly good then,' Ridley said loudly, the smug smile back in place. 'Now come on Brewster,' he said, 'you know this place. Let's assume he's lying in wait for us up the mountain path. Where do you think he is, and how do we get him without ending up like those other chaps up there?'

Brewster thought for a moment. 'There's a sort of bowl in the mountainside, another two or three hundred metres up. It would offer some natural protection from the wind, and you could perch on the southeast side of it and have a clear shot down the pass.'

'Right, so let's say he's holed up there, waiting for us. What do we do? There must be another way up?'

Brewster grimaced. 'There is a way. It ain't pretty – but he'll never expect anyone to try it.'

'Sounds perfect,' said Ridley. 'Lead on, Macduff.'

Chapter 23

Brewster wasn't joking, Abbie thought ruefully as they clambered over boulders and rocks at a gradient that seemed to get steeper with each passing minute. They were getting into the kind of terrain that would need proper climbing boots, ropes, crampons – the lot. On this side of the mountain and without the protection of the rock-lined pass, they were also now far more exposed to the wind. It seemed to be gaining in intensity too, each biting-cold gust threatening to rip them from the side of the rock and fling them off the edge. The gale felt like a malevolent sidekick to the island itself. Two bullies toying with them.

'How much further?' Ridley asked as he gripped a rock and pulled himself up another couple of feet.

Abbie watched him climb. He didn't look nearly as chipper as he had when he'd insisted they scale the mountain and apprehend Milton themselves. He might have looked fit enough at first glance, but she suspected he spent more time behind a desk than anywhere else. There was a world of difference between visiting a gym a couple of times a week, and this kind of brutal physical test on a rock face in deteriorating conditions.

'Not much,' Brewster whispered back.

'You said that twenty minutes ago,' Ridley said.

'Look, you were the one who wanted to do this,' Brewster snapped back. 'It'll take as long as it takes.'

Ridley didn't reply, he merely grimaced as he caught his hand on a jagged rock. He pulled it away sharply and went to grip another, but he hadn't planted his foot properly and suddenly he was sliding, his arms flailing as he tried to grab something solid, the rock face falling down away below him for several hundred feet.

Abbie flung out an arm and managed to grab a handful of his jacket, arresting his slide. But only for a moment, then she too was being pulled down by his weight. Ridley was scrabbling at the cliff face, desperately trying to find a solid rock, his boots scraping away dust beneath him.

Then she felt Brewster grabbing onto her coat from above. She looked up and saw his right arm hooked around a rock, his left keeping hold of her.

'Stop panicking and find your footing,' Brewster hissed at Ridley.

The scrabbling stopped. Ridley pressed his feet against the cliff and selected a secure rock, then leaned himself forward until he was flat against the edge. He nodded up at her and she released her grip on his jacket, anchored herself, and then all three of them took a moment and caught their breath.

'Be more careful,' Brewster instructed Ridley, who simply nodded in response.

Abbie pulled herself to one side to allow Ridley to retake his position in between her and Brewster, before they resumed their ascent.

After another twenty minutes of hard climbing, Abbie pulled herself over another ridge that snaked up to the very summit of the mountain. Brewster and Ridley had stopped ahead of her. She followed their gaze to see a man lying prone in the exact spot

Brewster had predicted – on the edge of a natural bowl some twenty-five metres across, rifle propped on a jacket on the rock. Lying. Watching. Waiting. It had to be Milton.

The breath caught in Abbie's throat. *There he was.* Just metres away, lying there. *Vulnerable.* She briefly wondered whether it was a good thing Ridley hadn't given her a gun – she wasn't at all sure she could've resisted shooting the bastard right then and there. She could feel the urge threatening to overwhelm her.

She studied his form, getting a good look at the man who had so utterly ruined her life. He didn't look especially imposing or impressive. He was dressed in blue overalls and lying in the dirt. She tried to comprehend the horrors that had taken place at his hand, the lives he had snuffed out in cold blood, the pain he had caused, the suffering. Not least her own.

She wanted to shoot him and watch him writhe in agony as she stood over him. She wanted to hurt him, to inflict on him even a fraction of the pain he had caused her. Make *him* feel the hurt, the hopelessness, the black hole of despair. The feeling coursed through her veins. She could feel the hate welling up inside her like water building up behind a dam. She heard her own breathing quicken, as if her body was preparing to strike.

She gripped a boulder, partly to steady herself on the slippery surface, and partly to keep herself from launching at the monster that lay before her.

Chapter 24

Ridley narrowed his eyes as he gazed down on the prone figure lying in the dirt beneath him.

Doing the kind of work he did meant that Milton wasn't the only skeleton in Ridley's closet. But now he finally had a legitimate reason to clean house. *She* had been very clear: he wasn't welcome back at the office until this was resolved, and resolved quietly.

But that wasn't quite enough for Ridley. He'd risen up through the ranks not just because he was effective at his job, but because he had a knack of seeing problems a long way off and working out how to neutralize them. Some things couldn't be avoided, of course – but that didn't mean they had to stick to him. And that was his other great talent: he had a skill for ensuring that if something did go wrong, it couldn't be pinned on him. And given *her* instructions, he knew that for this particular job he was going to need some insulation.

That was where this young sailor came in. He'd been keeping a watchful eye over her for the past four years. She was only one of dozens of people, all from different walks of life and in different jobs and locations around the world which he kept like chess pieces on a board. He never knew if, when or how any of them would become useful, but he kept them anyway, like arrows in his quiver, ready to draw if ever he should need to do so. Every single one of them was oblivious to his watchful eye.

And his job meant he had access to all sorts of helpful resources. For instance, he'd studied all of Abbie's Royal Navy personnel files – including the strictly confidential reports written by the psychologist assigned to counsel her after her husband's death. And what he'd read in those reports convinced him that, if he played it right, she could serve a very useful purpose. One that would allow him to solve this problem and keep his hands clean yet again.

He knew she hated Milton – hated him with a passion and rage. He knew too that she'd fantasized about killing him. And now, Ridley was about to make her fantasy a reality.

None of this would ever come out – he'd do his level best to see to that. But if it did, none of it would stick to him. He would, as ever, have his insulation.

The one thing he couldn't work out was the graves. Digging one for him was exactly the kind of sick stunt Milton would have savoured. And the one for Turner made sense too. But one for the girl? That was baffling. How could Milton possibly have known Ridley would engineer her deployment to the island? Did he have a leak somewhere in his own operation? Had Milton somehow overheard some radio comms between the girl and the ship? It was another mystery he'd have to solve before the volcano blew.

Brewster might have had a point on that – he could simply leave Milton to his fate with the eruption. From what he'd been told, it was going to be a big one. There'd be nowhere safe left on the island, and the clock was ticking. The latest data he'd seen predicted it would go before sunset.

Ridley would like nothing more than to leave the murderous

bastard to suffer that death, but two things ruled it out as an option.

Firstly, he needed information. He needed to question Milton. The intelligence report he'd received earlier was a problem. GCHQ had picked up a troubling amount of chatter about something called 'Project Reichstag' from Milton's old Cross of St George organization. Was it an op he'd planned before capture that his followers were now about to put into action? He needed to find out.

The second reason was much more elemental. Ridley only dealt in sureties. He couldn't go back to London and close the file unless he'd seen Milton with his own eyes. However destructive the volcanic eruption was, unless he'd *physically* witnessed Milton's demise, he could never – would never – be 100 per cent sure. There would always be a scintilla of doubt. And Ridley was not the kind of man who could live with that. No, whatever happened to Milton would not be left up to chance or fate or the volcano. Ridley craved control and certainty in all things. This would be no different.

Chapter 25

'What's the plan?' Brewster asked quietly.

'You circle round above,' Ridley whispered back. 'When I see you in position on the other side, I'll move.'

Brewster nodded and began to crawl around behind the ridge line.

Abbie stared down at Milton's form, the hatred coursing through her veins.

'There he is,' Ridley whispered to her once Brewster was out of range.

She nodded.

'I was there, you know. That night,' he added.

She didn't have to ask which night he meant.

'I was back on the ship, waiting for news.'

Abbie nodded. She'd known Drew was on drugs patrol. She'd known it was dangerous. But she had no idea what he'd be facing that night.

'I remember hearing Drew's voice over the radio,' Ridley continued. '"We've got him," he said. He was a hero.' He paused for a moment. 'A bloody hero.'

Abbie saw Drew's smiling face, and felt the pain stab her through the heart again like a stake.

'Then we heard the gunfire. We thought Milton had been taken down at first. Until Drew's number two got on the radio. They had Milton in cuffs in seconds. We sent in the helicopter for Drew. Brought him back to the ship. But it was too late. He was already gone.'

As he spoke, Abbie felt the grief wash over her anew. It felt as if she was being hollowed out.

'I saw them unload him from the chopper on deck. I saw what Milton did to him.'

Abbie fought back the tears forming in her eyes.

'Then they brought Milton back on one of the RIBs. I told him about Drew. I told him he was dead. Do you know what the bastard said?'

Abbie couldn't speak. She managed to shake her head slowly from side to side.

'He said Drew was a coward. Said he deserved to die for not having the guts to have killed him when he had the chance.'

Abbie felt her grief morphing into rage.

'He killed your husband and then he *laughed* about it, Abbie. Laughed like it was nothing. And you know how many other people he's killed. Women. Children. All innocent people. All dead because of him.' Ridley paused for a moment. '*Just like Drew.*'

'He's a fucking monster,' Abbie hissed, unable to control herself.

Ridley nodded. 'Yes, he is. He's caused so much pain, so much suffering. Not least to you.' He leaned in and whispered: 'I know you've thought about it. I know about your fantasy. I know you want to tell him who you are and what he did to you, to see the fear in his eyes before you end him.'

Abbie was so pumped with rage and adrenalin she didn't even have the capacity to wonder how he knew such specific detail about her innermost secrets.

'You've fantasized about this for four long years, haven't you?'

She found herself nodding.

'Ever since that night. All that time, just wishing for one thing, but thinking – knowing – it was impossible.'

He was right. Not a day had gone by when she hadn't thought about it. She wasn't proud of it. She knew it was wrong. She knew the bish was right, it wouldn't have been what Drew wanted, but she couldn't stop.

'But now it *is* possible,' Ridley whispered. 'You can fulfil your most deeply held fantasy – and rid the world of one of the most hateful and monstrous men ever to walk the earth.'

Abbie twitched. It was at that moment she knew there would be no capture; there would be no drugging, no transport to the *Northumberland*. Milton wasn't getting off this island. Not now, not ever.

It suddenly made perfect sense why Ridley had been so adamantly against calling in more back-up from the ship. Brewster was right: it had seemed like madness at the time, but now she saw the truth. Ridley never intended to take Milton aboard the ship. He had only one thing in mind, and he didn't want any more witnesses than were absolutely necessary.

It also explained why she'd been selected for the rescue team. Why *Northumberland* had been diverted from the exercise. And why he'd smiled so smugly when she let slip how much she hated Milton earlier. He'd been planning this from before he even arrived. She realized she was just another pawn in his game. And she didn't care one bit – not when it was about to get her what she wanted more than anything.

'Look at him down there,' Ridley continued. 'Look at him just waiting to kill us. Waiting to take more lives. But we – *you* – can stop him.'

Abbie gritted her teeth.

'I'm going to go down there,' Ridley said in a low voice, 'and reintroduce myself to him. See if he remembers me. I need to ask him a couple of questions. Then, when I give you the signal, come down and join me. And then,' he paused to make sure she was listening, 'you can have my gun.'

He didn't say the rest. He didn't need to.

She quivered at the tantalizing possibility.

Ridley moved before she could say another word.

Chapter 26

Ridley stood up to his full height and aimed his rifle at the rock face behind Milton, then let off a single round. The noise echoed around the bowl as the bullet buried itself in the rock and kicked up a puff of dust in its wake.

'You're surrounded, old chap,' Ridley called. 'Surrounded and outnumbered. Now be a good sport and throw the gun away, will you?'

Even from that distance, Abbie could see Milton's body tense up. He made no move other than to tighten his grip on the gun.

It seemed Ridley spotted this too. 'Don't even bother, Lindfield. My chum over there will have you before you can even get a shot off. Now come along, old stick. Just throw the gun away, there's a good chap.'

Abbie saw the body loosen, then she watched him pull himself up onto his knees and fling his gun towards Ridley. He turned and she saw his face. The 'leaked' images of his horribly disfigured head flashed across her mind. More lies.

He went to stand up but Ridley stopped him.

'No, no. On your knees is best I think, don't you? Now hands behind your head, please.' He was polite, but this was no request, and Milton complied as Ridley made his way down into the bowl, gun trained on the prisoner the entire time. He stopped about twelve metres away from him, as Brewster came down from the opposite side.

'Ridley?' Milton said as he squinted up at the black-clad figure before him. 'I should've known. So nice of you to pop in. Not a social visit, I take it?'

'Correct,' Ridley said evenly. 'Rather a bore, actually. Had hoped I'd never have to set foot on this bloody island ever again.'

'*So* sorry to have inconvenienced you,' Milton said sarcastically. 'Dragged you away from your club, have I? Or dinner with the minister?'

'How did you get out?' Ridley asked.

'You're so clever, you tell me.'

Ridley feigned surprise. 'What? Don't want to show off? Don't want to have the satisfaction of me knowing exactly how you escaped the cage I built you?'

'It's enough for me to know that *you* know it wasn't good enough. Falling down on the job, Ridley. They won't like that in Whitehall, will they? Not good for the old promotion prospects, I shouldn't think? Won't make the New Year's Honours list like that, will you?'

Abbie watched on. Milton was enjoying this. Sparring with an old enemy.

'I'd say my promotion prospects are rather better than those poor souls you murdered down there.' Ridley pointed his chin back down the mountain where the fallen Marines lay.

'They didn't have to die. They made their choice. They serve a corrupt and illegitimate state that I do not and never will recognize. They've contributed to the destruction of Britain, the greatest country on earth. They've stood by as the whole place has been taken over. Islamified. A Christian country for centuries that ruled the world, now on its knees. Brought down to nothing by hordes of foreigners with no Christian values, no respect for our Christian way of life, our families, our land.'

'I thought you were a man of God, Milton. What about Leviticus? Chapter nineteen, verse thirty-four, if I'm not mistaken: "The foreigner residing among you must be treated as your native-born. Love them as yourself, for you were foreigners in Egypt."'

'I think Isaiah one, verse seven is more apt,' he replied. '"Our country lies desolate; our cities are burned with fire; in our very presence foreigners devour our land; it is desolate, as overthrown by foreigners."' Milton continued as he warmed to his theme, perhaps simply enjoying having an audience again. 'As I look ahead, I am filled with foreboding. Like the Roman, I seem to see the River Tiber foaming with much blood.'

Abbie had heard him recite similar sermons before, usually a hodgepodge of lines and sentiments he'd cribbed from the likes of Enoch Powell, David Duke and Marine Le Pen, with a handful of Bible verses thrown in. She assumed it was an attempt to add gravitas.

After Drew's death, she had felt a strange compulsion to learn everything she could about Milton. Every mention of his name, every glimpse of his face brought stabbing pain to her heart, yet she couldn't resist reading more and more about him, watching more and more of his hateful online videos and self-titled 'sermons', as if somehow the more she knew, the less it would hurt. But it did nothing of the sort. In fact it had the opposite effect – every time she read about him, watched him, saw his face, it merely fuelled her pain and anger. And yet she hadn't been able to resist. She knew it would only hurt her more, but she couldn't stop. After Drew had died, grief, pain and anger were all she had. She had long forgotten what it felt like to feel anything else.

'Spare me the party political, Lindfield. And don't give me that biblical nonsense. Your Telegram subscribers might be buying it, but I'm not.'

'And he said to them, "Go into all the world and proclaim the gospel to the whole creation."'

Ridley rolled his eyes. 'Give it a rest,' he said wearily. 'I don't want to talk about God.'

'What do you want to talk about then?'

'Project Reichstag,' Ridley said, enunciating each separate syllable with crystal clarity.

Abbie looked back at Milton. He was smiling.

'Been doing a little reading, have we, Ridley? A little eavesdropping?'

'A little. Got most of it, but you could fill in a couple of gaps if you don't mind.'

'I don't know what you're taking about,' he said. He was being deliberately unconvincing, taunting his captor.

'Not to worry. As I say, we've got most of it anyway.'

Milton smiled. 'You've got nothing. That's why you've left your cushy little office and come all the way down here yourself, isn't it?'

Ridley shrugged. 'Ah well. Have it your way.' He tightened his grip on the rifle.

'How's your report going to read on this one, Ridley?' Milton asked. 'Gotta have something for the official form, surely?'

'Shot while trying to escape,' he replied. 'And the great thing is, it's true, isn't it? Finally I can close the file on you, even if it is four years too late.'

Abbie watched, unable to tear her eyes away. Ridley was nearly done. The moment she'd longed for, dreamed about for four torturous years, was almost here. The moment she'd thought would forever be a fantasy. Yet here she was, about to end the life of one of the world's deadliest terrorists, the man responsible for so many deaths, so much pain, so much misery – and the killer of her husband. The thief who'd stolen her whole life from her.

And yet.

And yet, she found herself conflicted. Wavering. He was un-armed, he was a prisoner. War is war and killing is never pretty, but there were rules. Then she thought back to the bodies they'd found down the mountain. Marines shot dead in cold blood. They got no mercy – and neither did Drew – so why should he? *Fuck it,* she thought as she watched the scene in front of her. *Fuck it, and fuck him.* She tightened her grip on the rock she was holding and could feel her heartbeat pick up as she waited for Ridley to give her the signal.

Her breathing quickened. This was her chance to end him, and perhaps start to rebuild herself. *Closure.* She knew Ridley was manipulating her for his own ends, but she didn't care. She gripped the rock as the urge began to overwhelm her. She waited for the signal and prepared to stride up to Ridley, take the gun, and finish this whole thing herself. For Drew. For the world. Who could blame her? Who *would* blame her?

But before she could move, the dead bodies of the Marines flashed through her mind again. Dead and cold and lying in a heap. But there was something wrong with the picture in her mind. What was it? She blinked and shook her head as she tried to work it out. Something didn't fit. Something wasn't right.

'Awfully sorry about this, old thing, but you know how it is,' Ridley said as he began to turn his head in her direction.

That was when it hit her. The picture. The Marines. It was wrong. There were only five of them.

There was one back in the radio room at the prison, and

Turner, already buried in a shallow grave down on the beach – that made seven.

Ridley had said the detachment was eight.

There was one missing.

Chapter 27

A single shot rang out and echoed back off the rock walls of the mountainside. Abbie watched as Ridley staggered forwards, dropped his gun, and let out a strangled cry that was more shock than pain. She could see Brewster on the opposite side of the ridge, desperately scanning the horizon for the source of the shot. He seemed to spot something and raised his gun but, before he could fire, he too was hit and fell back against the rock behind him, the Glock clattering to the ground. A second bullet hit him in the leg, apparently dissuading him from any notion of trying to retrieve his weapon. He roared in pain as he writhed on the ground, his uninjured leg kicking again and again at the rock as he howled in agony, as if he could somehow physically kick the pain away.

Abbie brought a hand up to her mouth to stifle a scream. She was shaking, shock and fear and terror and disbelief all fighting for prominence in her overwhelmed mind. As she crouched behind the ridge watching the scene unfold, she knew there was nothing she could do. She was unarmed – while Milton now had at least three guns – and there was clearly another shooter well within range. Despite every cell in her body straining to go to

Brewster's aid, she knew the only thing she could do was stay out of sight.

Ridley was crawling towards his gun, but Milton rose up from his knees, kicked the weapon away and then aimed a foot at Ridley's chin. The sickening crack that followed suggested a broken jaw.

Milton walked calmly over to pick up his own gun, then made his way to Brewster and casually fired off two shots at point-blank range, one in the head, one in the chest. The cries stopped.

Abbie watched on in utter horror, once again having to slap her hand over her mouth to stop herself from crying out as her friend was so casually murdered. The panic and shock was threatening to overwhelm her. '*Per mare, per terram*,' she whispered to herself as she tried to regain control. '*Per mare, per terram. Per mare, per terram.*'

Then the gravel was disturbed from the north and a man in Marines fatigues scrambled down the mountain pass.

'Good work, Robertson,' Milton said.

It was now obvious how Milton had escaped. An inside man. The only chink in Ridley's otherwise perfect containment system.

How dare he still be wearing the uniform. Abbie burned with anger at this traitor, as she watched him walk towards the prone Ridley. She'd never set eyes on him before, but she knew enough: she knew he was a Royal Marine. A Marine who'd taken an oath. And she knew he'd somehow been turned by Milton. She wondered if he'd been promised money. Or whether Milton had just worked on him, day after day, poisoning his mind with his hate-filled bullshit.

'Want me to finish him off?' Robertson asked, nodding at Ridley.

Milton shook his head as a smile crept across his face. 'Oh no. That particular pleasure will be mine alone.'

Milton walked up to the writhing figure of Ridley. 'Hide me away, leave me here to rot, to die? To die this slow death worse than death. How fucking *dare* you,' he spat, allowing his anger to show for the first time. 'The *arrogance* of it. Typical of you lot. Think you have it all under control. All your plans and schemes cooked up by the men in grey suits in smoke-filled rooms in Whitehall. Think you've got it all mapped out, don't you?'

Ridley said nothing. He clutched his wound, trying not to make a sound, as if he didn't want to give Milton the satisfaction.

'Well, you didn't see this coming, did you?'

Ridley looked up at Milton from his position on the ground. So smug just moments ago, now a beaten man.

'I *knew* you wouldn't be able to resist coming here yourself. Got your little code word, did you? "Elba" – ha! I knew it would be something unbelievably pompous but still – I'm almost honoured.' He smiled again. 'Do you know the funny thing? I had to torture that officious little gaoler Turner for hours – *hours*, mind you – trying to get him to tell me what the protocol was, so I could be sure you would come. Bless his fortitude – he held on for a long while. Longer than you would have. But after all that resisting, all that pain he endured, he finally cracked – and it turned out he'd already sent you his little code word message.' Another smile. 'I knew you wouldn't be able to resist. Then I just waited for you to scuttle down here to check up on your pet project, give me a good slap on the wrist. *Twenty lashes of the cane and double detention. Deduct fifty house points and no rugger for a fortnight.*'

Ridley couldn't help but let out a strangled groan as his pain intensified.

'It's tragic really. Your lot have had it your way for so long, you can't imagine it ever ending, can you? But mark my words, your time is done, *old chap.*

'My lot?' Ridley repeated between pained breaths.

'Yes, *your lot,*' Milton sneered. 'You and your self-satisfied, entitled, elitist fucking friends.'

'Elitist? You went to a posher school than me. Your father was a cabinet minister! You're as establishment as they come, despite what you like to tell your pathetic little followers. Your "man of the people" act. Tell me, how's the family estate doing these days? Still topping up the trust fund?'

Milton simply continued with his theme. 'You thought you could do this to me. To me! Send me down to this devil's island, lock me up and throw away the key. I told you I'd get you for that, Ridley. Do you remember? When you brought me here?'

'So all this was just about me? Luring me down here just to teach me a lesson?'

Milton laughed. 'There you go again. The arrogance of it is astounding. No, no. This was just my little bonus, the cherry on the cake. We have to have our little pleasures in life, isn't that right?'

Ridley said nothing as he looked up at Milton with fear and loathing in his green eyes.

'No, no. You are merely an hors d'oeuvre. And you have no idea what's coming next. No fucking clue. The only shame is, I won't be able to see the stupid look on your face when it happens.'

'Project Reichstag,' Ridley croaked.

Milton merely smiled in response.

'Killing me won't make any difference, Milton,' Ridley said as he clutched his arm in a vain attempt to staunch the blood loss.

'Oh, I have to disagree with you there, *old sport,*' Milton replied. 'Yes, I very much have to disagree with you there. I've been stuck on this island in the middle of nowhere for four fucking years with nothing to do, no one to talk to, no chance of ever getting out alive. Just sitting here waiting for death. And every night I've seen your smug, pin-striped, toffee-nosed fucking face before I go to sleep, and every night I've dreamed of the day I'd have you on your knees, *begging* me for mercy.'

Abbie felt a flash of unease at the similarities between this statement and her own obsession.

'I won't beg, Milton.'

'Oh, of course not. That would be beneath you, wouldn't it? Not right for a gentleman to *beg*, is it? Not right to do that – yet you can hide a man away, lock him up without trial and leave him to rot. That's all hunky-dory and tickety-fucking-boo by your fucked-up moral code, isn't it?'

'You're one to talk about a moral code, Milton,' Ridley managed. 'How much blood is on your hands?'

'Far less than yours, I'm willing to bet. I've never ordered a drone strike on a village square, or sent troops into battle to protect an oil pipeline. Don't try to pretend you're innocent in all this, you establishment piece of shit. Just because you order your kills from a desk in Whitehall on His Majesty's Government-headed notepaper doesn't make you any less of a killer.'

'You gonna start quoting the Bible again? Get me to repent? Save my soul?'

'Ah, that's where the Lord and I differ – you see, I think some people are beyond salvation.'

'Not very Christian of you, Milton.'

'Well, none of us is perfect, though we must strive for it. And as Mark tells us, "All things are possible to him who believes".'

'Tell me this, *Julian*,' Ridley said, 'do you really believe? Or is this God stuff all just a cover? Theatre? An act?'

Milton looked down at him pityingly. 'Matthew told us, "Whatever you ask in prayer, you will receive, if you have faith."'

He smiled. 'And, well, here you are.' He flexed his fingers around his gun. 'So it seems my faith has been rewarded by the good Lord.'

'Spare me,' Ridley spat.

'You should read your Bible, Ridley,' Milton said. 'The answers lie within.'

Ridley's breathing was coming faster and faster. 'So now what? Kill me? And then what? You and I both know there's only one way off this island – and on the other side of Neptune's Bellows there's a British warship with fifty Marines on board. There's no way out of here for you, Milton, and you know it.'

Milton smiled. 'You see, that's the trouble with you government employees, isn't it? Absolutely no imagination.'

Abbie watched Milton raise his gun. She saw raw, pure fear for the first time in Ridley's eyes.

And with one crack that echoed around the rock plateau, it was over. Ridley's body went limp, the whimpering stopped.

Just for a moment there was total silence.

'It's never as good as you imagine, is it?' Milton said, casually.

Abbie watched and tried to keep perfectly still. She looked to Brewster's lifeless body and felt tears forming in her eyes as the emotion threatened to overwhelm her. Poor Brewster. How had it come to *this*? Then a second horrifying thought hit her: it was all her fault. She'd asked him – pleaded with him – to stay, when he'd been so adamant they should leave. Her thirst for revenge, for a glimpse at the monster who'd ruined her life had blinded her to the insanity of it all. And now Brewster had paid for her lust for vengeance with his life. She let the tears flow, her eyes locked onto his body.

'Grab their guns and let's go,' Milton said, glancing at his watch.

'What about him?' Robertson nodded at Ridley's body.

'Leave him.'

'I thought you wanted to bury him?'

Milton thought for a moment. 'I've changed my mind. A grave is too good for that piece of shit. Leave him to the vultures.'

Robertson nodded and began retrieving the weapons. 'Any sign of the girl?' he asked.

Milton shook his head and checked his watch. 'Forget her. We don't have time to fuck about.'

Abbie took in another breath at his mention of her, but as she did so she shifted her weight slightly onto her right leg. The gravel beneath her foot slipped away, piercing the silence.

She ducked down as her heart rate shot up. A handful of rocks trickled down the slope behind her as Abbie held her breath.

A few seconds passed. Abbie didn't dare so much as breathe as she prayed the rocks would settle. Eventually she risked movement, slowly raising her head above the rock in front of her. She could see Milton and Robertson looking for the source of the sound they had clearly heard.

She ducked down, but with a little too much gusto, and her foot slipped on the rock again. Once more she tried to hold herself completely still, but she realized with horror that she'd started a chain reaction: the rocks below her began to shift.

She held her breath and prayed the two men hadn't heard it, but as she slowly lifted her head to look back over the rock, she could already see they were coming in her direction. *Shit.*

Chapter 28

Had they seen her? Or just heard the gravel and were being prudent enough to investigate? Should she hide? She quickly decided against that – if she hid, they would simply find her, drag her out, and add her to the pile of bodies that seemed to be growing by the minute on this hellish island.

She needed to get away from them. How or to where, she wasn't entirely sure, but that wasn't the immediate priority. She simply had to run. Now.

She knew she couldn't retreat the way that she, Brewster and Ridley had come up the mountain; it was such slow going that she would present an easy target for Milton or his accomplice to pick off. They wouldn't even have to be sure of hitting her with a fatal shot – getting hit anywhere would, at the very least, unbalance her, and the fall would do the rest.

No, she couldn't go that way. She had to get to the main path that snaked its way back down towards the prison building and the beach. She began clambering over the rocks in that direction, all the while keeping as low as she could and taking advantage of the natural cover.

She risked a peek over the rock and saw Milton and Robertson were walking towards where she'd been hiding, just eight or nine metres to the northwest of where she was now.

At the south end of the natural bowl cut into the mountain side was the entrance to the maze-like path that led down to the shore. It was too far from the ridge she was using as cover to slip into directly. Instead, she'd have to jump down into the bowl and then head for the trail. She'd be completely exposed – at least for the few seconds it would take her to make it to the path – but she had no choice.

She glanced back up the hill. The two of them were right at her former hiding place. It was now or never. She set her footing and made ready to make her stealthy move. But as she did so, she hit another patch of loose rock. Before she could do a thing about it, she set off a mini-avalanche. She looked up. They were staring right at her.

Panic surged through her veins.

She didn't hesitate.

She vaulted the rock ahead of her and landed heavily. Without looking back, she sprang to her feet, pumped her legs and made for the gap in the rock that led to the path.

'For fuck's sake. You take care of it,' she heard Milton bark at his little helper as she ducked in behind the rock and ran.

For once, the unique geography of the island was on her side: the path, walled by solid rock on either side, meant that as long as she could keep out of Robertson's direct line of sight, he wouldn't be able to fire on her. But that meant she *had* to stay ahead of him.

She could hear him crunching down the ash track behind her, his footsteps echoing off the rock walls so it sounded like an entire army was chasing her rather than just one man.

The footsteps were getting closer. He was gaining on her.

She also knew the path widened out in places, so she couldn't rely on its walls offering her cover all the way down to the beach. She needed a new plan. She thought fast – it wasn't anything particularly clever, but it would have to do. She pushed on, running as hard as she could back down the path towards the prison. Then she saw them: the lifeless bodies of the Marines. Her decoys, lying in a heap on the path. There wasn't much cover, but she wouldn't need much.

She darted left behind the rock opposite the bodies and slid to a halt, her pulse racing, her breaths short and fast. She placed a hand on the cold stone and tried to slow her breathing. Then she held herself as still as she could, and listened. She could hear him coming, the pounding of his boots on the ash and rock surface. She checked her footing in the loose ash, like a cat preparing to pounce, and waited, ears pricked up, eyes wide. Her whole body stiffened up, each muscle tensed and primed as she waited, poised and ready. *Not yet . . .* She would wait for the moment he too saw the bodies. She was counting on that to slow him, just for a fraction of a second. *Not yet . . .* Still she waited. *Not yet . . . Now!*

As soon as she saw the flash of green she moved, the tension in her body released like an arrow from a bow. She ducked her head down, launched herself from her feet and rammed into him as hard as she could, using Robertson's own momentum to slam him into the rock opposite. She heard his head hit the rock face with a crack, the wind forced from his lungs as he cried out in shock and pain, dropping his Glock. She knew she couldn't give him a single split second to recover or get his bearings; he was physically stronger than her and would overpower her in a fair fight. That just meant she had to make sure it wasn't a fair fight.

While he was still reeling from the initial hit, she took a step back and aimed a kick to his chest as hard as she could, slamming him back into the rock a second time. Caught off guard, he was winded, but he tried to stay on his feet to fight back. He aimed a punch at her, but she saw it coming a mile off, dodged his fist and used the base of the palm of her hand to land another blow, this time on his chin. He sprawled on his back against the rock – this was her chance; she knew she had to take it while he was still reeling. She turned to grab the gun he'd dropped in her first attack, scooping it up and aiming it right at him in one single movement.

'Don't move,' she commanded.

He looked up at her from under his eyebrows, his eyes burning with rage and pain, his jaw locked tight as he clutched his chest and spat on the ground, his breathing heavy and laboured. She studied his face for the first time. He was pale with dark rings under his eyes and mousy-brown hair that curled at the ends.

'You wouldn't shoot a Marine,' he gasped between wheezy breaths.

She flicked the safety catch off as she trained the gun on him. 'You did,' she said coldly, nodding at the bodies that lay dead in a heap off to her right.

He pressed a finger to his right nostril and forced out a torrent of blood from the other, then repeated the procedure on the left. 'They were all armed and trying to kill me. I only did what I had to do. Believe me, I didn't want to, but he convinced me it was the only way.'

She looked at him in disgust. 'He convinced you? What else did he convince you of? Why the hell are you helping him?'

He held up a hand as if asking her to wait while he tried to recover. His other hand went back to his face. 'I think you broke my fucking nose!' he cried out.

'I'm sorry about that.' She wasn't.

'Yeah?' he said, looking back at her. 'Well I'm sorry about this.'

Suddenly all she saw was black. She could feel a ringing in her ears. The pain came momentarily later, but when it did, it was excruciating and intense.

Chapter 29

Abbie slumped down on the ground, turning her head as she did so to see Milton standing behind her, from where he'd clearly administered the surprise blow that had felled her. She tried to crawl away, but Robertson was on her in a second, aiming a kick right into her ribs. She howled in pain and fell to the ground again.

Then Milton's hands were in her hair as he yanked her upright and propped her up against a rock.

'Are there more of you coming?' he shouted.

She was dazed and his words seemed to be coming at her through ten feet of water. Despite that, she felt acutely aware that – for the first time in her life – she was face to face with evil itself. The man who had killed and maimed thousands. The monster who had murdered Drew. Stolen her life. She felt revulsion along with her loathing, every cell in her body straining to recoil from him, desperate to get away, as if he was literally toxic and his mere proximity would somehow infect her.

Through groggy eyes she studied his features. The odd thing about him was that outwardly he looked completely normal. There was no Bond-villain scar running down his cheek, no glass eye, nothing. *But the eyes.* The eyes gave it away. They were small and dark. Blue in colour, but somehow black at the same time.

She remembered the photographs she'd seen of this same face, but horribly mangled after his supposed shooting. She decided he was uglier as he was now. Physically unscathed, but riddled with hate and anger, which flowed from every pore of his skin.

Hate and anger. The very same emotions she felt about him. That realization shocked her. She could see the ugliness of it in *him* – was that how *she'd* looked all this time? Was it that obvious?

'Are there more of you coming?' he shouted again, this time following his words up with a harsh slap to her face. 'How many?'

She could see Robertson composing himself behind Milton, dabbing at the blood leaking from his nose.

'Fuck you,' she said defiantly. She felt oddly disappointed, after waiting so long and spending so much time thinking about this monster, that she couldn't come up with anything better to say when confronted with him face to face.

He laughed. 'Try again.'

She stared back at him. She wasn't going to give him anything. *Not a damn thing.*

He pulled her head up by her hair, then drew his other hand back and slapped it hard across her face. 'Tell me!' he shouted.

It stung horribly, but the physical pain he was causing her was nothing – *nothing* – compared to the mental agony he'd inflicted on her these past four years. She could take the physical pain all day long; it was almost a relief, a distraction from the hurt in her heart which never left her. Still she said nothing, and stared at him with all the intensity and defiance she could muster. It wasn't hard to summon the hate she had for him.

'Let's try an easier one,' he said, his voice quieter. 'Who are you?'

She looked up at him through the pain and frowned in confusion. She flashed back to the grave. He *knew* who she was. He had to. Unless . . . it wasn't him who had dug her grave. But if not him, then who?

She declined to answer.

He seemed to sense he was wasting his efforts. 'I don't have time for this,' he said irritably, then took the rifle slung over his shoulder, turned it around and rammed the butt into her stomach.

Abbie dropped to her knees, a hand shooting out to balance her as she fell, heaving and retching on the black ash.

'I can't believe you let a girl take you down, Robertson. You're slipping.'

'She rushed me, but I'd have had her, even if you hadn't shown up.'

Milton looked sceptical. 'Well, deal with her, will you? I need to get down to the beach.' He handed the rifle to Robertson, then turned and began making his way down the mountain path.

Abbie was still prone on the ground, breathing heavily and coughing up blood. She spat out a mouthful, then peered up at Robertson, who was standing over her, Milton's rifle now slung over his shoulder, his Glock stowed in a holster on the front of his jacket. He scowled down at her.

'Better?' he asked.

She nodded. It was more of a reflex action as she could feel the pain in her stomach from where Milton had hit her.

'Good,' Robertson said before swinging his right leg hard, the toe of his boot connecting with her ribs.

The force of the kick knocked her onto her back and she howled out in agony, her hands instinctively clutching at her chest where the pain was. Then she was coughing up more blood in big, painful hacks. She rolled sideways as she moaned and tried to spit the blood out. A shadow loomed over her where she lay. Robertson, with his gun drawn, finger on the trigger. Vengeance in his eyes.

Abbie tried to block out the pain, put it on hold somehow, as she tried to think of a way out. She had no doubt what Robertson was about to do. He'd already admitted having a hand in killing the other Marines. What was one more death?

But there had to be a way out of this. She briefly considered rushing him again, but instantly dismissed it. The beatings from Milton and Robertson had weakened her. She knew she'd only got the better of Robertson before because she'd staged a surprise attack. Now, in her current state, and with him watching her closely, she knew she had no chance. And anyway, he had a loaded gun trained on her, and she was on the ground.

Physically, she was beaten, and she knew it. She had to find another way. She thought fast. 'I can help you!' she blurted out. 'I could help you get off the island. We could take Milton back to the ship together, then I could help you slip away when we get into port.'

He shook his head. 'Shut up.'

He wasn't buying it, but she persisted.

'Or better still, say you rescued me from him, took him down after he'd escaped and killed the others. The last man standing who saved the day. You'd be a hero!' She was nakedly appealing to his ego at this point – she knew there was very little as powerful as a male ego. And she suspected Robertson's was there to be exploited.

There was a pause. Was he actually considering it? Was it going to work?

'I said, shut up,' he said coldly, keeping the gun trained on her.

'Come on, Robertson. Is this what you signed up for? Is this what you call doing your job? I'm unarmed, for Christ's sake. Only cowards shoot unarmed prisoners. You know that.'

He hesitated for just a moment. Abbie could see he still had a sliver of his training, his old loyalty behind those eyes. Old loyalties die hard.

She pressed her point. 'You're a Marine. You don't kill without cause. What does it get you to kill me? I have no gun; I have no way of getting one. Please, I know you don't want to do it,' she paused just for half a beat, and then, more softly, 'I can see it.'

'Shut up!' he shouted.

He was breathing heavily; she could see confusion in his eyes. *Doubt.*

She knew he was a killer – and had killed right here on this very spot – but she was banking on the fact he'd been able to rationalize those acts to himself. And all his other victims had been armed and ready to kill him too. Abbie wasn't armed. She was already beaten. And she also calculated that the very fact she was a woman might count in her favour. Not very macho to kill an unarmed woman, was it? It wouldn't be the first time Abbie had been underestimated because of her gender.

'Come on, Robertson,' she pushed gently. 'You don't need to do this. Put the gun down.'

She saw the barrel dip just a fraction.

It was working.

He began slowly shaking his head and took a deep breath.

'You don't have to do it,' she said softly. 'It'll all be okay.'

The barrel dipped a fraction more. But then something seemed to snap in him. He steadied himself and raised the gun, a look of determination now in his eyes. The uncertainty was gone.

'No! Wait! Don't!' she shouted, as she instinctively pulled her arm in front of her face in some vain effort to protect herself.

Robertson raised the gun, took aim, and fired off two rounds over the ridge. 'On your feet,' he said. 'And if you try anything, I'll shoot you in a heartbeat.'

Chapter 30

Robertson shoved Abbie down the mountainside, the barrel of the gun in the small of her back on every single step, her mind whirring through options as she tried to think of a way out of her situation.

'Where are we going?' she asked.

'Just keep walking.'

She did as instructed as they crunched down the path. Without a weapon, she knew she was going to have to talk her way out of this.

'Why are you helping him?'

The only response she got was a shove in the back from the gun.

'Don't you know who he is?'

Another shove, still no verbal response.

'You must know what he's done?'

He didn't even shove her this time.

'The people he's killed?'

She tried a half-turn to see if he was listening.

'Keep walking,' he said gruffly.

'And even if you didn't know before, you do now. My PO up the mountain, and the other guy.'

No reply.

'And what about your mates? The five guys back up there? Turner. And the poor lad at the radio – what was his name, Berkeley?'

'Just shut up.'

'Did he deserve that? How old was he? Can't have been more than twenty-one. How long had you known him?'

'I said shut up.'

'Was that *him*? Or did you do that?'

Another shove. Harder than before.

'I just mean, even if he lied to you before, you know what he's like now. You don't have to go along with any more of it.'

'Look it wasn't meant to . . .' He stopped himself and pushed her again. 'Just shut up, okay? Come on, we're nearly there.'

'Wasn't meant to what? Wasn't meant to *what*?'

But he wouldn't respond.

They came around another bend in the rock, and Abbie found herself facing the dull green tin of the prison building.

Robertson shoved her forward. 'Open the door.'

She did as she was told, keeping her movements slow, deliberate and obvious so as not to make him twitchy with the gun, even if her eyes were darting this way and that, searching for something to help her. She saw nothing.

He pushed her through the door with the barrel of the gun. 'Hurry up. Through there.' He nodded ahead of her and, in that instant, she understood what he was going to do with her. She felt the familiar panic rising up inside her chest.

'No!' she pleaded, but he just shook his head.

'Come on!' he shouted as they walked through the building, past the control room and towards the reinforced steel door that led to Milton's containment cell. It was still open from when Abbie had investigated earlier.

'In there,' he said simply, nodding at the door.

'No, please!' she cried. She could feel the sand pouring over her body, closing her in. 'You can't leave me here!' she said pleadingly.

'I said, in there,' he repeated. He was getting impatient now. She guessed Milton would soon start wondering where he was.

'Please,' she begged. She could feel her limbs being pinned down and taste the sand in her mouth. 'Please! You can't leave me here! The volcano's going to go up at any moment. I'll be trapped!'

'Wait,' he said.

Her heart leapt for a moment – was he going to show her mercy? Had her pleading worked?

'Give me your radio,' he ordered.

She sighed and unclipped it from her belt. He held out his left hand and she passed it over. He slipped it into a pocket.

'Now in there,' he said again.

She shook her head. 'I can't. I can't!' she said, desperate now.

He moved towards her, but she wrapped her fingers around the door frame as she tried to resist.

He didn't bother arguing anymore. Her cheek cracked when the butt of the gun slammed against it. She released her grip on the frame and stumbled backwards in pain as she brought her hands up to where he'd hit her. She fell to the floor and, before she could make another move, he slammed the heavy metal door shut. It closed with a horribly secure and permanent clang. She looked up just in time to see him glance in at her through the porthole-sized reinforced-glass window in the door, before he turned and left.

She was trapped.

Chapter 31

The panic was overwhelming her. Abbie was trapped in a tiny prison cell on an island that was about to be engulfed by a volcanic eruption. There was only one person in the entire world who knew where she was, and he wasn't about to tell anyone. Robertson might as well have shot her, she thought grimly. At least that would've been quick and painless.

She felt as if the tiny room was already shrinking somehow, closing in on her as she crouched on the floor. She could taste sand in her mouth as her body reacted to her panic.

'*Per mare, per terram. Per mare, per terram,*' she chanted as she fought to regain control and stave off the terror.

The pain from Robertson slamming her in the face with his gun was fighting with the pain in her ribs and stomach from the beating he and Milton had given her, but she had no time to wallow in either. That would have to wait. She shuffled along the floor and then pulled herself up the door to peer through the porthole. She banged on the door again and again until her fists hurt.

'Robertson!' she pleaded. 'Don't leave me here!' She hit the door repeatedly. 'Robertson!' she tried again. 'COME BACK!' her voice already hoarse with the effort. 'Just come back and kill me!' she begged.

There was no answer.

She turned and slumped against the door, sliding down its smooth metal surface towards the floor as she tried to quell the rising panic with her familiar chant.

She had to keep a clear head and think rationally if she had *any* chance of getting out of this. She repeated her chant four times, then closed her eyes and took three deep breaths as she tried to regain control. Only then did she start to work through what she knew and how she might get out of here.

She knew Milton had escaped from this very cell, but that didn't help her – he'd had a man on the inside. Robertson had obviously busted him out before they'd made their break for it. And that meant Ridley's prison hadn't really failed at all – not in a mechanical sense. It was human error that had been its undoing. And that was absolutely no good to her right now.

She could feel her mind beginning to let the pain and panic back in. Her cheek and her chest burned with it. She thought Robertson might even have cracked one of her ribs. She was almost glad of the pain; it took some of her focus off the intense claustrophobia.

She tried to distract herself by taking a good look at her surroundings to see if there was anything she'd missed the last time she was in here.

She was in what might be termed the living and sleeping quarters. The tiny room couldn't have been much more than eight feet in length and less than that in width. It was small. Too small. She blinked and for a moment felt the sand on her skin, the taste of it in her mouth. 'No!' she said aloud, shaking her head in a desperate bid to fight off her fear.

She took in the rest of the room. It was as she remembered: single metal bed frame to her right with a thin mattress on top, and a chair tucked under a table on the left underneath the frosted glass window through which light could enter, but which offered no view of the outside world. She could imagine how mentally torturous that could become after even a short time. A small TV with a DVD player was perched on a shelf above the bed. She looked through the DVD boxes stacked next to it: *The Shawshank Redemption, Escape from Alcatraz, Papillon*. All prison movies. She suspected all of them chosen by Ridley himself. It was the kind of vindictive joke he'd no doubt have found funny.

There was also a small bookshelf with some Greek philosophy texts, an atlas, and of course, a Bible. She shook her head at that – Milton had co-opted it for his own purposes. He used Christianity as his shield: a cover under which he could wage his disgusting 'war' on Muslims. It wasn't even just Muslims, not really. Just anyone not like him. She found his assertion that Britain was a Christian country to be laughable. How many of his crazed, shaven-headed supporters were regular church-goers, she wondered? It was all just an excuse. He might have been a true believer, but he twisted and deliberately misinterpreted the words to suit his own disgusting and horrific purposes.

At the other end of the room from where she sat there was another door – the one that led through to the little wet room and the outside yard. She hauled herself up, one hand on her ribs in a mostly futile attempt to quell the pain, and walked the length of the room. She pushed it open then checked the wet room: nothing but a stainless-steel sink and toilet mounted next to a shower. Maybe there was some way out through the yard?

She made her way outside and was instantly disappointed. It was perhaps six metres square – a concrete box, with walls that stretched up perhaps five metres on all four sides, and at the top were thick metal bars covering the whole opening. It was clearly some attempt to give Milton access to what was technically an outside space. It was bizarre the self-imposed rules Ridley had apparently adhered to – he had secretly and illegally imprisoned a man on a remote Antarctic island, yet still ensured he was able to get fresh air whenever he wanted. The only break in the concrete other than the open bars at the top was a small grate about the size of a CD case in one corner of the floor for drainage, and the thick, frosted glass window into the cell.

She looked up at the bars. Even if she could somehow get up that high (she briefly wondered whether she could stack the bed on top of the table and climb up), she suspected the bars would be sunk into the concrete walls and totally unyielding. Still, she would try it if she couldn't think of anything else. Maybe the extreme weather down here had rusted one of the joints? Perhaps the cold had caused the concrete to weaken and crumble a little? She knew she was clutching at straws, but right now straws were all she had.

Then she had another thought – the wet room. There was no window, so there had to be an extractor fan to remove the moist air, and an extractor fan meant an air shaft – an air shaft that must lead to the outside. She ran back into the tiny room and was again immediately deflated. There *was* an extractor fan, but it was no bigger than the drain in the yard. She cursed herself for thinking it could ever have been a possibility. Only in Hollywood spy films did buildings come with convenient human-sized air ducts.

She walked back into the main room, eyes quickly scanning the scene, looking for something – *anything* – that might help. She walked to the door; its thick steel looked completely and utterly impenetrable, like the entrance to a bank vault. She felt around the frame, looking for any weakness, however small, that she could somehow exploit. Nothing. She glanced at the frosted-glass window, but that was no help either as it only led out into the yard. The walls, floor and ceiling of the room were all painted concrete. She'd need a jackhammer to break through – and even then, it would probably take her a week. She was trapped in a solid box. A *tiny* solid box. A cell with no way out. Her mouth went dry. She could taste the sand again. It was suffocating her, and she could feel the weight of it pinning her down.

She tried shaking her head again in a bid to snap out of the spiral.

Then the thought hit her that Milton had been trapped in here for four long years – and surely he'd tested every single inch of this place for weaknesses, but in the end had only escaped with help from outside. If he couldn't get out in four years, what hope did she have in just a matter of hours before the volcano erupted? She slumped down against the door again, defeated. Defeated and panicking. 'Help me Drew,' she whispered to herself, as she tried in vain to regain some level of control. Usually when she felt the claustrophobia threatening to overwhelm her, she could at least try turning to logic in an attempt to counter it. If she was in a lift, she knew the doors would open soon. When she'd been bailing out the water from the chain locker, she had known that if she really *had* to, she could have pulled her way out and up the ladder. In situations like that, she could tell herself her fear was a phobia – an *irrational* fear. But there was nothing irrational about her fear now: she was trapped in a tiny cell, halfway up a volcano that was about to erupt. Fear and panic were entirely logical responses, even for someone who didn't suffer from claustrophobia.

She looked around the room. She had to do something, to occupy herself to take her mind off her reality. Her eyes settled on the table. It was a long shot, but she had nothing to lose at this point. She hauled herself back to her feet and dragged the table out through the little hall and into the exercise yard, pushing it into the far corner.

Then she went back into the main room and pulled on the metal bed frame. It didn't move an inch. She yanked it again, but it wouldn't budge. She pulled off the sheets and the thin mattress to reveal just the bed frame beneath, and could immediately see why it wouldn't shift: it was bolted to the floor and the wall. 'Shit,' she hissed. Clearly Ridley and his builders hadn't wanted Milton to be able to move it, or even contemplate using it as any kind of weapon against his gaolers. But had Milton ever really tried to see how firm those bolts were? She yanked again at the frame, but still it wouldn't move. Another dead end.

She slumped down on the mattress. She was trapped. Out of ideas. Out of rope. Out of hope. She closed her eyes and saw poor Brewster lying dead on that rock. Tears formed in her eyes as she thought of his wife and daughter back in England. They would have no idea that he was gone. She knew exactly what they'd be going through when they learned the devastating news.

That took her right back to that morning four years ago. Back to Drew. Back to the pain. That inevitably led her to Milton. Finally she'd seen the monster face to face. She'd been so close to ending him. Would she have gone through with it? She could feel the rifle in her hands, her finger on the trigger, could see herself standing over Milton, his face full of fear. But now he was out there, and she was stuck in here. Trapped. Trapped and suffocating. She could taste the sand in her mouth again, feel the panic rising in her chest as the terror washed over her.

Chapter 32

Abbie lay on the thin mattress, tears running down her cheeks. She wasn't sure if they were triggered by the pain in her ribs, the hopelessness of her situation, or both. She rolled over onto her side to try to ease the pain in her chest, but that only made it worse. Something was pressing into her side from underneath the mattress. Something hard.

She sat up and reached under the foam and felt around for the obstruction. There was something trapped between the mattress and the sheet. It felt like a book. She pulled it out and saw it was a notepad. Not much bigger than a mobile phone, it was a deep red and clearly well used, with a cracked spine and a gold thread page marker hanging out the bottom. She let it fall open. The first few pages were apparently diary entries.

So I've finally discovered where I am. Some miserable little place called Deception Island in the Antarctic. Got that idiot Robertson to let it slip. Took long enough but I think he's coming round. I have been patient in tribulation and constant in prayer. Soon I shall rejoice in hope [. . .]

That bastard Ridley told me I was being held here 'temporarily'. More lies. That was more than three years ago.

And he was so smug about it all. Him and that common gaoler Turner. And the other one. The one that started it all. The one that put me here. I know our Lord would like us to turn the other cheek, but I'm afraid I prefer the Old Testament approach. When the time comes I shall go the full Exodus 21 – eye for eye, tooth for tooth, hand for hand, foot for foot, burning for burning, wound for every single wound [. . .]

There is something going on. There's been more activity. Turner came in yesterday and told me I'll be getting some injections. 'Inoculations' he told me. I told him to get fucked. He told me I have no choice in the matter.

I know it is the Lord's to avenge all, but soon I shall become his instrument for it. The moment is approaching. All will soon be in place [. . .]

So. It seems Ridley's perfect little prison isn't quite so perfect. Robertson tells me the volcano is waking. It matters only in that I shall be forced to bring forward one or two things. I've just got Robertson to send out another message for me. Things could happen quickly now. We must be ready to act fast. Matthew told us we must always be ready, because you don't know what day the Lord will come. It seems like he is coming now [. . .]

I can hardly believe how perfect it will be. It must truly be God's plan. Nothing could be so beautiful. I shall unleash pandemonium. And then I shall return. Risen from the dead, like our Lord himself. And then there will be no stopping me [. . .]

'Unleash pandemonium'? What did that mean? Clearly he had been planning to escape, but apparently that wasn't all he'd been plotting.

She kept flicking through the book until she came to a perplexing page filled with sequences of letters and numbers:

OT
P 5:8
II C6:30 P106:32 G18:25 N – D1:19 G17:4 G32:9 E
I C28:21 P19:17 N – N18:15 J52:3 W
I C21:16 E28:1 N – G12:7 G34:3 W
I C21:16 E9:7 N – G1:24 I22:16 W
II C18:31 E23:42 N – G45:27 D28:48 W

She furrowed her brow as she tried to understand what they were. She counted twenty-six lines. Some kind of code? Was this how he had been communicating with Robertson? She kept flicking and then saw a date with the words 'Project Reichstag' written next to it. He had ringed it twice in red pen: 11 September. That was just ten days away.

Project Reichstag.

She'd heard that before. Back up the mountain, Ridley had asked Milton about it just before the shooting began. What had Milton said? *You've got nothing. That's why you came all the way down here yourself, isn't it?*

Milton must be planning another attack, she realized. Ridley somehow knew about it but not the specifics. So *that's* why he wouldn't just leave Milton to the volcano. He wanted to question him, see if he could find out the details. And now she apparently had one of them: the date. And *of course* Milton had chosen that specific day – it was just his style to co-opt its power for his own ends. Just like he distorted and piggy-backed on the Bible to lend weight to his bigotry, so he would borrow what a marketing professional might term the 'brand recognition' of 9/11 to amplify and intensify his own terror attacks.

Then she felt it. It started as just a barely audible burble, but within seconds was growing and growing until the whole room was shaking, the metal bed frame was rattling and the books began falling off the shelf. An earthquake? Or was the volcano erupting already? Was she about to be buried under a river of lava? Was this it – was this the end?

After the distraction of finding the notebook, suddenly the fear flooded back into her body as she watched the walls shaking around her, turning to sand in her mind's eye and pouring over her body, ready to bury her alive all over again.

Chapter 33

Abbie was at a loss. Should she run to the yard? Or would there be smoke and ash raining down on her? Should she stay where she was, or would the concrete ceiling start to break up and crush her?

Maybe Robertson was still in the building. He hadn't left her that long ago. She prayed he was still here, and that he still had some shred of humanity deep within his soul. There was a chance – after all, he'd stopped short of killing her earlier.

She ran to the door and banged on it with all her might. 'Help!' she screamed. 'Robertson! Anyone? Help me!' She was getting desperate now as the whole room began shaking violently.

Abbie was seriously concerned about getting hit by falling concrete, so she ran out to the yard and huddled under the table, hoping it would give her some protection.

She pulled her legs up to her chest to tuck herself in, but as she did so the shaking slowed, and then stopped. After a few moments, it was almost as if it had never happened. She waited a few more minutes until she was sure it was over, then crawled out from under her hiding place and gingerly walked back inside.

She hoped the tremor might have weakened the cell

somehow, perhaps cracked the concrete around the door. But she found it just as solid and unyielding as before.

The only thing it seemed to have achieved was to shake all the books and DVDs from the shelf above Milton's bed, along with the TV which had smashed on the concrete floor.

She was still trapped. Still in the vice-like grip of this tiny room. Her eyes closed and she could feel the coarse sand rubbing against her skin, the taste of it on her tongue as the panic began to rise inside her chest. She needed a distraction.

She snapped her eyes open and looked down at the collection of films and texts knocked off the shelf by the tremor. The little Bible had flopped open. She slumped down on the floor, picked it up, and began flicking through the pages. It reminded her of her mother, who'd always been a believer and had taught Sunday school at plenty of the military bases they'd been stationed at over the years. Abbie had been forced to tag along. She couldn't remember when she realized she didn't believe any of it, but she'd been young, not yet a teenager. But she knew she couldn't tell her mum. She knew it would crush her. Her mum always seemed so sad. Looking back, Abbie suspected she felt trapped. A military wife no longer really in love with her husband, but forced to dutifully follow him around the world because she couldn't contemplate striking out on her own. So she'd retreated into her Bible and her gin, the twin crutches keeping her somewhat balanced. Abbie knew she couldn't kick one of them away by revealing her own lack of faith. She couldn't risk her mum leaning even more on the only crutch she'd be left with.

And so she went, week after week, to Sunday school. Reading the passages, listening to the parables. Helping keep her mum's faith alive.

She thumbed the pages of the book. The familiar names on

the page: Genesis, The Chronicles, Deuteronomy, Job, Isaiah, Jeremiah.

Suddenly she was struck with a thought. She picked up the little red notebook and found the page headed 'Project Reichstag' and that date: 11 September. She looked down at the numbers and letters listed on the page.

OT

P 5:8

II C6:30 P106:32 G18:25 N – D1:19 G17:4 G32:9 E

I C28:21 P19:17 N – N18:15 J52:3 W

I C21:16 E28:1 N – G12:7 G34:3 W

There was something about the way they were grouped together that looked familiar. The way there were two numbers separated by a colon. *Bible verses?* The more she looked, the more she was convinced that was exactly what they were – the first number represented the chapter, the number after the colon was the verse. And the letter before it was the book. 'II C' could be the second book of Chronicles, for example. The 'G' could be 'Genesis', the 'E' Ezekiel. The 'OT' surely had to mean they were all from the Old Testament.

The 'P' must mean the book of Psalms. She opened the Bible and found the page she was looking for: Psalms, chapter five, verse eight. It read: 'Be my guide, O Lord, in the ways of your righteousness, because of those who are against me; make your way straight before my face.'

What did that mean?

She looked down at the next line, and then flipped to the second book of Chronicles, chapter six, verse thirty. She read it aloud to herself: 'Then hear thou from heaven thy dwelling place, and forgive, and render unto every man according to all his ways, whose heart thou knowest; for thou, even thou only, knowest the hearts of the children of men.'

The hearts of the children of men? What was the significance?

It must be connected to the next passage in the sequence. She flipped through the Bible to Psalm 106, verse thirty-two. 'They angered him also at the waters of strife, so that it went ill with Moses for their sakes.'

She frowned. It still didn't make sense to her. She went to the next in the sequence, Genesis, chapter eighteen, verse twenty-five. 'That be far from thee to do after this manner, to slay the righteous with the wicked, so that the righteous should be as the wicked; that be far from thee: shall not the Judge of all the earth do right?'

To slay the righteous with the wicked. Was Milton referencing his own previous misdeeds? The innocent lives he had taken in the name of his cause?

She looked back at the line of numbers and letters. The next was the letter 'N'. That could mean the book of Nahum, Numbers, or Nehemiah. But there were no numbers alongside it to denote the chapter or verse. That didn't make sense. She frowned. She'd have to come back to it.

The next was 'D1:19'. Deuteronomy, chapter one, verse nineteen. Again she read aloud. 'And we journeyed from Horeb, and went through all that great and terrible wilderness which ye saw by the way to the hill country of the Amorites, as the Lord our God commanded us; and we came to Kadesh-barnea.'

She was getting more confused with every passage she read. The next two were both from Genesis. Chapter seventeen, verse four, and chapter thirty-two, verse nine.

'And for me, behold, my covenant is with thee, and thou shalt be the father of a multitude of nations.' Followed by: 'And Jacob said, O God of my father Abraham, and God of my father Isaac, O Lord, which saidst unto me, Return unto thy country, and to thy kindred, and I will do thee good.'

Then there was an 'E' at the end. Exodus? Ezra? Esther? Ezekiel? Again, there was nothing to tell her the chapter or verse though.

She read through every Bible verse mentioned in each of the twenty-six lines on the page, but could find no pattern, no logic that tied them together. Was he simply noting down his favourite passages? Possibly, but some of them were obscure in the extreme, and, on their own or in this group, didn't make much sense.

She went back to the notebook and tried to look for some other kind of clue. She looked again at the one on its own at the top that didn't fit the pattern of the rest. 'P 5:8'.

The book of Psalms. *Be my guide, O Lord, in the ways of your righteousness, because of those who are against me; make your way straight before my face.*

What did that mean? How did it fit in with the others? She looked closer and saw there was something else. Someone – presumably Milton – had underlined the first part of the verse in pencil. 'Be my guide, O Lord,' Abbie read aloud. My guide? Was it just a spiritual message, or did it mean something more literal? A guide leading the way? Like a map? A direction?

That triggered another thought. She looked again at the notebook. The letters that didn't fit the pattern. N, E and W. Could that be north, east and west? Her heart began to race as her brain rushed to connect the dots. Was she looking at compass directions? No, it wasn't that simple, but it could be . . . map coordinates?

II C6:30 P106:32 G18:25 N – D1:19 G17:4 G32:9 E

Perhaps the other letters were not actually part of the code? She needed to work this out. She went back out to the yard and dragged the table back inside. Then she found a pencil from among the possessions knocked off the shelf in the tremor, sat down, and wrote out the first line, leaving out the letters, other than the N and the E.

630106321825 N – 119174329 E

She'd read plenty of maps and coordinates over the years as part of her training and on live ops. It didn't look right. There were too many numbers. She tried the next two.

28211917 N – 1815523 W

2116281 N – 127343 W

The latter could be something, but as she worked her way down the list, time after time she found there were simply too many numbers for her theory to fit. She was stumped. Maybe she'd gone off on completely the wrong tack. She looked again at the list in the notebook. She tried to find something common in all of them. Something that linked them. The letter 'N' was the only one that appeared in every one. Always after the first sequence of numbers. And then either an 'E' or a 'W' after the second set. Surely those *had* to be compass directions, didn't they? Or maybe she was right first time, perhaps they referred to other books in the Bible. So if 'N' was the only constant, did that mean Nahum, Nehemiah or Numbers?

Another synapse sparked in her brain. *Numbers.* Wait . . . could it be that simple?

She went back to the first line and looked up the first passage referenced. The second book of Chronicles, chapter six, verse thirty. She noted down the page number that passage appeared on. Then on to Psalms, Genesis, Deuteronomy, and then back to the two verses from Genesis at the end. Then she grouped them all together.

53272819 N – 2171740 E

She had it. That *was* a map coordinate. She completed the same process with the other twenty-five lines of code. One by one they revealed themselves to her.

513320 N – 01647 W
524776 N – 18944 W
515101 N – 01342 W
515581 N – 02828 W
545983 N – 59253 W

And on and on. She read down the list as it hit her. She was looking at line after line of coordinates. Places. *Targets.*

Chapter 34

Project Reichstag.

She grabbed the big atlas from the pile of books and DVDs on the floor and thumped it down on the table.

She knew London was on a latitude of fifty-one degrees, so flipped the pages to the UK. She was right: there were several different targets in London, and more in Birmingham, Edinburgh, Cardiff, Belfast and on and on. All over the UK. She wondered how Milton had got such exact coordinates given the atlas wasn't so detailed. He must have had a more detailed map hidden somewhere. Or perhaps Robertson had helped him?

'Oh my God,' she whispered to herself as the scale of it hit her. It was far beyond any of Milton's previous crimes.

Abbie was an expert on his greatest hits. Mostly he'd targeted mosques in the early days, but then he'd widened his attacks to political decision-makers he deemed to be betraying the West with their policies. That's when the bombings on government institutions had begun. The Home Office, Ministry of Justice, and then the embassies. That's how he'd killed the US ambassador to Spain. One of his greatest coups, as he'd often bragged in his videos.

But this . . . this, it would dwarf everything he'd done in the past. Twenty-five different targets – and judging by the date she'd found ringed in red pen, it seemed like they'd all be at once – and just ten days from now. It would be huge.

She glanced back at the Bible. It was the New International edition. She'd seen copies like it in plenty of places before. In every church she'd visited as a girl with her mother, in hotel rooms, every chapel in every Navy facility she'd been stationed at. On every ship.

She remembered a line from one of Milton's diary entries.

'I've just got Robertson to send out another message for me.'

So he already had a line to the outside. All they would need to know is the exact edition of the Bible he was using, and his code would be easy to break at the other end. It was hardly *Enigma*.

She felt sick to her stomach as she thought of the carnage, the lives about to be lost, the pain that would be inflicted on the survivors and their loved ones. It was a pain she knew all too well. A pain she lived with every single day of her life.

And she could stop it all. She knew the location of every target and had the date of the attacks right in her hand. And yet she was trapped in an escape-proof prison on a tiny island in the middle of nowhere. No one knew where she was, her only companions were dead, and she might be buried under a million tonnes of volcanic ash at any minute – the key to saving potentially thousands of lives buried along with her.

She closed her eyes in desperate resignation.

Then it started again. First it was just a low rumble, more of a feeling than a sound, but it quickly got louder and louder, then the room started shaking, gently at first; and then without warning the whole concrete and steel box she was encased in lurched violently sideways and then back, as though its heavy-duty materials were nothing more than paper and string. Abbie was caught out and slipped over, landing with a thud on the concrete floor as the room continued to shake and shudder around her. The next noise she heard sounded like a giant groaning in pain – she suspected the movement of the quake was yanking and tearing apart the tin roof of the building. Then she could hear big thuds coming from somewhere, and realized with horror that heavy chunks of steel-reinforced concrete from the outer walls were starting to be chipped off by the power of the tremor. The metallic twisting noise got even louder and more painful and a huge thud followed. The structure of the building itself was starting to give up.

She looked up at the ceiling above her: it was concrete, just like the walls and floor. Heavy, thick, concrete. She knew even a small chip could easily knock her out. A bigger one could kill her. She needed cover, fast. She crawled over to the table, suddenly aware of just how flimsy it seemed against the power of the ground beneath her, which was literally shaking this previously immovable and solid building apart at the very seams.

Then there was a crack, bigger than before, and a chunk of the ceiling itself was chipped away by the force of the shaking and smashed down onto the concrete floor. Abbie risked peeking up at the hole it had left in the ceiling as a new hope began to wash over her: *maybe this was her way out?*

Perhaps this wouldn't be how she died, but how she escaped.

But as she looked up, the hope instantly evaporated. She could see into the concrete that lined the ceiling, and the chunk that had been carved out had barely left a dent. She could see the lines of exposed steel reinforcing it now, but above those was just more concrete. She'd be buried under tons of rubble before any kind of way out would emerge.

Another crack, and though she pulled her head back under the table as fast as she could, she wasn't fast enough. A sharp piece of concrete hit the top of her head like the blade of an axe.

As she howled in pain and withdrew under the surface, a hand reaching up to feel for blood, there was another huge crack and a big slab, at least a foot long and two feet wide crashed down where her head had been seconds before. Then another thudded down on the table top above her, bowing the legs with its force, and then a third somewhere behind her that was even bigger, and sent splinters of jagged concrete raining down on her. The table wouldn't survive another hit, and another hit seemed inevitable. She needed more cover. She looked around the bare room – it would have to be the bed. She'd be less mobile under there, but she hoped the mattress and the metal bed frame itself would offer her some protection.

More and more chunks of concrete were raining down now as the earthquake showed no signs of slowing. She'd have to pick her moment to make the dive under the bed. She pulled her legs up behind her and sat with her fists out in front of her and one foot anchored on the ground, like an Olympic sprinter waiting for the gun to start the hundred metres final. Another chunk hit the table above her and she flinched. She had to move before it was too late. Her body tensed up and she checked her footing, then she began a mental countdown. *Three, two, o—* she didn't even finish the thought, as a massive lump of grey concrete was torn from the ceiling and smashed down on the bed, the weight and power ripping the metal frame from the wall like it was made of matchsticks.

Abbie stared for a moment. Her last hope of refuge was now a twisted mess of metal, foam, springs and rubble. She looked behind her and wondered about the yard. Perhaps if enough of the walls collapsed, it might expose a gap at the top big enough to move one of the bars? She twisted her body and prepared to make a run for it, but even before she could get her feet set, there was another crash and she could just see the cloud of dust rising from the avalanche of concrete that must have fallen in the yard, before another wave came tumbling down and this time slammed the door shut, as chunks continued to pepper it from the outside. She was trapped. Again.

'FUUUUUUUCK!' she cried in desperate, angry, terrified, frustrated rage. 'FUCK FUCK FUUUUUUUUUUUCK!' she shouted again – louder this time, as if she was trying to outdo the noise of the earthquake that was about to kill her.

Because about to kill her it most certainly was, she now saw. There was no way out. This was it. She was going to die in this concrete cage – and in the most terrifying way she could possibly imagine. Buried alive in a box built to hold the very man who had killed her husband and ruined her life.

Her mind was filled with Drew as she huddled under the table, listening to more chips of masonry ping off its surface. His smile, his eyes, his silly sense of humour. A memory flashed across her brain: one day when they were only just married and trying to brighten up their drab, married quarters back at Bickleigh in Devon. They'd bought some shelves to put up in the living room and Drew had set her off into fits of giggles by pressing the stud finder against his chest and imitating its buzzing sound. 'Looks like it's working then,' he'd said.

She'd rolled her eyes but then caught the cheeky grin on his face and couldn't help herself from bursting into laughter. A tiny moment, a cheesy joke, but a precious memory that perfectly encapsulated the easy and comfortable way they were with each other. Drew. *Her* Drew. The one person in the world who had truly been hers. And she'd been his. Until that night.

Another crack, another smash.

At least the pain will be gone, she thought to herself as the room around her continued to shake itself apart.

She closed her eyes and saw Drew again as she waited for

the end to come. '*Per mare, per terram, per mare, per terram,*' she repeated to herself as she huddled under the little table. '*Per mare, per terram, per mare, per terram.*'

But then something compelled her to open her eyes. She looked up at the steel door that Robertson had slammed shut on her, and froze.

Staring back at her through the reinforced-glass window set into the thick steel door was a pair of deep blue eyes.

Chapter 35

Abbie crouched under the remains of the table, staring up at the eyes as they stared back at her. Then another chunk of concrete slammed down on the floor of the cell, splintering into a thousand dusty pieces.

'Let me out!' she shouted. She wasn't sure whether the eyes could hear her through the thick door, the rumble of the earthquake and the smashing of concrete around them, but she imagined her intent was pretty clear at this point. 'LET ME OUT!' she shouted again, louder this time as she gestured frantically at the door.

The rumbling beneath her feet was getting ever more intense, and suddenly she could hear what sounded like metal being literally twisted apart above her head. The whole damn ceiling was about to come crashing down on top of her.

'LET ME OUT!' she repeated, pointing at the door.

The eyes had been locked on her, as if their owner was paralysed with fear or confusion, but all of a sudden they blinked and the face behind them jolted into action. She could hear the bolts on the door clunk out of place before the din of the rumble, the cracking concrete and the twisting steel drowned it out as it got louder and louder above her head.

The heavy door swung open. Freedom beckoned. Abbie sprang from her hiding place under the table and ran through the open doorway. But as soon as she did a thought hit her. She spun on her heels and ran back into the cell, even as its mangled roof threatened to cave in at any second.

'What are you *doing*?' The eyes now had a voice and it was shouting in disbelief after Abbie as she ran back into the room.

Abbie ignored it, grabbed the red notebook, and with one final look up at the ceiling turned to run back out the door. The cracking sound that followed was like a deafening clap of thunder directly overhead. A split-second glance at the door told Abbie she wasn't going to make it, so instead she launched herself off her feet and dived as hard as she could at the opening. Now the eyes and the voice had limbs too, and his two arms were stretched out to her like a long-lost lover's. They made contact and he yanked her painfully towards him as he fell backwards and they landed in a heap as the rubble and steel and concrete came crashing down and dammed up the door behind her.

'Come on,' he shouted as he pushed her off him and scrambled to his feet. 'We've got to get out of here!'

Now the eyes had a voice, limbs – and demands.

The building was still shaking. All around them beams were snapping, walls were wobbling like jelly and the violent sounds of destruction were everywhere.

The stranger yanked Abbie up to her feet and began pulling her along the corridor, past the control room, through the boot room, and then finally they burst out into the glorious freedom of the open air.

Abbie gulped it down by the lungful and felt like her limbs finally had room to stretch, freed from the shackles of the tiny cell and her own deep-seated phobia.

They retreated to a safe distance, then turned and watched as the quake continued to shake and tear and pull at the building, until it was nothing but a heap of wood and tin and concrete. She shuddered as she thought of the young Marine Berkeley who was now entombed within it. It could so easily have been her too.

Eventually the tremor seemed to lose power until it tailed off entirely, and quiet and calm descended on them once again.

She turned to the man who had just saved her life. 'Who the hell are you?'

Chapter 36

Abbie stood staring at the stranger waiting for an answer. She looked him up and down. He was only about five foot four, she estimated, with red hair and wide, innocent eyes. He wasn't wearing military uniform and was instead dressed in green Gore-Tex trousers, hiking boots, a check shirt and dark blue jumper with a red winter jacket. He did not appear to be armed, and didn't look much more than twenty-one.

He seemed a little shell-shocked, and either hadn't heard her, or simply hadn't processed her question.

'Who are you?' he asked. 'And what are you doing locked in there?'

Abbie furrowed her brow. 'No, no. You first,' she said. 'Who are *you*? And what are *you* doing here?'

'I'm Spencer,' he said nervously.

She detected a Scottish accent.

'Spencer Munroe.'

'And what are you doing here, Spencer Munroe? Where did you come from?'

'I'm the volcanologist,' he said.

'The what?'

'The volcanologist – the volcano guy!'

For a moment it didn't compute. So much had happened that it seemed like months since she and Brewster had first set out to rescue the supposed 'research team' stuck on the island. She'd assumed there *were* no researchers once she'd learned the true nature of the base's purpose.

'I thought that was just a cover for the prison?'

'Partly, but the volcano is very real, and still needed monitoring. It was me who raised the alarm two days ago. This thing is about to blow, and blow big.'

'Was that an eruption just now?'

He shook his head. 'No, that was an earthquake, but it means the eruption is getting closer. We have to get out of here now. And I mean *now*.' He glanced at his watch. 'We're at alert state: RED. We've got a couple of hours at most. At *most!*' he added, to ram home his point.

Abbie nodded her head. 'We will.'

'Your turn,' he said.

'What?'

'Who are you? And how did you get locked in there?' He nodded back at the pile of rubble that was once the prison building.

'I'm from the ship sent to rescue you. Leading Hand Błaszczy-kowski-Fitzroy.' She suddenly felt a little silly being so formal with a civilian. 'Abbie,' she added.

'So if you were sent to rescue us, how did you end up locked in there?'

'You know the prisoner escaped?'

'I guessed. I heard a lot of shouting. Gunshots.'

'So where have you been?' Nothing had been what it seemed since she'd landed on this island, and she didn't trust this guy yet.

'When the shooting started, I stayed hid. One of the Marines told me to stay put and keep out of the way. I was only too happy to oblige. Eight Marines against one escapee? I thought they'd have him back in no time and it would all be over. I stayed in my lab. Hid in one of the cupboards. But then I heard more shooting up the mountain. Then, for a long time, no one came back.'

It was plausible. 'But we – me and my boss . . .' – she paused as her mind replayed the moment Milton had killed Brewster in cold blood before she could think to stop the memory resurfacing. She filed it away – something she would have to handle and deal with later. '. . . we came in here when we first landed. We looked around, we called out. We searched everywhere. You weren't here.'

'That was you? I heard you poking around. But I didn't recognize your voices. I had no idea who you were, so I hid. Robertson told me not to come out until he came back.' He paused. 'But he never did. And then,' he took a deep breath and looked down, avoiding her gaze, 'before you arrived, just when I thought it might be safe, I was about to come out and see what was going on. But then I heard these . . . noises.'

'Noises?'

He nodded.

'What kind of noises?'

'Screaming,' he said quietly. 'Awful, *awful* screaming – like insane asylum screaming. It was dreadful. It went on for a long time. I was scared,' he added in a small voice.

Abbie's mind flashed back to the kitchen with the steel benches and the tools. The blood. The finger. Munroe must have heard Milton torturing Turner.

'I'm not used to guns, all that shooting and shouting . . .' He trailed off, shaking his head and furrowing his brow. For a moment Abbie thought he was going to cry, but he took in another deep breath and composed himself. She felt herself softening. It made sense. She could see he was well out of his comfort

200

zone and even further out of his depth. He was clearly terrified. She felt for him. A civilian caught up in a war ten thousand miles from home. He looked so young.

'And no one came looking for you?' she asked more softly.

He shook his head. 'Maybe they forgot about me.'

'Or decided you were no threat,' Abbie said. She was thinking aloud, but hadn't meant it to sound so harsh. He didn't look offended by the remark. But then another thought occurred. 'Maybe he doesn't even know you're here?'

'Who?'

'Milton. The prisoner.'

'Maybe. They kept me well away from him.'

That didn't explain Robertson, who clearly knew about Munroe. But maybe he saw no point in mentioning it. He wouldn't have expected the timid young Scot to cause them any problems. Maybe Robertson still had a shred of decency and was trying to spare the kid's life.

'When the earthquake started, I realized I had to move, so I came out of the lab and I heard you shouting for help. How did you get stuck in there?'

'Robertson,' she said. 'There were three of us. We had no idea what this place was when we arrived. We didn't know about Milton.' She didn't have time to go into detail about the mysterious Ridley. 'He picked off the other two I was with.' She was avoiding being too graphic or literal about what had happened – she wasn't at all sure Munroe would be able to handle it. 'I persuaded Robertson not to . . .' she struggled for the right turn of phrase as she studied his face so full of fear, '. . . to . . . But he locked me in here instead. Left me . . .' she let the words hang.

'So Robertson is . . . ?'

She nodded. 'Yes. He's working with Milton. Must have helped him escape.'

'But why?'

'I don't know,' she shrugged.

'And what about the others? The other Marines?'

She sighed. 'He got them too, I'm afraid.'

He looked horrified. '*All* of them?'

She nodded.

Munroe was wide-eyed and twitchy. He wasn't focusing on her properly. 'We need to get out of here,' he said. She noticed he was fiddling with the cuff of his left sleeve with his right hand. 'I told you, the volcano is gonna blow at any minute. We need to get off this island.'

'You said we have a couple of hours until it blows?'

He nodded. 'From all my data, plus the venting and the quakes, I'd say less than two. But, Christ, it's a volcano – who knows when it will go?'

Abbie looked at her watch. She didn't want to be here a minute longer than was necessary.

'It could be any moment. There's no way of knowing. We just have to go now.'

'No arguments from me on that one. Do you have a boat?'

Munroe shook his head. 'No boats kept here. One of the security measures. You must have one?'

'We did, but it's probably long gone by now. I assume Milton and Robertson took it. I think that was their plan all along. Kill the Marines, lure us here, pick us off, then escape in our boat.'

Abbie stopped, as she wondered for the first time what Milton's plan was after that. Ridley's boat wouldn't get them far. And if he went aboard *Northumberland*, he would have to come up with a very convincing story as to who he was, and what had happened to her, Brewster, Ridley and the others they were supposed to be rescuing. She couldn't work out how he could possibly do it.

Munroe grabbed her by the shoulders and shook her, looking right into her eyes. 'We *have* to find a way!' He was getting manic. Panicking. 'From the data I've been collecting, this one's gonna be huge. *Much* bigger than the two eruptions in the Sixties. There won't be anywhere safe on the island. We *have* to get off!'

Abbie took his hands in hers and squeezed them, looking right back into his eyes. 'We will,' she promised in a soothing tone as he tugged and tweaked his jacket cuff. 'We will.'

'But what do we do if there's no boat? How will we get off? How?'

She squeezed his shoulders. 'We will. Trust me. Now let's go.'

'Go where?'

She moved past him on the trail and began crunching her way in the direction of the beach. 'First thing we always do,' she replied over her shoulder, 'go for a recce and see what's what.'

Half a beat later, she heard his footsteps following along behind her.

Chapter 37

Abbie made her way down the trail, Munroe following on behind her. She'd heard Milton tell Robertson he needed to get down to the beach, so she reasoned they would both be down there now, if they hadn't already left in Ridley's rigid inflatable.

But she still couldn't figure out what their plan was after that. They wouldn't get far on the open seas in such a small boat. Certainly nowhere near making landfall anywhere else – not with the nearest place a thousand miles away. Perhaps they were going to rendezvous with another ship? But how would they slip past the *Northumberland* undetected? Perhaps they would go to the *Northumberland* and pretend to be the researchers? Claim the others – and herself, Brewster and Ridley – had been killed in the earlier eruption and then the earthquake? But that would be extremely risky. It relied on Ridley having told no one – not even the captain – what his real orders were, and who was being kept on the island. It also relied on him persuading the captain there was no point in returning to the island to retrieve the bodies. Mind you, if Munroe was right and there was a big eruption coming in the next couple of hours, that might actually be the most feasible part of the plan. Lastly, of course, it relied on no one recognizing Milton himself. It was all far too risky for someone as calculating as him. She couldn't fathom it.

She led the way down the ash path from the prison building, until they rounded an outcrop of rock and got their first view of the beach below. Abbie stopped, crouched back behind the rock and motioned for Munroe to do likewise, bringing a finger to her mouth to indicate silence was necessary.

They peered down at the black beach below, the steam wafting across from the bay like a thick, ghostly carpet. Milton and Robertson hadn't left. They were still very much on the island. Abbie scanned the jetty. Ridley's boat was still tied up and apparently untouched. But between them and the boat were Milton and Robertson, and enough weapons to stop an entire regiment. All the guns they'd taken from the dead Marines, as well as the two Ridley had brought with him.

'Why haven't they left yet?' Munroe whispered.

Abbie frowned and shook her head slowly. 'I don't know. It doesn't make any sense.'

She looked back to Milton and Robertson. They were dragging a huge, rusted pipe along the beach. It was clearly very heavy, and they made slow progress, only stopping when they reached the edge of the beach, where they added it to a pile of junk.

'What the hell are they doing?' Munroe asked.

Abbie shook her head. 'No idea. But while they're on the beach, there's no way we'd make it to the boat before they saw us. And if they see us, they're not exactly going to wave us off.'

'Then what the hell do we do now?' Munroe said, his eyes darting this way and that, his breathing quickening.

Abbie could see he was starting to panic. She thought fast, assessing the situation as she'd been taught. Weighing up what was in her favour, and what was against. This was the kind of thing Royal Marines trained for: unexpected situations, impossible odds. This was what being a Commando was all about – what set them apart from ordinary troops. But was all that beyond her? Was she just part of the 98 per cent who weren't up to it?

Cons: she was unarmed. She knew Milton and Robertson had guns. And she knew the clock was ticking – the volcano could blow at any minute.

Pros: Milton and Robertson had no idea she'd escaped the cell – indeed, Milton may very well have no idea she was even still alive. If she could find a weapon from somewhere, she might be able to pick them off from her vantage point above the beach. Then she and Munroe could get to the boat and off the island. But for that she needed a gun.

'Do you know where the Marines kept their weapons?' she asked.

'In the control room, I think.'

She remembered the gun cabinet she and Brewster had found empty. Which was now under several tons of rubble anyway. 'What about another stash? Were any kept anywhere else?'

'I never paid much attention to the guns.'

She shot him an irritated look.

'I'm a pacifist,' he said with an apologetic shrug.

'Yeah, well, you're gonna be a dead pacifist if we don't find a gun. Think about it – did you ever see them anywhere else in the building? Ever overhear any of the Marines talking about it?'

He furrowed his brow as he tried to remember. 'Nothing comes to mind,' he said ruefully.

She sighed. 'OK, then there's only one thing we can do.'

Abbie looked back down at the beach to see Milton and Robertson hauling what looked like a large metal cartwheel to the edge of the beach. *What they hell were they doing?* It didn't matter right now. What mattered was finding a weapon.

'What?'

'We need to go back up the mountain and check the bodies. See if they missed any of the guns.'

She could see the colour draining from his face as she said it.

'But . . . the volcano,' he said meekly. 'We need to be getting down to the shore, not going *up* the mountain.'

'I know, but what choice do we have?'

He said nothing, but his whole body screamed reluctance.

'We'll be as quick as we can,' she said in as reassuring a tone as she could muster under the circumstances.

'But what if we get up there and find nothing? What then?'

Abbie said nothing as she pulled herself up and began crunching back up the ash pathway. She had no answer to that.

'Do you even know how to use a gun?' Munroe asked.

Abbie nodded. 'I'm a seaman specialist.'

Munroe cracked a smile. The first she'd seen from him. It was nice to see he had an expression that wasn't some variant on angst. 'A what?!'

'Yes, yes. Ha ha. I've heard all the jokes. That's my job – a sea spec. They call us "dabbers".'

'What's a "dabber"?'

'We're part of the warfare branch of the ship's company.'

'Isn't the whole ship a warship?'

'Well yes, but others have different jobs like navigation or working in the laundry, or the kitchen. The warfare branch are tasked with the actual fighting. So we're trained in small arms, boat handling, boarding other vessels, that kind of thing.'

'Makes you sound like a pirate.'

'Nope,' she said as they began making their way back up the trail. 'We're the good guys.'

Chapter 38

Abbie scrambled up the trail. She was light and nimble on her feet, though she had to keep checking herself to allow Munroe to keep up.

The Scot was talking fast as they went. 'It starts with these tremors we've been experiencing for the past few days, although that last one was the most powerful. Then the venting – the gas that will be pumped out at tremendous pressure. Then there could be steam explosions. Huge clouds of boiling hot steam emitted like a giant, deadly kettle.'

He was speaking faster and faster, entirely wrapped up in his subject. It seemed like a coping mechanism, a response to trauma. Abbie was happy to let him continue if it helped.

'Then will come the paroxysms – huge lava fountains many hundreds of metres high, millions of cubic metres of magma released with each one. We've already had a small flank eruption this morning, in fact.'

That must have been the one they'd heard from the ship, Abbie thought. God, was that really only a few hours ago?

'But the next could be much, *much* bigger. And any single one of these things could instantly kill us – especially the further up the mountain we are.'

It didn't take long for them to reach the point where the pass narrowed. Unlike before, Abbie did not approach with caution. This time she knew there was nothing waiting for her but dead bodies.

She sucked in a breath as she prepared to face the gruesome scene she knew lay just ahead, and motioned for Munroe to stay behind. 'You don't need to see this,' she said.

He nodded.

She pressed on and rounded the next bend in the rock. And there they were. Lured up the mountain path and picked off with horrifying brutality. She got her second look at the appalling scene of bloodied uniforms, twisted limbs and anguished, lifeless faces. Five more lives taken by Milton.

But Abbie had no time to ponder their fate now. She had a job to do and, though she didn't relish the task of searching the fallen men, it had become a necessity, and she knew each one of them would have done the same with her if the situation had arisen. She began frisking the bodies, heaving them over, looking for any weapon Milton and Robertson might have missed. She thought it unlikely, but perhaps one of them had a handgun stashed somewhere that had been overlooked in the murderers' haste.

But one after the other, the bodies yielded nothing. A dead end, in every sense.

She heard a retching sound and looked behind her. Munroe was vomiting.

She waited a few moments until he appeared to be finished, then turned and pushed him physically back out of sight of the bodies and guided his trembling body down until he was squatting on the ground.

'I've never . . . I've never seen . . .' he mumbled, his face pale and waxy.

'I know,' she said. 'I know. It's okay.' She unclipped her canteen from her belt and offered it to him.

He spat on the ground next to him, wiped his mouth on his sleeve and took the water bottle from her. He took a drink. His face was still pale, his expression pained. 'I've never seen . . .' he started again.

'I know,' she replied. 'It's okay. Happens to everyone. Believe me, I've seen guys twice your size who've done multiple tours in Kabul brought to their knees by a sight like that.'

He handed the canteen back to her.

She waved it away. 'You need it more than me,' she said. Frankly, she wasn't all that keen to have it back right now either.

He nodded and took another slug of water.

'Did you find anything?' he croaked.

She shook her head. 'It was always a long shot.'

He pulled his arms around himself. Suddenly he looked very cold. 'Then can we get back down the mountain, please? If we don't get off here soon, the fact that you don't have a gun will cease to have any meaning. We *need* to get back down by the shore.'

She shook her head. 'We haven't finished yet.'

'What do you mean? You've searched them all – let's *go!*'

'No,' she said firmly. 'We haven't checked them all yet.' She looked further up the path. 'There's two more bodies up there,' she added darkly.

Without waiting to see if he followed, she started back up the trail.

It was another long shot – she'd seen Milton and Robertson disarm both Brewster and Ridley. She knew Brewster wasn't carrying anything else, but Ridley? She hadn't trusted him from the moment she'd first seen him. Did he have something else secreted on him somewhere? She didn't think Robertson or Milton had really searched him – they'd been distracted when they heard her slip on the rocks in her hiding place after they'd killed him.

The mysterious and cocky Ridley had got them into the bloody mess, but maybe he could get them out of it – in death, if not in life.

She began the march, and soon heard the footsteps of Munroe behind her. He might be terrified of the volcano going up, but he was clearly more scared of being alone right now.

Now she could take the direct route up the path rather than Brewster's perilous mountain climb, it wasn't long before they emerged from the path into the natural bowl cut into the side of the mountain by the lava flow of a previous eruption.

Ahead of them was Ridley's lifeless body, and off to the left was Brewster. She turned to Munroe. 'Stay here,' she said forcefully. She didn't want him to get ill again. He didn't argue.

She turned and slipped down the ash towards Ridley, crouched down and began feeling up and down his body for a weapon. She rifled through his pockets and inside his jacket, across his chest and down each leg.

There was no weapon. He'd come with two, and Robertson had taken them both.

She glanced over to where Brewster's body lay and sighed deeply. Poor Brewster. The face of his wife Vicky flashed across her brain. She thought of their two-year-old daughter Rosie – the pair of them back in their military quarters in Bickleigh, happily going about their day, with no idea their husband and father was here, dead on the other side of the world, killed in cold blood by a murderous maniac, his body left to be consumed by the raging volcano on this tiny island filled with secrets and hate and lies.

She remembered when Rosie had been born. Brewster had been unsure how to act. Abbie reckoned he was holding onto some old macho idea that the birth of a child was something for the women to get excited about. She could see he thought he should be playing it all a bit cool – handing out cigars and heading off to the pub to 'wet the baby's head'. But she could tell he was totally overcome by it all. His whole life, his whole outlook, his *everything* had been changed by the tiny arrival, and he'd been totally unprepared for it. She smiled at the memory. He'd been a lot sweeter than he ever let on, and her heart broke for him, for Vicky and for Rosie. Another life taken, another family ripped apart by Richard fucking Milton – and all because of her insistence on facing him down. She felt a dreadful wave of guilt mixed in with the grief as she looked over at her fallen friend. How was she going to face Vicky?

She sighed again, then stood up and made her way reluctantly towards Brewster's body. She hadn't enjoyed the experience of searching the others, but she hadn't known any of the Marines, and Ridley had been in her life for less than two hours before he was killed. Brewster was different. He was her boss. Had been for three years. He was her friend. She remembered the promise she'd made to him as they motored towards the island a few hours earlier. At the time she'd agreed to it largely to pacify him and get him off her case, but at that moment she silently resolved that if she somehow managed to get off this island, she'd honour her pledge and send off her application for the Marines. 'I promise,' she whispered as she stood over him, her eyes filling up again.

She gazed down at his lifeless body. The faces of his family flashed up again. Poor Vicky. Another widow. Another widow in her twenties. And Abbie knew then she would be expected to know what to say to her – if she got out of this place alive herself. She could see Vicky's face, watery red eyes looking up at Abbie, waiting for her to impart the key bit of knowledge to make everything okay again. She'd been through it, after all. She *must* know. But in her mind's eye, as she looked down at the tearful, grief-stricken face of Vicky, she only saw herself looking back. Four years on and she had no answers, she had no key. She was just as lost and angry and flailing as Vicky would be. Time had healed nothing for her.

She blinked to try to clear the image from her mind. Right now there was no sense in worrying about what she would say to Vicky; she wouldn't be saying anything at all to her or anyone else if she didn't get off the island. She had to find a way, not just for her own sake, but also to warn the authorities about Milton's plot before it was too late.

She knew Brewster had come ashore unarmed, as she had, and she knew Robertson and Milton had taken the gun Ridley had given him. But as she looked down at him, she could see the outline of something on his chest. It wasn't a weapon – she knew that instantly – but it might, just might, be their ticket out of this mess.

Chapter 39

Brewster's radio. Robertson had clearly neglected to take it. It was a lapse. Then again, why bother stripping a dead man of his radio? She reached inside his jacket and pulled it out, then gently zipped his coat back up, as if protecting him from the cold. She took one last look at his face, pulled up his collar around his neck – a pointless gesture, she knew – then took a deep breath and stood up. She had to leave him now.

She turned away from his body and clicked the radio on. It hadn't worked when they were down on the jetty at sea level, but she hoped they were high enough now to be able to reach the ship.

She twisted the knob on the top, pressed transmit and held it up to her mouth. '*Northumberland*, this is Blaz, do you read? Over.' She and Munroe huddled round it, listening to the hiss of static. She tried again. '*Northumberland*, this is Blaz, do you read? Over.' After waiting for a good thirty seconds, she gave it one last shot, but got nothing in reply but dead air.

'What's wrong, is it broken?' Munroe asked.

She shook her head and waved to the ring of rock that surrounded them. 'It's the mountains. The signal can't clear them.'

'So what do we do?'

She turned the radio off and stowed it in her jacket. 'We go higher.'

He started shaking his head back and forth, faster and faster. 'Higher? The higher we go, the longer it will take us to get back down – what it if blows while we're up there? We won't stand a chance!'

He had that panicked look in his eyes again, and probably with good reason, but Abbie knew they simply had no choice.

'I wish there was another way, I really do,' she said gently, her hand on his arm. 'But there isn't, so let's get a move on.'

She turned and began walking up the trail. Just as before, she soon heard the crunch of his footsteps following behind her.

The ash path soon became little more than a hint of a trail as it gave onto the ridge that stretched right up to the summit, boulders and smaller rocks on their right, and a sloped bed of rock covered in loose, gravel-like ash fragments on their left, which fell away to nothing after ten or fifteen metres.

Every few minutes, Abbie stopped, pulled the radio out and tried to contact the ship. Each time getting the same result as before – a hiss of static and empty radio waves. She pressed on and was just about to pull it out for another try when she heard a low rumble. A rumble she'd felt before, when she was trapped in Milton's cell.

'Another tremor?' she asked over her shoulder as the earth began to shake beneath them. 'Or is this . . . ?'

Munroe shook his head. 'A tremor, I think,' he shouted over the noise. 'But they're getting more intense and more frequent. We have to hurry!'

Abbie pulled out the radio and hastily repeated her message. '*Northumberland*, this is Blaz, do you read? Over.'

Silence. Again.

She felt her shoulders slump at the lack of response, but she knew she had to stay positive; had to be the strong one for both of them, as Munroe was clearly teetering on the edge of all-out panic, so she took a breath and straightened her back.

They'd been climbing for almost an hour, and were so high they had a magnificent view of the island. Or at least it would have been magnificent, had they had time to appreciate it. As it was, they were merely being afforded a better view of the location of their death. She tried the radio again. 'Northumberland, this is Blaz, do you read? Over.'

More static, and then a crackle, then . . . wait. Was that . . . ?'

It *was*. A very faint and garbled voice. Between the patchy signal and the rumble of the ground beneath their feet, she couldn't make out what it was saying. 'Northumberland, this is Blaz, do you read?'

She turned the volume dial up as high as it would go, and pressed it to her ear. It *was* a voice. 'This is Northumberland. We read you. What is current status, over?'

For a moment, even Munroe seemed to forget his terror and huddled up to Abbie to try to hear better, as they shared a brief moment of relief and joy, smiles on their faces.

She pressed transmit and tried to speak as clearly as she could. 'Northumberland, request immediate back-up. Brewster and Ridley dead – killed by escaped prisoner on the island, armed and extremely dangerous. Request Merlin with armed team from Kilo Company immediately. Two enemies at large on the island. Treat as a Level Three boarding.'

There was another burst of static, then a reply they could only half make out. 'Northumberland . . . repeat . . . did not receive . . . signal . . .' then more static.

Abbie repeated the message again, as calmly as she could as the shaking of the ground beneath their feet began to intensify, adding, 'Approach with extreme caution – prisoner and accomplice armed and highly dangerous and currently on the beach at Whalers Bay. Treat as Level Three boarding. Repeat: Level Three boarding.' She looked away from Munroe, before pressing 'transmit' again. 'You have to take them out. There's no other way.'

The rumble was getting louder, the shaking more violent. 'Hurry!' she said into the radio. 'Volcano close to blowing.'

When she finished, she held the radio to her ear to try to hear the response. More static, and then just snippets of words from the other end that she could make no sense of. 'Losing signal, please repeat,' she asked, clutching the radio a little tighter, as if that might somehow boost the signal.

But before she could hear another word, the ground beneath them lurched sideways, knocking both her and Munroe to the ground as the earthquake intensified. Even as Abbie grabbed onto a nearby rock for some kind of stability, she felt the radio slide out of her hands. Before she could react, the little black box hit the ground, spun once, and then began sliding down the ash slope.

Her eyes went wide as she realized it was heading towards the cliff.

Before she even knew what she was doing, she flung herself after it. She landed with a painful thud on the rocky surface and threw her arm out in front of her as she slid.

She just needed to get a *little* closer, and stretched her arm and her fingers in desperation.

But she was too late.

She watched in horror as the radio slipped over the cliff edge, clattering its way down the sheer rock face on the other side, and was lost into the abyss.

She barely had time to process that loss when her feeling of horror took on an entirely new level: she realized she'd thrown herself after the radio with such force that she was still sliding down the loose, ash surface.

She was about to follow the radio over the cliff edge.

She tried to dig her feet into the ground, but it did little to slow her, and in her panic she began trying to grab the rocks with her bare hands, scratching and scraping at them in a desperate bid to halt her descent.

It wasn't working.

She was still sliding too fast, the cliff edge approaching too rapidly, and the shaking ground beneath her seemingly nudging her along.

The jagged rocks were cutting into her limbs, her belly and her hands as she slid, but not enough to stop her.

And then, just like that, she was at the cliff edge. It was over.

She briefly considered the fact that it hadn't been Milton that had killed her, not directly, nor had it been the volcano. Not that it mattered in the end. She also had time to think that at least the pain would be gone. The constant, devastating pain she felt every single day, every single time she woke, every single time the memory of Drew flashed across her mind. That would all be over in an instant. She slipped head first over the edge of the cliff and saw all the way down – it had to be a drop of over three hundred feet, punctuated by jagged rocky outcrops. Her arms were flailing to try and grab hold of something, anything . . .

And then she stopped.

She was dangling over the edge as the rocks rumbled and cracked and fell around and beneath her until, just as suddenly as it had started, the rumbling and the shaking and the cracking eased, and then stopped. She managed to twist her body, crane her neck, and look up behind her. And as the dust settled, she could see her left leg was being clutched tightly by two arms. Munroe.

Very slowly, he began to haul her up back over the edge. It was hard going, since he had all her weight, and the angle she was at made it difficult for her to help him, until he had her waist over the edge, when she was able to arch her back and roll sideways, away from the drop, as he yanked her by the belt, his hands gripping her tightly. Once they were some six or seven feet back from the edge, they collapsed into a heap together, holding each other tightly and breathing hard and fast, their hearts beating furiously in their chests.

When she'd finally got her breath back, all she could think to say was, 'That's the second time you've saved my life.'

'So?' he asked, brushing over her near-death experience and his subsequent rescue. 'Did they hear you? Are they coming?' His face was wide open and full of hope.

Abbie looked back at him. 'I . . . I don't know,' was all she could say. She shrugged and slowly shook her head. 'I don't know.'

Chapter 40

Abbie could find nothing more to say as they lay together on the mountainside. She opened her mouth to speak, but no words would come as she stared into Munroe's innocent clear blue eyes. He'd seen the radio fly off the edge of the cliff just like she had. The fact they'd found the radio in the first place was a minor miracle, as was them making high enough ground to get a signal. She'd pulled that whole plan from nowhere. She knew at this point she had no more miracles up her sleeve.

She stared at him in silence and watched the hope in his eyes wither and die.

Then, as if sensing the silence needed to be broken, the island spoke. Another deep rumble reverberated through the ground beneath their feet, and they could hear the sound of falling rock coming from somewhere above them.

'Come on!' shouted Munroe. 'We've got to get down to the shore!'

Abbie knew she'd dragged him up this far against his will because it was their only chance. But with the radio gone, they had no reason to stay.

'Is this it? The eruption?' she shouted back as they scrambled to their feet.

'Could be,' he said. 'It doesn't matter – we have to get down to the beach!'

Abbie wasn't about to argue. Milton or no Milton, they were dead if they stayed where they were and the volcano did blow. They began back down the mountain, Munroe in the lead this time, and constantly checking back over his shoulder to make sure Abbie was close behind, as if he was terrified she'd come up with some other hare-brained scheme and change her mind before making them go back up the hill.

Abbie's mind was whirring as they raced back down the trail. What *could* they do next? She guessed their only hope was if Milton and Robertson had already left on Ridley's boat. If so, she and Munroe could search the place and try to find the RIB she and Brewster had arrived on – if it hadn't been destroyed. If it had been, there had to be another one somewhere, surely; something for emergencies: an inflatable even – *something*.

On they ran, the rumbles and grumbles of the island beneath them matching them step for step. They reached the collapsed prison building, but it held nothing for them now. Munroe didn't even slow as he approached it, but upped his pace, pushing on and on further down the mountain. For a moment, Abbie envied his clarity of thought, his sense of purpose, his singular focus. His only thought was to get away from the volcano, get down to the shore. It was the only thing that mattered to him right now. And, she had to concede, she had no better plan.

On they ran, further and further down, until Abbie saw movement, way down in the distance. It was only for a split second, but she'd definitely seen something, and that was enough when her whole being was on a war footing.

She yanked Munroe back by the jacket with enough force that he nearly fell backwards onto her, then pulled him down into a crouch behind the rocks they'd used as a look-out point earlier.

'What is it?' he yelled, far too loudly for her liking.

'What the hell do you think?' she hissed. 'Milton. He's still on the beach. And keep your voice down!'

He looked a little stunned at the rebuke, but there was no time for her to tiptoe around hurt feelings right now. She put her finger to her lips and whispered, 'Stay down.' Then she slowly raised her head.

'Damn,' she cursed under her breath. Milton and Robertson were still there, still adding to their pile of rusty junk at the edge of the beach as the steam rose up from the ground like a ghostly blanket.

'Why haven't they left yet?' Munroe asked, his tone agitated.

'No idea. They must have felt the tremor as much as we did.'

'Exactly – and there's a boat right there,' he said, nodding at the jetty. 'It makes no sense.'

'And worse than that, it means we're stuck here too.'

'So what do we do?'

'Just be quiet a minute and let me think.'

She turned, her back against the rock, and slid down it onto her haunches as she tried to think of something, anything. But nothing was coming.

Come on – *think*. She saw Drew's face. What would he do?

The ground began to shake beneath them as another tremor took hold of the island. Abbie glanced at Munroe and immediately regretted her words about them being stuck. She could see the panic was rising in him again.

'We've *got* to get out of here,' he said.

Abbie looked down at the beach, where Milton and Robertson were still working, their rifles stowed nearby next to an old oil tank. Then she looked back up the mountain, just in time to see a chunk of rock blasted from the surface and some kind of gas begin pouring out of the crack.

Munroe had seen it too. 'Oh my God,' he said. 'More venting. We're out of time!' His voice was high-pitched. Panicked.

They were trapped, like two rats on a sinking ship. A ship which was about to explode.

The ground rumbled around them, rocks began tumbling down the mountain above and gas continued to rise from the vent.

Then the smell reached them. It was like rotten eggs.

'That's the sulphur,' Munroe said. 'It means the full eruption is getting closer.'

There *must* be a way out of this. Abbie scanned the horizon, looking for something that might help. She looked back to Milton and Robertson and glanced at their rifles, but there was no sign of the rest of the guns she'd seen before – the ones they'd taken from Ridley, Brewster and the other Marines.

Her eyes searched the shoreline. The beach house seemed relatively unscathed from the tremors that had destroyed the prison building. Had they stashed the guns in there? It was worth a try. Better to die trying than simply wait for the volcano to get them.

'Come on,' she whispered. 'Let's go.'

'Go where?'

'To get me a gun.'

Chapter 41

After slipping down the ash path to the beach, they dashed between the cover of the derelict oil tanks and abandoned buildings like would-be escapees in a World War II prisoner-of-war camp trying to make it to the fence without being caught by a sweep of the searchlights from the guard towers.

As they skirted out of sight behind the old church, Abbie noticed Milton and Robertson digging again at the graveyard. She remembered the freshly dug plot with her name on it, and wondered again how Milton had known she'd be coming – and yet why he didn't seem to know who she was when they'd squared up after she'd got the jump on Robertson. It didn't make sense.

Were they digging another grave? She didn't have time to give it any more thought as she led the way through the maze of rusted and broken pipes and tanks and other metalwork that had once served the whaling industry, moving quickly from hiding place to hiding place, a series of short dashes to cover the ground they needed before another rest out of sight. Eventually they reached the beach house, apparently still unseen. Ridley's boat was still tied up at the end of the jetty, bobbing enticingly in the chop from the harbour. Thanks to the layer of steam rising off the water, it looked as though it was suspended in mid-air, resting peacefully on a cloud. But Abbie knew if they made a run for it, Milton and Robertson would gun them down from the beach long before they'd escaped through Neptune's Bellows.

Instead they slipped inside the building and back into the boot room that Abbie and Brewster had found when they'd first landed, hours earlier.

'Stay out of sight of the windows,' Abbie instructed.

He did one of his little nervous nods.

She made for the control room first, the room containing the gun cabinet. But she quickly discovered both cabinet and room were devoid of firearms.

'So how long have you been here?' she asked as they made their way down the corridor to the mess room.

'About four months,' he said. 'I'm on secondment from my university.'

'Oh, which one?'

'Edinburgh. Doing a PhD.'

Abbie marched through to the kitchen area and began flinging open cupboards. 'Must have been a bit of a shock when you got here.'

'How do you mean?'

'When you found out what was going on here.'

'Oh,' he said, as he pulled open the big industrial freezer. 'You mean Milton?'

'Yeah. I still can't get my head around it.' She chose not to reveal her history with the prisoner at this point. Still wary. Still guarded. 'What did you think when they told you?'

'Officially,' he said as they moved on to the next room, one of the dorms, 'they haven't. I'm not even supposed to know there is – was – someone being held here. Before I came, I was told this was a cold-weather training base, that's all.'

225

It sounded absurd. Abbie couldn't imagine how anyone living on the island among the Marines wouldn't discover the true nature of the base.

'So when did you find out?'

'Some of my equipment was up at the prison building. I had a lab up there, so I was there most days. It was soon pretty obvious there was something weird going on. But no one told me anything.'

'And you never asked . . . ?'

'Of course I did. They said: "You don't need to know".'

She nodded. She'd been told that plenty of times. 'So the Marines wouldn't even tell you who was in there?'

'They, uh . . . didn't tell me very much at all,' he said quietly. 'Don't think they really . . . you know. We didn't have much in common.'

Abbie nodded.

One by one they searched the other rooms, and then re-checked them a second time until they found themselves back in the control room. The search had yielded nothing.

'Couldn't we make a run for it with the boat?' Munroe offered hopefully.

Abbie shook her head. 'We'd be dead before we could even get the engine started.'

He slumped down in one of the office chairs, defeated.

'So that's it. With no gun, we're stuck?'

'Looks that way.'

'And there's no sign of anyone from the ship, so I guess they didn't hear us after all.'

Abbie shrugged. 'I guess not.'

'And we have no other way of contacting them.'

She nodded at the dead radio unit on the bench. 'Nope.'

'So, what now?'

Abbie took a breath. She thought back over the hours she'd spent on the island. There had to be something, somewhere that could help them. She replayed the day in her head, like rewinding a videotape, from the search of the beach house to slipping past the oil tanks, their journey up the mountain, losing the radio, searching the bodies of the fallen, and Munroe springing her from Milton's cell. She remembered finding the notebook, his plans for an attack of unspeakable violence and cruelty. She put a hand to her chest and felt the outline of the book. She had to get off this island, or at the very least get a message out before he could be allowed to unleash more pain and misery on the undeserving and unsuspecting.

She scanned back to her fight with Robertson, watching him and Milton kill Brewster and Ridley in cold blood, finding the other Marines, meeting Ridley for the first time, the torture room. Her mysterious grave. Back to their initial search of the beach house, the alarm, their boat going missing, and their journey through Neptune's Bellows from *Northumberland*. She closed her eyes as she thought back over all of it. She played the tape forward and back in her mind, searching for something that could help them.

Wait – that could be it.

'There's something we could try,' she said cautiously.

Munroe looked up.

'We're going to need a torch and a pair of binoculars.'

Chapter 42

'I just don't see how it's going to work,' Munroe said as he returned from his lab with the items Abbie had requested.

'Trust me,' Abbie said, with far more confidence than she felt. She had no idea if it was going to work either, but she had to do something – she couldn't just sit in the hut waiting to die.

'Nice,' she said as he handed her a pair of expensive-looking binoculars.

'Birdwatching,' he said by way of explanation.

She nodded.

They slipped out of the hut and picked their way along the beach towards the east end, once again using the rusty remains of the whaling station to keep out of sight of Milton and Robertson.

Munroe, having assured Abbie he knew the way, led them right to the end of the beach to a gap in the rock. Then they began to climb.

'Do you think it's going to be dark enough?' he asked sceptically.

Abbie glanced up at the greying sky above them. 'We'll have to hope so.'

Just a few minutes later, they pulled themselves up another

boulder and stood at the base of their destination: the old lighthouse.

It speared up from the black rock into the sky like a moon rocket. The rusting metal structure was red at the base, white in the middle and then red again at the top, with a metal staircase winding around the outside of the tower to a lower gantry and then up to a second one at the summit.

'You know this thing hasn't been active in a hundred years?' Munroe said as they stood at the bottom. 'I've been up there. The mechanism and everything, it's all rusted up.'

Abbie ignored him and began climbing the metal staircase, passing the first gantry and continuing up to the very top. When she rounded the bend and got her first look inside the glass-house at the top, her heart leapt. Most of the panels had cracked or dropped out of their frames, and Munroe was right, the rest of the machinery was indeed stuck fast with rust. But the lens was still intact, and that was all Abbie needed. It was the first piece of good luck she'd had since stepping onto this cursed island.

She smiled as she momentarily slipped back in time.

She was eleven years old and tucked up in a sleeping bag in a tent in the back garden of their family quarters in Paderborn, Germany. Her digital watch told her it was nine o'clock. It was time. She flicked on her torch and turned the pages of her little green notebook, running over the contents of the page before her one more time. She needn't have bothered – she knew it off by heart by now, but it was important for her to get it right. She wanted to impress him, to please him.

She took out her pencil and laid it down next to the notebook at the ready. Then she flicked off the torch and unzipped the front flap of her tent. One last time she went over the sequence in her head, from start to finish. Then she looked out through the heavy blackness at the house that rose above her just thirty feet away. Then she began flicking the torch on and off. One second for a dot, two for a dash.

DOT DOT DOT DOT [PAUSE] DOT [PAUSE] DOT DASH DOT DOT [PAUSE] DOT DASH DOT DOT [PAUSE] DASH DASH DASH . . .

When she was finished, she repeated the message from start to finish, just like he'd taught her. Then she used the hook on the back of the torch to hang it from the tether at the apex of her tent, grabbed her pencil and notebook, and waited.

The flashes started in response from the kitchen window, and she noted each one down as they came.

DASH DOT DASH DASH [PAUSE] DOT [PAUSE] DOT DOT DOT [PAUSE] DOT DOT DOT [PAUSE] DOT DASH DASH . . .

The message stopped. She kept her eyes on the dark window, then it started again and she followed along with her notes, making sure she'd taken it down correctly the first time. She smiled. Not a letter out of place.

'Yes sweetheart I hear you. Daddy loves you. Time to go to sleep now. Over and out.'

When it was over, she grabbed the torch and tapped out a final message.

DOT DASH DOT DOT [PAUSE] DASH DASH DASH [PAUSE] DOT DOT DOT DASH . . .

'Love you daddy. Sleep tight.'

Then she tucked her pencil and notepad away neatly in her backpack, zipped the tent closed and snuggled down into her sleeping bag with a smile on her face.

She opened her eyes. Back in the lighthouse. No notebook this time, but she didn't need it. She'd studiously learned her

Morse code as a child and had never lost it. Apart from anything else, for her it was a precious link back to her dad.

She just hoped there was someone on the bridge of *Northumberland* who was watching – and who could read Morse, now that it was no longer compulsory in the Navy. She handed the binoculars to Munroe. 'Keep your eyes out there, and let me know if they signal back.'

The she took the torch, angled it to the lens and began clicking it on and off.

DOT DOT DOT DASH DASH DASH DOT DOT DOT . . .

Chapter 43

Milton looked up at the darkening grey sky above them, then glanced back at his watch. 'We need to hurry, we're losing the light.'

Robertson was struggling with the weight of a six-foot-long rusted pipe he was dragging up the beach. 'Give me a hand with this,' he grunted.

Milton walked over and lifted the other end of the pipe and they carried it the final few yards to the pile of debris at the edge of the beach, heaving it on top before it landed with a clang.

As Robertson caught his breath, Milton looked up at the sky again, scanning the air from the mountain top right around the bay to Neptune's Bellows. Then he stopped, his brow furrowing in confusion for a moment. It can't have been . . . he must be mistaken. Surely it was a flash of white from a circling bird or the sun bouncing off the glass . . . no – there it was again. And again.

He stood for a moment longer, taking in the sight, then turned to address his new assistant.

'Robertson, you did send that little troublemaker to the promised land, didn't you?'

'What?' Robertson was gathering a collection of old whaling hooks.

'You killed her? That girl?'

'Oh, yeah. Course,' he said quickly, chucking the hooks onto the pile with the other rubbish.

'Well then, would you like to tell me who in the name of the Lord is doing that?'

Milton pointed towards the Bellows, where the old lighthouse stood atop the rocks on the north side. And he and Robertson watched as light flashed intermittently from its very top.

Robertson took two steps closer, as if he couldn't believe what he was seeing. 'It can't be,' he muttered.

'Well it is.'

'It must be . . . that fucking geek,' Robertson hissed.

'Who?'

'Munroe.'

'Who?'

'Munroe. The volcano guy. Scientist. Monitors the volcano.'

'And he's just been running around the place the whole time? And you didn't think to mention it?' Milton couldn't believe what he was hearing.

'He's a nobody. Wouldn't say boo to a goose! I didn't think he'd be a problem.'

'Well, you were wrong about that, weren't you? Is there anything else you've neglected to tell me?'

Robertson shook his head. 'How is that thing even working? It's like a hundred years old.'

'I don't know,' Milton said evenly. 'But that hardly matters at this point, does it?'

'I suppose not.'

'Lucky for you, I'm a man of the Lord and I believe in forgiveness,' Milton continued. 'But would you mind being a good Christian solder and going up there to help him meet his maker?'

'I just—'

Milton held a hand up to silence him. 'I don't want to hear excuses. Just deal with it before he ruins everything.'

Chastened, Robertson turned and began marching up the beach, pausing only to grab his rifle and sling it over his shoulder.

Milton shook his head. How could Robertson have been so stupid to leave that scientist unaccounted for? He couldn't even follow an order – so much for His Majesty's Royal Marines. Frauds and clowns, the lot of them.

He glanced up at the darkening sky. A sky he'd been staring at for four long years. Day after day, night after night, hour after hour. Plenty of time to stare, to think, to plot, to plan. They could lock up his body and throw away the key, but not his mind. His mind was as sharp as ever. In fact, he'd had more clarity since he'd been stuck on the island than he'd had in years. While he was a wanted man, so much of his brain power and energy had been devoted to evading capture. It was a necessity, of course, but there was no denying it sapped his productivity and creativity when it came to his real purpose.

But then he'd been captured. At first it had seemed like his ultimate humiliation – and castration. Shorn of his power, dead in the eyes of the world – Ridley had boasted to him how they'd lied about that and faked his death. 'No one even knows you exist, except me and these Marines,' Ridley had told him with a barely suppressed smirk.

At first he'd burned with fury, raged against his incarceration. From having the might of the Cross of St George organization in his hand, the power of life or death over almost anyone he chose, he'd been rendered utterly impotent. No longer even in charge of when the lights in his cell came on and off.

He'd burned with that rage for months, years even. Mentally straining against his shackles.

And then one day he'd had an epiphany. A moment that

changed everything. He realized that, in truth, he'd been a prisoner for years. Ever since his last escape, in fact. Six years on the run. Six years living in a permanent state of fear that each day would be his last. Six years of suspecting everyone and everything. In its own way, it had made him weak – drained his strength, his energy, his creativity. His attacks had become predictable. Derivative. No longer shocking enough in scale or ambition.

But after he was captured, after he was put here with no one and nothing, suddenly, far from being imprisoned, he was . . . free.

Chained physically, but free of the shackles of the mind. He no longer had to plan and worry and expend precious brain power and energy on simply evading capture. In fact, he no longer had to expend brain power on *anything*. He lived in his cell, day after day. No work, no life, no decisions to make, not even what to wear or what to eat. Not even *when* to eat. And absolutely no distractions like women, alcohol or drugs.

Suddenly, he had realized he was in an almost unique position among his fellow citizens of the world. And when the thought occurred, he instantly felt more powerful than every single one of them – more powerful than ever. He remembered reading once that Albert Einstein always wore the same clothes every day; it was a way of ensuring he wasted none of his intellect on something as banal and prosaic as what to wear.

Milton realized he had now been stripped of the necessity to expend any brain power on *anything* at all. And it was the greatest gift he could have been given. Now was his chance to compose his masterpiece, his *pièce de résistance*. His Symphony No. 5. His *Mona Lisa*.

And so, he'd set to work. Freed from the chains that mere mortals had to contend with simply to survive, he directed all his intellect into his work. And he found he'd never been so productive. The ideas, the inspiration flowed through him as if he was channelling God himself. At least that was what he would tell his followers when the moment was right – though as the days, weeks and months had passed, he began to genuinely believe he was doing the Lord's work. He was God's vessel, the one man who could do what needed to be done. His mind fizzed with the power and the possibilities.

And what a thing of beauty his plan was. He realized he'd been going about his campaign all wrong. It was time to get more creative, more cunning. Targeting mosques was all well and good, but he'd been forced to admit to himself that it hadn't worked. The Muslims still walked the streets of Britain. The powers that be still protected them. He needed a new approach. And that's when he hit on what he'd code-named 'Project Reichstag'.

In 1930s Germany, the Reichstag Parliament building was set alight. Before anyone really knew the facts, Adolf Hitler and the Nazis had claimed it was the work of communist agitators and whipped up fear among the people that the legitimate government was about to be toppled. In response, Hitler demanded sweeping powers to confront the threat – and he got them. A host of civil liberties were suspended – supposedly temporarily – and were never reinstated. The Nazis weaponized the fear of the people to get what they wanted. No matter that a month later the head of the Berlin fire department was sacked, imprisoned, and later killed, after presenting evidence that suggested the Nazis themselves were involved in starting the fire. By then it was too late.

And so Milton began plotting. He too would use fear as his weapon. His twenty-five carefully selected targets were all designed to have maximum impact – and to represent the height of Western 'decadence'. A Premier League football match.

A concert at Wembley Arena. The biggest shopping centres in London, Edinburgh, Cardiff, Belfast, Manchester, Glasgow, Birmingham, Liverpool and Newcastle. A music festival. And even a school. That one had given even Milton pause for thought – but no, he decided, it *was* necessary. He had to be sure the attack would generate sufficient disgust – sufficient anger and fear – to achieve his aims. Of course he was aggrieved that British children would have to die; he was aggrieved for all the victims. But this was a war. And there were always casualties in war. They would die as martyrs for his glorious cause. Heroes of the revolution.

And the very fact that we was prepared to sanction such an act was, he knew, why he was God's chosen one. Most men would shrink at the prospect. Not him. He was brave enough to do what must be done.

And the attacks would just be the first part. The second was just as important – a series of doctored social media posts and videos claiming responsibility for the attacks by a Muslim terror group. Milton knew it didn't matter that they would eventually be debunked. That would take days, weeks. By then, the damage would be done. The news channels would show the videos, the social media sites would be awash with them. As people reeled from the attacks, the fear would take over. And then Milton would step in with the answers.

The fact he'd planned it all to happen on 11 September – a date etched in the minds of everyone in the West as synonymous with Islamic terrorism – was the final, exquisite brushstroke; the crowning artistic flourish.

It was beautiful and, once it had all been laid out in his mind, he'd waited for the one piece of the jigsaw he'd need to set his plan in motion. The thing he'd looked for ever since he'd set out down this path: a weak and malleable mind. And he'd finally found that in Lance Corporal Robertson.

It hadn't been difficult. The guards had eventually got sloppy. For the first three years, Milton did nothing but sit in his cell. He barely spoke to them, other than when it was absolutely necessary. He was one man. A beaten, broken man. He was no threat. Then, slowly, he'd tried to get one of them to open up. The first few wouldn't bite. But Robertson . . . he was a smoker. That was the key. Milton never had been. As far as he was concerned, it was a disgusting habit for the weak-minded. At its heart, simply a drain on one's wallet and health, with no discernible benefit other than a fleeting chemical-induced moment of pleasure, which only served to demand you repeated the process.

But when he'd noticed the packet in Robertson's hand that day, he knew he had his 'in'.

'I could murder one of those,' he'd said, nodding at the packet. 'Gave up years ago, but now' – he gestured around him – 'it doesn't really seem to matter anymore.'

At first, the Marine had said nothing, bar a sort of grunt of agreement. Milton had seen a flash of panic in his eyes. He'd probably been told not to talk to the prisoner, and was now mentally flailing as he tried to work out what exactly that meant in practice. Milton hadn't pushed it. Not that time. On that day he let the line out a little. It was a week before Milton saw him again when Robertson brought up his meal.

'Sorry about all this,' Milton had said in a half-apologetic tone. 'Bet this isn't what you signed up for – being a waiter to the likes of me all the way out here on this frozen rock.' He'd smiled. Robertson hadn't smiled back, but Milton could tell the ice was thawing, ever so slightly. He was being pleasant, non-threatening. It was a far cry from his reputation, and he suspected Robertson wouldn't know how to react.

Milton continued the routine, but only with Robertson. A little pleasant chatter – nothing too much, nothing overt. A wriggle of the hook, then let the line go slack. Still the Marine kept his counsel, though Milton felt he was conflicted.

Then one day when he'd brought in the food tray, Milton noticed there was a cigarette and a single match lined up together on the tray next to the beef stew and mashed potato.

Robertson still said nothing, but Milton had looked him in the eye and said: 'Thank you. That means a lot to me.'

Milton had banked on that secret code that exists between smokers. The code that means one would never decline the request for a light – or even a cigarette itself – because only smokers knew the particular and gnawing horror of going without. And having the means to end that suffering was a powerful feeling. You never knew when you might be the one in need, the one jonesing for a smoke. So you always gave.

And now Robertson had given in, and Milton had him exactly where he wanted him. Robertson had broken the rules for the prisoner; now they were in a conspiracy together.

On that day the Marine had left without speaking. Milton had eaten his meal and then taken the cigarette out into his tiny concrete yard, struck the match on the wall and lit up. He'd coughed and choked through that first one. He'd had no chemical stimulant of any kind enter his body since his incarceration, save for the tiny trace of caffeine in the weak tea he was served, and the nicotine and the smoke made him light-headed and nauseous. But he persisted and smoked it right to the end, practising so he could control the coughing. It was vital he mastered that – he had to look like a natural.

From that day on, every time Robertson had delivered his meal, there had a been a cigarette and a match included. And

Milton had smoked each and every one, getting more and more comfortable as he did so. The thought occurred to him that he would genuinely become addicted if this carried on, but he accepted that. It was a small price to pay. And unlike millions of others, Milton knew he possessed the requisite self-control to give up when the time was right. When the smokescreen had served its purpose.

And then one day he'd made his move. Robertson had arrived with his meal. Cigarette and match present and correct as usual. But this time Milton had looked at the tray. 'I don't feel hungry right now. Join me for a fag?' he'd asked casually as he picked up the cigarette and made for the yard. He'd just briefly glimpsed Robertson looking behind him as if checking whether the coast was clear, and he soon heard the footsteps following him outside.

Milton had cupped his hand around the match as he lit his own. Robertson appeared in the doorway pulling another cigarette from a packet, and Milton held the match up to light it. Another shared moment between two people who knew the joy of a cigarette on a cold night. A flash of exquisite pleasure amid the dull grey of another dull day in the middle of nowhere.

And after that first deep drag, that was when Robertson had spoken his first words to Milton.

'How long they had you here then?' he'd asked.

Milton suppressed a smile. It was a redundant question to which Robertson almost certainly already knew the answer, and it didn't make any difference either way, but clearly Robertson had felt the need to break the silence at last. *Got him*, thought Milton.

After that, their cigarette breaks became a regular fixture. Milton was careful not to overplay his hand. Some days they just talked about the banality of life on the island, or the latest news from Robertson's wife back in England. But Milton was clever. He knew exactly when to pepper in a few references to help water and nourish the seeds he was sure were already planted in Robertson's brain. A mention of Robertson's wife struggling to get a doctor's appointment was an easy way in to a throwaway line about immigrants. As was a story Robertson had seen on social media about asylum seekers crossing the Channel in small boats. It was almost too easy. Though Milton was careful to make sure he was subtle about it.

Eventually – and Milton was monk-like in his patience – the conversation turned to his own family. By now Robertson was full of tales about his wife and little boy. Milton knew his son Callum had started school last September, that his teacher was called Mrs Shorey, and that Michelle, Robertson's wife, was in a running feud with their neighbour – 'another illegal' – over a car-parking space outside their house. And he knew that Robertson's mother was waiting for a knee replacement operation that had already been postponed twice because the National Health Service was unable to cope with demand. 'There's just too many people, and they keep letting more and more in,' Robertson had noted, to Milton's nodding approval.

Soon Milton knew everything about Robertson and his family. And eventually, Robertson had asked Milton about his.

'You married?' he'd said, before a look of panic ran across his face. The two of them had chatted for weeks, months now, about most things, but they had never acknowledged the bizarre circumstances that framed their relationship. And Robertson had never brought up Milton's family before, perhaps because he knew the prisoner was never getting out of this place and was never going to see any of them ever again. But that day he'd spoken before thinking.

'Oh sorry, I . . .' he'd mumbled.

But Milton had smiled. 'It's okay. Really.' He'd taken a drag of his cigarette. 'I'm married too. The worst thing is . . .' he'd paused, '. . . she doesn't even know I'm here. Doesn't even know I'm alive! I just wish I could tell her, you know? Let her know I'm okay. That I miss her.' Another drag. 'Not for me, but for her. It must be so hard for her. Her and my little girl.' Milton glanced at Robertson and then looked away. 'But there's nothing I can do about it now.'

He'd stubbed out his spent cigarette and sniffed, as if on the verge of tears. And said nothing more.

Robertson had looked at his watch, clearly uncomfortable with the atmosphere after it had turned from pleasantries and idle chat to Milton's deep emotions. 'I'd better get back. That prick Turner will be on my back. He never fucking lets up.'

And so he'd left. And Milton had smiled again.

Patience was his greatest weapon and, luckily for him, time was the only thing he had. Robertson didn't need to know that Milton's wife had left him more than twelve years earlier, after he'd been arrested for the fifth time when a far-right protest march had erupted in violence on the streets of London. Or that his 'little girl' was in fact now seventeen years old, had changed her name, and hadn't had any contact with him since she was five.

He hadn't brought up his family again – time to let the line out a little. But then Robertson had done it for him.

'I was thinking about what you said,' he'd mentioned one day over a cigarette. 'About your wife. Your daughter.'

Milton had nodded casually.

'It's not right, you know.'

'I know, but what can I do? Stuck here?' He'd gestured around his quarters.

'They should at least know you're alive.'

Milton had replied with a 'what are you gonna do?' shrug.

'*You* can't do anything,' Robertson replied. 'But what if someone could get a message out for you?'

Milton had stopped and considered his response carefully. The fish was nibbling the bait, but this was the most critical moment – the moment when a less patient fisherman would panic, snatch back the line too quickly and scare the fish, allowing it to wriggle away. A less patient fisherman would go hungry. Milton wasn't about to let that happen to him.

'I've . . . I've given up hope on that,' he'd said quietly.

'Do you get what I'm saying?' Robertson had asked, his voice hushed.

Milton had sniffed, acted like he was choking back the tears again. 'I couldn't ask you to do that.'

'You're not asking, I'm offering. I want to. I told you, it's not right what they've done to you.'

Milton had looked him square in the eye, but had not overdone it. Robertson wouldn't have been comfortable with that. 'I don't know what to say. How would you even do it?'

'I've thought about that. Is there an email address she uses? We have internet access. I could set up an anonymous Hotmail account or something. You write down what you want and I'll send it. At night, like, when it's quiet. No one needs to know.'

Milton had briefly considered whether the internet access at the base was monitored. He wondered whether this had occurred to Robertson. Probably not. He quickly decided it didn't matter either way – he had nothing to lose. The worst that could happen would be Robertson getting into trouble. Very much a risk worth taking. And so, Milton had written a short note and ripped the page out of his notebook.

Dear Sarah, I know this sounds crazy, but it's me, Richard. I'm alive. Don't believe the lies the government spread about me dying (you know how they lie). I can't explain properly right now but someone is helping send this message. I love you and Olivia so much. Please don't worry about me. There is someone helping me. You can reply to this message if you get it. I love you.

PS. Remember 2 Timothy 4:7–8.

The last part was of course a Bible reference. Milton couldn't resist. He doubted Robertson would look it up, and doubted even more that he would understand it if he did. But Milton knew the passage well. 'I have fought the good fight, I have finished the race, I have kept the faith. Finally, there is laid up for me the crown of righteousness, which the Lord, the righteous Judge, will give to me on that Day, and not to me only but also to all who have loved His appearing.'

Robertson had slipped the note inside his jacket and tapped it out later that night from the email account he'd created for the purpose using the base's satellite internet connection.

Milton's ex-wife Sarah would not have been happy at all to hear from her terrorist ex-husband, but she was not the owner of the email account to which Robertson had sent the message.

Craig Compton, his former third in command, however, was shocked, energized, and immediately spurred into action by the message that he'd received to an email account that had lain dormant for four years. The account, and coded message, were both contingency plans Milton had laid out many years earlier when he was on the run. They'd called it paranoia then. But not now. Now it was genius.

A reply was sent within hours, with Robertson relaying the message to Milton on his next shift.

Contact.

And so regular correspondence began. They had to be careful. Robertson had agreed to facilitate a husband talking to his beloved wife and daughter, not a convicted killer contacting his terror group. So Compton had to write as Sarah but, once again, Milton's so-called paranoia was the answer. As far as Robertson knew, Milton was a deeply religious man. And so he used the group's old code system based around Bible verses.

Soon Milton, Compton and the rest of the group had it all planned. 'Project Reichstag'.

Milton had provided the vision, the impetus and, using carefully selected Bible extracts so as not to arouse Robertson's suspicions, a list of the kind of targets he had in mind. Matthew, chapter twenty-three, verse seven: 'And the salutations in the marketplaces', was one. Proverbs, chapter twenty-two, verse six: 'Train up a child in the way he should go', was another. Compton had understood, and had nailed down the specific targets, communicating their exact coordinates back to Milton, again using a Bible verse code. And Robertson had been their unwitting conduit for all of it.

The attack was a thing of beauty in itself. But that was only half of it. The real moment of glory would be Milton's return to the world. To his supporters he would have risen from the dead, like Jesus himself. *The Second Coming.*

He would return, triumphant – and ready for Judgement Day. He would expose the lies, the inhumanity of the British government. His very existence would do the heavy lifting. *Look how they lie to you: they told you I was dead – what else are they lying about?*

And after the attack, Milton would be there to offer the answers. His manifesto wouldn't seem so far-fetched then, would it? Not after innocent people had been killed. Especially the children. Milton would lead his followers in demanding action. He could see it now: a march through the streets of London to Parliament. He had no doubt he could draw a crowd in the tens of thousands, perhaps more. And Milton would be at the very front, leading his people to the Promised Land like Moses parting the Red Sea – metaphorically speaking, of course. He would have to do it all from a secret, remote location to avoid recapture.

But even from there he would be able to pull the strings of his tame MP, the leader of the small but growing British Values Party. The crowd and public opinion would demand a place in government for his pet politician. But even that was only the beginning. Milton knew he could never get the top job himself – his past precluded that – but he could and would be the power behind the throne. And everyone would know it. They wouldn't be laughing at him then, would they?

They'd had to change the plan, of course. Originally Compton had arranged for one of Milton's wealthy American backers to fund a vessel and fully armed mercenary crew to storm the island, pick off the Marines and free Milton. And thanks to careful probing of Robertson, they knew the exact layout of the base, all its defences, and details on the guard unit.

When the time came, Robertson would be offered the chance to join them, or join his colleagues in the ever-after.

But then the Marine had brought him news of the volcano, and the Royal Navy destroyer on its way. That had forced Milton's hand into bringing forward his escape – and then he'd realized that it was also his chance to enact his revenge on that smug bastard Ridley. And Turner for good measure.

Milton looked at his watch, one stolen from the wrist of his former gaoler. He glanced back up in the direction of the lighthouse. It was still flashing and it was almost time.

He hoped Robertson could at least handle this. So far, he'd

been a useful tool. A blunt instrument, even if he'd neglected to tell Milton about the volcano researcher. Still, it didn't matter now. He had been the key that unpicked the lock.

But the door was open now.

Chapter 44

Abbie flicked off the torch for the final DOT of her code. Twice now she'd sent the message in full:

S O S – S O S – S E N D – H E L P – H O S T I L E – E N E M Y – A R M E D – A N D – D A N G E R O U S – S E N D – M A R I N E S.

Now she stopped to allow a response from the signal lamp on the ship – if anyone had even seen her message. She hoped they'd been keeping a close eye on the island from the bridge, but would they have been able to see the light through the mist from five miles away? She could only hope.

'Anything?'

Munroe lowered the binoculars and shook his head. 'Not yet, maybe you should send it aga—'

His sentence was cut short by a burst of gunfire, followed immediately by two of the remaining panes of glass shattering around them into a thousand tiny shards.

They both instinctively ducked down, trying to find cover behind the old workings of the lighthouse. Abbie realized it was the first time in her life that she was being shot at for real. *How are we going to get out of this one?*

She risked a glimpse over the edge and saw Robertson

marching in their direction, rifle raised and ready to shoot, face locked in grim determination.

She pulled her head back. 'Robertson,' she whispered.

She knew he could simply climb up to the gantry and execute them, and there was nothing she could do to stop him. They were trapped, and without a gun she was powerless.

There was another burst of gunfire. They ducked their heads again as she heard the bullets ping off the rusting steel structure of the lighthouse. Abbie glanced at Munroe, who was crouched with his arms wrapped around his legs. He was holding on so tightly his knuckles were white. His blue eyes wide and scared, his curly red hair dancing in the wind. Guns, violence – she knew he couldn't cope with any of it. A pacifist who vomited at the first sight of blood. Abbie could feel the fear emanating from every cell of his body. He didn't deserve to get mixed up in all this. The poor guy had come out here to do some research for his PhD and somehow found himself in this unimaginable nightmare.

She knew that with Robertson heading their way with a loaded gun and a temper to match, she had to make a choice. *Maybe* she could talk him down again – she'd done it once already after all – but she suspected he would be far less accommodating this time. The bursts of gunfire coming their way weren't the measured, targeted shots of a man under control. They were the angry blasts of a killer shooting with anger. She glanced back at Munroe. It might be too much of a long shot to save both of them at this point, but if she couldn't do that, she could at least save him.

'He doesn't know both of us are up here,' she said. 'Get down to the gantry below and hide behind the tower. When he comes up to get me you can sneak away.'

'What?' He looked dazed, like he wasn't properly taking in her words.

'Get down there!' she pointed. 'Get down there, stay down and keep out of sight, then get away as soon as you can. Try and find a way off the island before it's too late.'

'What about you?' he protested.

'I'll come and find you as soon as I can,' she lied. 'But if you find a way off the island, then don't wait for me. Just go. Get to the ship and I'll meet you there.'

'What? How are you going to get past Robertson?'

'Don't worry – I have a plan.'

He looked unconvinced.

'But like I said, if you find a way off the island, don't wait for me. Get back to the ship and raise the alarm. If I haven't made it back by then, they can come and get me.'

They both ducked down as Robertson sprayed another round of gunfire at the lighthouse and another glass pane shattered above their heads.

'GO!' she hissed. 'Before he reaches the ladder!'

Munroe hesitated for a moment, but then more gunfire forced them to cover their heads again. When it stopped, Abbie physically pushed him towards the ladder. '*NOW!*'

This time he didn't argue and began hurriedly descending the rusted metal steps.

Abbie watched him go. She hoped he would somehow find a way to get off the wretched island and back home. From their current standpoint, that would be a success. It would be *something*.

Through the gaps in the metal gantry, she watched Munroe slide round to the other side of the lighthouse below her to take cover.

Seconds later she heard the clang of a heavy boot on metal. Robertson had reached the bottom ladder.

Chapter 45

Milton heard a burst of gunfire in the distance. He glanced at his watch. It was nearly time. He just hoped Robertson sorted this out before it was too late.

Despite how useful the Marine had been, he wouldn't hesitate to leave him behind if it came to it. None of this would have been possible without him – but then, Milton himself had put the work in. Months and months of softening him up, finding common ground, stoking the anger that he clearly already felt within him. Milton had simply poured fuel on the fire.

And it had all paid off the night Robertson had brought him news of the imminent eruption. Milton's original escape plan didn't rest on the Marine, but the volcano waking up changed all that. The original plan had to be abandoned – there was no longer the time. He came up with a revised strategy, but it relied heavily on Robertson. Milton was going to have to push him harder and further – and sooner – than he'd hoped would be necessary.

It was a challenge, but one that Milton relished. He was perhaps most proud of his ability to steer the weak-minded, turn them, mould them. Make them feel empowered, while simultaneously making them instruments for his use.

First of all he had to sow some seeds of doubt about what Robertson's superiors were planning.

'You know, this will be the end for me,' he'd said, as sadly as he could manage when Robertson arrived with his lunch rations and the news about the eruption warning.

'What do you mean?'

'Do you think they're really going to let me off this island?' He shook his head. 'It's too dangerous for them. They'll never let me leave. They'll probably leave me here to die. You lot will all be taken off. I'll be left to my fate.'

Milton watched for the young Marine's reaction.

'They can't do that!' he'd said. 'It's not right.'

Milton had shrugged. 'It's not right that they've kept me locked up here in secret for four years. But they did it.' He already knew Robertson thought this unjust. It was an easy starting point, a good thread at which to tug. 'They'll be glad to be rid of me,' he added.

'I wish there was something I could do,' Robertson said.

Oh it was tempting, so very very tempting to leap on that. But Milton felt it was a touch too soon. Robertson had to believe it was all his idea. He had to implant the notion in his brain rather than simply instruct him at this point – that would be far more powerful. So he shook his head again and slumped back on his bunk, the very image of a beaten man resigned to his fate. 'No, no. There's nothing you can do. And I wouldn't want to put you in that position. You're a good man, and I thank you, but I couldn't ask you to do anything to help me.'

Robertson sighed and left the room.

Milton was confident he would be back. And he was right. It was only a few hours later when he came in to deliver the evening meal.

'I'm on duty tomorrow night,' he said conspiratorially as he set the tray down on the table. 'Just me and Berkeley.'

Milton nodded. The fish was nibbling.

'Could you get someone here? I know you have contacts. Friends,' he said awkwardly.

'Get someone here?'

'On a boat or something. To pick you up.'

Milton feigned surprise that the very idea was being suggested. 'Well, I . . . perhaps I could. But how would I—'

Robertson cut him off. 'I've thought about that.' He looked left and right, as if to check the coast was clear, then leaned into Milton. 'I'll send Berkeley off on some sort of job down to the beach house. Then I'll let you out. You slip away, go and meet your pick-up.'

'But how will you explain that when they find I've disappeared?'

Robertson smiled. 'I'll say you pretended to be ill, dying or whatever, and I came in to help. Then you rushed me, knocked me out or something.' He pulled back, clearly pleased with the plan he'd thought up.

Milton paused and looked up at his guard. 'You think it'll work?'

Robertson nodded enthusiastically.

'And you'd do that, for me?'

Again he nodded. 'I told you: it's not right, what they've done to you here.'

Milton nodded slowly in return. 'Thank you,' he said, his voice cracking with faked emotion. 'Thank you.'

The following night, Milton had been ready.

Robertson had come a long way, but the most difficult part was yet to come. The biggest leap. Milton hoped he was ready.

Hour after hour had passed as the night dragged on. Milton had pretended to sleep in his bunk but really he was wide awake and counting the seconds. As the night passed, Milton began to think Robertson had lost his bottle. Chickened out.

But then, eventually, the heavy steel door of the cell had clanked open. It was time.

'What's going on?' Milton had asked, irritated. 'Where have you been?'

'I couldn't get rid of Berkeley till just now,' he said apologetically.

Milton shook his head as he walked out of his cell for the first time in almost four years. A first taste of glorious freedom – but only the first taste. He then convinced Robertson to let him into the control room. 'I need to see the map of the island so I know where I'm going.' And then, 'I'm going to need a gun,' he'd added. Another critical moment.

Robertson hesitated.

Milton spread his hands wide. 'Think about it – if I've knocked you out cold, the first thing I would do is take your keys' – he nodded to the keyring on Robertson's belt – 'and take a weapon. It's what they'll be expecting.'

Still Robertson wasn't moving.

'It'll make it more convincing. Better for you.'

After a moment's pause, Robertson made for the gun cabinet and handed a rifle to the now escaped prisoner.

Milton had then pressed him for details about the layout of the two occupied buildings, the other huts on the beach, and anything else he could think of. He was playing for time – he needed Berkeley to come back for the next part of his plan. The final test for his newest recruit.

When the other young Marine arrived, Milton didn't hesitate.

The younger man had opened the door and then stopped in shock at the sight of Milton out of his cell.

'What the fuck?' was all he managed, before Milton raised his gun and fired a single shot.

Berkeley fell to the floor screaming and clutching his thigh where the bullet had hit.

'What the fuck are you doing?' Robertson shouted, his eyes wide, his breathing fast.

Milton was calm, cool. He knew Robertson was seeing the whole situation get away from him in real time. He had to calm him down. 'It's okay, it's all gonna be okay,' he said soothingly, while keeping the gun firmly in his grasp, his finger on the trigger. 'We've just had to tweak the plan a bit, that's all.'

'You never said anything about this!' Robertson replied.

'I know, I know, but this is how it has to be. Your plan was good, but it wasn't all going to work. I can't get out of here with the detachment still active.' He shook his head. 'It's just not possible.'

'But . . .' Robertson stammered, but didn't have the words to finish his thought.

Now came the most crucial part of all. Milton took a breath. 'And this is decision time. For you,' he said.

Berkeley was groaning and thrashing on the floor.

Robertson was watching him closely.

'Look at me, Robertson,' Milton commanded.

The Marine did as he was told. The power balance of the relationship had just shifted through 180 degrees.

'You're a highly impressive young man. Everything you told me about your home, how bad everything is in the country, how it's all on the wrong track. I can do something about that – and I will. And this is your chance to help me. Join me – join me and help me make a real difference. Don't just sit on the sidelines and moan as your country is sold down the river. Join me and take a stand.'

Robertson looked from Milton to Berkeley.

'Remember what you told me: how when you go home and

you hardly see a white face in town? How you feel like a minority in your own country?'

Robertson nodded, his forehead glistening with sweat, his eyes wide.

'How your mum can't get that operation? It's just about fairness,' Milton said. 'That's all you're asking for, right? But it's not fair, is it?'

Robertson shook his head.

'Doesn't it make you angry? Don't you wish you could do something about it?'

'I . . .'

'Well, you *can*. You can help me. Help me save our country.'

Robertson's face was flush.

'You can *be* someone,' Milton said. 'Someone who makes a difference. A real difference.'

Robertson flicked his eyes back and forth between Berkeley, still writhing in agony on the floor, and Milton.

Milton needed to up the ante. It was another gamble, but he was confident it would pay off.

'Where's the alarm?'

Robertson looked confused.

'The alarm,' Milton repeated. 'That you're supposed to push if I ever got out.'

Robertson nodded at a round red button, a little bigger than a bottle top, set on a small metal electrical box on the breeze-block wall, a pipe leading off it up into the ceiling.

Without hesitation, Milton walked up to it and pressed down firmly. A deafening alarm began blaring out from a speaker somewhere in the room, with others echoing to the same sound throughout the building.

'What did you do that for?' asked Robertson, incredulous.

'You've got to help me get out of here. Do that and you can

really serve your country. You can be a hero. But you have to decide. Now.'

Milton studied Robertson's face as the alarm blared. The Marine's eyes were wide and the skin above his top lip slick with sweat. He glanced at the alarm button, then down at the writhing Berkeley, then at the door.

'Focus, Robertson!' Milton shouted.

The Marine flinched at the sound of his name, his eyes still darting between the door and Berkeley.

The alarm was unrelenting. Insistent. BwaaaaaaaaAAAAAA AAHHHHHHHH. BwaaaaaaaaAAAAAAAAHHHHHHHH. Bwaa aaaaaaAAAAAAAAHHHHHHHH.

Berkely continued to scream in pain, adding to the cacophony of noise assaulting the senses.

'Come on, man!' Milton said.

Robertson flinched again, wincing at the noise as panic crossed his face.

BwaaaaaaaaAAAAAAAAHHHHHHHH. BwaaaaaaaaAAAAA AAAHHHHHHHH. BwaaaaaaaaAAAAAAAAHHHHHHHH.

Milton wondered if he'd pushed too far. This thing could still go either way. He took a step towards the Marine to force the issue.

'Okay!' Robertson cracked. 'What do you need me to do?'

Milton smiled. 'You've got to prove you're with me. Prove you've got what it takes. It's not going to be easy, but that's the only way I'll know you'll really be up to this. Up to what needs to be done.'

Berkeley's agonizing cries now fought for prominence with the alarm.

Milton nodded at the gun cabinet, then at Berkeley.

Robertson's eyes went wide as he realized what he was being asked to do.

Milton pushed past him, pulled a Glock handgun from the rack and handed it to Robertson, who took hold of it reluctantly.

'Now's the time,' Milton said.

Robertson hesitated. He looked at the weapon in his hand, glanced at Berkeley and then back at Milton.

'Or was it all talk?' Milton taunted him. 'Are you as gutless as all the rest of them?'

Robertson was wavering. Milton gave another little push. 'Or are you someone with the courage to do what needs to be done? To do the difficult things to serve his country, even when it's hard – *especially* when it's hard. To fight for what's right.'

Robertson flicked his eyes back to Berkeley.

'The clock is ticking, Robertson. Turner and the others will be here any minute now. You have to make a choice. Are you with me, or . . . ?' With that Milton began to swing his rifle ever so slightly in Robertson's direction. The implication was obvious.

Robertson swallowed hard.

Berkeley screamed. The alarm pulsed. The clock was ticking.

'It's now or never,' Milton shouted.

Robertson took another deep breath, raised his gun, and fired two shots at Berkeley, silencing him.

Milton smiled. 'God bless you. You've just taken your first step on the path of the righteous man.'

Robertson was breathing hard and shaking.

Milton began barking further instructions – he didn't want to give his new follower too much time to reflect on what he'd done. 'Now you wait here for the others. Tell them you came to and found him like that. Tell them I was still here – you managed to get the gun off me but I got away and you saw me leg it up the mountain. Don't tell them I'm still armed. And remember, we need Turner alive. He and I are going to have a little chat.'

Chapter 46

'You fucking geek!' Robertson called up as he began climbing the metal steps that encircled the lighthouse. 'I thought you'd have the sense to stay out of the fucking way.'

So, he thought it was Munroe. Abbie tried to work out whether that was somehow to her advantage. She couldn't think how.

'Show yourself!' he demanded as he ascended the ladder.

Abbie looked over the railing behind her – nothing but a hundred-foot drop onto the rocks below that were being battered by the breakers. If the fall didn't kill her, which it almost certainly would, she'd be helpless against the ferocious waves. Either way, it would be terminal. A last resort, she thought, grimly. But before she could consider that, she needed to buy Munroe enough time to make his own escape.

'I'm up here,' she shouted down as she stood up and slowly leaned over the edge. She saw his face frown in confusion as he looked up at her.

'*You?* How the fuck did you get out?'

'The earthquake,' she replied. 'Shook the cell block to bits.'

'I knew I should have killed you up there.' He continued his climb. 'Get back.'

She didn't move. She wondered if she could aim a kick to his face if he got close enough.

'I said, get back,' he repeated. He paused on the ladder and slid his rifle around to his front with his spare hand, then aimed it up at her. 'Now.'

Still she stood her ground for a moment, but she realized he'd be able to get a shot off before she could get close to him. She sighed and walked slowly backwards.

He climbed the last few steps and pulled himself up onto the gantry.

Abbie watched him close in on her as the wind whistled through the glass house and the gaps in the steel of the lighthouse.

He slipped his right hand around the trigger of his gun. 'Get down.'

She began to kneel down in front of him.

'No. On your back,' he commanded.

She glanced behind her at the drop down to the rocks. If she was going to do it, the moment was now – now or never. But she knew if she did, she wasn't only condemning herself to certain death, but probably Munroe as well. And he still had a chance. She had to buy him some more time. She hadn't been able to save Brewster. She had to try to save Munroe.

'I said, get on your back,' Robertson repeated.

She looked back at him. 'Come on, Robertson, are you really going to kill me?'

'I should have killed you up on Mount Pond. Now get on your back. Slowly.'

She didn't move.

He began swinging the barrel of his rifle towards her.

He'd made his point. She closed her eyes. 'So this is it?' she asked as she rolled onto her back.

'Just shut up,' he barked back.

'You don't want to kill me,' she said, just loud enough for him to hear over the roar of the wind. 'You didn't want to do it then, and you don't want to do it now.'

His eyes flickered for half a beat. 'You don't know anything about me.'

'I know you're a Marine,' she shot back. This approach had worked on him up on the mountain. She prayed it would work again. 'I know you've got yourself in deeper than you meant to. I know about Berkeley, Turner . . . the torture – you never signed on for all that, did you?'

Another flicker. It was working.

'You never knew you'd be killing your own, did you?'

'He never . . . it wasn't supposed to . . .'

'What did he promise you? Money?'

'No . . . it wasn't like that.'

'I bet he never said you'd be in this situation, gun trained on someone like me.' She paused for half a beat. 'Especially as I'm unarmed.'

The eyes flickered again.

'Just leave me here. You can tell him you shot me. I promise I'll stay out of the way.' Did she just imagine it, or did he lower his gun by half an inch? 'He'll never know . . .'

He was sweating now, and it wasn't just from the physical exertion of climbing up the tower.

'Put the gun down,' she said quietly. 'Put the gun down and he never has to know.'

Robertson swallowed tightly. The gun lowered another half an inch.

'You don't have to kill again. I'm not your enemy.'

She saw his body relax.

'You're right,' he said. 'I don't want to kill an unarmed enemy. It's not right.'

261

It was working.

He let his rifle go slack around his neck and she felt the air leave her lungs.

Then he unzipped his jacket and reached inside, before pulling out his Glock. He gripped it from the barrel and offered it to her.

She didn't move.

'Take it,' he growled.

She still made no effort to move as her eyes flicked from the weapon to his face.

'An empty gun isn't much use in a firefight,' she said warily.

Without saying a word, he took the gun in his other hand, raised it up into the air above his head and fired it once, the crack of the shot slicing through the icy-cold air and howling wind. He'd made his point. He lowered the weapon and offered it to her again as she lay on the cold steel gantry. 'Go on,' he said.

Still she didn't move. She knew if she took the gun, she was dead anyway.

He lost patience and threw it towards her. It landed with a clatter. She stared down at the black weapon just inches from her left boot.

Above her, he slid his rifle back to his chest in readiness. The wind howled through the cracks and rusted joints in the old lighthouse as the two of them stared at each other, waiting for the other to move.

She saw him tighten his grip on his rifle, preparing for action. She thought rapidly through her options. None of them were good. She closed her eyes and pictured Drew's smiling face as the wind roared all around her. She felt a jolt of joy and grief surge through her heart. Her mind was made up.

She took a deep breath, and then with a kick of her left foot she flicked the gun off the side of the gantry. A moment later she heard a clang as it dropped down onto the metal platform below.

'I won't play your game, Robertson,' she shouted up to him. 'If you want to kill me, you'll have to do it with me unarmed. And you'll have to live with it.'

He shrugged. 'Have it your way.'

The wind was getting stronger, louder, angrier.

'Really?' Abbie looked up at him. 'This is *really* what you want to do?'

He hesitated.

'Just let off a couple more shots and leave me here. He'll never know. What can I do now, anyway? I have no weapon, no radio – nothing.'

He paused.

'I'm no threat to you or him. How can I be? Just tell him you killed me and leave me here.'

She thought she could sense doubt in his eyes. 'You don't have to do it, Robertson,' she shouted. 'You really don't.'

She watched the barrel of his rifle drop a fraction. She *was* getting to him.

But a split second later, he raised the gun back to a firing position.

'Sorry,' he said as he began to curl his finger around the trigger. 'It's nothing personal.'

There was a crack, followed by a second and then a third in quick succession, then a pause and then three more. CRACK. CRACK. CRACK. Then a click, followed by another and another and another. Click, click, click, click, click, click.

Robertson's arms dropped, his gun hung loose on its strap around his body. He looked down at her with an expression of confusion for a moment, before his eyes began to glaze over. He tried to turn to his right but – even as he did so – he was already falling. His body lurched over the railing and the momentum tipped him over the edge. He didn't even try reaching for a handhold as he fell over the bar and dropped like a stone down the length of the lighthouse and on down the cliff face until he thudded onto the jagged rocks below.

Abbie looked back up at where he'd been standing to see Munroe, ashen-faced and shaking, standing at the top of the ladder, the pistol still pointing right where Robertson had been just moments ago. The Scot was staring straight ahead, the wind toying with his curly red hair as his body trembled.

For a long time she stared at him. He was standing with his arms locked out in front of him, still holding the gun, his face devoid of colour, his eyes wide and distant.

'Munroe,' she said softly, as if trying to gently wake him up from a nap.

He didn't move. Not even his eyes, which were still fixed on a target that was no longer there.

'Munroe,' she said again. 'You can put the gun down now.'

Still he didn't move.

'Munroe,' she said a little louder as she slowly began to pull herself up by the railing.

He jerked his head towards her, as if snapping back into consciousness.

'You can put the gun down now,' she repeated.

He looked down at the weapon in his hands and seemed stunned to find it there. Shock turned to alarm, and without warning he flung it over the side of the platform in the same direction Robertson had fallen, as if he couldn't stand to have it touching his skin for one second longer.

Abbie watched as the gun clattered down the cliff face and then dropped into the black swell below. In between the ferocious waves attacking the rocky shoreline, she saw Robertson's lifeless body resting on the rocks, his rifle still slung around his body. She quickly assessed the cliff face and wondered if she would be able to climb down and retrieve his weapon but, before she could decide, a bigger wave crashed against the shore, lifted the body up and then sucked it back out when it retreated. A second wave then crashed Robertson violently against the rocks – a movement that would surely have killed him were he not already dead. This was repeated twice more, the body now looking more like a collection of rags loosely bound together than a person, before a third wave flung him against the rocks one last time, then sucked him away and down into the freezing dark waters below. He was gone.

Abbie took in a breath as she watched him disappear. Then she looked back at Munroe. He was still shaking and was staring down at the rocks where Robertson's body had momentarily lain before it was claimed by the sea.

'You did what you had to do,' she said calmly but firmly.

He didn't move.

'Listen to me, Spencer.' *That was his first name, wasn't it?* 'You did what you had to do,' she repeated as she slowly approached and gently put her arm around him.

He recoiled from her touch but she wouldn't let him go and held on tightly. 'Do you hear me?'

He was still staring over the edge and down at the water below.

She gently manoeuvred him by his shoulders so he was facing her. Then she took his head in her hands. 'Look at me,' she said softly. 'You did what you had to do. He was a murderer and he was about to kill me. If you hadn't done what you just did, I'd be dead now – and so would you.' She couldn't be sure if any of this was getting through. She knew he'd be going into shock. Taking a life was a profoundly transformative moment for anyone. Especially the first time. It was something Abbie had trained for – though she was yet to experience it for real – but not Munroe. He never would have imagined he'd end up in this situation. She felt for him. It would take a very long time for him to get over it. Maybe he never would.

'That's three times,' she said.

This seemed to register with him on some level. 'Three times what?' he murmured.

'Three times you've saved my life,' she smiled. 'Thank you.'

He pulled away from her, his skin waxy and pale. She knew what was coming next. He hunched over the railing and vomited, retching two, three, four, five times.

When he was done, he held himself over the metal bar, catching his breath as the waves crashed on the shore beneath them. She let him rest a moment and stared out to sea. She wondered if any part of her SOS call had reached the ship that lay somewhere out there beyond the mist.

After a few minutes she turned to him. 'You did great back then,' she said, 'but next time don't leave me hanging for so long,' she added with a smile.

He turned to face her and tried to smile back, but it came out more like a grimace. 'So, what now?'

Chapter 47

Abbie and Munroe clambered back down the rocks towards the beach in silence. She was keeping a close eye on him. He'd almost fallen apart at the sight of a dead body earlier in the day, but now he'd not only witnessed a death happen, but he'd been the one to pull the trigger.

The pacifist who'd never held a gun before – never had to deal with any kind of real violence – had committed the most violent act there was. He was still clearly in shock, so she'd decided to take them back to the beach, mostly as something to keep them busy – a way to distract him, give him a purpose. She had no idea what they were going to do once they got there, but it seemed the most sensible choice. For one thing they could keep an eye on Milton and see what he was up to, and it was the nearest place to the jetty should there be a chance for them to escape.

When they got low enough, they squatted down to survey the black beach below. There was no sign of Milton, but Ridley's boat was still tied up at the jetty, caressed by the steam carpet rising up from the harbour.

'We can make it,' Munroe said. 'We can get to the boat!'

Abbie shook her head. 'No. Not yet. He could be anywhere.

And he's the one with all the guns, remember. He could pick us off the moment he sees us.'

'But he might have already gone! What are we gonna do? Just sit here until the volcano goes up? We've *got* to get out of here,' he added.

Abbie glanced at her watch. Less than thirty minutes remained until Munroe's zero hour. She looked down at the beach, at the boat tied up at the jetty. She estimated the distance to be at least 800 metres. Even at full speed, it would take a few minutes. And it was across the beach. Open country. Then, once they reached the boat, they'd have to get it started, cast off – and they'd be sitting ducks until they got out through the narrows.

But Munroe did have a point. What if Milton had already made his escape some other way? How long would they sit here waiting? They could literally sit here and be burned and buried alive. She felt the notebook pressing on her chest – she couldn't let that burn with her. The attacks were scheduled for ten days from now; she had to get word to the authorities to halt them or thousands more innocent people would be added to Milton's list of victims.

The ground began to shake beneath them as another tremor took hold of the island. Rocks were being shaken loose up the hill and rolling their way down onto the beach. Abbie glanced at Munroe. She could see the panic was rising in him again. 'Is this it?' she asked.

'I don't know yet.'

She was almost at the point of agreeing they make a run for it; after all, if the island went up now, they were dead anyway. But the tremor had another effect: it brought Milton out of hiding. He came running out of the beach house, presumably fearing it would collapse in on him the way his cell had on Abbie. Even from this distance, she could see he had changed his clothes.

Gone was the blue jumpsuit he'd been wearing earlier. Now he was dressed in Marines fatigues. He must have stolen a set from one of the rooms. Dead man's clothes. She could also see he had a rifle slung over his shoulder. And now he was directly between them and the jetty.

Along with the tremor, there was another crack up on the mountain. Abbie watched as gas began spewing out into the open air above.

She turned to Munroe. He'd seen it too and was squinting up at it and moving his mouth as if talking to himself almost silently.

She strained her ears to hear what he was saying.

'Must get away. Must get away. Must get away!' he repeated. He was panicking again – and honestly, at this point, Abbie didn't blame him.

'Stop it!' she hissed. 'Just let me think.'

He stopped talking but was still breathing hard, almost hyper-ventilating. She tried to block out the noise and the wind and the cold, and her own sense of panic as she desperately tried to think of a way out. But try as she might, every avenue of thought she went down was a dead end.

It was hopeless. She looked back at Munroe. He was staring at her, wide-eyed, in the grip of panic and fear, but still looking to her for an answer. And in that split second her face gave the game away. There was no answer. She had nothing.

The ground rumbled around them, and rocks began falling down the mountain on the opposite side of the bay as the gas continued to rise from the vents. They instinctively huddled closer together – a primal, animalistic urge to be a tiny bit less alone at this moment of crushing realization as they stared death in the face.

Abbie's facade of confidence and strength was cracking. She'd tried. She'd tried her best. But now she was unarmed, with no radio, and no way to contact the outside world or escape this hellish island. She could feel her defences against despair and hopelessness creaking under the strain of reality.

She knew she still had to try to keep it together for Munroe's sake, but all of a sudden she felt utterly exhausted, physically and mentally. She felt as though her carefully constructed dam, keeping out the despair, was developing serious fault lines, with more and more pressure building up behind it. And she knew once there was just one tiny crack, the pressure would be irresistible, and the whole thing would come crashing down under the weight of the pain. She knew she hadn't just built the dam for Munroe, to try to keep him going, she'd been building it since the day Drew died. It wasn't for Munroe – it was for her. But she could feel it was reaching breaking point. And when it did, she'd be overwhelmed by the enormous weight of hurt and despair and anger that had been building up behind it, drip by drip, for four years, and just waiting for the chance to drown her. To bury her.

She opened her mouth to speak, but no words would come as she stared into Munroe's innocent clear blue eyes. She had to find something to say, some way of carrying on, but nothing came to mind.

And then she heard it. It was faint, and at first she'd been unable to distinguish it from the rumbling of the ground beneath them, but with every passing second it was getting louder and more distinct, until it was unmistakable.

A helicopter was coming.

Chapter 48

Abbie allowed herself a smile as the distinctive buzz of the approaching aircraft got louder and louder. She knew it would be packed with a unit of Marines, fully armed and battle ready. Milton would be outnumbered and outgunned. He would either have to surrender and be recaptured, or he'd be shot in the inevitable firefight if he refused to give himself up. Frankly, Abbie was hoping for the latter.

She and Munroe peered back behind them over the rocks as the unmistakable sound of rotor blades slicing through the frozen air got louder and louder. Then, to Abbie's utter joy, she saw the helicopter emerging from the mist curtain that was still hanging over the mountains which ringed the outside of the island. They watched as it popped through the clouds and thundered over them, full of menace and purpose.

'They *did* see it!' Munroe exclaimed. 'It worked! I can't believe it!'

He was giddy. She could hardly blame him – she hadn't dared to think her message had got through, but clearly it had.

Yes, thought Abbie, the cavalry was here. They were going to kick the shit out of that monster Milton, and she had a front-row seat for the show.

Munroe was beaming and pulled Abbie into a celebratory hug.

'We just need to stay out of sight while they go to work,' she told him. 'The Marines are the best. They'll soon have him under control.'

'And then we can get out of here?'

'Yes,' she nodded and smiled warmly. 'Then we can get out of here.'

She pictured the men in the chopper, lined up and ready. Even Milton – with all his evil intent and his past unspeakably violent deeds – would be no match for a dozen Marines. She wondered which of them had been sent; she'd spent a little time with most of them since they'd joined the ship three weeks ago, though she'd never told any of them of her ambitions to one day join their ranks.

Things would move quickly now. She wondered if Milton would try to run. Perhaps he would scamper back up the mountain, try to hide up on the ridge somewhere. It wouldn't do him any good. These Marines were used to hunting their prey. They might not even need to. If he ran, there would be nothing stopping Abbie and Munroe breaking cover, and they could all fly back to the ship and leave Milton to the eruption.

He could try to make a run for Ridley's boat, but they'd soon have him if he tried that. Maybe he would simply cower in the beach-house building – but room-to-room clearances were bread and butter for the Marines.

And if he tried to shoot his way out of it, there was only one way it would end: badly – for Milton.

Whichever way she sliced it, there was no way he could win.

She felt the adrenalin coursing through her veins as she readied herself for what was about to unfold. She found herself hoping Milton didn't surrender. She relished the thought of one of the Marines putting a bullet through the hateful little bastard. *Let him drop and leave him to burn*, she thought.

Then she saw him. He'd come back out of the hut wearing a dead man's uniform and was waving his arms back and forth at the helicopter as it closed in. *What was he doing?*

She began to think fast again: was the helicopter's arrival a possibility that master planner Milton was in fact counting on?

She looked back up as the aircraft thundered over their heads with a THWACK THWACK THWACK as it approached the beach. It was close enough for her to see it clearly now – and something was wrong.

She could see high-vis orange jumpsuits. The side door was open, but there was no gunner in position, and no rows of camouflaged Marines behind him clutching rifles. Instead, the winch-man sat in the open door. A sudden jolt of fear ripped through her as she realized what was about to happen.

Chapter 49

Abbie knew in that moment that *Northumberland* clearly hadn't received her full message. Perhaps they had got the mayday part but nothing more, or perhaps they hadn't seen any of it. And Ridley had made such a fuss about secrecy, he almost certainly hadn't told anyone onboard about Milton and their real mission.

The captain hadn't sent armed Marines ready to engage the enemy, she realized with a feeling of horror surging up from deep down in her stomach – he'd sent the search and rescue crew. She looked back down at Milton waving them in, and her blood ran cold as what was about to happen fell into place in her mind. *They were flying into a trap.*

She had to warn them, but how? She had no radio, no gun, no nothing. She considered pelting down the hillside and trying to warn them off, but they certainly wouldn't hear her, and probably wouldn't even see her at this point. As far as the crew knew, they were being waved in by a fellow Marine.

Shit. Shit shit shit.

Milton was pointing them down to a flat, concrete pad just up from the beach, and the pilot seemed to be complying. In a panic, Abbie wondered if she could somehow tackle the bastard before it was too late.

But then it happened.

The noise of the helicopter almost drowned it out. Almost. She heard the first shot, and then a second right after it, his rifle now held up to his eye, the barrel pointed directly at the helicopter.

The aircraft began lurching towards the ground at a sharp angle as suddenly the noise of the engines increased. He'd shot the pilots.

The helicopter was lurching out of control, heading straight for the old shipwreck beached on the black sand. Within seconds the first rotor blade hit and began slicing up the ancient timbers of the boat like a wood-chipper, turning the wreck into matchsticks and flinging splinters high up into the air before the fuselage itself collided with the hull and began to roll onto its side. The rotors continued to turn in vain, smashing and tearing the old boat to ribbons, the fuselage crumpling and crushing the hull underneath its weight. The whine of the engines got louder and louder and louder as the rotors turned in the ash, jolting the aircraft like a fish in its death throes, writhing on dry land.

Something must have fused then, as the engine seemed to cut out and the rotors gradually lost power and momentum. When they finally stopped turning, there was silence. There was no explosion. No fire. Just silence.

Abbie wanted to scream. She wanted to run to the downed craft as fast as her legs could carry her and begin dragging out survivors, just as her training had taught her. These weren't just survivors; these were her colleagues. Her friends. But she didn't dare move. It wasn't cowardice, it was logic. She knew that if she gave herself away, she'd be dead too.

Munroe was watching open-mouthed and seemingly too terrified to even take in what he was seeing. It was no less horrifying for Abbie.

Then she saw movement: Milton was walking purposefully

towards the wreck. He was still carrying his gun. Once he was within range, he stopped.

Abbie knew what was coming and turned away, yanking Munroe around as well to spare him the sight. But they couldn't escape the sound. She closed her eyes tight, clenched her jaw, and felt every muscle in her body tense up as she heard the horrifying sound of Milton unloading round after round into the hull of the crashed aircraft. They huddled together as bullet after bullet pierced the metal. Abbie could feel every single one of them as if they were plunging into her, tearing her flesh apart with white-hot accuracy, her body jerking with each round as Milton peppered the helicopter with enough ammunition to take down an army. Then it was quiet again.

She turned back and heard the sound of twisted metal scraping against itself, as one of the helicopter's doors was forced open. Even from this distance she could recognize Andy Stokes, the helicopter winch-man from *Northumberland*. Clearly bleeding heavily, he nonetheless managed to push his way out of the craft. He staggered a few yards and raised an arm as if to ask for help. Abbie knew none would come. Instead she watched, her head shaking furiously, her body trembling, as Milton raised his weapon once more and fired two rounds.

Stokes's body hit the ground.

Chapter 50

Abbie and Munroe watched on in utter horror as Milton murdered the crew. There was no mercy shown, no effort made simply to capture them and leave them on the island. Milton had apparently let loose all the years of hatred stored up inside him. All the rage he'd channelled into his so-called 'war on Islam', all the fury he'd used to justify the killing of thousands of innocent people, and the anger he felt at the British government for capturing him and keeping him locked up on this tiny, frozen hell. And as Abbie thought of the notebook tucked away in her jacket, she knew that this was only the start – just the first chapter in his next book of violence.

She saw Drew. In her mind's eye he was falling, felled by a bullet from Milton's gun, just like Stokes was a moment ago. She wanted to reach out and catch him, cradle him in her arms, will him back to life.

Now there were even more victims on Milton's kill list. More loved ones who would have to live with the grief.

She felt sick with guilt: it might have been her distress call that brought them here. If she hadn't sent out that SOS from the lighthouse, who knows what would have happened?

The deaths of the seven Marines stationed on the island had

been tragic, but Abbie could not blame herself for those. But the bodies that now lay in the wreckage of the bullet-riddled Merlin? She felt the blood of every one of them was on her hands. Just like that of poor Brewster. She'd pleaded with him to stay and go hunting for Milton, and he'd agreed, against his better judgement.

She glanced at Munroe. His face was so white it almost seemed translucent, his eyes locked onto the scene below, his mouth hanging open in shock and fear. He hadn't thrown up yet – apparently he was getting used to seeing death, Abbie noted grimly. Even if they did somehow get out of this alive, she knew he would never be quite the same again. Then again, getting out of this alive was looking less and less likely by the minute.

She knew she'd have to look after him. At that moment she was glad he was here – left alone she didn't know if she had the strength to keep going, but she would have to be strong for both of them.

'What the hell do we do now?' he said.

Abbie spoke quietly and as calmly as she could. 'We wait here. We wait for Milton to leave, then we find some way off the island.'

Munroe seemed not to hear her. He was looking off into the middle distance.

'Did you hear me?' she asked, taking him by the shoulders and looking directly into his eyes. 'He'll be leaving soon, and then we'll go too. We'll find a way to get back to the ship. We'll be safe there. Do you understand?'

She still wasn't sure he'd taken it all in, but he nodded slowly. He was still very pale and she wondered if he might even pass out from shock.

'We'll be back on board with a cup of tea in no time, you'll see. Then you never have to see this place ever again.'

He nodded again, but still didn't reply.

She popped her head back over the rock and looked back

down to the shore. Milton had left the helicopter and had also stopped whatever it was he was doing with the rusty junk on the beach. But he was still there. *Why hasn't he taken Ridley's boat?* she thought as she glanced to the end of the dock and saw it was still tied up. Milton was sitting on the wooden jetty, his legs hanging over the side. Steam rose up from the surface of the water, obscuring his feet. *What the hell is he doing?*

She glanced back down at Munroe, who was slumped against the rock, his eyes glazed over, somehow detached from the whole situation. For a moment the wind died away and she could hear Munroe whispering to himself. She leaned in to try and hear what he was saying.

'Must get off. Must get off. Must get away. Must get away.'

He wasn't talking to her, just chanting it to himself like some kind of mantra. He turned and began staring at the boat tied up at the jetty. His chant was getting louder and very insistent.

'Munroe,' she hissed. 'Keep quiet!'

He didn't stop or even look at her. She didn't think he'd even heard her. It was as if she simply wasn't there anymore.

'Must get off. Must get away,' he repeated again and again, his gaze now fixed on the boat gently bobbing in the bay next to the jetty, just a few yards away from Milton. He was now gripping the rock with his hand, his knuckles getting whiter and whiter as he held it ever tighter.

'Must get off. Must get away.'

He shifted his legs, bringing one up so his foot was planted on the ground.

'Must get off. Must get off. Must get away. Must get away.'

'Munroe!' she hissed again, to no avail.

His eyes were now locked on the boat like laser pointers, as if the rest of the world was falling away around him, and only the little inflatable craft remained.

'*Must get off. Must get off. Must get away. Must get away.*'

He'd lost any sense of rationality. She could see he'd become like a prisoner of war who'd gone wire happy – ready to risk the fence even though it would mean certain death in a hail of bullets from a guard in the watchtower. He was beyond sense, beyond reason. She looked at him again: he was about to go, to make a run for the boat, Milton or no Milton. And that meant he was dead – and so was she.

'Must get off. Must get off. Must get away. Must get away!' He tightened his grip on the rock and began to bring his other leg up, sliding it across the loose rock.

'Munroe!' she cried, but still there was no acknowledgement.

She grabbed his arm, but he simply shrugged it free without even looking at her.

And then he bolted.

Chapter 51

'Munroe!' she called after him, but it was too late. He was off and running like an Olympic sprinter reacting to the starter's gun – running to his certain death if he got anywhere near Milton, who still had his rifle slung around his neck.

'Fuck,' she muttered to herself as she sprang to her feet and pumped her legs in pursuit of Munroe. He was heading directly for the jetty, some 700 or 800 metres to the northwest.

He was lucky Milton was sitting facing in the other direction, or he'd already have been spotted. The howling of the wind and the still-ticking engines of the downed helicopter were also cloaking the sound of his crunching footsteps on the black ash beach.

Abbie kept one eye on Milton as she gave chase. Munroe was quick, but she was quicker. She was gaining on him, but she'd have to do it fast. He seemed utterly single-minded, focused only on reaching that boat – which, of course, he never would. Milton would gun him down the moment he saw him. Abbie just prayed she could catch him before he got them both killed. She redoubled her efforts as they pounded along the beach. But as she did so, another thought occurred to her: what was she going to do when she got to him? If she tackled him to the ground and he struggled or cried out, which surely he would, it would alert Milton to their presence.

Then she saw her way out of this. She would have to time it just right, but she was getting good at that.

Munroe continued to run, his ungainly gait deceptively quick.

Abbie altered her direction of travel slightly, tacking off to Munroe's right, before she changed the angle once again to arc back towards him, like a footballer curving their run to avoid the offside trap.

She was now off to his right and still behind him, but now, ahead of him in her line of sight was the old warehouse to the left of the concrete slipway – specifically the gap in the northeast corner which, judging by the rusted metal rails running along it at the bottom, was once closed in from the elements by sliding doors.

Abbie drew on her reserves and went up a gear, and with her window of opportunity closing, she took her chance and slammed into Munroe from the right-hand side. She felt the intense pain of her possibly broken rib as she made contact with him, but blocked it out as she used the momentum she'd built up to propel them both through the opening and into the warehouse. They fell and landed hard on the dusty concrete base inside it, and she wrapped herself around Munroe and locked her arm over his mouth and nose to subdue him.

She'd successfully got him off the open beach and out of Milton's sight – and done so before he could shout too loudly. But there was something she hadn't counted on: inside the warehouse were dozens, if not hundreds of birds – Abbie was no ornithologist so had no idea what kind they were – which had apparently been sheltering from the wind and were perched on every beam, ledge and roof truss in the great building. But Abbie and Munroe's entrance had disturbed their peace, and within seconds the whole space was a blizzard of feathers and flapping wings as the creatures took flight, escaping through the open end out onto the harbour, through the doorway to the north, and through every other exit point – from broken windows to holes in the roof – in a mass exodus.

Abbie was breathing hard as she held tightly onto Munroe, until she felt him relax a little in her arms. She whispered menacingly in his ear, 'Stay here and stay down,' with a tone she was certain conveyed how serious she was. 'Nod if you understand me,' she added.

He moved his head up and down, and she removed her hand from his mouth and released him from her full-body grip.

Then she got on her knees and crawled along to the small, fogged-up window on the northwest corner of the building and peeked through, praying she wasn't greeted by the sight of Milton walking their way and cocking his gun.

She froze as soon as she brought her face to the window. He was staring right in her direction and walking towards them. He pulled the rifle around on its strap, slipping his finger onto the trigger as he went. *Shit.*

Chapter 52

It felt as if Milton was staring right at her, those blue-black pins of his eyes boring through hers, as Abbie watched him walking purposefully down the beach towards the warehouse. Instinctively she wanted to duck down but she fought the urge. Logically she knew it was dark in the old building, and the window was old and cloudy. He couldn't actually be looking at her, not from that distance and in the dying light. Movement would only risk giving her away. So she stayed stock still and watched as he continued to walk, rifle in hand.

Munroe crawled up beside her and followed her gaze. His face dropped when he saw Milton coming towards them. She'd apparently knocked him out of his mentally absent state when she'd rugby-tackled him into the warehouse, but she feared he could snap again at any moment. She slipped her hand down and took his, squeezing it tightly, as much for her sake as for his. She realized the strange little Scottish scientist's hand was the first she'd held since Drew's. Once she had that thought, she expected to feel guilty. Instead she felt comforted.

She focused back on Milton who, without warning, stopped in his tracks, turned and looked up into the darkening sky.

Abbie followed his gaze and tried to see what had grabbed

his attention. She narrowed her eyes and searched the dark grey expanse above. Then she saw it – except it couldn't be. It did explain why Milton and Robertson hadn't left in the boat, and what they'd been doing on the beach.

Munroe saw it too. 'Wait, is that . . . ?'

A small, twin-prop plane had punched through the cloud cover and ducked down into the inner ring of the island. They could hear the whine of its engines now as it got closer. Abbie estimated it could be no more than an eight-seater.

Suddenly, what Milton and Robertson had been up to made sense. Ridley was right, there was no airstrip on this island – but there *was* a long, flat beach, which, if cleared of all the rusty junk that had littered it, would serve the same purpose. And the two of them had spent the last few hours doing just that. Now she knew why Milton had been so concerned about the time – they had to get the beach cleared before the plane arrived.

But what didn't make sense was how the tiny plane was here at all. She knew Robertson had clearly been Milton's conduit to the outside world, and must have arranged it with some remnant part of the Cross of St George organization (and they were rumoured to still have supporters, some extremely wealthy, all over the world), but that wasn't what didn't add up right now. What was confusing her was how such a tiny plane – with a correspondingly small fuel tank – was able to operate all the way out here, more than a thousand kilometres from the nearest mainland airfield in Argentina.

She couldn't work it out, but the plane's arrival did explain why Milton had been entirely unconcerned when Ridley had told him *Northumberland* was just five miles away, and his only way off the island. Milton already knew that wasn't the case, and he had no plans to go anywhere near the ship.

As they watched the plane circling, presumably as the pilot

assessed the makeshift airstrip, Munroe became animated, almost manic.

'This is it!' he said excitedly. 'He's going to leave on that plane, and we can be on a boat and out of here as soon as they take off!'

He'd seen a way out that just two minutes ago simply hadn't been there. He had hope again, and there was no more powerful force in the world.

But he was right: much as she hated to think Milton was about to escape and there was nothing she could do about it, him leaving on the plane did at least mean she and Munroe could get off the island, hopefully before the volcano erupted.

The buzz of the little plane suddenly faded to nothing, drowned out by the biggest bang Abbie had heard yet. She jerked her head in the direction of the sound – it was coming from the west, on the shoreline across the harbour opposite Whalers Bay. She gasped as she saw an enormous column of steam, gas, mud and rock shoot up into the sky. It looked like the giant exhaust cloud triggered by the firing of the engines at a space rocket launch, only there was no cigar-shaped craft at the top of it: this was an entirely natural phenomenon. Abbie felt the whole warehouse structure shake as the sound wave from the explosion hit the old building.

Munroe was at her side and watching just as intently. 'Holy shit,' he said quietly. 'I've never actually seen . . . I mean, not in person. Holy shit,' he repeated.

It seemed like he'd switched from abject terror to awe, as if his professional curiosity and passion for his chosen field was overriding any rational fear he might be feeling.

'What is it?' she asked as they watched. There was a central grey column, with offshoots squirting up from it, surrounded by clouds of steam billowing up into the sky above.

'A steam explosion,' he said. 'The heating up of the volcano has melted snow from the peaks. This water has then trickled down into the magma chamber where it's been flash boiled. But steam takes up much more space than liquid water, so the pressure builds and builds and builds until that happens.'

'Jesus.'

Munroe nodded. 'Incredible, isn't it? All that power.'

'I presume it's not a good sign?'

'Not for us,' he said, shaking his head. 'All the venting has so far been on Mount Pond, so the fact this is happening on the other shore means the whole island could be getting ready to go.'

'Don't worry,' she said. 'We'll be on that boat in a few minutes.' She thought of the red notebook inside her jacket. She had to get back to the ship pronto and show the captain its contents so the authorities could stop the attacks before it was too late.

But even as she spoke, movement from the jetty caught her attention. She looked back and saw Milton making his way back down to the end of the dock. Then he pulled his gun up and fired round after round into the craft, puncturing the tubes that ran around the rigid hull and piercing holes in the bottom. Water from the harbour bubbled up through it and began pulling the little vessel down. As a final act, he fired off another dozen rounds into the engine for good measure.

When he was satisfied, and the boat was already looking low in the water, he turned and made his way back down the dock.

Abbie turned back to Munroe, who had watched the scene with the same look of horror he had had on his face when Milton had downed the helicopter.

'That was our last chance,' he said in a quiet voice.

She turned back to watch Milton. He'd just taken away her last hope. Their last possible chance of escaping the island. Abbie knew then that she and Munroe would die here. And suddenly she felt not despair, but rage.

The plane had disappeared from view. Abbie guessed it would be behind them, completing its approach before touching down on the black ash of the beach in front of them, into the westerly wind – assuming the steam explosion hadn't spooked the pilot off the whole idea.

But no, she could hear him pulling back on the engines now as he made his final approach, while Milton had made his way to the side of the beach, waiting for his transport to land. If she was going to think of a way out of this, she was going to have to do it very, very fast.

Chapter 53

The pilot was on his final approach now. Abbie knew what would happen next: after the plane landed, Milton would board, and then they would taxi back to her end of the beach, turn through 180 degrees and take off into the wind. And then Milton would be gone forever.

She knew the massive effort that had gone into catching him the last time. He'd been on the run for six years, having already escaped once. Surely he would never be found again – at the moment nobody even knew he was alive, other than she and Munroe, however many of his old supporters Robertson had got word to, and presumably some employees of whichever government department or agency Ridley had worked for. In a matter of minutes, he would be free and out there again, ready to unleash a new wave of terror. She thought of the notebook in her inside pocket, of the scale of the violence he was set to inflict on the world.

She thought of the pain he'd already caused her: Brewster and all the men aboard the helicopter, callously and mercilessly gunned down; the Marines they'd found halfway up the mountain. Even Ridley. But most of all she thought of Drew. For four long years, she'd thought of little else but how she'd been robbed of her love – her *life* – by this monster. She found the anger rising up inside her, as unstoppable as the tide. It felt like lava in her chest getting hotter and hotter, higher and higher, the pressure building and building as the rage bubbled up in her chest. *No*, she thought, *no, no no*. He was *not* going to get away. Not just like that. Not if she could do anything about it.

All was lost now anyway – her only hope of escaping the island herself had been the boat Milton had just sunk. He'd taken *everything* from her. First her love. And now he was going to leave her to die. She had nothing left to lose. And all she felt was pure, distilled rage.

The whine of the engines was getting louder and louder as the plane bore down on them from behind. She looked at Munroe, broken and terrified, then out through the window at Milton. He stood waiting, his jacket flapping in the wind as he watched the plane intently.

She tried to think fast: what could she do? Could she rush him before the plane landed? He would cut her down before she got within a hundred yards. No, that wouldn't work. She could wait for them to take off, then see if they'd left behind any guns and try to hit the plane? Doubtful. Firstly, it required him having left at least one gun behind, and secondly, by the time she'd run down the beach and grabbed one – if she could even find one – the plane would likely already be out of range. And even if it wasn't, her chances of hitting the thing would be slim at best. No, that wouldn't work either. Come on, *think!*

She heard the groan of the plane's twin engines as it swooped over her and Munroe's hiding place. It was so low she almost ducked as it came over them, then watched as the pilot cut the power and the little plane glided the last few yards. It looked like the carpet of steam rising from the beach cushioned the little plane as it gently touched down on the surface.

Once he'd slowed sufficiently, he swung the aircraft around and began taxiing back to the mid-point of the beach where Milton was waiting, then pulled to a stop, killed the engines, got out and hooked the door on a catch to keep it open. When Milton got close enough, she could see the pilot salute him. Pathetic. Milton styled himself as a military hero, but he was nothing of the sort. She knew he'd joined the Territorial Army as a teenager, but he hadn't even completed basic training before being asked to leave, apparently because his training officers were alarmed at some of the rhetoric he was espousing, even then. But clearly he promoted this ridiculous charade among his supporters. He was about two steps away from forcing them all to wear black shirts, she thought.

Think!

Milton boarded the little plane and then the pilot climbed back in himself and pulled the door shut behind him. The engines started up and, after a brief pause, the aircraft began edging forward. She knew, the moment it reached them, it would turn to face the wind and Milton would be gone forever. It was getting closer and closer – so close she could see the face of the pilot behind his controls, Milton sitting next to him up front. Behind them she could see the rest of the cockpit was taken up with a massive auxiliary fuel tank. So *that's* how this tiny plane had made it all the way out here.

The engines got louder and louder as the aircraft got nearer and nearer.

She was out of time.

Chapter 54

The plane was getting closer and closer. The pilot looked as if he was staring back at her through his aviator glasses. She could see the hateful face of Milton staring ahead with a smug grin on his face, and she felt a bolt of rage surge through her body. He was going to get away, he was going to kill again, and there wasn't a thing she could do about it.

The little plane was now just yards away from the end of the beach. She could see the pilot reach down, and then the right-hand engine suddenly ratcheted up in power as he used it to begin turning the plane ready for take-off.

Time up. Game over.

Her brain was whirring, her eyes darting left to right and up and down the shoreline. They fixed on the pile of old harpoons and whaling hooks on the concrete slipway that led up to the warehouse. Brewster had pointed them out to her when they'd first landed, explaining how the whalers had used them to hook into the animals and haul them up the slipway on chains anchored into big winches.

Could she . . . ?

She studied them, looking for one suitable for her purposes. The main winch in the centre looked rusted solid and too heavy anyway, but there were three other, smaller hooks – perhaps two feet long – connected to chains embedded into the concrete slipway. The ones Brewster had explained helped keep the carcass steady while they stripped its flesh.

Could it really work? She had no idea, but at this point she was willing to take the chance. She had to. She had nothing left to lose.

'For you, Drew,' she said in a barely audible whisper. Then, the instant the plane began to make its turn, she launched herself from her hiding place, through the open door, and sprinted towards the pile of junk, grabbing the hook she'd already selected for the task. She momentarily broke stride as she grabbed the handle, barely having time to be relieved that the chain wasn't so rusted up as to be stuck fast. She heard the engines increasing their tone as the pilot completed his turn and revved them ahead of take-off.

Her legs burned as she yanked the chain behind her. The plane was starting to move; she kicked up into a gear she didn't know she had, fuelled by the pain of losing Drew, Brewster, and everyone else this monster had killed and maimed. The whine of the engines went up another notch as the pilot gave it full power for take-off and, with one last, lung-busting burst of speed, Abbie pounded across the surface, then threw herself as hard as she could towards the back of the aircraft, throwing out her right arm as she did so. Time seemed to slow down and as she flew through the air and came to land on the black sand, she watched, eyes as wide as saucers, as the rusty metal hook grabbed onto the right rear wheel strut of the undercarriage.

She rolled out of the path of the rapidly unfurling chain as the plane continued down the beach, picking up speed all the way until it had just defied the constraints of gravity and lifted up off the ground. And at that moment, the chain ran out of slack.

The instant the chain went taut, the plane's acceleration was halted, and it was yanked right as the speed and lift it was generating were countered by an unexpected anchor. The right wheel strut was ripped off when the competing forces between the plane's forward motion and the chain collided, snapping a link at the winch end which caused the chain to whip back towards the hook. But the break came too late – the plane had lost the vital momentum needed to change the air pressure under its wings and, even though the pilot was fighting it, he was losing the battle. It veered off to the right, crunching back down hard on the black ash beach. Abbie watched, mesmerized, as the little plane bumped over the ground and headed straight for one of the giant rusty metal tanks that lined the top of the beach.

With a painful sound of tearing metal, it punctured through the hull of the huge tank, sparks flying as the propellers continued to turn, ripping through the metal of the tank as if it was paper, and flicking razor-sharp shards of rusty tin high up into the air before the fuselage itself collided with the structure.

Each slice of the props through the tank created a thousand tiny sparks and, within seconds, they combined with the remnants of the whale oil once stored there by the gallon. Now, with a ready supply of oxygen thanks to the gaping hole in the side of the structure, the oil ignited, just as the plane itself finally came to a stop, the front half now buried in the burning tank, its engines finally silenced at the centre of the inferno.

Chapter 55

Breathing hard, Abbie pulled herself to her feet and observed the destruction she'd wrought on the plane as the fire picked up in intensity. Her plan had extended no further than simply stopping the aircraft from taking off. She had no idea what she was going to do next. She looked back towards the warehouse and could just about make out the tiny, pale face of Munroe peeking out from their hiding place.

A noise coming from the plane grabbed her attention, and she saw the rear door being kicked out of its frame. It detached from the plane entirely and hit the beach with a clang.

And then she saw his face. Blood running down from a cut above his eye, but very much still alive, Milton hauled himself out of the wreck, rifle still slung around his body, and roared in anger as he staggered away from the fire.

He was scanning his surroundings in the half-light of the dusk when there was an almighty crack from above and a rumble from below. Up the mountain, Abbie could see another vent spewing hot gas from the volcano. Further up she saw a bright red line beginning to snake its way down the mountain. It was happening. The lava was coming for them. Endgame.

'*You!*' he spat.

Abbie's head snapped back in the direction of the plane. Milton was standing in front of it, the flames dancing and licking up behind him as he stared at her, hate in his eyes.

'Why aren't you dead?'

She was momentarily frozen to the spot but then he started to move. As he went to swing his rifle around to his chest, Abbie knew he was preparing to fire, and in the same instant, she ran.

She made for the nearest cover there was: another huge rusty oil tank to her right up the beach. She pumped her legs hard and heard three metallic pings in quick succession as he hit the tank with his first three shots.

She had to keep moving. She heard another two shots slam through the tank from the east side. He was circling around, which made her decision for her. She made another dash for the next tank, then saw there was a small hole at the bottom where it had rusted away and the black sand had leaked inside. She crawled through the hole and made her way to a similar, slightly wider opening on the other side, pulling herself out.

She ran to the next boiler and rested a moment on the other side, ducking her head down as she heard more bullets rain into the metal behind her.

In front of her was a mess of pipes, boilers, crates, and sheets of rusty tin that stretched for perhaps a hundred yards to the next big tank. Not perfect cover, but it would have to do. She took a breath and then set off, pounding along the ground, ducking and dodging around and between the decaying detritus of the whaling industry as Milton fired off round after round at her.

She took cover and a moment to breathe as she crouched behind a huge U-shaped pipe that had collapsed and lay abandoned in the black sand. But as she sat on her haunches, breathing hard and scanning her surroundings, she knew she couldn't simply keep running. She needed a plan. She needed to fight back. She needed a weapon. But where had he hidden the guns?

She'd been well trained in small arms handling, and she knew she was a good shot. If only she could actually get her hands on a rifle, she could turn the tide, get on the front foot and hunt rather than just evade. Again the tantalizing vision crossed her mind of him kneeling, vulnerable, beaten and terrified as she stood over him, her finger caressing the trigger . . . She felt electrified by the prospect – but she needed a gun to make it a reality.

Had she missed something at the beach house? Milton had been hiding in there before the helicopter arrived. Maybe he'd left one of his guns in there? She had to get in there to look. But between her and the building off to her left was open ground. She shook her head; it wasn't going to be easy but, if she was going to try it, she had to go now while he was making his way through the rusty mass of metal behind her.

Then there was another huge bang – this one wasn't natural, but came from the direction of the crashed plane, presumably as one of the fuel tanks had overheated and exploded.

She glanced back and saw Milton looking back towards the aircraft. This was her chance. She sprinted out from her hiding place. She was out in the open now, running as fast as she could across Milton's makeshift airstrip. There was no cover to protect her here – it was a desperate move, but she *needed* a gun. She needed to get back on the front foot, back on the offensive.

She ran hard and she ran fast, devouring the distance between her and the beach house, willing herself on.

But then she heard it. A crack in the night. A bullet – right past her left ear.

He was on to her, and he was close. The beach house was too far away. She wasn't going to make it. It was just too far and she was defenceless out here in the open.

Another crack, the whizz of another bullet. *Too close.*

She had no choice. She threw herself to the ground, landing hard on the black sand, feeling the pain in her ribs all over again.

She was grateful for the layer of steam wafting up from the harbour. She'd thought it creepy when she first landed, but now it would give her some level of cover. Now it might save her life.

She stayed still for a moment as she peeked up and took in her surroundings. She couldn't stay here. He was coming towards her – coming to kill her. But she wasn't close to anything that would offer her any kind of decent protection. There was no way she would be able to crawl to the beach house before he got to her. She looked back to the old tanks. Too far away – and anyway he was coming from that direction. She looked to the church, but that wasn't close enough either.

She glanced to her right down to the shore: nothing but open beach until the water. She swivelled round and looked behind her; perhaps if she could make it to the mountain path . . . ? But then she saw the lava lighting up the trail like a long neon sign, slowly making its way down the track with red-hot inevitability.

She was trapped.

Chapter 56

Munroe crouched down in his hiding place in the warehouse. He could hear gunfire out on the beach. He'd never heard a gunshot in his life until yesterday. He'd only seen it in the movies, and even that always made him flinch. But in the last twenty-four hours he'd heard a man tortured, seen dead bodies, watched a whole helicopter full of men die – and, worse than that, *so much worse than that*, he himself was now a killer.

With every shot he heard, a vision of Robertson flashed across his mind. The look of shock and confusion on the Marine's face as he fell over the railing atop the lighthouse was seared onto his brain. He'd watched the Marine fall the length of the lighthouse and on down the cliffs until the body had thumped and cracked against the jagged rocks below. Dead. He'd watched the waves toss the corpse around like a wild animal toying with its prey, until a bigger breaker washed over the rocks and sucked Robertson out to sea on its retreat. And then he was gone, lost in the surf and the black waves of the Southern Ocean.

Munroe shook his head, as if he might erase the memory from his brain like an Etch-a-Sketch drawing. He tried to ground himself in the present to avoid a panic attack: he felt the old warped wood of the window ledge he was gripping. He wriggled his toes in his boots and sucked in a deep breath. He tried to shut out the gunfire and focus on another sound – *any* other sound. In the breaks between shots, he could hear the wind whistling through the gaps in the roof and walls. Then the flapping of wings as one of the storm petrels nesting in the beams launched into flight – perhaps, like Munroe, spooked by the gunshots.

The firing stopped. He could hear the gentle lapping of the ocean. A moment later, he realized the sound of water was coming from *inside* the warehouse. He looked left towards the slipway, and noticed that the roof above him extended further to the left than the concrete surface. He stood from his crouching position and made his way across the space, climbing over the piles of old rotted rope, huge rusted buoys, hooks, harpoons, and massive boiling pots that were piled high and crammed into the warehouse.

As he climbed higher, he saw the building's roof and west wall extended out over the harbour for perhaps twenty metres alongside the slipway – presumably so the whalers were able to sail straight in with their latest catch? Whatever the reason, it didn't matter now: what did matter was what he saw on the other side of all the old kit rotting away and slowly being covered by decades of bird shit.

A boat.

Escape.

This was his way out of here.

He paused for a moment as the joyful prospect reverberated through his body, then he climbed back down the pile of junk and risked another peek out of the old window.

He could see no sign of Abbie, only the camouflaged figure of Milton stalking the beach with his gun raised. *Where was she?*

He remembered her words from when they'd been up at the lighthouse. '*If you find a way off the island don't wait for me. Get back to the ship and raise the alarm. If I haven't made it back by then, they can come and get me.'*

He closed his eyes as he thought it through, then opened them again and scanned the beach. Still there was no sign of her – only Milton, marching up the black ash.

Then his attention was grabbed by another bang piercing through the open air, and a flash of bright red as a column of lava shot up from another vent up on Mount Pond. This was followed by a second bang from off to his left – another steam explosion from the shore on the far side of the harbour.

He desperately searched the beach again but there was still no sign of her. He'd heard Milton shooting; perhaps she was already dead.

He took a deep breath, then clambered back over the junk pile and began untying the rope holding the boat in place. With the failing light and noise of the eruptions and explosions, he reckoned he could probably fire up the engine and be halfway to Neptune's Bellows before Milton even spotted him.

He climbed into the boat and examined the engine, soon finding the ignition and starting it up. He looked out onto the water to the gap in the rock that led out of the harbour to freedom. Safety.

'If you find a way off the island don't wait for me.'

He set his jaw and took a deep breath. His mind was made up.

Chapter 57

Abbie had the harbour to her left, lava flow dead ahead, a maniac with a gun coming towards her from the rear, and nothing but open ground between her and the closest building. She had nowhere to go, nowhere to hide.

There was only one thing anywhere near her that might offer some cover: the graveyard.

She began crawling along the black sand towards the rows of little wooden crosses in the ground. But they were not her target. Instead she headed for the stone obelisk, the one Brewster had told her was a monument to ten poor Norwegians who'd drowned out in the open sea when their whaling ship went down.

She pulled and heaved and dragged herself through the mist and steam blanket that covered the beach, keeping as low as possible to try to remain out of sight as Milton continued letting off potshots at where she'd gone down under fire. She wondered if he thought he'd hit her? If so, that might buy her a little time as he went to investigate.

She reached the stone and crawled around to the side opposite to Milton, then flipped onto her front and risked a look in his direction. He was marching towards the spot where she'd dropped to the ground.

'Come out, come out, wherever you are,' he called in a mocking, sing-song voice.

She stayed perfectly still and watched him as he scanned his surroundings. He continued to walk on the line she'd been on, heading for the beach house. Perhaps if he went back inside, she could make a run for it. But to where? She still needed a gun. Running and hiding again would only delay the inevitable.

She watched Milton reach the hut. At least if he went inside and searched for her there, it would give her a little time to think of something.

But he didn't. He stopped at the door, turned on his heels and began walking in her direction. Her heart dropped as her pulse quickened. She assessed her options. Could she reason with him? She suspected not, given his current state of mind.

Could she run? She glanced around, but nothing had changed about her position. She was simply too far away from any other cover. But she had to do *something*. He was coming right at her, even if he didn't know for sure she was there.

If she couldn't run, couldn't escape, maybe she could find somewhere to hide, just long enough for him to pass. *But where?*

An idea popped into her brain. And as it did, it triggered panic deep within her. She felt dizzy and physically sick at the very idea. *Please not that. Anything but that.*

But even as she desperately searched for an alternative, she could hear the crunch of his footsteps getting closer.

She was out of time. She knew she had no choice.

She took a deep breath and tried to steel herself for what lay ahead. She could already feel her heart rate going up yet another notch, and a tightness clutching at her chest as her body was gripped by anxiety. She knew she had to fight through it.

She took one last look through the mist at Milton, who was still heading in her direction, then dropped back down onto her belly and began to crawl, pulling herself across the sand until she reached her destination.

The makeshift cross marked the spot. The inscription was illuminated by the red glow of the lava flow coming down the mountain:

A. Błaszczykowski-Fitzroy

1/9/2026

She took another breath and slid into the open hole. Then, starting at her feet, she began hastily scooping the black sand over herself.

If she was going to survive, she was going to have to bury herself alive in her own grave.

Chapter 58

Milton stopped momentarily and listened. She'd gone to ground, but had he hit her with that last shot? He paused and waited for cries of pain, but could hear nothing. He resumed his march, scanning the beach in front of him, his hands gripping the gun tightly.

Had she somehow sneaked back past him? He slowly turned around and looked down the beach. Something caught his eye. *Movement.*

He brought his gun up and narrowed his eyes to try to see better in the fading light. Someone was moving in the old warehouse. But he knew it couldn't be the girl. It was too far away – there was no way she could have got past him and all the way down the beach in the few seconds since she'd disappeared from view.

That meant that volcano guy must still be running around as well. So Robertson had even failed on that front, despite all the shooting he'd heard from the lighthouse. What a disappointment he'd proved to be in the end.

He squinted through the gloom and watched the pale, skinny form through the cracked windows of the warehouse. He could see him clambering around inside. *What was he up to?* He instinctively took a step forward, ready to deal with this latest irritant, and then stopped himself. *No.* He was no threat. A minor inconvenience. He could be dealt with later. Milton would not be distracted. This stupid fucking girl had ruined everything: downed his plane, killed his pilot and damn near killed him. His months – years – of planning would be wasted. Everything had been so carefully coordinated, so meticulously laid out. Every step of it designed for maximum impact, every stage more glorious than the last. He seethed with rage. This was not how it was supposed to play out. God had spoken to him! Why would the Lord let this happen?

Perhaps he was being tested? Maybe the good Lord wanted to see how committed Milton really was, just like Milton himself had tested Robertson when it came to the moment of his escape. If so, Milton would not fail the test. Not now. Not after he'd come this far.

As he always did when he was uncertain, he thought back to his Bible. He remembered James, chapter one, verse twelve, and recited it aloud to himself as he stood out there on the beach. 'Blessed is the man who remains steadfast under trial, for when he has stood the test he will receive the crown of life, which God has promised to those who love him.'

He knew God loved him. He *would* remain steadfast under this trial, and the crown of life would be his. Of that he had no doubt.

The girl had ruined his escape. She had to pay for that. He would *make* her pay. And then he would find a way out. His glorious Second Coming could still happen. It could all still happen. It *would* all still happen.

He turned away from the warehouse, back in the direction he'd last seen her. Perhaps he *had* clipped her? If so, he would go and finish the job. If not, he would hunt her down like a rat. *Everything else could wait*, he thought as he resumed his march through the mist.

Chapter 59

Per mare, per terram. Per mare, per terram, Abbie silently chanted as she tried to keep her panic at bay. With each scoop of dead, black earth she moved over her body, the panic increased and another little part of her disappeared as she buried herself in the grave. It was as if she was erasing herself from the world. She felt like the picture Marty McFly carries with him in *Back to the Future,* in which he and his siblings gradually fade away.

She hurried to pull the sand over her as Milton got closer and closer. She knew he still hadn't seen her – he was still taunting her, trying to get her to reveal herself.

'You can't hide from me forever,' he called. 'I'll find you. And then I'll make you pay. As Matthew says, seek, and ye shall find . . .'

She scooped more and more grit on top of her body, until her legs, torso and her left arm were all entombed. She fought against the rising panic as her mouth dried up and her heart rate got faster and faster when she began what she knew would be the hardest part.

She laid her head right back and pulled handful after handful of dirt over her face, fighting the overwhelming urge to shake it all off and free herself from this living nightmare.

Still he got closer.

She furiously pulled more and more dirt until it covered her mouth and nose, sucking in a final long deep breath before she did so, and then she closed her eyes and covered the last part of her face. She had to stifle a scream as she took away her own vision.

Per mare, per terram. Per mare, per terram.

She smoothed over the dirt as best as she could, and then, figuring she was out of time, she burrowed her right arm under the dirt next to her.

She knew it was far from a perfect job but, in this dying light, with the steam rolling over the beach and with blood already running down his face, she counted on the fact it didn't have to be. It only had to be good enough for a few moments – just enough time for him to pass by without seeing her. She hoped he would presume she'd scrambled up into the church or one of the other old buildings. If it didn't work in a few minutes, she'd suffocate anyway.

That thought sent another wave of panic rising through her body. She felt faint, dizzy. Her mouth was dryer than sandpaper, but she didn't dare try to swallow, lest even that tiny movement might give her away.

Per mare, per terram.

The ground beneath her was warm and getting warmer. The thermal heat was getting more intense as the volcano below continued to stir from its long slumber. She imagined the lava underground bubbling and boiling. It was as if hell itself was located beneath this very island and was threatening to surge up into the realm of the mortal.

She was already in hell, of course – her own personal version of it. She fought hard to quell the thought and not dwell on the reality of her situation. Every millisecond she remained – trapped and immobile under the dirt in a grave with her name on it – was the purest form of torture, as if the devil himself had built this place, dug this grave for her, and then contrived for her to willingly lie down and bury herself in it before she was even dead.

The claustrophobic's greatest fear is being trapped and unable to escape or move, and Abbie was now in that exact scenario. She was desperate to shake off the dirt from this godforsaken island and free herself, but she knew she'd be dead the moment she did so. To stay alive, she had to stay dead and buried.

Per mare, per terram. Per mare, per terram.

She fell back in time. She was nine years old again on Fistral Beach. Trapped under a mountain of sand and certain she was going to die. She tried to distract herself as she lay, wondering how long she could keep this up before she ran out of air, or the panic overwhelmed her.

Inevitably, she thought of Drew. Her wonderful Drew. She silently prayed for him to give her the strength to block out her panic, somehow section it off so she could remain perfectly still and avoid detection. But even as she did, she suddenly saw an image of his body, buried in *his* grave, exactly like she was. Dead and buried and rotting away. Was her fate to be the same as his? Would Milton notice the grave which had been empty was now occupied, or would the darkness and the steam that wafted over the beach obscure his view? Would her deliberately crawling into an open grave simply be the last thing he was expecting?

She had no way of knowing. She only had hope.

But hope of what? Her hiding place would save her for – at best – a few minutes. She'd be forced to free herself soon. Worst-case scenario, he'd simply be waiting for her, dispatch her with a shot of his rifle and then she'd slump back into place in her grave. How neat.

Best case, he'd have walked on past her, continuing his search elsewhere. But then what? What was she going to do then? He was armed, she wasn't. And she couldn't simply run away – there was Munroe to consider. She couldn't just leave him. But even if she wanted to run, how could she? The volcano was about to erupt and Milton himself had sunk the boat that would have been their way off the island. The plane was a wreck, as was the helicopter.

The hope was slipping away by the minute.

Then she could feel movement. She tensed up as she heard his boots crunching on the ash beach above her. She held her body as still as she could and squeezed her eyes shut.

Crunch, crunch, crunch.

He must be barely yards away now.

The sand was leaking into her mouth but she didn't dare make a move. She pictured him standing over her, just waiting for her to give in and pull herself from the ground. *No,* she would *not* give in, she decided. She thought again of Drew – of his dedication, his mental strength and all he had achieved as a Marine. She summoned that energy, that resolve and resilience as she lay in the ash, living out her very worst nightmare.

Crunch, crunch, crunch.

He was moving again.

Crunch, crunch, crunch.

The noise was getting a little fainter, the movement less pronounced. *He was walking away!* But still she didn't dare move.

She clenched her jaw and tried to think of something to distract her from the unbearable horror of being so closed in. *Where had he hidden those bloody guns?* She knew Milton and Robertson had stripped the other Marines of their weapons, and had grabbed the two Ridley had brought with him. Two of those guns were now sinking to the bottom of the sea along with Robertson's body out by the lighthouse.

Milton had at least one of the others. That left possibly seven unaccounted for. But where else could Milton and Robertson have stashed them? She thought back to when she and Munroe had watched them collecting up all the rusty junk.

Then she remembered their stealthy run from the prison right along this very beach to the hut, ducking behind the church and then the oil tanks and boilers as they slipped past the prisoner and his accomplice working in the dusk. Her train of thought screeched to a halt.

That's it.

She knew exactly where the guns were.

Chapter 60

She was going to pass out. She felt oddly proud of herself at the realization that lack of oxygen was going to get her before she gave in to panic. A small, Pyrrhic victory. But she had no time to celebrate. She had to take in some air, or she would indeed die right here in her grave.

As gingerly as she could, she began to wriggle her right arm. She pulled it backwards and bent it at the elbow as she shook off the sand that covered it. Once her arm was free, she slid it up to her face and cleared handfuls of dirt from around her mouth until she had an air hole. She sucked in the fresh air her brain so badly needed and felt clarity returning as the oxygen made its way around her system.

She braced herself for a gunshot – perhaps her movements had given her away – but after ten, twenty, thirty, forty seconds, none came.

She risked more movement and began scooping off the dirt from around her eyes. Still no gunshot. She cleared her face as quietly as she could and then blinked her eyes open. They stung from the dirt and grit, but she tried to ignore that as she swivelled her eyes around to check her surroundings.

She was relieved to find Milton wasn't standing over her ready to fire.

After waiting another minute or two, she began the next phase of bringing herself back from the dead, scooping and shaking off the ash and dirt she'd buried herself in, gradually revealing more and more of her body as she emerged from the grave. The faded photograph was being restored, pixel by pixel.

Once she was free of the black ash, she pulled herself out of the hole in a movement that felt as if she was being reborn. She'd come back to life; she was *out*. It was utterly joyous. She wanted to shout from the rooftops and run and dance and jump to revel in her regained freedom. But as she pulled herself out, she scanned her surroundings and was brought straight back down to earth. There he was. Milton. Probably a hundred metres away now and walking in the other direction, back up the beach. Her ruse had apparently worked. At least for now.

She dropped back down to the ground to keep out of sight in case he should turn around, and crawled past her grave marker to the one next to it – the one marked for Ridley, which he had never occupied.

She knew there was no body buried under the sand here; she was banking on something else entirely. She remembered back to when she and Munroe had sneaked along the length of the beach. Milton and Robertson had been digging.

She began scooping the sand away until she saw a flash of dull metal against the black earth.

They hadn't been digging anything up at all. They'd been burying. Burying the guns.

With a triumphant yank, she pulled the rifle she'd found from the ground and dusted it off. She looked back up to where Milton had been. He'd stopped and was casting his gaze far and wide, still looking for her – and no doubt baffled as to how she'd got past him.

She confirmed the rifle contained ammunition, then pulled

it up to her chest and crawled along the dirt, back past her grave to the stone monument. She came up to her knees, brought the gun up to a firing position and then swivelled around the side of the stone.

There he was.

She gripped the rifle tightly and brought the sights up to her eye.

'Come out!' he roared. 'Come out and face me!'

She briefly considered the fact that she'd never actually shot a rifle at another human being before. She remembered Munroe's reaction when he'd killed Robertson up at the lighthouse. Would she go into shock like he had?

'Come out and show yourself!' he bellowed again.

He was going to turn in her direction at any moment. She curled her finger around the trigger and prepared to fire.

Chapter 61

Abbie held the rifle steady, just as she'd been trained to do, and stared down the sights with her right eye.

Milton still hadn't spotted her.

She took a breath and squeezed the trigger.

The rifle violently kicked back and she cushioned the blow against her shoulder.

She saw Milton recoil. She reckoned she must have just grazed his right arm.

He whirled around in a fury and began firing his gun in any and every direction. She crouched down behind the stone monument as he fired off round after furious round. There was nothing targeted, surgical or precise about what he was doing. He was a toddler lashing out. A child furious that he was being thwarted. He simply fired his gun again and again and again.

Abbie held her position. She prepared to turn and fire again.

Round after round went off, and then the firing stopped. Suddenly she could hear him roaring in anger and frustration. Was he out of ammunition?

She waited another moment and then peeked around the corner of the monument, all the while keeping aim on Milton. She did so just in time to see him let out another roar as he pulled the rifle strap up and over his head and then threw the weapon away in a fury. A little boy having a tantrum about his broken toy.

She stood up, keeping her aim on him as she did so.

'Stay where you are,' she shouted as she held her rifle steady.

He looked up and saw her position behind the obelisk. 'Hiding behind dead men,' he shouted back. 'How heroic.'

She ignored his taunt. 'Put your hands behind your head.'

He did as he was told.

She had him. She had him right in her sights, gun raised. He was out of ammunition and out of ideas. This was it. This was the moment she'd dreamed of, fantasized about. She took a deep breath and raised the sight to her eye. It would all be over in a few seconds. *She would have her revenge.*

'Abbie!'

She could hear someone shouting her name. Munroe.

She turned towards the source of the noise and saw the Scot racing towards her across the beach. 'Abbie! I found it!'

It was all Milton needed.

'I found it!'

Abbie shook her head and turned back to Milton, but he'd seen his chance and taken it, ducking down out of sight.

Abbie quickly scanned her field of vision, but somehow he'd slipped away. *Fuck.*

Munroe arrived panting. 'Didn't you hear me shouting?'

'For fuck's sake! You let him get away!'

Abbie resumed her visual search but there was no sign of him. It was getting darker, and with the mist and now the smoke from the plane and tank fires blowing across the beach, there wasn't much visibility. The roles of hunter and hunted had been reversed.

Munroe was pulling at her jacket. 'We have to go *now!* Believe me, it's about to blow. It's happening. The big one.'

She shook her head. 'I lost him . . .'

'It doesn't matter,' he said. 'I found a boat tied up in the warehouse. We can get out of here!'

Abbie didn't move; she simply gripped her gun tighter.

'Come on!' Munroe pleaded.

Abbie clenched her jaw. 'No. Not yet. I'm going to finish this.'

Munroe shook his head in disbelief. 'Do you not see that?' He pointed up at the lava that was already flowing down the mountainside towards the beach – towards them. 'That is coming to kill us.'

As if to make his point for him, there was another huge crack from the opposite shoreline and steam and mud and rock were thrust up hundreds of metres into the air.

'Come on!' Munroe pleaded. 'Let's go!'

He grabbed her by the arm but she pulled away. 'Not yet,' she said. 'Not yet.'

'You're going after him? Why? He'll be dead soon enough!'

'I have to,' she said grimly. 'For Drew,' she added, as she left him standing on the beach and set off in pursuit.

'Who's Drew?' Munroe called after her.

She didn't respond.

'But he could be anywhere!' he shouted in protest.

'I know exactly where he is,' Abbie muttered under her breath as she marched away.

Chapter 62

Abbie was aware she had to be careful – the cache of weapons was in the grave behind her, so she knew he hadn't been back there to get another gun. But she didn't know if he'd hidden one somewhere else earlier. It was possible.

She crunched up the beach with her weapon in her hands and one goal in her mind. Finally, she would put an end to this monster. Destroy him like he'd destroyed her.

She walked purposefully away from the graveyard. Some thirty-five men were buried here, she was about to add one more to their number.

She soon reached her destination: the derelict building that had once been the church.

She knew Milton wouldn't have been able to resist. The self-styled 'military padre' would surely seek sanctuary on holy ground.

The tremors had shaken yet more of the tin roof sheets free, opening the entire building out to the elements. The old wooden door at the entrance was wedged open, though that didn't mean much. The building itself was in a sorry state: all the windows had long since blown in and most of the roof had collapsed, with the walls soon to follow by the look of them – though somehow the little spire was still standing, with its sad little cross hanging down limply, held on by one remaining defiant screw.

She made her way 'inside' and began walking slowly up the aisle.

For a moment she was transported back to five years earlier. The last time she'd set foot in a church. Her wedding day.

Initially she hadn't been that keen on a church wedding, but Drew was, so she had gone with it; she knew it would make her mum happy as well. And on the day, she was glad she had. She'd never really imagined that type of thing for herself, but as she got out of the car and stood at the door with her dad linking his arm with hers, she'd been glad of the setting. The ancient stone walls and solid oak door lent the occasion a permanence she relished – it was exactly how she felt about her relationship with Drew. This was forever, she was certain of that.

She'd never been a 'dress' kind of girl either, but she'd made an exception that day. The fact that she so rarely wore one actually made it feel all the more special.

She blinked as she slowly made her way past rows of pews. Suddenly it wasn't a rifle in her hands, but a bouquet of flowers. She could feel her dad's arm linked with hers, holding her tightly. *Her father's shadow.* They'd shared a moment together as they stood outside the church waiting to go in, her dad sniffing back the tears as Abbie dabbed her eyes to try to stop her make-up running.

She felt the eyes of her friends and family on her as they walked towards the altar. Her cousin's little baby boy was crying somewhere at the back, people were holding up their phones and taking photographs of her. She blocked it all out, fixed smile on her face as she got closer to Drew. He looked a little stunned – he wasn't used to seeing her in a dress, after all – but her heart flooded to overflowing as she neared him. Her dad had given her a kiss and she'd squeezed his hand tightly before he stepped away and sat down next to her mum in the front row.

Abbie and Drew shared a smile. 'I love you,' he mouthed silently, as the minister began the service.

She blinked again. She was back in the room. Drew wasn't here. But his murderer was.

'Show yourself, Milton,' Abbie shouted. 'Come out and show yourself. I know you're here.'

She heard another huge crack, and through the open roof could see trails of lava being hurled up high into the dark skies above. The eruption had begun.

'I said show yourself!' she shouted.

'Ask, and it shall be given you,' he said. He stood up slowly, looking down at her from the wooden pulpit off to the left of the altar, which had been cracked in half, perhaps by a falling roof beam, at some point in the past.

She stopped and gripped her weapon tightly. She recognized the line as one from the book of Matthew.

'You really think God is on your side?' she asked.

'God is always on the side of the righteous man.'

Righteous?! *How dare he.*

'Do you even believe? I mean do you *really* even believe in God? Or is that just another con?'

'My faith is what's given me purpose, kept me alive.'

'Not for much longer,' she said, raising her gun.

'So what now? You going to shoot an unarmed man? A man of God? And in a church, no less? You'll go to hell for that.'

There was another blast as yet more lava was forced high up into the air from the mountainside above. Ash was raining down on them, and the stench of burning aviation fuel and smoke from the aeroplane fire filled the nostrils and the eyes. A new river of lava coming down the mountain from the bank to the north illumined the scene as it flowed towards them, slowly devouring everything in its path and getting closer and closer to the church itself.

'Look around you, Milton – we're already there.'

She got a good look at him in the red glow of the lava as he stood in the pulpit. A gash above his left eye was seeping blood down over his face.

'You think this is hell?' He shook his head. 'I think Jude had it right. "Hell is a prison of everlasting chains from which there is no hope of release." That's hell,' he said. 'That's what my life has been this past four years. A place of excruciating misery "where the worm does not die, and the fire is not quenched." Mark, chapter nine, verse forty-eight,' he added.

'Jesus called it the place of final judgement,' Abbie said. 'I'd say that's pretty accurate, given the situation,' she added, keeping her gun trained on him.

'Very good,' he smiled approvingly. 'You know your Bible. "Then he will say to those on his left, 'Depart from me, you who are cursed, into the eternal fire prepared for the devil and his angels." Matthew, twenty-five, forty-one.'

Abbie kept her gun up.

'And you're the one who's going to judge me, are you?' he said.

'Someone has to. And I don't trust God to get the job done.'

'"Judge not, that ye be not judged".'

She shook her head. She was getting tired of him quoting scripture at her. 'Before I do, I want you to answer me one thing.'

'So now you want something from me?'

'How did you know I was coming here?'

He looked confused, but said, 'The eyes of the Lord are everywhere, keeping watch on the wicked and the good.'

'Give it a rest, I want to know how you knew I'd be here.' She waved the gun at him. 'I mean it.'

'What do you mean?'

'Out there.' She nodded to her left in the direction of the cemetery. 'The grave you dug. It had my name on it. And today's date.'

He frowned. 'What's your name?'

She shook her head. 'You *know* my name!' she shouted in frustration. 'I'm Abbie Błaszczykowski-Fitzroy.'

His right eyebrow raised to what was left of the roof.

And then he began to laugh.

Chapter 63

Earlier that morning

Milton knelt on the beach over a wooden cross he'd fashioned from two bits of wood that had once been part of the old BAS hut. He held a paintbrush in his hand and was carefully dabbing at the wood as he added the inscription. Ridley's had already been completed and he was now halfway through the second. He dipped his brush back into the tin of white emulsion that Robertson had found for him in the storeroom of the beach house. Neither the paint nor the brush – one more suited to painting cornices and skirting boards than its current purpose – were ideal, but Milton was content to make do with what he had. The effect would be sufficient.

'I still don't get the point of this,' Robertson said from over his shoulder.

Milton looked up at his new accomplice. The young Marine – was he still a Marine, Milton pondered, after what he'd done in the past few hours? – was sweating, his pale face clammy and glistening in the morning sun.

'It's fucking hard work, this.'

Milton sighed inwardly. He found it absolutely insulting that he had to explain himself to this imbecile, but for now he needed him, so he indulged his accomplice.

'Remember Ecclesiastes two, twenty-four: "There is nothing better for a man, than that he should eat and drink, and that he should make his soul enjoy good in his labour."'

Robertson looked back at him, his face a picture of gormless confusion.

Where do they find these idiots? Milton wondered. 'It means hard work is good for the soul.'

'I'd rather have something to eat and drink,' Robertson replied.

'Oh you will,' Milton smiled. 'We shall soon be in the land of milk and honey, my friend.'

'Sod the milk and honey, I want a pint and a burger. Five months I've been here without a single beer. Fuckin' joke.'

'We'll get you one soon, don't worry. In the meantime, if you wouldn't mind . . .' Milton nodded at the half-dug grave.

Robertson returned to his work, and then Milton to his.

'Who are these people anyway?'

'Ridley is the bastard that stuck me here. Never did find out exactly which government department he works for. One of the security services, anyway. Stuck me here and loved every minute of it. The little shit probably got a couple of promotions out of it as well. Smug bastard.'

'And why are we digging his grave?'

'You know what they – he – did to me. Brought me here, locked me up and threw away the key. Told the world I was dead. Never given a trial. Nothing. Just left me here to rot. Scrubbed me from the face of the earth. He tried to bury me alive here. But now, when we get off this island, I shall be reborn. Just like Jesus Christ himself I shall be risen again. My second coming.'

Milton closed his eyes. He saw himself back on his Telegram channel – no, that wasn't big enough. Back in front of a crowd. A huge swathe of his supporters cheering and chanting his name – that was better. He saw himself on a stage address-ing them. Whipping them up into a cauldron of fury and energy and hate. He would bring the microphone up to his lips and wait for the chants to die down. Then he would quote scripture. He already knew the very line he would use. Acts, chapter two, verse twenty-four. 'God raised Him from the dead, releasing Him from the agony of death, because it was impossible for Him to be held in its clutches.'

It was impossible for him to be held in its clutches. Milton smiled at that. Death couldn't hold him. Nothing could. He would be risen again. It was almost too perfect.

The impact of it all would be beyond belief. The British gov-ernment had lied, had held him in secret without trial. And soon the whole world would know. He would be back from the dead. He hated Ridley and the rest of them for what they'd done to him, but he had to hand it to them: they'd given him a far better nar-rative than he could ever have spun for himself. He would seem super-human. God-like. It would give him a status, a mythology that would go far beyond anything he'd ever created for himself. It was glorious.

And even better than that, their lies would be exposed. Every-one suspected their government lied to them, but perhaps not on this scale. But he would be the living, breathing proof. And he would do everything he could to exploit that to the fullest poss-ible extent. He would cultivate that mistrust like a farmer would a particularly fertile field. Everything they said would be under-mined. Every slick politician in a grey suit would be mistrusted even more. He would stir up his followers into a frenzy like never before. He was almost frightened at the thought of the power he would hold. What would he do with it, he wondered. Anything he liked, probably.

And with his biggest attack yet timed to coincide with his

rebirth, the effect would be even more potent. The West – the *world* – would tremble at his power.

'They tried to bury me on this island. They didn't know I was the seed,' he said, more to himself than Robertson, who had stopped digging again. 'Ridley tried to bury me here, but now it's my time. Now it's time for my revenge. And I shall bury him.'

'And you're sure he's going to come? I don't see how.'

'Oh he'll come, believe me,' he said in a low voice. 'I know him – he won't be able to resist it. He never thought he'd have to worry about me again. But here I am. And this time, I'll be waiting for him.'

'Turner I get,' Robertson said, nodding at the one fresh grave already occupied by the base commander. 'But who is the other one for?'

Milton added the final letters to the cross and held it up for Robertson to see it.

The young Marine narrowed his eyes as he tried to read it. 'Blazcry . . . Blazyk . . . Blaz . . . who the hell is that?'

Milton seethed with rage at the memory. 'That is the bastard who caught me. Major Andrew Błaszczykowski-Fitzroy.'

Robertson looked confused. 'But I thought he died the night they caught you?'

Milton nodded. 'He did. I shot him twice in the head at point-blank range.'

'So what's this for?' he asked, nodding at the grave as Milton dug down and planted the cross he'd made at the head.

Milton stood up and brushed his hands together to remove the dirt as he looked down at it with disdain. 'I may have killed him that night, but he still won. He caught me. Helped put me here. But now, today, is the time I finally get out of here. Out of that cell. Out of my head. Away from having nothing to do but sit and think of getting my revenge on him. On all of them.' He looked up at Robertson. 'Yes, I may've killed him that night. But today is the day I finally bury that bastard.'

'But who's actually going in it?'

Milton shook his head, the concept of symbolism apparently entirely lost on Robertson. 'It doesn't matter,' he replied. 'Whoever Ridley brings with him. They all represent the same thing. Turner, Ridley and the Pole. My "unholy trinity" of captors. When these three graves are full, then I will have my revenge. Then I will have closure.'

They looked up in unison as they heard the buzz of an engine in the distance. A boat, coming through Neptune's Bellows.

'Come on,' Milton said, 'into position. And let's turn the alarm back on. We may need the sound to cover us.'

'What time is the plane arriving?' Robertson asked as he shovelled the last few loads of dirt to the side of the grave and then followed Milton down to the jetty.

'Should be here about five,' he said. 'That little crate doesn't have much of a top speed, but it's the only thing small enough to land here.'

The Marine ducked inside the beach house and started up the alarm before the two of them made for the old warehouse next to the concrete slipway.

Secreted in the building, they watched as the boat arrived carrying two people in dark blue Royal Navy uniforms.

'Is that him?' Robertson asked.

Milton shook his head. 'No.'

'So what now? I thought you said he'd definitely come?'

'He will. I know he will.'

'So what do we do now?'

Milton thought for a moment. 'We make sure these two, whoever they are, don't leave. And then we wait.'

'Wait?'

'For Ridley.'

'For how long?'

'For as long as it takes. I've waited four years. I'll wait another few hours if I have to. Another day, a week – another year if that's what it comes to. We wait for as long as it takes.'

He took another look out the window and watched the visitors making their way down the jetty towards the beach house.

'Come on,' he said. 'If they leave it long enough, we'll grab their boat, and then go and cut the power. That should slow them down a bit.'

Chapter 64

'That grave wasn't for you,' Milton smiled down at Abbie from his position up in the pulpit. 'What was he – brother?'

She stared back at him and clenched her jaw as she saw Drew. She felt him at her side in his wedding suit, a goofy grin plastered across his face as it dawned on her: the 'A' on the grave wasn't for 'Abbie'. It was 'Andrew'. That just made it worse – he never used 'Andrew'. He hated it. Not even his mum had called him that. It was always 'Drew'.

'No,' said Milton. 'Husband.' He smiled again. 'That's right, isn't it? He was your husband.'

A. Błaszczykowski-Fitzroy. It had been Drew's idea that they combine their surnames, and he was happy for hers to be first in line. 'We'll be the only two people in the world with that name,' he'd smiled, and she'd fallen even harder for him at that exact moment.

Abbie burned with rage at Milton. 'This is for him,' she said as she raised her gun and took aim.

He laughed. 'You think you've won? You think I die and this all goes away? You think if you kill me, the pain will leave you?'

She shook her head. 'I'll never be rid of this pain,' she shouted back. 'But the world can be rid of you.'

There was a screech of metal followed by a snapping of

329

timbers as the northeast corner of the wall collapsed, crushed by the force and weight of the lava flowing down the mountain. The ancient beams in its path caught light as they were overwhelmed by the thousand-degree temperatures of the molten liquid.

Abbie could feel the heat radiating from the flow, and was forced to take a step back as the slow-moving river began collecting pews and tin and wood from the walls of the church on its journey. She knew it wouldn't stop until it reached the sea. The lava was slicing through the remains of the building like a butcher's knife – just like it had in 1969 with the Biscoe hut.

She heard a noise behind her and glanced around briefly to see Munroe enter the church.

She ignored him and returned to her task. She still had time, and raised her gun once again.

'Do it!' Milton yelled. 'Do it! Kill me! Martyr me! I can see now: *this* was the Lord's plan for me! And you shall be my Pontius Pilate. In death I shall become even more powerful than in life. My work will continue in my name.'

He stood with this chest puffed out, spread his arms out wide to his sides and began reciting the Lord's Prayer.

'Our Father, who art in Heaven, hallowed be thy name . . .'

Abbie gritted her teeth and tried not to be distracted by his grandstanding. All this Christian business, all the Bible quotations, she saw it for what it was: just a cloak he wrapped himself in to justify his shockingly violent and evil deeds. Even if he did believe, he was nothing but a murderer, and she saw now he wanted nothing more than to be shot down by her – killed by the state.

He was such an egotist she knew now he would see that as the perfect ending to his story. If he couldn't escape, couldn't 'rise from the dead like our Lord himself' as he'd put it earlier, he wanted to be a martyr. Be in death what he couldn't be in life. She felt the red notebook in her pocket. *Because his legacy would be the dreadful attacks he'd planned. Project Reichstag.* She knew his supporters – the rump of the Cross of St George's terror group that was still active – would spread the message far and wide about his imprisonment on this island. The attacks would all be done in his name. To his pathetic supporters he would become immortal. It could spark a new wave of hate and violence.

'. . . Thy kingdom come, thy will be done, on earth as it is in heaven . . .'

He had his hands clasped in prayer, his eyes shut and his face raised to the night sky above.

'Give us this day our daily bread and forgive us our trespasses . . .'

She saw that death wouldn't hurt him. To pull the trigger would be to give him exactly what he wanted, to play into his plan yet again. Not to mention Ridley's plan for her.

'As we forgive those who trespass against us . . .'

She blinked and pulled her eye from the sight and instead looked directly up at him.

'And lead us not into temptation, but deliver us from evil . . .'

She lowered the gun.

'For thine is the Kingdom, the power and the glor—' He stopped mid-word and looked down at her.

She was forced to take another step back as the raging heat from the lava came closer and closer. It had reached the bottom of the pulpit now, the wooden steps bursting into flame as another part of the north wall behind him collapsed and smashed down onto the rotten altar, crushing it before it was swept along with the lava flow.

'What's the matter – lost your bottle?' he called out to her.

'You don't deserve to live, but that doesn't mean I'm going to kill you,' she replied. 'He didn't kill you when he had the chance, and I won't either. That's not my job. That's not what I do.' She

331

would not allow herself to be manipulated. Not by Ridley and not by Milton.

'Weak! Just like your pathetic husband,' he shouted, his holy facade cracking under the heat. 'You think this somehow means you win?' he asked. 'You kill me, or you leave me to die; either way it won't change a thing.' He smiled again as the flames began licking up around his feet. 'It's far too late for that. You've got no idea what's about to happen. No idea at all. Like Mulciber, I'm about to unleash Pandemonium itself.'

Abbie couldn't understand how he was standing the heat as the lava surrounded him and the flames licked higher, claiming more and more of his pulpit.

Then she felt another rumble coming from deep underground. This time the south wall collapsed in its entirety and two more roof beams caved in. Up to now the volcano had apparently only been flirting, but she felt the real eruption was now just moments away.

Still Milton stood defiant in his flaming pulpit, his arms once again outstretched to his sides as he stared down at her.

She felt a tug on her sleeve. Munroe.

'We've got to go – this is *it*. The place is gonna blow!'

She wrestled free of his grip and turned back to Milton. He was still smiling that smug smile from up in the pulpit, sweat beading on his brow as the heat finally began to get to him.

She locked her eyes with his as she slowly reached into her jacket pocket and pulled out the red notebook she'd found in his cell. With her feet firmly planted, she raised it in her right hand – never taking her eyes off him as she held it aloft defiantly.

'"Be my guide, O Lord, in the ways of your righteousness, because of those who are against me; make your way straight before my face", she recited at the top of her voice.

It only took a moment before she saw a flicker of recognition flash across his eyes. A split second later, the smile ran away from his face and his arms dropped back down to his sides as his whole being seemed to slump.

She narrowed her eyes as she held the book up triumphantly and let out a long, deep, cathartic breath as she watched his defeated form.

In that instant she could see he was beaten. Utterly crushed. The only thing he'd held onto all the time he'd been imprisoned would come to nothing. His life's work ruined. The theatrical swagger he'd had just moments ago had withered and died. Now he was just a pathetic, hate-filled little man.

He roared in frustration and fury as the pulpit finally began to collapse beneath him as the lava and fire consumed it.

Abbie revelled in the knowledge that – thanks to the information she'd found – none of his horrific plans would come to fruition. She let the feeling wash over her, and as she did so she felt four years of pain and anger and fury and hatred flow through her like the lava that was engulfing him. It was like a pressure valve had been released and the flood of hurt and anguish and grief and fear and loathing that had been building up inside her mind and her heart suddenly had an outlet.

She'd thought for years she wanted nothing more than to kill that evil bastard, but this – this was *so* much better. This hurt him in a way killing him never could.

The flames were getting higher, the lava was getting hotter and the very ground beneath her feet shook once more. She lost sight of him as the pulpit collapsed into the river of lava that had now destroyed almost the entire building.

All that remained of him were his anguished cries as he burned.

Munroe grabbed her again and this time she didn't resist. 'Come on!' he shouted.

They turned and dashed back down the aisle as the remains

of the church finally gave in to the force of the lava flow and the tremors. The final beams came crashing down as they escaped back out onto the beach.

She heard a creaking noise over the rumble of the volcano and turned her head just in time to see the old spire splinter and crash down under its own weight into the lava, cross and all.

She saw Munroe had a boat tied up at the jetty – and not just *a* boat, but *her* boat. The RIB she and Brewster had arrived on.

'Where did you find it?' she shouted as the two of them ran towards the wooden pier and the shaking beneath them became ever more violent.

He waved an arm in the direction of the old warehouse. 'In there – tied up under a tarp!' he shouted back.

The lava had reached the jetty now, and though the sea would eventually cool and stop its flow, the wooden dock was yet more fuel for it to hungrily devour. They had to jump the first few feet to get past it, then thundered down the wooden planks to where Munroe had left the boat idling.

'I'll get the rope!' she called.

Munroe nodded and jumped into the boat. He took the controls as Abbie unhooked the rope, flung it into the craft and then jumped in after it. Her feet had barely left the jetty when Munroe turned the wheel and slammed the engine into full power as he aimed straight for Neptune's Bellows.

Abbie looked back at Whalers Bay and the erupting Mount Pond behind it. She was just in time to see the big warehouse give in to the earthquake and collapse in on itself, while the lava flow was now spreading down the beach, setting fire to all the rotten wooden timber that had once made up this little village. The whole shoreline itself now seemed to be alive with flames, while behind it lava spewed up into the darkening sky from the crack atop Mount Pond. It was quite the show.

'Hey Abbie,' Munroe shouted over the noise of the engine and the blasts coming from the shore.

'Yeah?'

'That's four times I've saved your life,' he said with a smile.

She smiled back. 'Maybe they'll give you a knighthood.'

He shook his head. 'I'd never accept. I'm an anti-monarchist.'

She laughed. 'Of course you are.'

They motored on as fast as the boat would carry them, and soon reached Neptune's Bellows. Abbie glanced up to her left as they passed the lighthouse. She wondered if anything would be found of Robertson, or if the relentless Southern Seas pounding the rocky outer ring of the island would already have torn his body to shreds.

She looked back one last time as they motored through the narrows. One last look at the island that had nearly become her final resting place. She hadn't ended up buried there, but had her demons? She thought back to the look of shock, fury and helplessness on Milton's face when she'd shown him his notebook. She patted her jacket and felt its outline in her pocket.

She watched the flames dancing on the beach until the rock walls of the island closed up behind them as they powered away at top speed. She scanned the horizon and saw in the distance the blinking lights that must be the *Northumberland*. The captain must have sailed further away out of caution when the eruptions began. Munroe tweaked his course to head right for the ship.

A flash of light in the sky caught Abbie's attention and she swung her neck round to see a giant column of ash shoot up into the night sky from the volcano as it finally unleashed all its incredible destructive power and fury. A few seconds later a deafening crack followed as the shockwave reached them, shaking the little boat and echoing through the half light of the dusk.

She thought of Milton being buried under the ash, his body surely never to be found.

They pushed on until they reached the ship, great plumes of ash soaring into the sky behind them as the eruption took hold of the island.

Northumberland was just getting underway when they pulled alongside and scrambled onto the ship, as the boat crew began the job of winching the RIB aboard.

Abbie waved away their shouts and questions and instead made her way quickly and purposefully to the bridge – Munroe following closely behind – where she found the captain barking orders as he tried to get the ship out of harm's way.

'Sir!' Abbie interjected.

'Błaszczykowski-Fitzroy,' his eyes went wide in surprise and confusion. 'What the hell's been going on over there?'

'We need to get on to Northwood,' she said, ignoring his question as she pulled Milton's red notebook out of her inside pocket. 'Now.'

Chapter 65

Two months later

Abbie pushed open the door of the pub and stepped out into the cold of the night. She hadn't said goodbye to anyone – she knew if she did, the rest of the lads would never let her leave. They were in for a session now as they toasted the memory of Paul Brewster. He had always enjoyed a few pints and his crew mates would be sinking plenty tonight in his name. But she had something else to do. Her own way of honouring his memory.

As the door swung shut behind her she heard a whistle and then saw a burst of red light in the sky off to her left, followed by a sharp crack.

For a moment she was back on the RIB, motoring away from Deception Island as the volcano erupted behind her.

She glanced at her watch: 5 November. Guy Fawkes Night. She'd completely forgotten that was today. Another burst of fireworks shot up into the black sky from somewhere near the harbour, the bright lights and the cracks and bangs so reminiscent of that night down at the bottom of the world. The night when she'd come so close to death; so close to joining Drew.

Simply going by the odds she shouldn't even be here, she thought, given everything that had happened on that island.

She'd even discovered what it felt like to be buried alive – and in what she'd thought was her own grave.

But she'd *survived*. She'd come through it. She'd escaped her would-be grave in the black, dead sand.

Not only that, but thousands of others had also survived because of her. After getting back to the ship, she'd explained everything to the captain and the information she'd gleaned from Milton's notebook was transmitted back to London. Within days the police had rounded up the remaining members of Milton's terror cell in a series of raids that had also led them to an abandoned factory in Luton, one corner of which had been repurposed to manufacture explosive devices.

Milton's attack had been thwarted, his associates now awaiting trial, and the secret of his imprisonment on Deception Island now revealed to the world as the powers that be scrambled to pin the whole thing on Ridley, who was already being labelled as a 'rogue officer' by unnamed government sources.

For a split second she saw a flash of Milton's face, beaten and humbled, in his final moments before the fire had consumed him.

Then she pushed that monster out of her mind and instead closed her eyes and saw Drew. He was walking away from her, smiling at her over his shoulder as he went. She felt a tear come to her eye as she watched him go.

She'd had to say goodbye to so many people in the last two months. She'd been to enough funerals to last a lifetime. One for each of the helicopter crew members Milton had murdered, and then, today, Brewster's. His had been the last, and the most difficult.

His wife Vicky had asked Abbie to sit up front with her and their daughter Rosie, and they'd hugged and cried their way through it together. Abbie had summoned all her strength to recite Tennyson's *Crossing the Bar* to the congregation, and then they'd cried a little more.

Two months of mourning. A parade of sadness and tears and reflection. Though in truth, that described her whole life for the last four years.

But now, at last, she sensed it was time to stop living in the past. It was time for the future.

She knew this wasn't the end of it. She wasn't 'cured'. She wasn't *over it*. Four years of holding onto grief and pain and anger didn't just disappear in a moment, a day, or even a month.

No, this wasn't the end, she knew as she blinked her eyes open. Not yet. But something was different.

She saw Drew again as he walked further and further away from her. All this time she'd been trapped in this half-life. Mourning him. Mourning them. She knew then he would want her to find happiness. She would never forget him, never lose him. But she couldn't carry on just existing like this.

Enough now, she decided. It was time to try. It was time to live.

And she had to start with a promise she'd once made to a friend. She turned to her right and began walking down South-side Street, the chatter and laughter from the pub fading a little more with each step, the fireworks illuminating the sky above with their bright colours.

She passed the Greek restaurant on her left, and glimpsed the families inside enjoying their meals. She walked on past the fudge shop on her right. A young couple was coming in her direction on the other side of the road, arm-in-arm, and laughing about something. He was wearing a long coat and she had a bright red bobble hat. Abbie watched him pull open the door of the pasta bar for her and the two of them ducked inside. Abbie smiled, and walked on. She had to sidestep a father pushing a small child in a pushchair, with a toddler walking alongside. The toddler slowed and was pointing at something in a shop window. 'Come on, Harry,' the father said. 'We're going to meet mummy at the fireworks. Let's go,' he added taking one hand off the push-chair to grab the boy and pull him along.

Abbie walked on, past the little art gallery and the pasty shop, and stopped at the red post box outside the Morrisons. She reached inside her jacket and pulled out an envelope. Her application for the Royal Marines.

'I promised you I would,' she said as she held the letter up to the slot. She looked up into the night sky, as the lights and bangs of the fireworks died away for just a moment. 'Fair winds and following seas, buffer,' she added.

She took a deep breath and dropped the envelope, then turned back towards the harbour and walked on into the night.

Acknowledgements

My debut novel *Whiteout* was published in February 2025. It was a lifelong dream realised for me, and came only after many years of trying to write something that anybody would be remotely interested in reading. I had written *Whiteout* mostly in secret, under no pressure and with no deadline. If I failed, the world would never know. And, once I'd written it, I had years to hone, tinker and tweak it before it finally found a publisher.

And when we did find a home for it (with the brilliant team at HarperFiction), they were kind enough to offer me a two book deal. I was overwhelmed that they had such faith in my first book that they were confident I could deliver a second. This was faith I wasn't sure I had in myself.

Suddenly I *did* have a deadline. I *did* have people counting on me. And the clock was ticking.

I was going to have to change my *modus operandi* to deliver a whole new book in a much shorter time-frame than I was used to. I had to get away from the distractions of home, so I took myself off to a series of old farmhouses out in the countryside (known as the 'Camp' here in the Falklands) for a week or ten days at a time, where I would write intensively, before going back home to my day job. And, as the months wore on and the deadline loomed, somehow the book came together.

So my first thanks must go to Sammy and the team at Falklands Landholdings, and the managers and staff at Fitzroy, Walker Creek, and Goose Green farms for providing me a distraction-free environment to get the words on the page (and for the inspiration for some of my character names). I must also thank Leon, Helen and Sammy Marsh at Fox Bay West for the use of the very cosy Black Shanty House, where the proof-reading and editing was done.

As mentioned at the very beginning of this book, Deception Island is a real place in the Antarctic. It really was a whaling station and is an active volcano which erupted twice in the 1960s, forcing the evacuation of the scientists working there. It's also true that it has what is said to be the largest graveyard in the Antarctic.

That said, I have used some creative licence, which I hope readers will forgive. In reality, Deception Island is part of the South Shetlands archipelago, and unlike in my book, it is a popular destination for tourists on visiting cruise ships and expedition boats, so the mysterious Ridley would likely not have chosen it for his clandestine purposes.

A huge thanks must go to my brilliant editor Morgan Springett and the whole team at HarperFiction who have worked so hard to whip this book into shape. In particular, a fantastic suggestion from Morgan was crucial in making the whole thing hang together, so thank you for a brilliant bit of editing expertise which really saved the day. The cover art team and the ever eagle-eyed copy and proof editors have also done a brilliant job.

I also want to thank my tireless agent Jemima Forrester, without whom, none of this would have happened. I find it difficult enough to keep one book at a time in my head, so I'm constantly amazed and impressed you are able to spin so many plates so well for all your clients. You are always there with sound advice and guidance, and given my first draft of *Deception Island* was, in some places, little more than an outline, both you and Morgan had your work cut out on this one.

Thanks also to everyone at David Higham for your hard work, especially Giulia Bernabe in the foreign rights team who brokered the deal which means the book will be coming to German readers in 2027.

I would also like to take this opportunity to thank all my friends and family for their support when *Whiteout* was published. I was blown away by the reaction and the messages I've had since it came out.

Thanks also to everyone who's helped me with the new book, however that help has come. In particular to my old friend Stephen for his generous and invaluable advice on naval matters. Any errors on that score are mine alone. Thanks also to Dan, for your atlas, and Anna for Winnie's Bible! And of course thanks to Tamara for all your encouragement and support.

Finally to the readers – thank you so much for picking up the book and taking a chance on it. I hope you enjoyed it.

Want more from R.S. Burnett?

'Gripping debut . . . Cracking'
The Times

'My favourite sort of thriller . . . tons of fun'
Guardian

'Immensely exciting and moving,
this is adventure fiction of the best sort'
Literary Review